This Raging Flower

Lynn Erickson

Weston, Florida
32136 - 701

This novel is a work of historical fiction. Names, characters, places and incidents relating to non-historical figures are either the product of the author's imagination or are used fictitiously, and any resemblance of such non-historical figures, places or incidents to actual persons, living or dead, events or locales is entirely coincidental.

EXCLUSIVE DISTRIBUTION BY
PARADISE PRESS, INC.

The cover image was obtained from IMSI's MasterClips® and MasterPhotos™ Premium Image Collection, 1895 Francisco Blvd. East, San Rafael, CA 94901-5506, USA.

ISBN #1-57657-411-3

Printed in the U.S.A.

They Were Slaves of Pride and Passion on Afghanistan's Savage Slopes!

REBECCA MERIDETH crossed an ocean to discover a world of love and rebellion—and a legacy of passion with a man she despised!

WILLIAM ST. CLAIRE vowed to make her his no matter what he had to do to win her. Then his evil secret would be buried at last, when death did them part.

AZIM. Afghanistan had stripped the civilized veneer of the former Alex Drayton. England was far behind the man with the haunting gray eyes, the man who took without asking until Rebecca walked into his life and brought him back again to a world he hated—and could not live without!

This Raging Flower

*To the loving patience
of my family.*

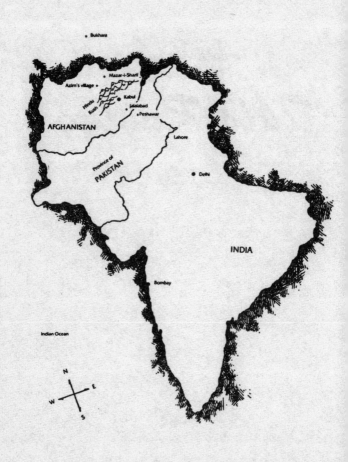

Bukhara

Mazar-i-Sharif

Azim's village

Hindu Kush

Kabul

Jalalabad

Peshawar

AFGHANISTAN

Lahore

Province of PAKISTAN

Delhi

INDIA

Bombay

Indian Ocean

N
W E
S

This Raging
Flower

CHAPTER 1

The sun, a crimson fireball, was dipping below the horizon; its evening-warmth causing a haze to collect over the ocean as it does so frequently off the West African coast. Never before had Rebecca seen a sight so elegant, so awesome. It was a dreamlike spectacle to the young English girl, lost in contemplation. Waves stroked the tall ship's giant hull, rocking it in gentle harmony with her thoughts.

Evening had become her favorite time to stroll about the decks. The colorful western sky seemed to raise her spirits before dining at the captain's table. It was not that she disliked her meals, or for that matter, the captain, but more that she preferred solitude and reflection before beginning her new life in a distant land. Only yesterday, it seemed, she had roamed lazily through her grandfather's gardens. Did she really miss the carefree hours spent with young suitors? Perhaps it was too soon after Grandfather's death to be certain of anything. What mattered now was the new role she must assume. Her future was a mystery at best; Kabul, an unknown entity.

The mellowing sun slipped into the great sea and fog swiftly curled up onto deck, chilling the air. As Rebecca became more engrossed in thought, she failed to notice William's silent approach. The soft evening light cast a golden hue on her honey-wheat hair and emphasized the rich creaminess of the fair English skin gracing her cheeks and long slender neck.

William St. Claire watched her green skirt billow in the moist breeze, the image silhouetted against the white canvas of the sails. God, but she's only in need of a frame to be the most beautiful picture on earth, he mused. His eyes perused her chiseled profile and found strength and intelligence, a proud British heritage. He continued his mental caressing of the girl; she radiated youth and purity, her long dark lashes demurely lying over large brown eyes. Eyes with such untold depths, William thought, that he would surely drown in them if he did not speak at once.

Aloud he ventured, "If you'll pardon me, Miss Merideth, your lovely gown will certainly not protect you against the evening air. Please allow me?" He gently draped his cloak around her pale naked shoulders.

"Thank you, Mr. St. Claire," she said as she turned to face him. "I'm afraid I was lost in thought and most forgetful of the time of day. But please call me Rebecca, as we are sure to see much of one another in the weeks to come."

"I'd like nothing more, Rebecca, except perhaps if you will call *me* William, and allow me to escort you to the captain's table."

Rebecca laughed coyly and took his proffered arm. It was pleasant to be in the company of a young man again. Perhaps it would put behind her the brief, but painful, mourning period for Grandfather George. After all, wasn't it he who had said, "Never look back, girl, lest you stumble for naught!"

Dear God, how she missed him! His gentle humor was forever gone, but she would try not to think of that now. Her future would be with her father, as it should be. His beloved foreign land, Afghanistan, would become hers as well. Rebecca knew she must make every effort to please him and to keep her sharp tongue subdued. Grandfather had appreciated her ready humor and quick wit but she had no way of knowing if Lawrence, her father, would find intelligence in a woman entertaining.

"A penny for your thoughts?"

"Oh, I'm afraid I was thinking of my father and wondering if he will approve of me. After all, it has been five years since last we saw each other, and I'm so accustomed to my English luxuries that I'm certain he will find me a nuisance."

William laughed heartily. "A nuisance, lovely lady? That will never happen!"

For the first time Rebecca looked carefully at William. She saw a somewhat handsome man of about thirty years of age. He was a trifle heavyset, of medium height and rather sallow complexion. His heavy English features told of hidden intensity. Perhaps there was security in that face, she thought. The voyage promised to be tedious and she longed for a friend in whom to confide her hopes and fears. She idly wondered if he would often continue to seek her out.

When they entered the captain's quarters, his officers stood appreciatively to greet Rebecca as did the other voyagers. William possessively seated himself next to her. Captain Brownsley grinned at the young couple and asked Rebecca in a rather fatherly fashion, "And how, may I inquire, my dear, do you like life at sea?"

"I find it quite tolerable, sir, and I thank you for providing seas that swell thus!" She indicated a calm ocean with a feminine sweep of her hands.

All joined in a hearty laugh at her gesture and assured Rebecca that they, too, preferred a smooth voyage.

The evening passed quickly. Rebecca found herself enjoying the ribald humor and implausible stories that passed among the men. She silently compared the crew with William, who seemed pensive and a bit bored with the revelry. He was, after all, older than most of the lads on board, and perhaps he found their boyish humor tiresome.

Most of the passengers sailing aboard the *Star of Bombay* in the early spring of 1882 were either military men or members of families traveling to India to seek out new adventures or adopt a more exciting way of life than existed in England.

The ship's command was a gently-bred lot who loved their simple life at sea, and Rebecca found this new type of person more and more to her liking.

Before Grandfather's unexpected death, she had known many suitors who were really more the dandy than she cared to admit. Now, seeing a more responsible group, she found herself wondering if they found her as attractive as had her London beaux.

Indeed, if Rebecca could have read their minds, she would have blushed from head to toe, for at eighteen she could hardly have known the effect her budding beauty had on these seafaring men. She was unaware that the high-strung gaiety among the officers was due to her low-cut bodice, or that William's bright mood stemmed from the same white cleavage.

After awhile both the intense heat of the cabin and the bulk of the fare began to take its toll on Rebecca. She excused herself, pleading overindulgence, and started toward the door. William was immediately at her side, begging to see her safely back to her quarters. She assented and they bade the others a good night. Once out on deck, the cool breezes revived her flagging spirits, prompting her to stroll more leisurely.

"I hope you'll allow me to escort you to breakfast, Rebecca, before one of the officers beats me to your door."

"William," she sighed, "whatever makes you think they have the slightest interest in me? Why, at any rate, they have their duties to perform!"

William mused to himself, is it possible that she does not know the effect she has on a man? Aloud he offered, "Lovely lady, let me just say that, to these sailors, you are a flower cast on a sea of thorns." He smiled at his own cleverness.

Not knowing quite why, Rebecca blushed, said good night and retired. Her cabin was stifling and she lay awake thinking, as always of late, about what her new life would be like. Captain Brownsley had known of her circumstances and was more than happy to give her passage as far as Bombay. There, as her father's letter had indicated, Lawrence Merideth would be on hand to greet her. Her father and Captain Brownsley had become acquainted on their initial voyage to India some five years earlier, and her father had immediately booked passage for her with his trusted friend. He was confident that the captain would see to his daughter's welfare aboard the *Star of Bombay*. Time had flown by swiftly. The letters and arrangements for her voyage were made, and Rebecca barely had had time to mourn Grandfather's death. Here she was, an uncertain future, a father she barely knew. Her grandfather, George Merideth, had been a wealthy man, leaving one living son to inherit his estate. Unfortunately, his only son, Lawrence, had chosen to live in the Far East after the death of his loving wife. Naturally, Rebecca became the favorite companion of her eccentric grandfather. As she lay awake reflecting upon the past, she realized that she was far from destitute. George had left her, in trust, a large sum of money to be paid upon her twenty-first birthday. She would also receive a number of small, but treasured, trinkets he had collected on his various travels. She could remember begging him to allow her to play with the priceless objects, but he always had laughed and told her that someday, when he was gone, she could toy with them all she pleased.

Sleep was gradually taking over. Rebecca allowed herself to drift along, until a small creak at the door brought her instantly back to reality. She sat up, pulled the covers over her scanty lace chemise, and wondered fleetingly if it were the captain.

The door opened slowly and a man's profile was revealed against the bright moonlight. Rebecca parted her lips, ready to scream. Then a familiar but slurred voice hushed her. "It's only me, my love! I've come to see if you are abed, safe and sound."

"William!" Even from across the room Rebecca could smell the stench of liquor on his breath. "You must leave this chamber at once! Why, you could be flogged for this intrusion!"

"There are things I would tell you . . . unable to—sober . . . I have longed for you since I first . . . I'll speak with your father. Please tell me that I may hope."

Rebecca's mouth was quivering with anger. "Get out! How dare you break into my cabin! Oh, you . . . you drunken imbecile! Get out immediately!" The man's audacity is too much to believe, she thought. The utter gall!

When William made no attempt to leave, she could contain her temper no longer. Rebecca's anger unleashed like a whip snapping in a quiet room. She jumped out of bed, raced toward him, her long hair streaming behind her, totally unmindful of her scarce attire. William groaned at the sight of her heaving, half-exposed bosom that was illuminated by the moonlight shining through the porthole. Overcome by desire, oblivious to the gentlemanly air he had tried to project earlier, he grabbed Rebecca's arms and slammed her against the wall. Crushing against her with the weight of his body, his sweaty hands groped at her breasts and he began to bite her delicate skin in a frenzied attempt to kiss her. Reacting instinctively, she clawed wildly at his face in desperation. She was horrified by both the sudden change in his demeanor and the pain he was inflicting.

At last William released her, almost sobbing. "I'm terribly ashamed, Rebecca," he choked. "But God, if only you knew the powers of your body! I want you so . . . I'm drunk . . . talking too much . . ." His voice trailed off as he stumbled out the door and down the narrow passageway.

Exhausted and in shock, Rebecca sank into the bunk

and grasped the wooden frame with her fingers until
her knuckles turned white. She squeezed her eyelids
shut, trying to suppress the flood of tears that threatened to cascade down her cheeks. Her efforts were
useless, however. Giving in, she wept convulsively and
rocked back and forth. Never had she been so close to a
man before, nor had she realized to what extent desire
could drive them. Recalling the image of William
standing there, heavy beads of perspiration running off
his brow and the look of a beast in his eyes, made her
shudder.

Finally she was able to calm herself and see the
simple truth. William, she feared, was a passionate man
who could only express himself with the assistance of
spirits. It must surely stem from great shyness, for what
else could the explanation be? And yet, was there more
in his declaration she failed to see? Perhaps she had
pushed him too far by attacking him in her half-clothed
state.

Rebecca was fully aware of, and slightly embarrassed
by, the fact that her contours had, in the past year,
filled out to near perfection. Although she considered
her breasts almost too full, she did like her small waist
and was proud of her height, which lent a willowy
appearance to her figure. Was it truly possible that
William found her so irresistible? Was her recently
blossomed shape at fault? She must seek him out in the
morning to apologize and seek some solution to this
problem. After all, it was *she* who had been offensive,
driving him to grab and bruise her bosom, and it *was*
William who had broken off the assault. She could not
judge him so quickly. After all, having had no other
experiences with men's advances she ought not to be so
harsh.

Whereas sleep came slowly to Rebecca, it did not
come at all to William. He lay awake in his cabin
cursing himself for taking that first drink to gather his
courage. If only he had courted her in the slow fashion
he had intended. But then he had seen her beautiful

body and felt such unfulfilled promise. God! Were his plans ruined by drink and a moment of lust? Why couldn't he have waited for the time that her body would belong to him alone, with a marriage certificate to confirm it?

Was it only a year ago that his future had held all that any English gentleman could hope for? William rolled onto his side, but rest still would not come. He thought of his father, now dead, and of the accursed bankers who would not allow him the needed time to redeem his father's bankrupt estate. *Damn!* If only he had bothered to read the diary before the bank auction, he would still be comfortably back in England.

William tossed and turned. The effects of the alcohol gradually diminished, leaving his eyes wide open and his mind reeling. He must cease this wicked drinking that had begun only months ago. Damn the blasted diary! How could he get back into the good graces of Rebecca? He had come this far; nothing would stop him now. Certainly, he would cease his drinking and take control. How easy Rebecca would be to handle then; she was now in a most vulnerable state, far from home and traveling to a father whose love she questioned.

At dawn the ship dropped sail and docked at Dakar on the West African coast. Supplies were already being hoisted aboard when Rebecca sat down alone to breakfast. She was anxious to see this famed African port, and hoped that Captain Brownsley would allow her to go ashore for a few hours. It would be pleasant to have William's company, if for no other reason than to have her little talk with him.

The door of the cabin opened and William humbly eased in his head. "Rebecca," he started apologetically, "before you toss me out, please let me explain. This is a rather awkward situation. I beg you to listen!"

She presented one of her sweetest smiles. "William, before you continue, I shall say that you were very rude to enter my cabin. I don't wish to condone your action. However, I should not like a rift between us. Perhaps we might start our friendship anew. After all, neither you nor I should dock at Bombay as enemies."

William beamed, this was going to be easier than he thought. "You are the most understanding woman on earth! I feel that I do owe you an explanation, nevertheless." William was determined to make use of his lie, having lain awake the entire night contriving it. "I have suffered a great loneliness since my father succumbed to a fever . . . My need for comfort overcame me last night . . ."

"Say no more, William. Besides, I was so hoping that you would ask the captain if you could see me ashore today so that I might purchase some native crafts. Do you think I should also purchase a gift for Father?"

Overjoyed by his victory, William rushed to speak, "We must leave at once. The ship is due to sail before noon, so hurry now!"

Rebecca grabbed her lace shawl, drained the last sip of morning chocolate and went with William to seek the captain's permission.

The morning in Dakar was a complete success for William. Rebecca was like a small child in a sweet shop. He felt certain that before arriving in Bombay, the young beauty would be eating out of his hand, tamed and ready to ride. William smiled cunningly to himself.

The sun set, lending beauty to the earth as the *Star of Bombay* prepared to head due south toward the Cape of Good Hope. Soon they would round the Cape. A new world lay ahead.

CHAPTER 2

The currents around the Cape were rougher than the crew cared to admit which caused most of the voyagers to spend the last week of April in their cabins. By the time they reached Port Elizabeth the wearied passengers badly needed a day ashore.

Rebecca and William made the most of the sojourn in Port Elizabeth, delighted to find it much more civilized than their previous stop. Rebecca even braved some of the local foods and therefore spent the next few days at sea flat on her back in bed.

One such day, William stopped by to see how she was faring. He said sympathetically, "My dear, I must say that *I* knew better than to try those greasy cakes, but I do envy the spirit of adventure you seem blessed with."

"Oh? But my stomach does not feel adventurous!" she laughed. "In fact, when we reach Mombasa I fear I shall only eat aboard ship. My shopping from here on out will be strictly for inedibles!"

William enjoyed the lighthearted banter. He was pleased to find her accepting his company with trust rather than suspicion. Indeed, his plans were going according to schedule.

Rebecca did not feel altogether well until they had

neared Mombasa, on the eastern coast north of Madagascar. The city was far from being the garden spot of Africa, and even those who ventured ashore were not unhappy to leave the bug-infested place and head out into the great Indian Ocean toward their final destination. So far, the trip had been totally and unbelievably without incident. The sooner they arrived in Bombay the better, for the Indian Ocean could be treacherous in the late spring.

It would still be a couple of weeks before they docked, but on this final leg of the journey the passengers seemed more pensive than usual. Undoubtedly it was due to the new land and the new life they were adopting.

Rebecca spent the remainder of her time aboard organizing her wardrobe for the days in Bombay and the overland journey through India and into Afghanistan. She tried not to think of her father's reaction to her now that she was grown. She remembered him as a quiet-spoken man who had been deeply devoted to her mother. When Mrs. Merideth had passed on—Rebecca, just a young girl then—Lawrence Merideth had thrown himself into his awesome job as Representative of the East India Company. Rebecca wondered what his home was like in Kabul. Would it be elegant? She cleared her mind, pulled a loose thread on her blue day dress and went about the business of sorting her trunks.

The notions going through William's head were not quite so innocent. He spent much of his time leaning over the rail remembering events of his past that had led to this voyage to India. William's father had left India nearly thirty years before, carrying his infant son home to England. Until a year ago, William St. Claire had thought himself the son of a military man of noble upbringing and of an English mother who had lived in India. She had always been a sketchy figure in William's mind. His father had been extremely vague when asked about her relatives living in England. It had always puzzled William why he had no family on her side in London, even though his father had said she was originally from that city.

Several weeks after his father had succumbed to a fever, William sat brooding over the auction that had been held the day before in his home. One of the representatives from the bank had been very understanding, but had held little hope for the recovery of the funds necessary to redeem the estate. William's father, although a St. Claire, had been an army officer, and had fallen into some bad habits, gambling being the main cause of his financial downfall.

William had been leafing through his father's remaining personal belongings when he had spotted the diary. Thumbing through it, he had seen an entry concerning himself. Thinking back, William recalled staring at the page for an eternity. Finally the words had become all too clear. He was an *Indian*—a bloody half-caste! His mother had been a woman from Bombay, a dark-skinned native! But his insipid father had evidently loved her desperately and had planned to bring them all home to England, careless of the shame it would cause the St. Claire family. As it turned out she had died before sailing, leaving the man and his infant son alone to face the world. William's father had thought that his son's skin would be light enough to pass the child as a full-blooded Englishman. He had gone so far as to concoct a ficticious British mother.

The diary went on, and William wondered if anyone alive knew of his shame. He had come to an entry that described a small jeweled box. The box had been a treasure left to his mother and contained a hidden compartment. Inside was concealed his parents marriage certificate and his own birth certificate naming him as a person of *mixed race*.

Mixed race! he had thought at the time. I certainly don't feel half-caste! I don't feel like one of those dark-skinned servants bowing and mumbling to their mistress. I feel like an Englishman! I have been brought up as a white, attended the finest public schools, and no one ever suspected!

But the proof of his mixed blood did exist, duly embossed and imprinted, signed and stamped legally for anyone to see.

My God! If anyone found out I'd be shut out of my lodgings. I'd never get another position. I'd never even receive a commission in my father's regiment! No decent Englishwoman would look at me, much less marry me! No hope of a good marriage, he thought panic-stricken; only a barmaid would have me if my true color were known! He would have to find that box, remove the papers inside, and burn them. Then no one would ever discover his secret.

William knew that he had seen the box at the auction. Yes, he had clearly remembered an elderly gentleman making a fuss about the rarity of such a jeweled treasure. A casual question to the auctioneer had given him the information that it was one G. Merideth, of Faroaks Manor. My God! What if the buyer had examined it before William had a chance to buy or steal the box back? He had known the document would undoubtedly cause a scandal and make him the laughing stock of London. He would have been totally ruined, without friend, and without hope of a wealthy marriage! An utter disgrace!

That was the beginning of his plot against the Merideths. As he stood musing and looking out over the Indian Ocean, he could find no other solution than the one he had decided on several months ago. Marrying George Merideth's granddaughter was still his only access to the box, which was now locked in the London bank vault with her other valuables. At least he knew that for the time being he was safe from discovery.

Thinking back to the decision he had made, William

became even more vehement in his determination to conquer Rebecca. He must make the most of the situation before the final docking. By the time they arrived he must secure her promise of marriage. Perhaps he should have gotten her with child, then her father would be forced to allow the wedding. But no, her soft mouth that promised so much was undoubtedly cold and hard, and he might only have alienated her forever.

"Damn her beauty," he muttered aloud. But William had no intentions of being taken in by a beautiful face or a sensual body. He must bend her in every way to his will.

"Why, William, do you realize that you have missed dinner?" Rebecca asked, coming up behind him.

At that moment he could have strangled her slim neck! After all, *she* was the cause of this insane journey to a heathen land. He answered sharply, "Can't a man have a moment to himself?"

His sudden retort startled her. She looked up noting his stormy dark eyes and unusually sallow complexion. This man has many sides to him, she mused silently.

"If you prefer to be alone with your thoughts, all you need do is tell me. After all, I, too, enjoy my privacy. And now I shall bid you a good night."

As she turned to leave William noted the deliberate pout to her full rosy lips. Despising himself for lying, he soothed, "My darling, please don't be angry with me. I was merely wishing that I could speak my mind to you. I asked you once to consider me. I am asking you again." He hoped this was not too sudden. He also knew that she must think him in earnest or she might soon start looking elsewhere.

Rebecca considered his face for a moment. She viewed him as somewhat less than handsome, but attractive nevertheless. She definitely did not feel a flutter in her stomach. Her girl-friends had assured her that love was like a sickness that would leave her dizzy.

Certainly William did not make her feel this way. Was she different from her flighty friends?

Slowly, choosing her words with care, she said, "I'm uncertain as to how I should feel. I do care for you and I enjoy your company. But what of love? Is what I feel love?"

"Darling, love comes over the years spent together," he offered. "Surely you realize that life and love must both be cultivated. May I be so bold as to ask for a kiss so that you may feel the love that I have for you?"

Rebecca wasn't sure whether she would like to feel his lips on hers, especially after the scene in her cabin, but she knew there was only one certain way to find out. She nodded her assent. As William gently gathered her soft body into his arms, he could feel the rise of her bosom beneath her bodice. Her narrow waist was lost in his embrace. Her breath was sweet and warm. He kissed her slowly at first, then with more passion. She began to feel stifled in his arms, but endured his caresses with an open mind. Had he not just told her that it took time? William was nearly eleven years her senior; he must be experienced in these matters.

Finally he broke away from her. When he stood back he saw that her lips were still parted. She seemed visibly shaken to him. William, mistaking her discomposure for passion, decided to leave her unfulfilled. In the morning she would be begging him to speak to Lawrence Merideth at once. William was almost gloating when he silently led her to her cabin and kissed her good night on the forehead.

Later, when Rebecca was donning her nightgown, she was far from longing for William's hardness against her naked flesh. Quite the contrary. She was wondering how she would endure his embraces if she did marry him. She supposed that in time they would become bearable. After all, marriage was a union necessary to bring forth children, and Rebecca did have a longing to have many small ones. She had been an only child herself and had missed the companionship of brothers and sisters.

While Rebecca fell asleep fantasizing about her children, William drifted into an easy slumber envisioning her responding body lying beneath his own. The sea rolled and lapped against the ship's hull and the strong breeze carried them closer each hour to their destination.

CHAPTER 3

Lawrence Merideth left word at his hotel to notify him immediately upon the sighting of the *Star of Bombay*. He had dressed in his lightest waistcoat, as the early May heat in Bombay could be stifling by midday. He was certain that this was the day of his darling daughter's arrival, and prayed that the warmth of the day would not bring an onslaught of insects. Her coming must not be marred by the threat of humidity or stinging bugs.

Lawrence had arrived by train from Delhi nearly a week ago. He was glad for the extra time to prepare for Rebecca. The few unwanted pounds he had shed for her made him feel years younger. She would of course not notice the effort, but Lawrence did not want to appear stout and aged. His luck had been extraordinary this week. Not only had he seen many friends at the Bombay Staff Club, but one old comrade had found Meera for him. Meera was a youthful lady's attendant who came with the highest recommendations. She had already prepared Rebecca's rooms with a style and feminine touch that delighted Lawrence. Meera spoke and read English, cooked, styled ladies' hair in the latest fashions, did laundry, and most important, was a girl of exceptional good humor and cheer.

As Lawrence sat waiting with friends in the Staff Club, he could barely contain his excitement. Rebecca's mother had been one of London's rare

beauties. She had been sought after by so many worthy
suitors that Lawrence could hardly believe his good
fortune when she had said "yes" to him. Their married
years had been pure bliss. Up until the day of her
untimely death, Lawrence had known only happiness.
Then, even though he had to leave his daughter with his
father, George, he felt he must take the job offered him
by the East India Company. It was necessary to throw
himself as wholeheartedly into his work as he had into
his marriage. He wondered if his little girl had changed
in the five years since he had waved good-bye to
Rebecca; due to his remote post in Kabul, communication had been very difficult. Still, at thirteen, her
likeness to her mother had been astounding. She had
hair the color of autumn wheat, eyes like deep pools,
skin a pale shade of cream. What nonsense, mused
Lawrence. Obviously, all parents must feel an enormous pride in their progeny; it is only my deep love for
her that makes her seem so beautiful.

Shortly after noon, a breathless messenger burst into
the club. He had run all the way from the lookout point
atop the hills. The *Star of Bombay* would dock in half
an hour! Lawrence left immediately for the shipyard,
his excitement growing with each second. He took
Meera with him, hoping to please Rebecca with his
thoughtfulness.

As the ship rounded the inlet, Rebecca prayed that
she had dressed properly. Already the sun was causing
the heat to rise in shimmering curtains over the city of
Bombay. The effect was ethereal, exotic. She was sure
that she could see Lawrence as the ship edged its way to
the dock. She began to wave frantically, unable to
contain her pleasure, forgetting all doubts about how
they would get along. William stole up behind her
feeling that the most important moment of the journey
was rapidly nearing; her father's first impression of him
must be one of admiration. He hoped that Rebecca
would introduce him as having been a kind protector

during the long voyage. Certainly Lawrence Merideth was no buffoon—a man did not hold such a prestigious position by title alone. William had dressed accordingly; not too foppish, not too severe. The name of St. Claire was not unknown in India, and he hoped that his father's good deeds would be known to Mr. Merideth.

As Lawrence scanned the decks he hoped to spot Rebecca before she picked him out of the waiting crowd. A sudden shock passed through him when he saw the image of his lost wife, waving and smiling back at him. Lawrence's features darkened momentarily, then lifted. He realized Rebecca was here not as a ghost come to torment him, but as a gift of love sent to comfort him.

"Meera, have you ever had a vision?"

Meera understood immediately once she saw where his gaze fell. "Sahib Lawrence, your daughter is being far more beautiful then I am imagining! Yes, Sahib, I too am seeing vision," Meera replied in her unique version of English.

The gangway in place, Rebecca almost broke into a run trying to disembark. Gone was all her resolve to be ladylike! Once she saw him looking at her with open warmth and anticipation, she could no longer contain herself. Her joyous face alone parted the waiting crowds: Soon she was in the sweet embrace of her father. Not a word had been spoken, but both laughed while wiping a flood of tears from the other's face.

Lawrence broke the silence first. He choked, "Rebecca, Rebecca . . . how I have missed you! But I must compose myself lest my old heart burst with happiness. Now here, let me introduce you to Meera. She is a treasure that I have found for you."

Rebecca's voice was full of emotion. "Oh, Father! You have thought of everything. Meera, you say? I hope you can stand to attend me! I vow I can be a bit naughty at times as my father has surely told you."

Meera laughed good naturedly. "Missy Sahib, last

lady Meera attending weighed nearly as much as ship, had three teeth, and fewer hairs on head! You bringing sunshine to my life. I am not believing my luck!" Her bright eyes sparkled merrily over her veil. Rebecca vaguely wondered if Meera's hidden smile was as cheerful. Her instincts told her that it must be.

It had been months since Rebecca had known such peace of mind. Already she realized how sincerely glad her father was to see her again. His procuring of Meera was still further proof of his concern for her comforts. How could she have doubted his need for her?

Captain Brownsley approached the merry group and talked at length with Lawrence. They had not seen each other since the ship's last voyage and the reunion was full of quickly related news.

When William St. Claire joined the cheerful banter, no one took notice. He felt slightly miffed. He coughed, shooed a pesty fly from his brow, and began, "Ahem, excuse me, Mr. Merideth, I am an old friend of Reb . . . Miss Merideth's, and I should like to introduce—"

"How could I be so thoughtless?" Rebecca broke in. "William St. Claire, this is my father, Lawrence Merideth. Father, William has been so kind to me during the past weeks, and I nearly forgot to introduce you! It must be all the excitement. Why, William is traveling all the way to Kabul also. Isn't it a coincidence?"

Lawrence hesitated. A coincidence such as this was hard to believe. He replied casually, "Very decent of you to watch out for my daughter. How interesting that you are to travel to Kabul. I presume that business takes you so far from England? Let me see, St. Claire, there was a distinguished captain in the army I believe. Yes, that's it! Here in India. Wasn't it some twenty years past?"

William was delighted that Merideth had recalled. All was going well; he smashed a fly triumphantly on his coat sleeve, and answered, "That, sir, was my father. It was nearly thirty years ago, however. Sir, I was rather hoping that I might accompany your party to Kabul. I have received a position there as secretary to the governor." Why not assert myself? he added silently.

Lawrence wondered if perhaps he was not a nice chap after all. Was he just overreacting to the time William had spent with Rebecca? Aloud he offered, "We should be most delighted if you joined us. The journey is both long and hard. Sometimes we shall require military assistance along the way. Yes, indeed, it would be much safer to come along with us. It's all settled then."

William beamed openly. Rebecca was a bit apprehensive, but had she not expected her father to say just that? She hoped that William would not approach her father about a marriage between them—at least not until they had arrived safely in Kabul.

Rebecca's trunks were unloaded at last. The small group agreed to adjourn to the hotel. Plans were made for dinner at the Staff Club where Captain Brownsley had promised to join them later. The reunion was guaranteed to be a gay affair.

As they traveled to the hotel, located in the district of Colaba, Rebecca noted that Bombay was a series of islands. The port was a thriving shipping and commercial hub, lying on the coast of the Arabian Sea. Lawrence entertained Rebecca and William by relating some of the local history, his knowledge and humor proving to be a delight.

"Actually, the Portuguese first acquired Bombay as a trading port. It wasn't until the 1600s, when Charles II of England and Catherine of Portugal married, that the British began to influence the city.

"Father, why do women still wear veils after two centuries of British influence?"

"Because, my dear, the population is overwhelming-

ly Hindu. The English can build rail systems and
modernize many things, but you will still see an entirely
different culture here. I hope you will come to love it as
I have."

They arrived at the hotel in time to find rooms for
William. Bombay was a busy port just before monsoon
season, which begins early in June. Lawrence hoped
the travelers would be rested enough to begin the long
overland journey in a few days time.

Meera spent a long time in dressing Rebecca's hair
that evening. The effect was stunning. Her waist-length
curls were piled high on her head, as was the latest
fashion. Her gown was pressed and given a last minute
check for threads. Rebecca stood admiring herself in
the mirror while Meera laced the tight-fitting bodice to
her slender form. The frock was beige in color, with
yards of peachy lace gathered around it. The bodice
enhanced Rebecca's swelling bosom, while the skirt
flowed gracefully over her hips. All in all, she would be
the talk of the town for many months to come. Finally,
a single strand of tiny pearls was placed around her
neck in choker fashion. Meera stood back, mouth
agape.

"Missy Sahib, you will be doing much credit to
Meera's work. Tonight, gossiping ladies will want
Meera to come to work for them too! You are looking
like evening flower to me."

Rebecca laughed. "Oh, Meera, I know I shall like
having you with me during this long trip. You will keep
me giggling like a school girl! A flower indeed!"

Long before the party arrived at dinner, Rebecca had
turned nearly every head in Bombay. The officers they
encountered were clamoring for an introduction. She
was indeed a sparkling jewel. Her head began to swell,
although she was sure it was only due to the noticeable
lack of young women. Most of the ladies present were
married to military men, or were spinster daughters.

The attractive ones had been sent to relatives in England to meet eligible young men.

William, who was seated next to her at dinner, was well aware of her beauty and the effect her gown was having on the many soldiers seated around them. He nurtured mixed feelings about Rebecca. On the one hand, he was certain she was virginal. On the other, he was beginning to resent her beauty and vivaciousness. There were so many rivals around that he wondered if she weren't a bitch in heat, just waiting for the opportunity to lie in as many beds as possible! How else could she radiate such sensuality?

Rebecca noticed his intense brooding. "William, you are lost in thought. Is dinner not to your liking?"

"Quite the contrary. I have so overstuffed myself, and the flies have so annoyed me, that I was wondering if you would care to stroll in the fresh air of the gardens?" He looked irritably around him at the many brown-skinned servants dressed in white livery, their skinny arms tugging tirelessly at the corded ropes of the punkah fans. Why didn't someone do something about these disgusting insects! The Club was reputed to be the finest in Bombay and never in his life had he felt so stifled.

Rebecca regained his attention by lightly tapping his sleeve with her hand.

"I would love to get out of this overbearing heat. Will you wait until I ask my father? After all, he is now my chaperon. I would not want to offend him." She swirled around and sought Lawrence Merideth.

He assented, although he wished William would not pay such close attention to his daughter. By God, she deserved a far better man than him! No matter how charming young St. Claire was, Lawrence simply did not trust the man.

Rebecca could feel perspiration trickling down her bodice. She was glad for the fresh air in the garden and waved her fan to cool her hot cheeks. She sensed the ringlets tightening around her face as the humid air made her hair a mass of curls. William noticed her discomfort, so like his own, and could not help but suggest, "Perhaps if we shed these earthly garments our discomfort would cease!" He chuckled at his own cleverness.

Blushing profusely, Rebecca added, "I should leave at once and return to a more polite company, but somehow I find myself quite in agreement." She laughed deeply.

William was not laughing now; instead he was approaching her, trying to draw her into his arms.

Rebecca, bracing herself against him, squared her shoulders and snapped, "You, sir, seem to think you can kiss me at any given time. Just because I allowed *one* kiss, does not mean there will be more! Now if you will let me pass, I shall return to my place by my father's side."

But William was not to be so easily put off. He pulled her toward him, crushing her to the front of his starched ruffled shirt until she felt smothered. Suddenly she was free, and William was standing back from her, looking furiously at a stranger who held William's arm tightly. Rebecca's breast heaved from William's recent attack until she recovered her composure. Then two spots of angry red covered her cheeks.

"I say, old man," drawled a deep, lazy voice, "are you bothering this *lady?*" She could not help but notice his emphasis on the last word. Rebecca braved a look at the intruder while William stammered indignantly, trying to defend himself. He was tall, impeccably dressed in formal attire, dark-haired. She could only see him dimly in the faint moonlight, and his features seemed terribly strong and virile.

William had detached himself from the man's grasp and was looking sulky, standing by a lantern on the flower-lined path.

"Thank you, kind sir," said Rebecca, her voice

quavering slightly. "My . . . ah . . . fiancé and I were merely taking a breath of fresh air and I stumbled," she lied. "But I am quite all right now." She feared a scene might erupt causing her father embarrassment. Perhaps if she called William her fiancé, the man would think no more on the matter.

The stranger turned toward Rebecca, his features shadowed, almost frightening in the lush, hothouse atmosphere of the garden. "I trust you have received no injury from your . . . stumble, miss. It would seem that I have made an error in judgment. My apologies." His tone was serious, but she had the uneasy feeling that he was laughing at her. How dare he! And the way he made his excuses sounded as if the man had never erred before!

"Come on, luv, ain't you interfered enough in the lady's affairs? Leave 'er be and let's have a dance!"

The voice, Rebecca discovered, belonged to a garishly painted woman who had just emerged from the shadows of the undergrowth along the path. The woman, certainly not a lady, was pretty in a common sort of way, snub-nosed, blond with blue eyes and the smoldering magnetism of a woman of the streets. She was, at least, dressed decently in a white frock. She was quite obviously put out by her escort's attentions to Rebecca.

"Lucy, darling," said the man, "we'll be going in a moment, be patient."

Lucy sulked and hooked her arm in his as if to draw him away. Why, thought Rebecca, he was chiding *me* for taking a stroll in the gardens and he was doing the same thing with that, that creature! The very nerve! And what poor taste he has, dragging that trollop about on his arm in front of decent women!

Rebecca swirled, turning her back on both men and gathering her skirts about her furiously, deciding to put this rude stranger and William from her thoughts for the evening. She was determined to enjoy herself.

She hurried from them and returned to the gaiety and brighter lights. As she was searching through the guests, a new acquaintance, a Mrs. Cutler, literally snatched her arm. Major Cutler was attached to the army garrisoned in Bombay, she had been told by her father.

"Why, when Sam told me you were to travel all the way to Kabul," Emma Cutler began, "I could not eat a bite of food!"

Judging by the woman's figure, Rebecca doubted that anything could steal her appetite.

"Sam and I know for a fact that these heathen Sikhs would like nothing better than to kidnap a white girl! Why, you must have heard of the slave markets? Usually the poor dears are raped so many times that they barely care who buys them," she ended in a conspiratorial whisper.

Rebecca was uneasy. She knew that this puffy old woman was only trying to scare her, but somehow the thought of a turbaned, dark-skinned tribesman made her spine tingle. Yet she did manage an icy reply. "Mrs. Cutler, I'm sure I shall be very well protected. Why, it just wouldn't do to let the daughter of Lawrence Merideth by taken by some heathen. I'm certain that the army will protect me. Do you doubt that the British army lacks the strength to provide proper escort?"

Justly taken aback, Mrs. Cutler bid her a safe journey and went off in a huff to tell her friends what a rude little hussy Rebecca Merideth was.

While Rebecca was being reproached by the rapacious Dame Cutler with her horror stories, the dark stranger in the garden was trying to disengage himself from Lucy's cloying hold.

"Lucy, I have spent the entire day with you. I've brought you to dine at the Staff Club as I promised and scandalized everyone here in the process. I do realize that you receive a certain thrill from the adventure, but sooner or later your husband is bound to hear of your

flirtations. Come now, let me see you safely home for I
have pressing matters to attend to and the hour is
getting late."

"Alex, luv, spend the night with me. 'Arry won't be
back 'til tomorrow . . . and ya might not be back for
years!"

"Lucy," he repeated patiently, giving her voluptuous
backside a playful pat, "I have an appointment, a man I
must meet tonight or I shan't be able to set up another
meeting in the future and that will mean no more visits
to you at all."

"I'm sure of that! I am! A man to meet! What do you
take me for, a fool?" She pouted.

"Lucy, it's true. Have I ever lied to you? And I'm
serious about not being able to travel to Bombay again.
Now let's hurry. There, that's a good girl."

"All right, luv, I'll go home," her eyes lit up and she
smiled fondly at him, "but you don't know what you're
missing, Alex, ducky."

"Oh, yes, I do," he breathed to himself. "Oh, indeed
I do."

After delivering Lucy safely to her home, the man
slipped quietly through the close hot streets to the dock
area of Bombay, striding purposefully past the hoardes
of beggars that reached scrawny hands out to him,
crying "*baksheesh, baksheesh*" weakly and piteously.
His black cape almost hid him from view and he made
as little sound as did the scurrying rats in the open
sewers. He kept a light hand on the knife stuck into the
waistband on his trousers, for attack from poor starving
Hindus was commonplace here. But he saw no one
dangerous as he neared his destination—a small door
on a side street from which the light needled through
the cracks. He knocked and the door eventually
opened, showing a bare room lit by a single candle. He
slipped in cautiously. The door closed silently behind
him leaving the street empty again save for the
scavenging rats and sickly mangy dogs.

"Good evening, Singh. Have you any news for me?"

"Good evening, Sir Alex. It being fine weather, is that not so?"

"Yes, Singh, very fine." Alex spoke patiently, knowing that the social amenities had to be gone through. The merchant, Singh, was not about to give out his knowledge so quickly . . . nor without some gain to himself. The small brown man was spare, as were most of the Hindus, but his white shirt and pants were at least clean and his turban was wound elegantly, telling of his relative wealth.

"And how is being your friend, Mahmud? You did not see fit to bringing him this time to visit Singh?"

"No, Mahmud stayed in our village. His favorite mare was about to foal and he could not bear to leave her, so this time I have come alone. The journey is long, Singh, and I must return shortly." Alex was growing impatient to find out if the wily merchant had accommodated his needs. He thought about the shipment of ammunition waiting back in the village—the shipment that two of the men had lost their lives over to acquire. Now they needed the guns, he thought grimly.

"Ah. So you are wishing to return to Afghanistan soon, and you are wishing to know if Singh has found your merchandise?"

"That is true, my man. And have you located any guns for us?" Perhaps, at last, they could get down to haggling over the price.

Singh suddenly looked despondent. His very flesh seemed to sag in gloom. "Alas, sir, there are being no guns to be found in Bombay. I have been searching everywhere, but the shrewd English lords are having them all locked up tight. Even the guards are of very honest nature." Singh's eyes lit up momentarily. "If you could but stay a few weeks—"

"Damn!" The word exploded from the man's lips. "So there is nothing and I've made this long trip in vain!" His black brows drew together in irritation.

"Oh no, sir, not in vain! If you must go so soon it

shall not be with empty hands, for I have wonderful cargo for you to bring back. I am selling to you cheaply and you will be making a great profit back in your home."

"Yes?" growled Alex. "What have you in mind, Singh?" His disappointment showed clearly in his tone.

"Women's corsets—big shipment—I am selling you very cheap. Make your Turkoman ladies so beautiful . . ." His thin, brown hands carved voluptuous curves in the air.

The tall, deeply tanned man swirled his cape and stalked out of the door so quickly that Singh was left speechless and in the dark, for the draft of the slamming door had snuffed the guttering candle.

Alex silently retraced his footsteps in the muggy night, cursing the stubborn British for both their abysmal stupidity in Afghanistan and their shrewdness in keeping guns out of the natives' hands. He stalked the dank, narrow streets feeling his impotence keenly in this matter. He cursed under his breath, then thought of what his friend would say were he here.

"It is as Allah wills, Azim," Mahmud would intone. "There is nothing more you can do. Do not rage against fate. Our time will come in the end, never fear." So the man tried to calm himself, searching inwardly for a train of thought to blot out his frustration. Women's corsets, indeed! he mused, remembering Singh's offer. He almost laughed aloud, recalling the merchant's hands curving through the air. Unexpectedly, he found his mind straying to the young girl he had seen in the garden of the Bombay Staff Club. That one hardly needs a corset, he remembered with a lewd chuckle. What a rare beauty! And who was she? New here, and certainly a bit hot-blooded, it would seem, if her stroll in the garden with her gentleman was any evidence. It might be worth while to cultivate her acquaintance, he notioned, remembering the damply curling gold tresses, the heaving white bosom, the curving waist. But then he remembered that he was leaving shortly for

Kabul. Ah well, she's most likely a narrow-minded British officer's daughter, he told himself, and treats her servants worse than her dog. But as he neared the British section of Bombay and saw again the lighted lanterns of the Staff Club, he could not help but wonder if she were, at this moment, walking in the garden with a new beau. He quickened his pace as a misty warm rain began to fall on his face and shoulders.

Rebecca should have been inwardly laughing at Mrs. Cutler and her friends, but the mental vision of a swarthy grinning native raping and selling her would not leave her mind. As she tried to shake the queer feeling, her father found her in the crowd. He suggested that they all retire to the hotel, for the morrow would be busy. He had promised to buy her some cool native gowns to wear in her private chambers. There would also be the sights to see, people to meet, and more exotic meals to share. Rebecca was overjoyed with the prospects.

On the way back to the hotel Lawrence asked, "How was your walk in the gardens?" Rebecca shot a wicked glance at William, which her father quickly and silently observed.

"Oh, it really did not seem to cool either of us off. Did it, William?" Rebecca batted her lashes coyly at William.

Awkwardly William stammered, "No. Indeed, I find the climate here far too tropical to suit my taste." *Damn,* but she had put him on the spot!

Rebecca added, "*I* rather like the heat and the sweet smell of the blossoms. Why, just look at the size of the moon! Father, please tell us about the monsoons?"

Lawrence spent the remainder of the trip back describing the rather grim time of year when the southwest monsoons could bring a staggering four hundred and fifty inches of rain to the area, causing flooding and great loss of life.

Rebecca was glad they would already have arrived in

the more temperate climate of Afghanistan and the mountains of the Hindu Kush by then.

At their hotel Lawrence bade them a good night and retired, hoping that the trip would not be too much for his daughter. He also determined to find out if William had overstepped himself in the garden. God help the man if he had!

CHAPTER 4

The train chugged its way north across seven hundred and forty miles of dust and rock to reach the city of Delhi. Rebecca was anxious to arrive there, it would mean most of the long trip would be behind them. Thinking back on the days spent in Bombay, she was nevertheless glad to have left that city ten days ago and see some of the country. She had enjoyed the attention of the young men there, and Meera had rattled on and on about India. Besides, thought Rebecca, simply debarking from the ship was excitement enough to last her a lifetime.

Although the train ride was hot and uncomfortable, she realized what an engineering feat the Indian rail system was considering the vast distances it covered. The terrain barely changed as they moved slowly northwest. The local villages and scenery along the route provided Lawrence with endless topics of conversation. He seemed to know the name of every village, every crop.

Lawrence could see that his daughter was intelligent and grasped the significance of his ramblings. He made clear the interest the British had in keeping a strong foothold in India; their desire being keen in the export of many goods. He told her the importance of tea, spices, cotton, wheat, rice, and nuts, to name only a few commodities essential to the economy of England.

Rebecca was totally fascinated as she had so often used all the exported goods in her everyday life at home.

The trip went rapidly as an easy relationship developed among Lawrence, Rebecca, and Meera. Only William remained aloof. Rebecca could see that her father did not particularly care for him. She admired Lawrence, though, for being more than civil to William. If only her father approved of him. Her decision, whether or not to marry him, would be less complicated because she would never marry without her father's consent.

By mid-May the train rolled wearily into the outskirts of Delhi. Even William could not help but be impressed with the landscape. The dry, arid countryside lent a beauty to the much used red sandstone. The buildings seemed to rise out of the earth, creating an eerie effect.

"William, my father tells me that he must spend several days here attending to business matters. Would it be too improper if I asked you to chaperon me while we are in Delhi? And yes, you, too, Meera," she added automatically.

Cheerful for the first time in days, William replied, "Nothing would please me more, but with your father's approval, of course." His wide smile was distasteful to Mr. Merideth, striking him as being insincere in some respect.

Slightly frowning, Lawrence nodded. "You may start at once. I have much to do in our short stay here. Just a fair warning though. The gold and filigree here are world renowned, so, Rebecca, please do not stretch my purse strings!"

"Oh, father, I think my taste shall run to the ivory and embroideries. Would that not be cheaper?" she giggled.

The party was laughing mirthfully when the train pulled to a jerky stop. The days spent here promised to be full of sight-seeing and shopping.

On one such spree, while they were standing beneath

the Great Mosque, William dared, "Meera, why not wander on down to the Chandi Chauk and see the bazaar? Here, take these coins and we shall join you in a moment. I would like to have a word alone with Rebecca." He scowled at Meera.

She had little choice, although she was not at all sure she should leave her mistress. Sahib Lawrence had asked her to accompany them at all times. Rebecca bade her to do as William asked and assured her that they would only be a minute.

William began slowly, "Rebecca, we have had so little time alone. I only wanted to ask you if you have mentioned me favorably to your father. After all, my dear, we have come halfway around the world together and it should not surprise him."

Rebecca hid her dark eyes beneath long lashes. "I just don't know yet. I realize that I must someday soon think about marriage, but I cannot honestly say the notion makes me happy. At least not yet. I feel like I am beginning a new adventure here and already there is so much that is different in my life. Can you give me a few months to think about your kind proposal?"

William assented, although he felt that his foothold was slipping. Vowing not to mention it again they took off down the hill to join Meera in the bazaar area. They entered the walled portion of the city and soon found Meera, who was still uncertain how to spend her coins.

The days were passing quickly. Lawrence completed his business for the East India Company and they once again boarded the train, heading first north and then west to Lahore.

The land along the way was extremely arid. Passing by the mud hut villages, Rebecca was somewhat depressed by so much deprivation. She often saw the insect and disease-ridden corpses of cows covered with huge voracious vultures. Half-naked children, their bellies distended miserably, passively stared at the train churning up the dust of their impoverished villages. Rebecca averted her stare and lost all appetite. Yet, she could not help but notice the beauty there, too. Her mood lightened to see a variety of colorful parrots in the tree-lined streets and a multitute of shades blending into the earth.

On one particularly hot afternoon, Lawrence commented on the varied scenery. "I think that if we stop for a moment and look beyond the poverty, we shall see an ageless, highly refined culture. I think watching the veiled women drawing their water from ancient wells has a timeless quality to it, something seen for centuries by travelers. Where have we seen a culture that has survived on so little yet remained seemingly unchanged throughout history?"

Rebecca thought that her father had tears in his eyes, tears of love and compassion. Her heart welled with a pride for him and for a deep understanding of his emotional response to the land that he had chosen to adopt.

William, not entirely in agreement with Lawrence's viewpoint, but wishing to sound interested, said, "Yes, I find it terribly absorbing. To live here, though! I must say that I hope Kabul is a bit less beggarly. I cannot see all this decorative cow dung on the walls of *my* quarters! I shall find other means of fuel to warm my home and cook my meals."

Silently, Lawrence thought, that man has a way of being a total bore. I certainly hope that Rebecca does not find him attractive!

"If you find the train ride not to your liking," Rebecca baited, "then how do you think you will fare on the back of a camel for the rest of our journey?" She chuckled, teasing him.

Even Meera could not suppress a giggle. William shot the Indian girl a murderous glance, shifted his weight on the wooden seat, swatted at an insect. He felt she was stepping out of her place expressing her opinion and was annoyed with Rebecca for permitting it.

They disembarked at Lahore to join a commercial

caravan heading to Jalalabad via Peshawar, province of Pakistan. There, Rebecca rode her first camel. Although she was an experienced horsewoman, this was a totally new area of challenge. The beasts were odorous and cantankerous, slow to obey and often tried to nip or kick at their riders.

Rebecca found riding the creatures an adventure, but William detested every second of the journey from the moment he first mounted the camel's back. Meera kept silent on the subject, although she would have preferred the more modern train ride.

The caravan was carrying munition supplies to the outpost garrison in Jalalabad, then onto Kabul. First they must pass over the border into Afghanistan by way of the Khyber Pass.

They spent no time at all in Peshawar, but headed out instead for the Pass. The trip had been uneventful up until the day they began their ascent. The country was still hot and dry with barren slopes that lent an eerie setting to the landscape. Massive boulders threatened to topple at any moment. Rebecca tried to keep her eyes from the towering rocks that hung precariously over their heads.

To make matters worse, her camel, who was called Abdul, liked the climb less than Rebecca. He tried more than once to sink his teeth into her soft flesh, but she would stand for no part of his cranky nature and finally dismounted to give the brute a swift kick.

Lawrence approached her with a warning. "Rebecca, please get back on Abdul at once! I do not mean to alarm you, but the soldiers inform me that this is an area where the local clans have staged many attacks. They may know that we carry arms to the garrison, so we must not linger here for even a minute!"

"Father, surely with such protection they would not dare!" Nonetheless she remounted quickly.

She was to be proven wrong. Not seconds after his warning, shots were heard coming from the rear of the caravan. The camels and pack horses bolted at the first sign of trouble. William's camel stumbled over a rock, nearly throwing him into a deep ravine. Both Lawrence and Rebecca tried desperately to reach him. Rebecca crossed the short distance reaching William before her father could. William's camel was struggling for balance perilously close to the edge. He lunged from his precarious perch and clung to her camel's neck. She half-dragged him to safety, but feared that he had been injured.

Minutes later, the rear guard joined the main party and began to round up the stray animals. It appeared that after a brief exchange of gunfire, the bandits had wisely withdrawn. Two natives lay dead. Only one British soldier was injured but would be able to ride. The captain informed them that the robbers might soon return, so they hastily headed toward the summit.

William was uninjured, but was trembling when he finally spoke. "I could be lying dead now, Rebecca, if it weren't for your quick reaction. What can I say to thank you . . ." His voice trailed off to a whisper.

She was also visibly shaken, feeling embarrassed at the sight of William's scared white face. Lawrence, however, seemed to be taking control of the party and tried to keep some semblance of order.

Meera, momentarily putting aside her anger at the bandits, said in awe, "Missy Sahib, you are bravest of all women! Meera thinking army be giving you medal, yes?"

"No, Meera, women do not receive medals. At any rate, look at how I am trembling all over. I vow, the sight of Jalalabad will be the sweetest I have ever seen!"

Rapidly recovering, William saw the absurdity of his position. Why hadn't *Rebecca's* camel stumbled? He could have rescued her, winning the immediate approval of Lawrence Merideth! Instead, it was he who was made to look the fool. He gave a sidelong glance at her sitting upon her camel. She was like a dusty rose, covered with dewlike perspiration that he knew was trickling down her white cleavage. Her hair was blowing free in the wind like thousands of petals catching the sunshine. She thrived on the excitement of the danger while he cowered in fear. Damn, but he detested her! No, not that—he wanted her, badly.

"William, I say, are you all right now?" Lawrence inquired when he came up from behind.

"But of course I am!" William sneered.

Lawrence thought that he was indeed a strange and umbrageous fellow. He even had a fleeting thought that if St. Claire had gone over that ravine perhaps Rebecca would have been better off.

Instantly, he dismissed the notion as ridiculous and unworthy, and set his mind once more to the scenery and history surrounding them. In the five years that he had been with the East India Company to establish trade relations with the Shah of Afghanistan, Lawrence had become an expert historian on local cultures. He enlightened the group on almost all aspects of the countryside they passed through.

That night, around the fires at the base of Khyber Pass, Lawrence was enjoying the respite from the day's heat. The mountain airs were cool and fresh in the evening, although the dry, rocky landscape still held much warmth. Their small group of civilians, with many of the soldiers, gathered around the flames while Lawrence began his nightly tales.

His soft eyes twinkling, he began, "Now that we have descended the mountain, the attack, thank God behind us, I feel safe to tell you some of the history of Khyber. To begin with, due to the barren, rugged cliffs and the lack of mountain greenery, travelers have forever encountered strong and unrelenting winds. These never-ending breezes have provided a dusty cover for such invaders as the notorious Nadir Shah. The Afghans have also used the Khyber Pass for centuries to invade India."

"Mr. Merideth, sir," a young soldier ventured, "please tell of the attack on the British column back in the forties. My uncle Emmet was killed here, and I know little of the circumstances."

Lawrence started again, picking up the story a few years prior to the slaughter. His vivid descriptions of the military, their dress, and the Afghans, held all who listened spellbound.

"Apparently the day was hot, much like today. The winds were whipping up so much dirt that the unsuspecting column did not see the Afghans until they were on top of them. What ensued then is hardly fit to relate in mixed company. Let me just say that the battle was a total bloody massacre of all, save one, in the column. The British have not before, or since, fought in such a fury. It was, I dare say, the first defeat the armies had suffered. Days later, a lone figure stumbled into Jalalabad. He was the single survivor of the horror."

A pensive hush fell over the audience. The air had become calm and slightly warmer, or so it seemed. Behind the group, the moon was casting grotesque shadows on the rocks. Silently, wistfully, they departed the fires one by one, and sought out the safety of their bedrolls. No one would rest peacefully that night. Visions of the mutilated bodies laying slaughtered on the ground filled their minds.

Rebecca lay curled up in her blankets; her eyes gazing at the splendor of the stars. The heavens, the mountains, and the people of this ancient land compelled her to know more of them. When she finally drifted into a restless slumber, her dreams were filled with the mystique of this exotic country of legend.

The exhausted party arrived several days later in Jalalabad without further incident. They were greeted by a friendly young lieutenant, Rufus Smithers. The garrison inhabitants, as always, came out to meet the weary travelers begging for any news from the outside world.

After a brief tour of the fort, Rebecca sought out a hot tub of water and scrubbed her aching body until she tingled all over. Meera, too, was delighted to wash off the grime from the long journey that seemed to cover every inch of her body.

Rebecca took her evening meal in the privacy of her quarters. Before the sun had set she decided to relax on her cot for just a minute, but did not open her eyes again that night.

Mr. Merideth had mustered enough energy to dine with the post command, but soon followed his daughter's example and retired early for the night. He was immensely relieved to once again be within the walled protection of the garrison. Before he drifted into a peaceful sleep, he thought of the surprise he had for Rebecca in the morning. His heart beat proudly. Dusk came through his open window and bathed his eyes in pale soft light. In a short time now he would have Rebecca safely back in Kabul with him. He was happy, his life was in order, and his daughter returned to him.

CHAPTER 5

In the morning, Rebecca was awakened by Meera, whose large dark eyes sparkled with excitement. "Wake up, Missy Sahib! Your father is saying put on riding habit quickly this morning, Missy! He is having surprise for you!"

She sat up in bed, rubbing the sleep from her eyes, stretching languorously.

"What is it, Meera? Why are you so excited?"

"I cannot be telling you, Missy. Come, get dressed, and you will be seeing," replied Meera, smiling mischievously.

Rebecca arose from the army cot and went about her toilette. The heat was beginning to seep in around the tightly closed windows, a few errant rays of sun stealing between the cracks of the shutters. Sounds of men's voices, jangling spurs, snorting horses, and hoof beats came into her room, muffled by the thick mud walls.

Attired in her stylish gray-velvet riding habit, Rebecca felt prepared to face the new day. The tailored lines of the outfit did little to conceal the rounded figure underneath. One last glance in the cracked mirror to adjust the small hat perched on her golden curls left Rebecca ready to meet her father.

Rounding the corner of the building, she saw him speaking with an officer and called across the courtyard to him teasingly, "Father, what is this surprise Meera has awakened me so early to see? I think—"

She stopped, her words caught in her throat, her eyes wide at the sight of a ragged stable boy holding the reins of an elegant dapple-gray filly. Her father had turned toward her and was smiling broadly.

"This is Alia, my dear. I hope you like her." He beamed.

"Oh, father, she is lovely! Is she mine?" cried Rebecca, stroking the velvety black nose of the young horse. "May I ride her now, please?"

"Of course, my dear, but not for too long. We must have breakfast and then be on our way. I want to get to Kabul before June and it is still several days travel."

Rebecca gracefully mounted Alia, hooked her leg around the sidesaddle and arranged her skirt. Taking up the reins, she immediately felt the alertness and spirit of the beautiful mare. Alia stomped, then turned her head to nicker softly to the girl. A little heel pressure and Alia bounded forward, her ears pointed ahead, all aquiver with eagerness.

William St. Claire, emerging into the courtyard at that moment, was in time to see one of the most charming tableaux he had ever witnessed. Rebecca, lips parted and eyes sparkling, leaning low over Alia's neck, was flying through the gate, leaving a puff of dust in the still air.

William bit his lip in frustration at the sight. He *must* have that girl, not only to satisfy his lust for her young and voluptuous body, but also to protect his future. Putting a smile on his face, he approached Lawrence Merideth.

"Quite a sight, sir, wouldn't you say? Your daughter seems to be a skilled horsewoman in addition to her many other accomplishments." William sounded rather envious.

"Yes, she certainly is a fine rider," replied her father, politely, but as coolly as he could without seeming rude. There was something false about this young man. He did not feel comfortable around him.

"I assume you slept well, Mr. St. Claire. We have

some hard days of riding ahead of us. Excuse me now, sir, as I must check with Lieutenant Smithers about our escort and supplies."

Lawrence Merideth walked away, a small worried frown on his face. He wondered just how much Rebecca was attracted to this St. Claire. He knew there were not many eligible men in Kabul and that Rebecca was certain to see a lot of this fellow, the British colony in this capital being so small, and the same faces appeared at all social and official functions. Alas, I'll simply have to trust my daughter's good common sense.

The road to Kabul was extremely dry, the heat rising in oppressive waves. The air was clear and brilliant, so different from the damp, soft English climate. Here, everything stood out in relief, bright and stark against the horizon. Colors were sharp, clear, totally unlike the gentle English greens, blues, and browns. The plain in front of them stretched out, seemingly forever, in shades of ocher, rust, and beige. In the distance, small walled villages, deserted for unknown and mysterious reasons, melted back into the earth from which they were made. And they were formed from the soil itself, as trees were scarce on this high barren plateau and all buildings were made of mud bricks.

Occasionally, a line of camels and small figures swathed in dark clothing could be seen inching across the landscape. These were the nomadic people, traveling in their unending cycles with the seasons. At this time of year they were headed toward the north, toward the high and mighty Hindu Kush mountains where melting snows fed meadows of lush grass for their sheep, goats, and their essential camels.

Rebecca was spellbound by the scenery and by what she learned from her father.

"This is a strange and forbidding land, Rebecca," he said. "The people also are strange and difficult for us to understand. They are a fiercely proud, independent race, these Afghans. I'm afraid we British have not always respected that particular side of their character, even though we respect such qualities in our own. I suspect we thought they would succumb to our overwhelming power as have the Indians. Nothing could be further from the truth. Indeed, there are bitter feelings between our people and theirs because they will not bend under our yoke. There have been many revolts against us, and even pitched battles, some of which we have lost. The British Empire, I believe, has met its match here in this proud nation. Why, only three years ago, the entire British population of Kabul was massacred by Afghans, for the second time in half a century! I'm not even sure, Rebecca, my dear, that I should have brought you here to share the possible dangers of my post."

"Father, dear, surely things are going better now. And besides, I am so happy to be with you again. Do not even speak of my not staying!" Rebecca replied with sudden anxiety in her voice. "I want so much to make your home comfortable and to assist you in any way I can, and then there is this fascinating country to learn about. Why, this is an adventure beyond anything I had dreamed of in those stuffy drawing rooms back home!"

They were riding in a small caravan: Lawrence, Rebecca, Meera, William St. Claire, Lieutenant Smithers and his score of soldiers which formed their escort, followed by a line of donkeys carrying their supplies and personal belongings. The days were long, hot, and tedious. Muscles ached from the unaccustomed hours in the saddle. Eyes became red and irritated from the dust and pitiless sun. Everyone suffered from the heat equally: Rebecca in her velvet riding habit, which became somewhat more bedraggled each day; Lawrence and William in their riding jackets and white linen shirts; and the soldiers in their heavy tunics. The English were always the last to adjust to new climates.

They stopped at twilight and made camp in a

caravanserai, a walled sanctuary found throughout Afghanistan. The structure always consisted of a central space for animals, surrounded by high mud walls with one gate and a water supply. Any traveler who entered a gate of a *serai* was safe for the night from any other travelers who might gather there in a tradition older than time itself.

The soldiers usually camped together, a short distance from the Merideths and William St. Claire, each group having its own tents and campfire. Meera was a skillful cook in the primitive conditions afforded them. Sometimes there were small groups of native travelers in the caravanserai. Their strange language and exotic music haunted the night air. They were a fierce looking people, proud to the point of arrogance, and usually ignored the Europeans completely. Always they were gone without a trace in the mornings.

Day followed day, alike in the heat and boredom of the trail that was still fascinating to the English girl. Her unfailing cheerfulness and surprising strength on the journey pleased her father greatly and made the trip easier for everyone.

William was biding his time. He used his natural, but lately forced, charm whenever he could grasp a chance to be alone with Lawrence. He did realize that the older man felt a faint distaste for him. He could even see the resemblance between Lawrence and George Merideth, Rebecca's grandfather . . .

The portly old gentleman had also felt a slight distaste for the young man who had been ushered into his comfortable study at Faroaks Manor several months before. William could remember the room with perfect clarity. The image caused cold drops of sweat to burst out on his forehead in spite of the heat.

The room had been large, lined with books, and had a great desk between the two tall windows. The walls were papered in a dark green and gold brocade and the carpet was a rich shade of red. Tobacco smoke filled the air from George Merideth's pipe. The whole atmosphere had been one of comfort and security, precisely those things William lacked.

William had taken the opportunity to fortify his courage before the interview by throwing down a couple of quick shots of brandy at a pub near his lodgings, then one or two more before he was to face Mr. Merideth. He felt that he was under perfect control, nevertheless.

"Mr. Merideth, my name is William St. Claire, lately of Mosswood House," William had begun his interview. "I understood you to have purchased a small jeweled box at the auction of my father's estate last week."

William had hesitated; how to best present his case? "Mr. Merideth, the box belonged to my mother and was very valuable—"

"Well, yes, Mr. St. Claire, I do remember the item. It is an exquisite piece, East Indian workmanship, I believe. I bought it for my granddaughter, Rebecca."

William had been a trifle miffed by the interruption. "I do not now have the funds to purchase the piece back from you, as I realize that you paid a goodly sum for it, but I wondered if I might look at it once more. I thought perhaps there might be some small memento of my dearly departed mother still inside. I'm sure you can understand my concern, sir." He had tried desperately to keep his voice calm. His whole future hinged upon getting those papers out of that accursed box!

George Merideth had seemed slightly irritated. "Mr. St. Claire, I would certainly let you see it again, but unfortunately, I gave it to my granddaughter and it is in our bank being appraised. Perhaps you could take the matter up with her in the future. And now, sir, as I am rather busy . . . ," his voice had trailed off.

William remembered precisely how he had felt at the time; a red haze had swum before his eyes. His head had sunk onto his chest in the deepest misery. His brain had whirled with despair, fear, horror, and a goodly amount of brandy.

He had thought, this old man thinks I am nothing more than a pest while I am fighting for my very existence!

He had tried again. "Mr. Merideth, I must insist. The box is very important to my family. I believe there is something inside that would prove vital to me. Perhaps you could arrange for the bank to release it to me for a short while."

"I repeat myself, Mr. St. Claire, speak to my granddaughter in a month or so. She is much too occupied at the present time." George Merideth showed his irritation. This young man was really too insistent for his own good. And he even smelled suspiciously of spirits!

"I cannot wait a month!" William shouted, desperate then. He stood up abruptly and swayed. The room lurched around him. George instantly reached for the bell cord to ring for Stokes.

Something had snapped in William's alcohol-clouded brain. In one long stride he had reached the elderly man, grabbing at his arm to prevent him from summoning assistance.

"Why, what do you think you are doing?" Merideth sputtered, jerking his arm away. William lunged again. A short struggle took place, accompanied by several grunts and wheezes from George.

Suddenly, William had felt the resistance against him gone. George had lost his balance and was teetering backwards, trying unsuccessfully to regain his footing. His face was red with strain, arms flailing in the air while he toppled over. The struggle had seemed to take an eternity to happen and yet it was over in an instant. William heard a thick sound as if something heavy were cracking open; George's head had struck the sharp corner of the desk. Silence hung heavily in the dimly lit study.

William had stood frozen and shocked. That damned old man! He's ruined my chance to get the box back. That had been William's first thought, only as an afterthought had he bent down and listened at Merideth's chest. No heart beat! The fool was dead!

Self-preservation had taken over William's instincts. They'd never believe he had not meant to do it! He'd be locked up in jail for life, or even worse! The hangman's noose dangled menacingly before his eyes.

William St. Claire had hastily picked up his hat, brushed it off, put a casual expression on his face and sauntered out of the study, closing the door carefully behind him. There had not even been a servant to see him leave. What confounded luck!

Two days later, William had read in the newspaper:

The Honorable Mr. George Merideth, of Faroaks Manor, was found dead in his study by the parlor maid. It is presumed that he had an attack of apoplexy, thereby falling, and hitting his head in such a manner as to cause his demise. He is survived by a son, Lawrence, stationed in Afghanistan, and a granddaughter, Rebecca, of London.

The article continued: the police were evidently trying to locate him as he had been the last person to see George Merideth alive. The funeral was to be held at such and such a place and the burial would be at, etc., etc . . .

William had pondered his choices upon reading the article: he could go to the police and admit to having been there and then try to brazen it out and say he'd left Merideth alive, or he could avoid his lodgings, change his name, and eventually leave the country. But, he must keep his eye on the granddaughter, this Rebecca Merideth. She just might be the key to regaining the incriminating documents.

After much thought, he had decided on the latter—hiding from the police. The London bobbies were an incompetent bunch anyway. They would never pursue him—they had never found Jack the Ripper, after all.

So, for a few weeks he had lived in new lodgings, calling himself William Stafford, and meanwhile went to see an old friend of his father's who, being retired from his father's regiment, worked in the foreign office.

William had told the man that he had recently suffered an unhappy love affair and wished to leave England for a lengthy period. The man said he would see what could be done to find William a post, and fortunately, it seemed that there were many available. It was several days later that William had read in the newspaper that one Rebecca Merideth was to travel to Bombay, where she would join her father on an overland trek to Kabul. Miss Merideth would sail on the *Star of Bombay*.

He recalled rushing back to the friend from the foreign office where the man was quite taken aback that anyone should wish to be posted in Kabul, but yes, there was a good position there for a man of learning. The job of secretary to the Governor was at present vacant. Just when everything, his whole life, seemed in ruins, Williams had seen a glimmer of hope, a small, tenuous ray of light.

William snapped back to the present as he heard Rebecca saying to him, "My goodness, William, you certainly seem preoccupied. Whatever are you thinking about?"

Realizing that he had been musing for much too long, he replied, "Just tired of this endless traveling. I am anxious to arrive in Kabul and begin my new duties."

"Well, Lieutenant Smithers says we shall be there by noon tomorrow, so it will not be too much longer. But I must admit that I am almost enjoying this trip. Everything here is so different, so new! I have much to learn. If only a certain part of my anatomy were not so sore!" At this, she made a delicious little *moue* of discomfort and then laughed at herself. "At least Alia is more comfortable than Abdul, that nasty old camel I had to ride!"

For the remainder of the afternoon hours, William could only think of the suffering he had been thus far forced to endure these past months. By dusk, he had a bitter and foul taste in his mouth and a bilious stomach. He did not have the slightest interest in his new job nor to be in such close contact with the uncivilized natives of Afghanistan, who would only serve as a constant reminder of his ignoble origins.

CHAPTER 6

That evening, the last day of May, they stopped at a
particularly large caravanserai. It was situated by a
spring with the welcome presence of several large
overhanging trees nearby. The spot was one of the
loveliest they had seen in weeks and everyone was in
high spirits because of the nearness of the journey's
end, Kabul. Their evening meal completed, Meera was
cleaning up by the fire and Lieutenant Smithers had
gone to see about one of the horses that had gone lame.

Lawrence Merideth sat with a very full stomach
staring into the fire. The leaping flames mesmerized
him.

"Rebecca, my dear, I must retire immediately or I
shall never be able to move from this spot! I should like
you to retire also. You will, won't you?"

"Yes, of course, Father, I'll go shortly." Her voice
was preoccupied. Rebecca was also staring into the
embers, but her thoughts followed a different line. She
was thinking about going to the spring just outside the
gate to wash her hair. It was filthy, stiff with sweat and
dust from days on the road. What a wonderful feeling
to be clean again—she could hardly resist.

William was saying something, but she only heard
the end of it, ". . . go to bed now. We are to rise very
early tomorrow morning to reach Kabul by noon,
Rebecca."

"Yes, William, I know. I think I'll just stay here for a

few more minutes. It's so peaceful tonight," she fabricated.

William rose and went to her. He took one of her small white hands and raised it to his lips. "Then good night, my darling, and sweet dreams." He disappeared into the tent's shadowed doorway.

Rebecca waited for a few minutes until the camp was quiet, then she quickly slipped out of the gate of the caravanserai. The water from the little spring made a cool black pool in the darkness. She took off her heavy skirt, her gray jacket, and her blouse. The night air caressed her hot skin as she stood by the pool in her petticoat, taking the pins out of her hair. Quietly, she knelt by the pool and began to wash the long heavy tresses of honey-colored hair. It felt heavenly to her after the days of torrid heat and endless dust.

After she finished her task she put on her skirt and decided to allow her mass of dripping hair to drip freely down her back since she had nothing clean to towel it dry. Briefly, she considered how wonderful it would be just to stroll to the tent without having to redress completely, to let the evening breeze caress her chest and back. Quickly, she forced the hedonistic thought from her mind, knowing if she had the nerve to act on it there would be an incredible scandal that could never be lived down. Still, it would be lovely to give into such an impulse some day, provided she were in an isolated spot.

As she turned to reach for her blouse, her hand froze in shock. William was standing just behind her watching her every move. His face had an intent look upon it and his lips were tight with suppressed emotion.

"William! What are you doing here? How dare you spy on me!" she whispered. "I thought you were asleep." She was quickly buttoning her blouse, aware of his eyes on her white skin and swelling breasts.

"I was restless, I couldn't sleep," he said in a strange hoarse voice, stepping closer. His rather small hand reached out and his fingers brushed the skin of her bosom. His other hand held her arm tightly. Rebecca looked up at his white face. His eyes were like dark, burning holes. His mouth was slightly open.

"You have no idea what you do to a man, do you, my innocent little girl?" He sounded as if he were in pain. "I've tried to keep away from you. On my honor, I have tried. But you are too much for even the strongest man to ignore."

Rebecca heard his words and despite the fear of her position she was a little excited by them. She had never been so close to a man before when her own thoughts were so sensual. She could feel the tenseness of his body, the pure animal force of him.

"I must go." she said weakly. "William, you must let me go!"

"Not so soon," he rasped. Then he pulled her close and covered her lips with his own hot searching mouth. She felt the strength of the whole length of his body pressed against her. She felt the hard bulge of his maleness thrust into her stomach; her breasts were squeezed hard against his chest. His tongue found hers and probed it. Rebecca began to tremble, whether from fear or from reaction to his nearness, she did not know. William covered her neck with kisses and was beginning to undo the buttons of her blouse. She pulled back from him in panic, but he held her tightly and continued to fumble with her clothing. She began to twist in his arms and brought up her hands to push against his chest. Suddenly he stiffened. Then Rebecca heard a worried voice calling her.

"Missy Sahib, Missy Sahib, where are you?" It was Meera, her voice on the edge of panic.

Rebecca gave one last wild shove. At last she was free! With one hand she snatched her jacket from the ground and with the other holding her blouse together, she ran back to the gate of the caravanserai.

"Here I am, Meera! Don't worry. Nothing has happened to me. I was just washing my hair in the spring. See? It's still all wet. Come help me comb it out.

It's in a terrible tangle." The words came tumbling out over each other. Meera looked at her mistress strangely. With such red cheeks and her air of excitement she hardly looked as though she had been washing her hair. But her long curls, wet and plastered to her back, needed brushing badly, so Meera followed her into their tent. The flap was closed and only a dim candle light flickered through the canvas.

Meera finally succeeded in combing the knots out of Rebecca's hair and the honey-colored curls hung clean and shining down to her waist.

Sleep was a long time in coming to Rebecca. As she lay on the hard cot, foreign images were whirling around her head. Her last coherent thought before sleep claimed her was confusing, but she acknowledged it anyway, as truthfulness was second nature to Rebecca. Had she really been relieved when Meera interrupted William tonight?

CHAPTER 7

After an early start the next morning, they made good time and had nearly reached Kabul by noon. Everyone was anxiously watching the horizon to see the first buildings of the capital city. Rebecca cantered Alia up to the front of the column and finally saw the city she had traveled so many long months to reach. It was not prepossessing. The buildings were mostly earth-brown; a few were whitewashed. There were hardly any trees, no parks, no boulevards, no elegant facades. It was an ancient middle-Asian city, sacked by conquerors more times than the inhabitants had bothered to count. Genghis Khan had been through here, as had Tamerlane and Alexander the Great. Kabul still dozed in the harsh light of the Afghan steppes, waiting for destiny to touch her once more.

The Shah of Afghanistan did not live in the city, but had his residence outside of Kabul in an ancient walled palace. The British compound was also outside of the city itself, and this was where Lieutenant Smithers led his small caravan.

The soldiers were obviously very glad to have arrived with so little trouble along the way. They looked forward to joining the British force here. There was strength in numbers to combat the dangers of this country.

Lawrence Merideth was relieved to be home with his daughter safe at his side. He hoped she would settle in well here and enjoy the rest of the British colony. There were very few English women in Kabul due to the primitive conditions and constant danger of native attacks. Several hardy officers' wives, a few wives of East India Company employees, and government officials constituted the whole contingent of English ladies. There was also a handful of French wives and one Russian lady who had accompanied her husband, the Russian commercial agent.

They rode up to the British compound which was surrounded by high mud walls. A private opened the gate and they entered a transplanted English town. Everything possible had been done to make the two-story, mud brick houses attractive. They were whitewashed and neatly kept. The streets were clean. There were even some bedraggled flower gardens scattered here and there. But the heavy gate was always guarded and the foreigners, or *ferangi*, as they were called, were not able to move about as freely as they might wish.

Lawrence Merideth's house was very comfortable, containing a wing for servants, a large suite upstairs for Rebecca, and a comfortable sitting room downstairs. There was also a courtyard in the rear protected by the ever-present mud walls. The furniture was simple, but tastefully arranged, most having arrived from India by pack mule or camel. Lawrence had a cook who lived in and two men who did everything else, as Afghan woman were heavily veiled and rarely left home. It was fortunate that Rebecca had Meera as a companion and maid because no Afghan woman would be allowed to work in the house of a ferangi.

The soldiers unloaded the Merideths' luggage for their two male servants to take care of while Rebecca said good-bye to Lieutenant Smithers who had escorted them so far. William waited impatiently for the young lieutenant to depart so that he could have a word with Rebecca. He finally saw a chance to talk privately with her while Meera was seeing to her trunks.

"I must see you again," he said softly. "I hope that last night has not given you too poor an opinion of me, but I am only human . . . Your beauty overcame my better sense, I'm afraid. I don't know what to say except that I pray for your forgiveness." He looked earnestly into her eyes.

"Yes, of course I forgive you, William," she said, unable to meet his eyes. "I fear it was partly my fault. I assure you that there will be no repeat of last night's . . . performance. And now I must really retire to my rooms and try to get settled. I know we shall be seeing a lot of each other in the future, and I would like us to be friends."

William's face lit up with happiness. "As long as I can hope, Rebecca, I am content." He turned and followed the manservant sent by the governor to show him his own lodgings.

Rebecca had found it easy to adjust to the routine of her father's house as it was a casual pleasant residence. She had met several of the English wives in the compound. Each Englishwoman had taken it upon herself to visit the new arrival, had exclaimed over her dresses which were the latest fashions from London, and had warned Rebecca not to go out alone in the streets of Kabul. She found them all narrow-minded, provincial, and alike in hating their present post. The exception was a rotund, jolly, middle-aged lady named Polly Swanson, who was very likable and gentle and who had a habit of saying too much about almost everything. She was the only one who had a good word for the natives of Afghanistan or the country itself.

Rebecca had tried to change the monotonous fare that Lawrence's cook prepared. *Pilau,* rice, greasy with mutton fat, and mutton stew were his specialties. He rarely deviated from these dishes. Rebecca went to the kitchen one morning with the purpose of introducing some varied meals to his repertoire. He only knew a few words of English, but through pointing and pantomime, she got him to understand that she would like some fresh vegetables and fruit served and perhaps some chicken. The cook was a tiny frail old man, bent and seamed by the years in this harsh climate. Nur Mustafa had shrewd black eyes that looked out from heavy folds of skin.

Nur Mustafa did not show it but he was mortified to be addressed by this brazen ferangi female whose face was uncovered. He mumbled and nodded, agreeing to everything she said so she would remove herself from his kitchen as quickly as possible. Meanwhile, he assured himself inwardly that he would continue to cook precisely the same dishes he had heretofore.

Rebecca left the kitchen feeling very proud of herself. She had already begun to organize her father's house more suitably and felt that he would be pleased. As she entered the cool sitting room, one of the servants brought her an envelope addressed to Mistress Rebecca Merideth. It was from the governor's office, and was an invitation from William to show her around Kabul and explore the bazaar together. Could he have the pleasure of her company around two in the afternoon tomorrow? Rebecca sent her reply that she would be happy to accept the kind invitation. Then she ran upstairs to select a becoming outfit for the next day.

CHAPTER 8

The next day promptly at two, William drove up in a small carriage he had borrowed from the governor. Rebecca was ready for him, looking demure in a frilly white blouse that framed her lovely throat and brown taffeta skirt. Her hair was flowing loose, tied back by a velvet ribbon. She was highly excited about seeing the exotic capital city and its inhabitants. So far she had seen only the British compound for scenery and her father's three servants for local color.

"Oh William!" she cried exuberantly as he helped her and Meera into the carriage. "I want to see everything . . . everything in this fascinating place. I want to know it as I know London!"

"Well, I hardly think you would want to know Kabul as well as you do London," he said dryly.

"Of course I would." She looked at him in surprise as he whipped up the horse, then settled back to take in the atmosphere of the area.

Lawrence had been pleased that she had something with which to occupy her time while he was at work, although he would have preferred almost anyone else to be her guide. He had insisted that Meera accompany Rebecca and William everywhere. The thought of his daughter out with that man made him shake his head to himself.

Shortly after leaving the compound, they entered the city itself. They were headed for the bazaar which was located in the old right bank section. The narrow streets were full of men dressed in sandals, baggy white pants, long white shirts worn outside the pants, and often beautifully patterned vests over it all. Rebecca was surprised to see guns being carried openly and bandoliers across many a broad chest.

To Rebecca, the bazaar had the allure of the unique. It was full of tiny shops selling everything from nuts and bolts to silver tea services of exquisite workmanship. All around the young English couple were Afghans bartering and haggling in *Pashto,* the *lingua franca* of Afghanistan.

The men sitting placidly in a *chaikana* sipped their strong tea and inhaled smoke, bubbling it through the water of the *nargile.* When they saw William and Rebecca they nudged each other, silently mouthing the word ferangi. Their malevolent scowls made Rebecca hurry past the open shops nervously, feeling very much the intruder in their ancient world.

The aroma of the bazaar was compounded of spices, dirty sheep, human bodies, and the open sewer that ran down the middle of the street.

"William, what kind of man is that? Where is he from?" Rebecca whispered, unable to contain her fascinated stare. The man walked arrogantly through the crowd which parted respectfully in front of him. He carried a vicious looking whip stuck in the sash which belted his long striped coat. A turban and leather boots with high heels completed his outfit.

"He is a Turkoman from the north. They are the famous horsemen you have heard your father speak of. Governor Mountstuart has been trying desperately to gain their trust, but they seem disinterested in our overtures. To tell the truth, we are afraid they're going to give their allegiance to the Russians—a bad thing all around, I should say. Do you recall meeting Madame Potrofsky? She is the Russian agent's wife. He's here to influence them against us, you see. Those Russians are sly ones!"

"I should say so!" answered Rebecca, agreeing with him, although she personally thought Madame Potrofsky charming.

Exploring the bazaar on foot was an adventure for Rebecca. She stopped at every shop exclaiming, touching, comparing. The merchants smiled happily at her, recognizing an easy mark, proudly dragging merchandise from piles of items that they could not sell to their own women who were sharp at bargaining.

Rebecca loved the narrow old streets that wound along the river. She was excited by the teeming humanity and was not in the least put out by the strange and sometimes unpleasant aromas that emerged from the crowds. Neither did she mind the jostling and curious stares given to them as ferangi. She found the whole experience thrilling.

After shopping for a time, Rebecca decided to buy a graceful pair of gold hoops for Meera's ears, a length of Chinese silk for herself, and an exquisitely embroidered vest for Lawrence.

"He will be able to wear it at home in the evenings," she told William teasingly, "even if he doesn't choose to wear it out."

"It certainly appears to be fine workmanship. I am sure your father will love it," replied William, trying to picture the dignified Mr. Merideth in this brightly colored garment.

"Now I simply must attend to the real reason I had for coming to the bazaar. Oh, not that your company was not enough reason, William! But truly, I must replace a worn carpet in the sitting room. Shall we look for the street of carpet merchants?"

They picked their way through the malodorous streets, avoiding donkeys, camels, and small children, finally arriving at the street of the most prestigious merchants—those who handled the traditionally hand-woven wool carpets, slaved over for months by veiled wives and daughters, tediously reproducing the ancient patterns and colors. Each was a work of art.

One shop in particular caught Rebecca's eye. It was large and prosperous looking. The owner was quite repulsive—obese and squat as a toad, with a pendulous lower lip that showed a froth of spittle as he talked. Foul breath emanated from the gaps in his stained teeth. He spoke English reasonably well, however, and addressed Rebecca effusively as she entered his place of business.

"Madame, welcome to my humble shop. I am Suraj Mal, best carpet merchant in Kabul. You have not picked wrongly to enter my store. Here you find the dreams and ambitions of my people, woven into design, color, texture. Look, see this one, a poem in crimson, or this, a blue fantasy. I have whatever you are wanting."

She was quite overcome by his attention, as well as his breath, and did not know what to reply.

Suraj Mal, seeing her confusion, took the opportunity to turn to William and say to him quietly, "And if there is anything *else* the fine gentleman is wanting, only let Suraj know. He can get you anything you need." He winked, suggestively.

"Oh, William, look at this one! Don't you think it will go well in the sitting room? Look at the colors! What a beautiful pattern," cried Rebecca, holding up a corner of a deep red carpet.

"Beautiful."

"An excellent choice," broke in the fat merchant. "The lady is a connoisseur! This carpet is soaked with the tears of a lovely young widow who wept as she created this treasure, wept for her young husband, brutally slain by bandits, and for her fatherless children. And it will only cost you one thousand afghanis! A bargain!"

"One thousand," sputtered William. "You are a bloody thief!"

"Now, now, young gentleman, do not become upset. Perhaps we can discuss the price further . . ."

An hour of haggling followed, with Rebecca happily

getting her carpet for six-hundred-and-fifty afghanis, and Suraj Mal making a clear profit of four hundred afghanis.

By the time Rebecca turned to leave the stuffy shop her velvet ribbon was slipping and her cheeks were flushed with pleasure. She wound her way through the narrow aisles between the piles of carpets, watching her feet carefully to see that she did not trip over a stray rug. Suddenly, she bumped headlong into a substantial figure. Looking up, she was startled enough to drop a package. Rebecca had to run her hand through a mass of stray curls that had bounced loose into her face in order to see clearly. Strong hands braced her waist while she tried to regain her composure and balance.

She had an impression of keen gray eyes, thick dark hair, a wide humorous mouth, an animal sensuality. He was obviously an Afghan, extremely handsome—dressed like the Turkoman she had seen earlier.

She was completely astonished when he smiled and said to her in perfect, unaccented English, "Excuse me, Madame, but I believe you have dropped something. Allow me."

He bent to retrieve her package, and handed it to her politely with the barest trace of a smile on his lips. Because of his tall stature, Rebecca had to tilt her head up to get a complete view of this singular man. Their eyes met as his strong hand touched hers inadvertantly while giving her the parcel. She felt a tingling spread out from her fingers; her eyes could not tear themselves away from his coolly appraising gray ones. A small nagging sense of recognition clouded her brain for an instant but then quickly receded.

His stare broke away first, searching behind her for something. He caught sight of Suraj Mal in the shadowed rear of the shop and left her standing there. She wondered how she could have allowed him to affect her so.

William and Meera came up to her, having arranged the delivery of her carpet. She recovered herself and they left the shop, reentering the stream of humanity that thronged the street.

Rebecca had loved every second of their tour. She looked charmingly disarrayed as the afternoon drew to an end. Her hair was tangled, her blouse had a small tear in it from the jostling in the bazaar, and her cheek was smudged with dirt. Meera was exhausted, William was trying not to show his foul mood, but Rebecca was still enthralled by all she had seen.

As they drove through the gate of the British compound, she felt a small cloud descend upon her. She was cut off from the life and excitement of the city, returned to the dull security of home.

When they arrived at the Merideth's house, etiquette required that she invite William in for some refreshment. To her slight annoyance, he accepted with alacrity.

One of the servants, a young boy of thirteen or so, brought them tea in the sitting room where they sat and chatted about the afternoon, especially of fat Suraj Mal.

William was rising to leave, when they heard Lawrence Merideth arrive home.

"Good evening, Mr. St. Claire," he said, nodding to William. "Good evening, my dear, and how did your afternoon go? More than satisfactory, I would say by the look of you! I'll wager she led you a merry chase, Mr. St. Claire. I know my daughter."

"That she did, sir, but I must admit to having enjoyed it thoroughly."

"I have some interesting news for both of you," Lawrence went on. "Governor Mountstuart is planning a ball for all of the British nationals posted in Kabul. He usually plans such an event to get us through the summer doldrums, but this year it is to be a special affair. He has planned it especially in your honor, Rebecca, to enable you to meet everyone here. What do you think of that, my girl?"

"Oh, Father, what a wonderful idea! How nice of the governor, and he does not even know me!" cried Rebecca, her eyes sparkling. "When is it to be? And what should I wear?"

"Isn't that just like a woman!" exclaimed Lawrence, smiling fondly at her. "It will be held next Saturday evening at the governor's residence and I shall be happy to be your escort, my dear."

Rebecca turned to William, "I expect you will also be going William, won't you?"

"Yes, of course. I had heard the governor mention such a plan the other day, but I had no idea he meant to put it in effect so soon. It should prove to be the social event of the year," he replied. "Do save me a dance, Rebecca, as you are sure to be overwhelmed by invitations."

"Do you really think so?" she asked, her large eyes wide with anticipation. "Oh William, what *fun* it will be, I can hardly wait!"

"Waiting will be harder for all the young men who have heard there is an unattached young lady newly arrived here," replied William. "I really must be going now. It has been a charming afternoon which I hope we can repeat soon. Good-bye, Rebecca. Good-bye, Mr. Merideth."

As the door closed behind William, Lawrence could not but help to put his feelings into words. "Rebecca, Mr. St. Claire seems to be an upright young man, but he gives me an eerie feeling at times. He is so smooth, so collected, yet I feel there is something intense under the surface. And I'm not sure he has good intentions toward you."

"Mr. Merideth!" Rebecca replied jokingly, "You sound like an overprotective father! William has been a good friend to me . . . He is harmless. You should be glad he is around to protect me from all those dangerous natives I hear about!"

"Rebecca," Lawrence said sternly, "that is not a

joking matter. You did not travel all this way to be kidnapped by a bandit *or* to be foisted off on a self-seeking adventurer."

"Of course, Father. I did not mean to be flippant. But with all there is to see in this country and the ball coming up, I just cannot bring myself to take William seriously at the moment."

She felt a little guilty at this statement, knowing that William desperately wanted to bring up the subject of betrothal with her father. At this point she felt she could easily hold William at bay, not upset her father, and have a delightful time herself. It was just a matter of keeping the men in her life in their proper places. And they say *women* are the weaker sex, thought Rebecca to herself, almost giggling aloud at this revelation.

CHAPTER 9

The day of the governor's ball had finally arrived. Meera was even more elated over Rebecca's gown than she was herself. There were many dilatory preparations to be made at the Merideth house that afternoon. Lawrence had never seen such a fuss over a ball, at least not since his adored wife had also spent her entire day in a tither over a prospective party.

In the early evening, Meera prepared a scented bath for Rebecca. She insisted that Missy Sahib soak until all the perfumes were fully taken into her skin. Rebecca, trying to remain good-natured, complied until she thought her skin would turn into a mass of wrinkles if she stayed in the water an instant longer.

She winced as she stepped into the waiting towel. "Look at my skin. Why, I'm lucky I don't look as old as Methuselah!"

"Missy, Missy, please to be having faith in Meera! Now, come to bed and be lying down on stomach." Her mistress complied, knowing a massage would help her relax.

Rebecca's nostrils were at once assailed by a most delightful fragrance. It was an oily lotion that Meera had made from local flowers and herbs. Rebecca was charmed by the care Meera had taken to prepare the balm. She lay giggling softly while Meera gave her a complete rubdown, head to toe. Rebecca's skin gleamed with a soft peach glow and she found her nerves completely soothed.

Mounds of petticoats were put in place before the tedious job of hairdressing commenced. Rebecca's hair was done simply, piled high on her head with a few golden locks falling softly around her shoulders. Meera then placed several pink flowers into the swirling masses of hair. Rebecca had never seen this done before and was completely delighted with the effect it had of enhancing her coloring. Certainly no rouge need be applied here!

The dress came next. The fabric was a lustrous, pale mint-green silk. It had a flowing skirt and a daring deeply-cut neckline. The tight bodice did much to heighten the swelling curves of her breasts, pushing the globes higher than Rebecca was sure would be proper. Meera thought her mistress looked like a flower; pale green dress, graceful neck curving into a ring of golden petals. A delicate, shimmering gold locket of her mother's was placed around her slim neck just in time to hear Lawrence bellow, "My Lord, woman! The ball will be over before we even leave this house! May I enter?"

"Of course, Father. Why *I've* been waiting for *you!*"

He had been ready to reprimand his daughter for telling such a fib when his eyes fell on her. Lawrence knew, then, that he had been far wrong in comparing her to his wife. Rebecca was much more beautiful, but in a sensual way. Her long dark lashes lay silky and thick over her eyes as she realized that he was at a loss for words.

Meera saved the situation, saying quickly, "Missy is beautiful, yes? She was not looking very prettily before Meera making her so!" The tension was broken as all laughed at Meera's lightheartedness and hurried out to the awaiting carriage.

Kabul was cloaked in a warm darkness, the shimmering moon casting a serene glow over the city. As the open coach rolled to a stop in front of Governor David Mountstuart's mansion, Lawrence became slightly apprehensive over the attention William would undoubtedly pay to Rebecca. He knew that, at least tonight, William would have to wait in a long line to chance a talk with her. Somehow the thought was comforting to him.

The Merideth party was indeed later then most of the other guests. Rebecca's entrance was more dramatic than she could have dreamed. A whisper fell on the crowd and all eyes were upon her. The radiance of her dress topped with the soft petals in her hair would be the talk of the tea-circuits for months to come. She glistened with perfection; the overall effect far outshone any other woman present. Introductions were made when the young civilian and military men gathered around her. Polly Swanson, seeing Rebecca's predicament, came to the rescue with a glass of punch. She hurried the girl away to a quieter spot among the ladies, for the music had yet to begin.

Rebecca finally had a chance to observe her surroundings. The mansion had been prepared for the ball with a touch of elegance she had not seen since London. There were bright lights for the feasting area, while the ballroom was adorned with softer candlelight, creating a dreamy effect. The rooms were both spacious and airy so that the guests would remain cool. A myriad of native male servants, dressed from head to toe in starched white cotton, scurried to produce heavy silver trays of hors d'oeuvres, while others kept their posts near the walls as they pulled endlessly on the thin ropes of the overhead punkah fans. The veranda was lit with warm candles and a punch bowl with exotic fruits had been placed near the garden area. Varied flowers were in bloom, sweet-smelling in the balmy Asian night. Rebecca knew that she would enjoy this evening and would relish each minute.

Casually approaching Rebecca and Polly, William pronounced possessively, "Darling, your entrance was planned perfectly. I really could not get through the crowds to wish you a good evening. I trust you saved me a dance?" His eyes were hot.

Rebecca, feeling a trifle daring, replied, "Oh, William, I really had hoped to save some moments to acquaint myself, at last, with some of the other guests. I've had so little time to meet the English people here. So many of my days have been taken up by you. I'll try to save you a dance, but I would like some time to circulate." She tapped him lightly with her ivory fan.

She had not meant to rebuff William, especially in front of listeners, but enough was enough! William, bowing too deeply, disappeared. Rebecca felt rather mischievous, if not a touch guilty. But, after all, she really couldn't give him her total attention. What would people think!

The party was a complete success, at least as far as Rebecca was concerned. Before the first set of music had begun, she had met many handsome men, and flirted outrageously with them all. Out on the veranda, between waltzes, Rebecca was introduced to an attractive woman a little older than herself. The woman, Catherine Mansfield, was married to a gentleman nearly the age of Lawrence Merideth, Thomas being the colonel at the outpost of Mazar-i-Sharif. It seemed to Rebecca that the young lady was terribly lonely for a companion her own age, as Catherine implored her to visit the outpost. The garrison at Mazar-i-Sharif was apparently small, remote, and boring for a sole woman. Rebecca promised to speak with her father about a visit the very first opportunity she had.

Rebecca and Catherine had struck an almost instantaneous friendship. They laughed and chatted for some minutes before Rebecca was again claimed for a dance. She felt faintly embarrassed to have forgotten her latest partner's name. There had been so many introductions, so many attractive young men!

When a cool breeze swept across the hard wood floor, Rebecca felt the air lift her hem a few inches and she felt so free, so gay. How long had it been since she had whirled around a ballroom with so many attentive men? Aeons, she thought. After her grandfather's untimely demise, she had been compelled to clothe herself in black mourning attire. Naturally, there had been no balls, no dancing and very little opportunity to talk with young men.

When the music stopped for a few minutes, Rebecca spotted Eleanor Mountstuart, who was waving at the vivacious girl and beckoning her to come over. Rebecca politely excused herself from her escort of the moment and headed toward the older woman.

Her skirts billowing and swirling gracefully, she crossed the dance floor. Eleanor watched her glide, feather-light, poised and confident, and thought that Kabul would hear much of this rare newcomer. Rebecca was indeed a vision that night, her coloring high and glowing, her skin healthy and slightly tanned from the hours spent in the sun and fresh air. Even her hair sparkled with pale yellow streaks of gold, contrasting sharply with her deep brown eyes and lashes. Yes, indeed, Eleanor Mountstuart thought, this charming young lady shall have few dull moments in her life here.

Rebecca stopped in front of the woman and curtsied deeply. They stood at the foot of the elegant staircase leading to the ballroom. A silver candelabra behind Rebecca cast a faint glow of peach and gold on her hair and bare shoulders.

She spoke gaily, "Oh, Mrs. Mountstuart, I cannot tell you how much I am enjoying the party. How can I ever thank you enough?"

"No need, my dear. David and I have welcomed the opportunity to entertain you. In fact, I shall be quite hurt if you don't come to tea in the next few days."

Rebecca was truly glad that Mrs. Mountstuart was so gracious a hostess. So many of the matronly women in England could easily pretend a smile and play at hospitality, while all the time they were bored to distraction. The governor's wife was an openly warm person, whom Rebecca liked instantly.

Rebecca was about to excuse herself when she hesitated and looked over Mrs. Mountstuart's graying hair. At the head of the steps standing magnificently tall stood a dark-complected man dressed in elegant native attire. Rebecca first noticed his high soft-leather boots; they were well shined but reminded her of harder days spent astride a horse. His tight-fitting breeches outlined fine muscular thighs, partially covered by his raw silk *chapan*. The coat was striped with deep shades of emerald and ivory. His Afghan dress was completed with an intricately wound turban. Rebecca realized that she was staring at the man, but her eyes could not tear away from his dark gaze. The piercing gray color of his eyes held her frozen to the spot. All movement stood still around her. She felt her breath catch in her throat.

The man was coming down toward them, his stare never leaving Rebecca. She wanted desperately to flee, but could not. There was something so physically compelling about this handsome man that she forgot all modesty and boldly returned his gaze.

"My dear, I must introduce you to our friend, Alex Drayton." Eleanor felt the tension in the air between them. She would have to speak to this Mr. Drayton about his manners. A man did not go about glaring at a young girl. He was behaving like a complete rogue. ". . . and this is Miss Rebecca Merideth. I believe you have met her father, Lawrence—" Eleanor was unable to continue, Alex Drayton had interrupted her.

"My people call me Azim." His voice was a hauntingly familiar low drawl, seductive in its manliness. "Eleanor prefers to call me by my given name. Actually, Miss Merideth and I have met once before—"

"I hardly recall meeting you," Rebecca broke in, her tone higher than she expected. But she did have the feeling that they had indeed gazed into one another's eyes before. But where? Why couldn't he wipe that infernal grin off his face? She fanned her warm cheeks nervously.

"Ah yes, you have forgotten. It was one day in the

bazaar, I believe. You dropped a package. A rather stocky man accompanied you." His stare fell directly to her neckline, making absolutely no attempt to be discreet.

Must he insult William? she thought. But her voice came back, "Why, yes. I suppose I do remember now," she fumbled. How dare he rake her body with his eyes?

"And now I believe we have this dance." It was not a question, but a command. Rebecca would have put him off then and there except that he was already steering her onto the floor. His grip was gentle but firm enough that she thought her arm would surely come off if she resisted. What impertinence!

Eleanor watched the entire scene with mixed emotions. What a divine couple they made! No doubt there would be many envious ladies here tonight, for Alex was the most devilishly handsome man any of them had ever met. But poor Rebecca, what if he decided to pursue her? Had any woman ever survived his attentions without much heartache? Eleanor decided to warn the innocent young woman before Alex could add her to his long list of conquests.

Rebecca recalled later that her next few minutes at the ball were like living in a dream. The edges of her perception were clouded and fuzzy. Contrarily, the core of her vision remained sharp and clear. Time hung motionless before her.

The musicians were playing a slow waltz that Azim followed gracefully. Rebecca glided along with his movements, floating on a sea of confused emotions. She felt herself reddening under his bold glances. But Rebecca could not move from him. When she dared to look at his face she found him more and more attractive. His nose was not altogether British, but from the side, hinted at Gallic ancestry. It was his mouth that held her fascinated, a wide curved smile with a sardonic twist. His lips were sensuous and tempting.

Rebecca could have stayed in his embrace forever,

even though it was too close for propriety's sake, but she felt an odd sensation of fear beginning to tingle her spine. What was the matter with her? Was she so fickle that a man need only touch her to send her senses spinning? She stiffened slightly and tried to calm her nerves.

"Mr. Drayton, I do not recall accepting your offer to dance. Now if you will—" His hand tightened around her narrow waist causing a small gasp to escape her rounded lips.

"My beautiful little flower." He tilted his head to sniff her petalled hair. "I thought that I told you to call me Azim." He finished by looking into her outraged face with his keen gray eyes.

Rebecca's head was light and she trembled delicately. "Sir, I don't think that I should continue to dance. You are rude and ill-bred. No man has ever spoken to me that way!"

Azim laughed aloud at her retort. "It would seem then," his eyes held her spellbound, "that you find a man's physical attentions more to your taste."

"I . . . I fail to understand . . ." she was utterly confounded and fell speechless.

"Either you are a good liar, or you really do not recall our brief encounter—"

"But, I do, sir! It was the day I purchased the new carpet—"

"Hardly." He whirled her effortlessly around the dance floor, the heady smell of her sweet scent causing his blood to boil. "Did you not dine, once, at the Bombay Staff Club?"

She looked quickly up into his intent gaze, and in her confused thoughts she wondered how she managed to keep step with the music. And then suddenly, shockingly, the memory of that night flooded her mind. Yes, she had indeed met this man before the day in the carpet shop, but the incident was cloudy in her memory—it had seemed of little importance at the time, a ridiculous misunderstanding. And the garden had been cast in night shadows, she recalled. So *this* was the brash stranger who had come to her unwanted assistance and confronted William!

"Yes," she whispered, still in dazed disbelief. "As I recall the time, you were quite out of turn, sir."

"I sought only to protect a lovely lady from possible danger . . . but now I see plainly that the man's attentions were welcome."

"Oh!" She wished she could find words to throw in his arrogant face, but the music had stopped for the moment and she turned to leave instead.

Yet her escape was not to be so simple as he deftly caught her upper arm and turned her back to face him. "I should hate to cause a scene—"

"*That*, sir, you have already done!"

"Then stay, and for God's sake, smile. Act as if you enjoy the ball!" The music began again and there was no help for it. Azim drew her into his arms once more and led her helplessly into the throng of dancers. Suddenly, she felt herself unable to resist his bold attentions. Certainly, the man had a way about him, a fascinating charisma that weakened her will.

She determined not to let him see her nervousness. "My father is the East India Company representative here, and I'm sure he would not take kindly to your abusive manner!" Had she been firm enough?

Azim's face was all but kind, his tone mocking her. "Ah! So soon after we've met and already you fear for my safety. How touching."

Tears welling in her eyes, she parried, "Why, I should slap your face! How dare you . . . Oh!" A single tear slipped down her cheek. She was frustrated to be at a loss for words.

His features grew dark, the suntanned face showing a thin white line from a slanted scar on his forehead. "Even a rare beauty, such as yourself, would be wise to think twice before striking a man. I suggest that we finish our dance and stop taunting one another before we create a scene." His tone was decisive and she would normally have responded, but his logic was too sound.

Trying to forget his crude manner and to compose herself, Rebecca relaxed again in the cradle of his arms and once more enjoyed his nearness. Azim's confident stare continued to fall on her. She knew that she really should have slapped the vile smirk from his face.

Although Rebecca was not short, Azim still stood at least a head taller, affording him a delightful view down her low-cut bodice. Her bosom rose and fell rapidly, not from the dance, he was certain, but from her confusion. The full swells rounded perfectly above the green silk gown. Her flesh was soft and peachy—his lips ached to touch her there. He wondered how soon he could maneuver her into the garden, never doubting that she would come. This goddess had almost made him feel a tenderness for her, but she was probably like all the rest, ever ready to act the role of virgin, ever eager to roll in the hay if it got her what she wanted.

Rebecca gathered the courage to raise her eyes to him, "I'm certain that you are often asked this, but why are you dressed like an Afghan?" Immediately she wished she had not bothered to show an interest in him, but still, he did hold a strange fascination for her.

Azim held her apart from him. The music had stopped without her even noticing it. "Your curiosity, my sweet, is easily satisfied. I have, through peculiar circumstances, chosen to live my life in the steppes of Afghanistan. I find the people and their customs eminently more exciting than the rather dry British ones back in England." He ended his explanation while leading Rebecca out to the veranda.

She was not fooled by his ploy to distract her. Did this Afghan, or whatever he called himself, think that she was so taken by his good looks that she would obediently follow him?

Rebecca pulled her arm away from his grasp. She steadied her voice, "Where do you think you're taking me? I vow you are much too forward for my taste!" Her voice, however, did not match her brave words. The man had an animal attractiveness and Rebecca was not immune to his charm.

Where was William? He was forever under foot when she least wanted him and now she could not find him. Rebecca looked around for assistance, but only a few of the women had noticed her position, their glares anything but helpful!

Azim knew that he was losing ground. He was a little baffled by her resistance. Most of his conquests had succumbed with ease, but this sweet rose was not, seemingly, of the same mold. He felt the game: His body responded to her coyness. This chase would definitely be worth his full attention—the prize, a treasure more precious than any before.

Azim smoothed his normally harsh voice. "Miss Merideth, I only thought to get you a sip of punch, but, if I frighten you . . ." This usually brought the sought after reaction.

"Well, I guess a glass of punch would not hurt, but then I must find my father, I haven't seen him in hours." Rebecca had fallen prey, she had taken his bait and knew it. The game had become intriguing and left her breathless with anticipation. But victory would be hers when she showed him her back and left him standing on the terrace alone. Let him remember her in William's embrace. The thought caused her to smile.

Azim was almost disappointed when she had given in so easily. The delightful creature was just like all the rest. Too easy! He ladled Rebecca a cup of punch and eased her over to the garden's edge.

Somehow Rebecca had waited too long to make her move.

They stood apart and eyed one another. Azim was taken aback by her beauty. She appeared so young, so delicious, that his look boldly stripped her. Rebecca was totally involved in her confused senses. Something hidden, something gnawing was growing in the pit of her stomach. She blushed too easily from his caressing eyes. What was this unusual man doing to her composure? She quickly raised the ivory fan to cover her confusion and lowered her eyes.

Azim saw her skin redden from his gaze. The deep coloring fell all the way to her full breasts. God, she was lovely! He tried to step nearer. She backed instantly. After all, she was going to turn and walk away, any minute now.

"Don't look at me that way." Her words fell like a caress, not at all the way they should have!

"Do I frighten you? I won't hurt you. Come with me, only for a second . . ." Azim took her trembling hand, leading her just out of sight of the veranda.

His manner, his maleness were hypnotic to her and she ceased to think clearly. What if he touched her? But of course he would! She knew that she wanted him to kiss her, to feel his strong arms around her!

Rebecca panicked. She jerked her arm free, but only for an instant. Azim pulled her shoulders toward him. She was both terrified and dizzy at the same time. His lips came close to hers, he moaned hoarsely, "You want me. Your eyes betray you, Flower."

His mouth covered hers tenderly at first. Azim knew what a woman liked. Rebecca felt a wave of warmth surge upward from her stomach. Never before had she known desire. She knew it now. Her mind said, run, he's dangerous. Her lips responded instead with a will of their own.

Azim's mouth moved harder now, his tongue parted her lips, and then he moved his head suddenly and looked into her glazed eyes.

"Tell me what you like . . ." His voice was a faint whisper. His lips moved to her neck, to her soft golden curls and down to the hollow at the base of her throat.

"Please . . . don't. I feel dizzy . . . My head is spinning." Rebecca could barely control her mixed sensations. He was so powerful—so handsome.

Azim eased her weakened body against a tree. He pressed himself against her, hard, and his mouth took hers, brutally. He was sure that Rebecca was on fire, that she would herself raise her gown. Instead, she was struggling against his male hardness grinding into her belly. She twisted and turned, fighting to free herself. Though in one respect she found this experience exciting, all she could think of with growing panic were the two forced, unpleasant attempts William had made. She couldn't breathe, she desperately needed air.

Azim was confused. He thought that perhaps she wanted more, that she was too *ready* for him. The girl was, of course, not innocent!

His mouth fell to her swelling bosom, his hand pushed upward from beneath them. Rebecca gave a weak gasp and her whole body slid into his arms. Her head fell backward nearly snapping her slim neck.

By God! She had fainted dead away!

Some minutes later Rebecca slowly opened her eyes to find herself lying on a settee in an unfamiliar room. Still in a daze, she could vaguely hear Azim's voice.

"Mr. Merideth, I'm glad you've come. Rebecca passed out in the garden, and I fear this is all my fault."

She sat up abruptly and interrupted him before he totally shamed her. "Oh, Father! It was awful, I was dancing, you see . . . Well, the air was so stifling, and I needed to . . . I guess . . . I simply fainted," she finished her fumbling explanation.

Lawrence raised a disbelieving eyebrow, but chose to remain silent. Azim had an amused expression on his face and unashamedly gazed into Rebecca's eyes.

Unafraid to fully explain his role in the mishap, Azim began again to relate what transpired. "I was saying, sir, that your daughter and I were in the garden and—"

"Mr. Drayton! I have already told my father what happened. I'm feeling much better now, so please, let's just drop the subject." When Rebecca shot him a threatening glance he decided to let her have her way.

Lawrence would normally have called the younger man out on the affair, but he feared that Rebecca's reputation would suffer further embarrassment. The three guests agreed to rejoin the party and were leaving the library when William bolted through the door, nearly bowling Rebecca over.

"Rebecca! I've just heard about your, ah, accident. Is there anything I can do?" She shook her head but that did not satisfy William St. Claire, who turned his attention to Azim.

His tone was low and menacing. "And you bloody . . . I saw you outside with Rebecca and I must demand satisfaction! Name your time and place!" William made sure that Mr. Merideth overheard his challenge. He prayed silently that Azim would not accept the invitation.

Azim laughed aloud at William's discomposure. "And where, may I inquire, were you hiding when I escorted Miss Merideth to the garden? Filling your punch cup, I presume?" Azim's amused expression seemed more of distaste than of humor. "I'll gladly fight you, sir. But make no mistake as to whom the victor would be. Are you certain that you wish to have your blood spilled?" His voice was mellow, but Lawrence and Rebecca knew that he was seething and would undoubtedly best poor St. Claire.

Placing herself between the two quarreling men, Rebecca hissed, "Enough of this! I have a reputation to uphold and I shan't allow this duel to take place. William, please mind your own business!" She hoped her obvious rebuff of him would end the whole hideous affair.

"There will be no duel," she scolded Azim. "If I felt that you behaved in any way improperly, I would myself insist on satisfaction." Rebecca hoped that her father would believe that the affair was innocent.

Azim was smiling down at her, completely unworried about her statement. He really hadn't expected the gorgeous creature to be so innocent and naive, but she certainly had not pretended to swoon. He could see no reason to humiliate her further. Azim directed his attention again to his adversary. "The lady would be done with the incident. Consider yourself lucky this night, St. Claire. I would advise you to think twice before interfering again in my personal life." Turning sharply, he bade Merideth a good night. He left the room, tall and lithe, disappearing into the midst of the dancers.

Rebecca gave a sigh of relief and, taking her father's arm, left William alone in the library. She felt that a "thank you" to him was unnecessary, as William had blundered in uninvited and had almost caused a worse situation to develop.

When the military band finally played the last melody for the night, Lawrence began searching for Rebecca. It was nearly two o'clock in the morning and he felt they must return home before he fell asleep on his feet. She was standing with Eleanor Mountstuart and was deeply engaged in conversation. Lawrence left the ladies for a few more moments, strolling, thinking to himself. First William, whom I can handle easily enough, but Alex Drayton! Well, that's a whole different problem. The man is an enigma. Perhaps that is why the ladies find him irresistible.

Eleanor Mountstuart was, at the same moment, telling Rebecca much the same thing that her father was brooding over.

". . . And I would not be interfering, my dear, except that without a mother to guide you, I feel that it is my duty to warn you about the man. Of course, this is simply gossip, but Alex Drayton normally leaves at least one broken heart behind him when he returns to his northern village." Eleanor felt awkward giving her warning for she usually would not have bothered, but Rebecca was so lovely, and Alex had spotted her immediately. Eleanor had every intention of talking to him also, but he would not listen, she felt sure.

Rebecca barely heard the woman's words. Her mind was on the encounter in the garden, which she viewed with both excitement and shame. Eleanor's speech brought her back to the present.

"It's rather a long story, but now Alex has chosen to live out his life in the steppes. His brother, Lord Blackstone—"

"Lord Blackstone! You don't mean to tell me that this Azim is Sir Stuart Drayton's brother! But that's remarkable. My grandfather was well-acquainted with him. I just cannot believe that he would allow his own brother to behave this way!"

Eleanor really could not fathom it either, and said as much. She explained that his brother wrote often to Alex and implored him to return home, but the young rascal would not even consider the matter. After his parents had been slain on some godforsaken pass he had been taken in by natives and would not leave them.

Rebecca felt that she was beginning to know something about the handsome stranger and, unfortunately, he only became more fascinating to her.

Lawrence finally interrupted the chatting ladies. He spoke with a barely suppressed yawn. "Rebecca, we really must be going now. I'm unable to stay awake another moment. You ladies will drive a man to an early grave if you don't allow him a rest."

The women laughed gaily and bid each other a good night. Rebecca took a few minutes to thank everyone for a lovely evening, and then they gathered their cloaks. At the head of the stairs, Rebecca frowned, noticing Azim gaily conversing with an attractive woman, rather older than himself. Her heart took a slight leap when his eyes followed her out of the door. She wished that the rogue had not seen her reaction to the other woman. Rebecca determined not to think about him again. He was apparently all that Eleanor Mountstuart had said! Apparently he felt no compunction about forcing his attentions on several women during the course of an evening! No, she would not think about him again. She had William to distract her. But the stranger's gaze mocked her as she turned away, leaving the room much too hastily.

On the way home, Rebecca looked lovingly at her sleeping father. Lawrence was propped comfortably against the side of the vehicle. He had fallen into a restful slumber before the carriage had left the drive. She wondered what his reaction would be to Catherine Mansfield's invitation to travel with them to Mazar-i-Sharif. She would love to see more of the country here, and it wouldn't hurt to get away from this Azim fellow for awhile—not to mention William. Rebecca spent the remainder of the ride home adding up all the advantages of just such a journey.

CHAPTER 10

The next afternoon, after Rebecca's late luncheon, Meera came into the dining room. It seemed that William was waiting for her to finish eating. She sighed, neatly folded her napkin, and went to join him in the garden. She was wearing a pale-pink summer frock, and had considered rouging her cheeks as the late hours at the ball had left her pale. No, she thought, not the late hours, but the lack of sleep. Rebecca had tossed and turned all night, unable to free her dreams of clear gray eyes, and a tall masculine body.

Shaking her head to clear her thoughts, she said, "William, don't you ever have duties to perform? Oh! Please forgive me. I'm just extremely sleepy today. What can I do for you?" She smiled as sweetly as she could.

"I only stopped by to see if you were all right. After all, that upstart, Drayton, frightened you terribly. Also, I wanted to explain why it took me so long to come to your rescue. I was talking to Governor Mountstuart when he—"

"Drayton, Azim! Whoever! I'm sick to death of that name! Let's not ever again mention him. Promise me? Between you and Father I rather think I shall go with the Mansfields next week."

William frowned. "Rebecca, we won't talk of him again, I promise. Now swear to me that you will not go on this absurd journey. It's not only dangerous, but I would miss you so terribly."

Seeing a way to silence him, she said, "I shall go. Yes, that's exactly what I need. Oh, William, don't you see? If I go now, you can approach Father while I'm gone. When I return, if Father agrees, I'll promise to give you my decision within a day. Now let's not have any words over this. My mind is quite made up."

"I'll not mention it again, but do you swear to give me a favorable reply?"

Rebecca was silent, but smiled enigmatically, closing the subject. Shortly thereafter, William left her to her thoughts, which she had vowed would be free of Azim, and which were not.

Thomas and Catherine had been invited to dine with them the following evening. Colonel Thomas Mansfield, commanding officer at the outpost of Mazar-i-Sharif, was an old school friend of Lawrence. Rebecca spent the early evening hours, before the guests arrived to dine, trying to convince her father that the invitation to stay with them was a sound idea.

Having put on her prettiest summer frock and her most beguiling smile, she implored, "Father, don't you think that I need some time away from William? I would not mention it otherwise, but perhaps if I stay here I might run into that scandalous Azim again. Besides, my knowledge of the country would be increased vastly. Imagine what an asset I would be at our business dinners?"

Lawrence could not argue the point. As of late, she had been winding him around her little finger. He did realize this, but he found it nevertheless difficult to say "no" to her. By the time they arrived at the dinner table, Rebecca had completed her coup and only needed Thomas to formally extend the invitation. She was as good as there!

Long before the final courses were served, Lawrence had indeed agreed to allow Rebecca to accompany them. Catherine was delighted and suggested that they go straight up to Rebecca's room to begin selecting dresses for the trip. Lawrence and Thomas were glad to be rid of the endless female enthusiasm and adjourned to the sitting room for brandies.

Lawrence hesitantly began, "Thomas, please understand that what I'm about to say in no way reflects on my high opinion of you. My girl is all that I have left in the world and I have only recently rediscovered her. Her safety is of the utmost concern to me."

"I can quite understand your feelings, especially having met her. Believe me, I would not even suggest her visit if I were not completely satisfied as to her welfare. Rest assured, my dear friend, that she will come to no harm."

Upstairs the ladies were having a gay time discussing all that they would do and see together. Even Meera was becoming caught up in the excitement. Rebecca had already begun tossing things into her trunks.

Thinking aloud she said, "How lucky I am to have found a friend such as you, Catherine! Before we depart we must lunch with Polly Swanson. I know you will get on famously. My, but I feel lucky to be setting out once again on an adventure!"

Catherine laughed at her vibrance, saying, "I should think that after your encounter with Alex Drayton at the ball, you would want some solitude for at least a month!"

Rebecca flashed a glance at Meera, who stood listening intently. That was the first mention of the experience in front of Meera, and she likened it to opening Pandora's box. She hoped Meera would not say a word to her, but she doubted it. She knew Meera could hardly wait to question her!

"Catherine, I really have put the whole thing from my mind. Besides, it's not likely that I shall ever see him again, especially where we are going! Now, let's go join the men. I think they may await our company." The girls laughed and went down to the parlor.

Meera was brushing Rebecca's hair later, when she began to pull and tug at one stubborn curl. Rebecca thought that Meera was deliberately trying to get her attention.

She grimaced. "Ouch! Meera, whatever has come over you tonight? You're hurting me!"

Still tugging, Meera replied, "Missy Sahib is not telling Meera about ball. Meera is seeing sleepless nights for Missy. Meera worrying, but Missy is not caring."

"All that happened was a kiss. The man was a total bore. He kissed me and I fainted. Father and William know. Now you know. Does that satisfy you?"

"Missy Catherine is saying it was Azim, the English. Meera is knowing many ladies swooning over that good looking man. Meera is hearing that Sahib Azim is very hard to have by woman. You are being lucky, Missy, to have so big a man kissing you."

Rebecca was irate. Rising rapidly, she turned on Meera. "That will be enough, Meera! You forget yourself!"

Meera gathered up Rebecca's dress, shoes, and underclothes. As she was leaving the room, a hurt look on her face, she muttered just loud enough for her mistress to hear, "Meera is thinking that Missy is liking kiss too much." Her exit was followed by the hairbrush striking the door.

The week went quickly and soon all was ready for their departure. William had said his farewells at least a dozen times and Rebecca was glad to see the last of him for awhile. She faintly wondered what her father would say to him about his proposal. She was sure it would be negative, and she was pleased that she would not have to face William for several weeks.

The morning of the departure arrived and they all set out on a somewhat gloomy note as Lawrence had been on the verge of tears. As the sun began to rise, Rebecca's spirits lifted and she began to look forward to her new adventure.

CHAPTER 11

Azim had put Kabul several hours behind him. He was indistinguishable from the other travelers on the great road toward the Hindu Kush, except perhaps for his height and expertly bred mount. He was accompanied by Mahmud, his best friend, companion, protector, and advisor. Mahmud remained in the background when Azim visited Kabul and the ferangi, preferring to stay with his second cousin in the old section of the city. He came very much to the fore as they headed back to the north where their friends awaited them. Mahmud was of indeterminate age, of medium height, but with great breadth of chest and huge gnarled wrists and hands. His legs were somewhat short and bowed from years on horseback. He had dark flashing eyes under bushy brows and a luxuriant black mustache of which he was inordinately proud. Mahmud was not formally educated, but Azim had never met a finer person, no one endowed with as much natural wisdom and dignity. He rode a homely jug-headed roan named Ghazal, with whom he would never voluntarily be parted. Both horse and man were covered with old scars of battle and sport.

Azim rode with a scowl on his face. He flicked his whip nervously and touched his stallion's glossy black shoulder. The horse tensed at this unusual display and he swished his tail in annoyance.

"I'm sorry Khaled, old friend," said Azim apologetically. His mind was occupied with several problems; Kabul always disturbed him. Governor Mountstuart never tired of trying to convince Azim to give up his life in the north and return to England to take up his "duties and responsibilities." He could not seem to make Mountstuart understand the deep feeling he had for his adopted people and his sense of injustice at what the British were trying to do to them. They were a wild, free people, and could not live under the British cloak of respectability with all that it entailed. They were far better off being left to their own type of life: raising their fine horses, tending their fat-tailed astrakhan sheep, playing *buzkashi,* and rearing their children in the same proud heritage.

As a matter of fact, Azim was at the moment planning an attack on a British military troop traveling to Mazar-i-Sharif in a few days. He occasionally felt slight pangs of guilt when he led his men against British soldiers, but he knew that he had to harass the English constantly. He was quite aware of the British notion of moral and military superiority, and their tenacity in this type of situation. They simply would not give up even though they had been shown in countless ways, over the years, that the Afghans did not want to become another province of the British empire. Azim had learned at Mountstuart's ball that a Colonel Mansfield would be traveling back to Mazar-i-Sharif with a contingent of soldiers and a supply of weapons for the small garrison already there. It was the perfect opportunity to snatch a supply of weapons from under the very noses of the British, especially since he had been so unsuccessful in Bombay. This would supply the village with the latest weaponry—the guns to fire the ammunition that still lay useless, hidden in his own home. To return empty-handed this time would be bad for the morale of his adopted people.

He was going over the familiar trail in his mind,

choosing the best place for an ambush when Mahmud
interrupted his thoughts. His mind automatically began
thinking in Pashto.

"Azim, here is the path to the village where the
others await us. You almost missed it, my friend."

"You are right, Mahmud." He showed his white
teeth in a wry smile. "It must be that my head is still
fuzzy from the big city!"

They turned their horses west, off the main road
through the great mountains, and followed the path to
a small cluster of mud huts where five men from their
village had arrived earlier.

The five were all strong, fiercely independent men,
handpicked for the dangerous job of guerrilla warfare.
There was a great deal of backslapping and embracing
when Azim and Mahmud rode into the tiny village. The
men were like brothers.

The villagers left them strictly alone, as they feared
these arrogant men from the North. Only a few of the
young women looked their way, finding these seven
horsemen very attractive. The seven did not notice the
veiled women, being more interested in their mounts.

Azim and his men cooked a simple meal over their
fire, then sat around the leaping flames perfecting
strategy for their ambush. When they were satisfied
with the plans, they rolled up in their wool-lined
chapans and fell asleep.

Only Azim remained awake, still staring at the red
embers. Tonight, for some undefinable reason, he felt
restless and torn between his two selves, Alex Drayton
of England and Azim of the Afghan steppes. He
reflected back on how he had first become Azim, how
he had been adopted into the people of the northern
grasslands. The beginning of this saga always brought a
scowl of pain to his handsome face . . .

Sir Godfrey Drayton, his wife Sarah, and their
fifteen-year-old son Alex had been traveling from India
to Kabul escorted by military troops. They had been set
upon and massacred by a wild Pakistani tribe near the

Khyber Pass. Sir Godfrey and his wife had been killed, the soldiers slain or scattered, and young Alex left for dead with a slight head wound. He had regained consciousness a few hours later to find himself surrounded by a group of fierce-looking men who stared curiously at him.

The wounded boy tried to stand up, but was overcome by dizziness. Sitting down with his back propped against a rock, he had surveyed the scene of carnage around him. The sight of his parents' bloodied corpses lying in the dust, covered with a cloud of flies, had been too much for the youth. He had bent his head and wept for them and for himself.

Alex had waited until his head felt clearer to begin the sad task of burying his parents. The best he could do was to scrape a shallow grave and pile boulders on the bodies so the wolves could not reach them. When he looked up from his work, the strange men had been standing at a respectful distance, watching him solemnly.

Alex had made an attempt to talk to them, but they knew only a few words of his language. They did understand that he was English and had just buried his mother and father. They had led him to know by their gestures that he would be welcome to travel with them. They were returning to the north with new mares for their stallions. Bowed with grief and painfully confused, Alex had gone with the quiet-spoken, proud men—

Mahmud interrupted Azim's somber thoughts by appearing at his side and throwing another log onto the fire.

"I could not sleep, my friend. The stars are too bright tonight and my body restless," offered Mahmud.

"I, too, am discontent, beset with many doubts. Why is man such a restless spirit, never content with what he has, always looking for more, or better . . . ?" asked Azim.

"Ah, my friend, Allah decrees that we be thus. Men always yearn for a distant star."

"In that case, perhaps *my* God would serve me better. But no, the English are forever dissatisfied themselves. I was thinking before of how I met you. What a sight I must have been!"

"You were a brave boy, Azim, burying your parents and traveling with us so far. Many another boy would have fled in terror."

"I never regretted it, Mahmud. It has been a rewarding life in so many ways."

"Do you remember the first time you saw the Hindu Kush? We thought your eyes would fall out staring at the peaks!"

"We don't have mountains like that in England," laughed Azim. "I was impressed. You know, old friend, that was one of the first words I learned in Pashto—mountain." He laughed again. "And I think the next word was horse. I still get annoyed when I think how long you kept me doing children's chores before you let me work with the horses! Those smelly sheep!"

"It was not so long—only a year or so. But I must admit, we were surprised at the skill you showed with them. You have a natural feel for the animals. It is a talent one is born with. That is why I named you Azim. He was a legendary horseman of the steppes, and since I could not pronounce your ferangi name, it seemed only natural—"

"Mahmud, do you remember the first time I played buzkashi? I'll never forget! Khaled was nervous. I was terrified. Could you tell? The poles seemed *miles* apart and the goat's body weighed so much I could hardly hold onto it when I got it for a moment. What a fool I must have looked!"

"No more a fool than any beginner," chuckled Mahmud. "And better than some. It is best to remember how you improved, not how you were at the beginning."

"Yes, Mahmud, but I have many scars to remind me of the learning process like this one on my forehead."

Mahmud yawned hugely. "I think I will try to sleep

now, Azim. Your reminiscing has made my old head tired."

He rolled up in his chapan and soon throaty snores were heard coming from his dark form. Azim smiled fondly at the sleeping man, recalling many incidents from the past when he had been glad to have the staunch friendship of the Afghan. He fell to musing again, searching his past, trying to understand his present restlessness. . . .

Five years had passed so quickly that he could hardly believe they were gone. He had realized one spring that he was twenty years old, tall, strong from his many hours in the saddle, and not at all the typical young nobleman of England. He had often wondered where he would be now, given different circumstances—in a London drawing room, married, perhaps, a country squire? He had toyed, occasionally, with the idea of embracing Islam, but could not bear the thought of all the study involved. More truthfully, he still felt a strong affinity for the religion in which he'd been raised.

That spring, a representative of the East India Company had arrived in the village, lost on his way to Mazar-i-Sharif. The man had been astonished to find a young Englishman living in this place and offered to take him back to Kabul. He had been even more dumbfounded when Azim refused, but asked the man to convey to his brother in England the news that he was alive and well. The East India Company employee was David Mountstuart, later to become the English governor of Kabul. In this way, the world learned of Alex Drayton's existence again.

Another event was of more immediate interest to him. He would be allowed to enter his first real buzkashi game on Khaled. He had developed enormously strong arms and hands from hours of snatching the headless goat from his adversaries in practice. He was taller than most of the men in the village, with a correspondingly long reach. His finely tuned muscles could hold him in the saddle in any position while he raced toward the *halal*. Khaled had been a little young to have reached his peak of skill—he was only four—but his incredible speed and ferocity in the contest awed even the older men. Azim was expected to become a *chapandaz*, an expert, the highest honor that could be bestowed upon the buzkashi player. The young Englishman and the black horse made a natural team, there was no doubt about that.

It had been an autumn day, he recalled, when he was to play in his first game at Mazar-i-Sharif. There was a gusty wind blowing and gray clouds scudding overhead. The signal given, the men threw themselves upon the goat carcass. Above the milling horses and men, suddenly appeared someone's arm holding the goat. The player tried to break away from the howling mob as each man used his whip, hit, kicked, to grab the prize. The horses kicked, struck out, whinnied with rage along with their riders. The goat was suddenly seized by another who managed to ride clear of the throng. Immediately the others whirled and set after him. Khaled was swifter than any horse there and gained on the goat-carrier. Azim reached across his mount's neck at a full gallop and plucked the goat from the other player. A wolfish grin on his face, he rounded the pole, galloped back toward the other pole, only to have the goat jerked from under his arm by Mahmud who had been waiting for him. He remembered Mahmud flashing his white teeth in a broad smile as he had galloped away.

Back and forth sped the carcass until finally a bruised and bloody player managed to throw the goat into the halal, howling his victory as he ended the game. Only one man had died that day as a result of the game and not one horse had been seriously injured. It had been considered a great success by all involved.

Azim yawned. His long vigil at the fire had finally made him drowsy. He got up to check on the horses once more, then rolled up in his chapan by the dying embers.

The next morning the seven men set out for the spot they had chosen for the ambush. They traveled quickly and easily for several days along the rocky trail deep into the Hindu Kush. They had chosen a well-known caravanserai for their ambush. Knowing they were at least two days ahead of Mansfield's party, they settled down in the rocks with primeval patience to await the arrival of their unsuspecting prey.

CHAPTER 12

Thomas Mansfield's party left their encampment in the early dawn hours. The road north was, at first, much the same as those they had seen east of Kabul. As the small caravan inched its way along the trail, the sun bathed the ancient road of kings in shimmering waves of heat. Rebecca could feel the intense warmth on her shoulders as the day wore on. There were few trees to offer any shade and they were forced to stop along the way at a chaikana which served tea and food, but also proffered some welcome relief from the sun. At this rest stop, Rebecca and Catherine took off their hats and slightly opened their blouses.

Catherine sipped her scalding tea. "This afternoon we pass through Charikar, then north still to the Shibar Pass. This road we are traveling has been used for centuries by men trading, conquering. Oh, isn't it all so romantic!" The two women gratefully settled themselves in the shade and viewed the many facets of human traffic on the route. They were fascinated by a saffron-robed Buddhist monk begging for his daily ration.

Rebecca laughed. "If only he could see our well-fed priests in England! But it's the Hindu merchants over there that interest me most. I'm longing to barter for their wares in those donkey sacks. I spoke earlier today with one of them. He almost sold me a marvelous bolt of silk, cheaply, too, but wherever would I put it?"

The women continued to compare their impressions of the caravan trail. Thomas sat nearby watching them with a content expression. He thought, what other well-bred Englishwoman would find beauty here? My Catherine has at last found a lovely friend whose enthusiasm for this land equals her own. Pleased with Rebecca's reactions to their trip, he ushered them back out into the harsh sun. They had planned to stop after Charikar in a caravanserai for the night; the walled shelter would offer them protection. Thomas was grateful that there would be many serais on their way, one approximately every three miles. He knew the women must long for a respite from the hard ride, as he noticed them discreetly shifting their backsides in their saddles.

They wound their way through the dusty little place that was Charikar. The town seemed unusually empty, shops closed up, windows shuttered, a ribby dog slinking around a corner being the only sign of life. As the troop reached the northern outskirts of Charikar, the reason for the abandoned town became evident. There on an open field was a crowded circle of men, howling and shouting raucously.

"What is it, Thomas?" asked Catherine, mystified.

"I don't know, Cathy, but I'll take a look. You ladies wait here."

"Do be careful, Thomas."

"Yes, dear," he called over his shoulder as he cantered his horse toward the wild gathering.

They could see him shoulder his way through the throng. In a moment he galloped back, excitement lighting up his face. He looked like a boy.

"Hurry! You must see this fight!" He was breathless. "It's a camel match. What luck! We've just happened on a spectacle few English have been allowed to see. You understand, they have to bring together two male fighting camels, each in rut. These matches are very rare. And, by heaven, we've just stumbled on one!"

They approached the edges of the crowd, and

Rebecca could hear the noise of the shrieking hoards mingled with the guttural groans of two camels battling to the death. She was appalled at the sight once she was close enough to see the horrible spectacle.

The beasts were struggling to kill one another, blood and dirt sticking to the open wounds made by their teeth and hooves. The camels rolled and twined their hairy necks around each other. The onlookers were in a frenzy of excitement, shouting words of encouragement to their favorite. They had no doubt bet their meager earnings on the outcome. Dark pools of blood covered the dry earth as dust rose in clouds around the infuriated animals. A terrible scream was heard as one of the camels appeared to be mortally wounded.

Rebecca, barely audible, whispered, "Take me away, please. I feel sick . . ." Her words were lost in the commotion of the primeval battle. Her head began to swirl as the odor of mixed dust, blood, and urine assailed her nostrils. Thomas was lost up in the fighting and momentarily forgot the presence of the women.

"Come, Rebecca," Catherine offered, "you are pale and must get out of this intense heat." She started to lead Rebecca away from the sight, her stomach also rising.

Suddenly a hush fell over the crowd as a low deep groan came from the fallen camel. Rebecca turned just in time to see a long bloody string of saliva and foam spew forth from the dying creature. She tore behind a rock and vomited.

Thomas, turning from the gory scene, amid the cheering crowd, went straight to the women and, shame-faced, led them back to the waiting horses. Rebecca's nausea was subsiding and the tiny caravan once again began its trek north to the Shibar Pass.

An hour or so later, Thomas brought his mount up to Rebecca and apologized, embarrassed. "I fear I became lost in the battle back there. I can only be honest in saying I have, for years, wished to witness the spectacle. Up until today I have only heard of such fights. Few white men have ever seen one. I am afraid I gave no thought to your feminine sensibilities. I am so terribly sorry."

She replied weakly, "No, Thomas, I came along to learn and see everything. I am the one who should apologize for allowing myself to see only the horror. I, too, know that in these matches there is something worth learning. This is their country, and who am I to judge?" Thomas was pleased that she had an open mind; at least Catherine would not be reprimanding him quite so severely.

High midday sun turned into late afternoon gold as the group neared their nightly destination in the hilly terrain of the lower Hindu Kush. Once stopped for the day, Catherine and Rebecca sat pensively viewing the brown landscape. They lounged tiredly on the small terrace of a walled hut while food was prepared by Meera. Sleep came slowly to their weary bodies as the heat had not yet given way to the coolness of night.

The next day promised to be cooler as they began their ascent over the pass. By midday they were overtaking a large nomad caravan. Rebecca had to tie a scarf around her face to avoid choking in the heavy clouds of dust kicked up by camels, fat-tailed sheep and the hundreds of tribesmen. The nomads moved slowly, enabling Thomas's troop to pass in a short time. Rebecca commented to Catherine about the lack of veils on the women, whose dark eyes glowed with the strength of centuries of wandering through the vast stretches of the Hindu Kush. Loosely clad in robes, they suckled their babies while moving endlessly through the barren lands. Rebecca wondered what such an existence would do to her creamy skin. She banished the thought.

Climbing the steep approaches to the Shibar Pass, they were at once awed by the splendor of the Hindu Kush. The high, majestic chain was nearly impassable, except for this one breach in the sheer walls surrounding them. Rebecca stopped Alia frequently, resting her, as the thin mountain air left her horse breathless. The crystal clear skies promised a cooler night ahead.

Looking back down the twisted path, she ventured to Thomas, "Look there! See the nomads far below us now? A marvelous sight, isn't it? They look like tiny ants from here."

He glanced in that direction. "Yes. They are moving north and will not return this way for some time to come. Can you imagine forever roaming the Kush and the steppes, living off this forbidding land?"

She stretched out her arms and indicated the vast, snow-covered peaks before her. "What beauty God has made here. Oh, Thomas, I hope that we English never, never change it!"

They remounted and once again began the hard, steep ascent. Pushing, breathless, they were wearied almost beyond endurance when finally they began the descent on the north face of the mountains. Thankfully, the numbers of travelers had required many a stopping place along the winding cliffs. Rebecca ventured a look over one such crevice. She wondered if any merchants or soldiers had ever fallen into the bottomless void, there to be forever lost on the jutting rocks below. She shivered, not from the cooler air, but from the dizzying heights. It would be heavenly to stop for the night; her stomach was gnawing from hunger. She had heard that the high mountain altitudes increased one's appetite and made for a heavy sleep.

Finally they came to their resting place, another serai, built impressively out of the rocks and cliffs. Catherine brushed her riding habit and smoothed her wrinkled sleeves. "I vow this trip will age me too quickly. Why, look how out of breath I am! Even Meera seems too tired to prepare our dinner. Perhaps we should assist her, at least until we reach lower altitudes on the morrow."

Rebecca readily agreed, but first felt she must attend to her exhausted horse. As she was mothering Alia, she reflected on how glad she was to have her deep blue riding habit along. She had not worn it until this morning. The heat of the plains had kept her in a cooler outfit. Rebecca wished there were a warm spot to shake out her heavy velvet outfit, but she knew that she should remain clothed, as the air was too cool.

Watching Meera prepare the fire, Rebecca tenderly fed Alia her grains. The dapple-gray mare gently nudged her neck, causing a few hair pins to loosen. She laughed and, pulling her golden curls free, threw her head forward and shook the day's dust out. Tossing her head back gracefully, hair flowing gently to her waist, she had the odd feeling that she was being watched. Rebecca was sure that the soldiers rarely took their eyes from her and therefore attributed her uneasy notion to the troopers. She finished her task, gave the horse a pat and set out to find Catherine.

The small camp was still busy preparing for the night as the sun dipped below the snowcapped peaks. Daylight was fast giving way to a softer pink hue, lending an array of colors to the surrounding cliffs. Rebecca was stooped over the burning embers, stirring a stew, when she heard a strange, high warbling cry pierce the still night. Looking back later, she remembered only confusion. Everything seemed to happen in slow motion, as the animal-like yells continued to create a frenzied atmosphere in the frantic campsite.

The few soldiers were engaged in defending themselves against gunfire issuing from the shadows. Rebecca saw one trooper fall, then another. They had been totally surprised by the ambush. The soldiers were scattering for shelter. Pandemonium prevailed. Startling Rebecca, Thomas came swiftly up from behind. He was pulling Catherine along with one hand and grabbed Rebecca with the other. Then they were shoved behind the protection of a boulder.

Thomas was saying, "Quiet now and listen! Edge your way to the horses. Don't take time to saddle them. Get as far away as possible! Stop that sniveling, Catherine! Now go!"

The two terrified women worked their way to where the horses were tethered. Gunfire rang out in their ears, the sounds of battle echoing off the treacherous cliffs. Catherine was astride her horse when Rebecca felt a sharp sting in her left shoulder. She staggered slightly and tried desperately to mount her plunging Alia. Catherine's animal bolted as a bullet nearly missed him, ricocheting off the rocky wall behind. Rebecca cried out in hysteria as she futilely tried to pull herself up onto Alia's back. The pain in her arm was spreading, her strength leaving her. Suddenly her wrist was being grasped, strong hands turning her around. Looking into the face of her captor, she saw hard gray eyes opening wide in recognition.

"My God! It's you, Azim! What are you doing?" Her voice trailed off as the reality of her situation dawned on her. She had never known such horror. Before she could protest, he had swept her easily up into his arms. With the agility of a cat, he placed her onto his mount. She began to struggle, but his iron grip held her in place securely in front of him. Reaching over, he grabbed Alia's reins. His horse reared slightly, nostrils flaring, and shot off into the night.

Rebecca was acutely aware of his hard thighs grinding against her own. She felt lost in the wide expanse of his chest and began to shake uncontrollably. His right arm was wrapped around her breasts causing her pain. She tried in vain to turn her body this way and that, but still he held her with ease.

Moonlight was casting grotesque shadows on the barren cliffs above them and Rebecca was sure she would die from terror. Where was Catherine? Were all the troops dead? Was anyone going to rescue her? Questions ran through her mind as they put more and more distance behind them. Eventually Azim slowed his mount and seemed to concentrate on the rough terrain.

With furrowed brows he thought, If only she had not recognized me! Perhaps I could take her back. No!

That would ruin my plans. She'll surely tell them who I am. Why in God's name was she traveling in a troop caravan? His arm loosened its grip, realizing he was hurting her. In a moment of tenderness he reached his hand up to caress her shoulder to reassure her. To his dismay he felt a sticky substance on his fingers.

Rebecca winced in pain, a groan escaping her lips. Azim reined Khaled in, dismounted quickly and tenderly lifted her down into his arms. She could feel his warm breath on her hair. His masculine smell of leather and horseflesh reminded her of the tackroom at Faroaks. Azim was trying to place her gently on the dry earth when Rebecca broke away, nearly escaping him.

Desperately trying to stop her without causing her further injury, he growled, "Woman! Will you please stop struggling? I'm only going to look at your wound. Do you want to bleed to death?"

Still fighting him, she spat, "Help me? You could have helped me by leaving me alone! Am I supposed to lie still and let you put a knife in me?"

Realizing that she would never lie down on her own accord, he decided he could knock her senseless or just hold her down. He chose the latter and pushed her shaking body to the earth. With one hand he held her wrists above her head, and with his knee, he held her legs still.

Talking with surprising gentleness, he quieted her. "We can stay here in this position all night or you can behave. The choice is yours. I suggest you stop struggling because otherwise you will either bleed to death or pass out. Now what will it be?"

"I don't trust you! My blouse must be removed, and I . . ." Tears were dropping off her long lashes and her next words were inaudible.

He laughed. "Is that all you were worried about? So like a female to worry about her vanity when she lies in the arms of her kidnapper, possibly seriously wounded." His eyes found hers, large dark pools glistening from the sobbing spell. Her lovely mouth was parted slightly, lips still quivering. Rebecca's hair was spread out on the hard ground in golden disarray. In spite of her terror, he could feel his desire for her harden his loins. Trying to keep control of himself, he said too harshly, "Well? Answer me! Damn you, woman! Here let me undo this button."

Rebecca's struggling began all over again. She said, her voice tremulous, "No! I'll do that myself! Please, I'll be still now. It's just that no man . . . I mean not even my father . . ." She was at a loss for words. Azim silenced her by placing a finger tenderly on her lips.

Rebecca sat up and, turning her back to him, took her blue jacket off. Azim had to help her with the left sleeve. Next, she hesitantly tried to undo the tiny pearl buttons of her blouse. Once again he brushed her hands aside and with great care he unfastened the remaining buttons. She should have been shaking from the cold. Instead, she was burning all over from shame. His bold gray eyes found hers and she was reminded of how handsome he was. Even the scar on his face lent a certain devil-may-care charm to his features.

Azim gently helped her out of the blouse. Only her scanty chemise stood between his fingers and her bosom. Rebecca felt her cheeks burning and tried to turn away.

He stopped her. "Do you think that I have never seen a woman unclothed before? Now lie down here, Rebecca. That's it."

She obeyed silently. Azim could not help but laugh inwardly at his own words. He had seen many breasts, but these young, firm ones were more beautiful than he had imagined possible. The pink tips were straining at the bodice, which concealed little from his eyes. Soft round mounds pushed up and over the neckline of her slip.

His breathing almost labored, Azim fought his instinct to feel her warm flesh in his hands. God, he mused, give me the strength to tend her wound, not to tumble her . . .

Gaining some semblance of control, Azim managed to probe the wound. Rebecca grit her teeth and was determined not to scream. His fingers were gentle in spite of their strength, but the pain was becoming unbearable. She shivered involuntarily and a moan escaped her lips. Azim gathered her up into his arms and whispered assurances into her ear. He stroked her arm, saying, "Rest a minute. I need a pouch from my saddle. Soon all the pain will be gone. I promise."

He walked swiftly to where his horse stood. Bringing a small leather bag back with him, he noticed that Rebecca was trembling from the cold. Azim knelt down alongside her and tenderly smoothed a salve into the flesh wound. She felt a burning sensation, then a tingling that was not unpleasant. She marveled that he had taken the time to tend her arm when she was still sure he meant to kill her. Azim took her riding jacket and placed her good arm in the sleeve. He put her wounded one in a sling made from his sash, then tried to button the front.

Rebecca was so cold by then that she almost begged him for a blanket. Pride, however, held her back. She stood, straightened her attire as best she could, and asked coolly, "Will I live?"

"It was a flesh wound. The bullet only grazed your skin, but caused a lot of bleeding. Yes, I think that you will live." He took her good arm and led her back to his horse.

"Where are you taking me?" Rebecca protested.

"Not back to your friends, if that is what you think. Be a good girl and keep silent while I think of what to do with you." He smiled wickedly, bringing a rush of fear to Rebecca's heart.

He insisted that she ride with him. Her horse, Alia, was led behind. Rebecca was certain that he held her close to ensure that she did not escape. She would have been quite surprised to know that he feared she might fall, further injuring her arm. Part of Azim's nature, however, was to keep his thoughts to himself. He had learned that silence could be a trusted ally. Rebecca was normally a very open person, but something in this man's hard eyes told her to beware lest she give herself away. She hardened herself against the chill and rode in front of him silently.

They found their way down the treacherous mountainside and then were able to make better time. Khaled did not seem to tire as they threaded their way north. A gently sloping road lay ahead of them as the sun's first golden rays warmed Rebecca's face. In her exhaustion she was unable to control a sudden flow of tears. She had been thinking of her friends, still high up in the Pass. She wondered if Azim knew of their fate. That, at least, would be *one* question he could answer before her fate was sealed. She would see to that! She fell asleep silently. Her head rolled back, resting uneasily on Azim's chest.

When her silent tears had fallen on Azim's hand, his body had momentarily stiffened. How cruel destiny had been to him. His small band of men had failed to tell him about the presence of women in the troop. If he had known, he would never have allowed the attack to take place. Azim knew that he would never tell her that. Thinking back, he realized that kidnapping her was the only choice given him. But now, what was he to do with her? Did she really believe he meant to harm her? Ridiculous! As her head had rested against his chest, Azim had once again felt a tenderness for this rare beauty. She had frightened him half to death with that wound, and then she had been so brave, so soft. Up until that point, he had doubted her virginity, but when he had seen the embarrassment on her face, amidst pain, he knew she had never lain with a man.

Rebecca's eyelids opened reluctantly when Azim finally found a stopping place. He gently lifted her from Khaled's back, laying her carefully on the cool ground. The sun was casting morning shadows on the brown rocks around them. Rebecca was trying desperately to awaken but found it impossible to keep her eyes open.

Azim looked down on her resting form and had the sudden urge to take her in his arms and reassure her. He saw the sun dance on her tangled curls, making them shimmer like spun gold. Her dark lashes contrasted sharply with the pink and cream of her skin. Rebecca's lips were parted slightly, reminding him of the night in Mountstuart's garden. Was it possible that all Englishwomen were as lovely? He thought back to a time past, nearly fifteen years ago. No, he was certain that Rebecca would stun men, at any time or any place. Azim had taken his share of women, some better than others. All of them had soon bored him and he found it difficult to rid himself of them once he tired of their endless prattle. Would Rebecca become a nuisance? Would he tire of her so soon? Azim thought that, although she was the most radiant flower he had ever seen, she would soon bore him, too. At any rate, his life was too dangerous to allow himself the time to find out.

Coming back to reality, Azim wondered why such thoughts were going through his mind. He went off to gather what scrub he could for a morning fire. He would awaken her when the food was prepared. From now on, though, she would rise and tend to the chores! It was just that without rest she would slow him down. Azim wondered then, where was he going with her? He had to rendezvous with his men at the village and Mahmud would be worried about him. That man! He was sometimes more a mother-hen than a comrade-in-arms. Azim knew that Mahmud had seen him tear out after the two women and Mahmud would know that Azim was safely on his way to camp. The outcome of the battle was a mystery to Azim, although he had little doubt that the ambush had been a success, winning the Afghans more weapons.

He was only yards from their resting place when he heard the horses stir. A moment later quick hoofbeats sounded. He quickly dropped the pile of sticks and rushed back to the encampment.

"Damn the bitch!" he muttered. She was riding hell-bent for a deep ravine, not visible unless you knew the terrain. Azim leaped up onto Khaled's back and sped after her. He saw a spot in the rocks where, if he maneuvered through them skillfully enough, he might reach her in time. Khaled had the training and ability for such a trick and Azim had no time to doubt his own skill. His talents were in earnest use as Rebecca's life might very well depend on them. As he burst through the narrow cleft, all that stood in his way was the speed of her mount. The little dapple was swift, but no match for his own horse. Overtaking her, perilously close to the edge, Azim grabbed her reins and jerked Alia to a stop. Rebecca's eyes were wild, unshed tears glistening in them. Her arms flailed out at him. Then she kicked furiously at him from her horse's back.

"You damn stupid little bitch! Hold still!"

Rebecca had rarely heard such words before, particularly directed at her! She started to really fight him now, using even her stiff arm to scratch at his face as he pulled her off her horse. Brutally, Azim struck her cheek hard with his open hand. Her hands automatically went to the reddening spot. The slap had done its work. Rebecca was totally subdued, half in shock. Never had anyone treated her this way! She was utterly terrified of him now, more aware than ever of the powerful strength this tall stranger possessed.

Azim roughly dragged Rebecca with him. She was trembling violently from the aftermath of the slap and could hardly keep up with his impatient stride. Leading her none too gently to the edge of the steep-walled ravine, he forced her to look down into the deadly sight below. Rebecca tried to cover her face with her hands because she refused to let him see how embarrassed she was. He realized that Rebecca understood why he had hit her and led her meekly back to Alia. Then he gave her some time to calm herself.

Streams of tears flowed down her cheeks as they walked the horses to the campsite in silence. Rebecca wondered why, once again, Azim had bothered to save her. A new strength began to envelope her. She decided that she would not just lie back and let him kill her. She would fight him tooth and nail. Somewhere, in the recesses of her mind, she heard her grandfather, George, saying, "Child, never let anyone take from you what you treasure for yourself." By God, she would cease this weeping and show the beast that she was as brave and untamable as he. What had he called her, "bitch"? That was it! If that was what he expected, that was what she would be!

Dismounting, they tethered the horses. Azim went to gather up the sticks he had dropped earlier. When he returned and began to build the fire, Rebecca came up to him. She was a sight: swollen eyes, filthy blue habit, curls falling at random.

Bravely, she started, "Thank you for saving me. It was a foolish thing to do and I won't try to escape again, at least not today."

His gray eyes met her dark ones, his eyebrows joined, his lips twisted wolfishly. He had the sudden urge to shake her. Why hadn't the slap done its job? She was daring too much to openly defy him.

Azim rose to his towering height. He would set her straight as to who the master was here! Rebecca almost hesitated, but she refused to be intimidated by his size and overpowering masculinity. She had planned this moment on the walk back and even if he killed her on the spot it would be worth it.

"I believe I also owe you this." Her small hand shot out, taking him unaware, slapping his face with all the force she could muster.

At first, Azim was totally shocked. When anger finally replaced surprise, his features darkened into a black scowl. Rebecca was horrified by his look. She slowly retreated, fearing the repercussions. What Azim saw in her face made him check his wrath. She stood before him with naked emotion showing in her every move. He recognized fear there, also fierce pride, and he had to respect *that*. Rebecca's face was streaked with tears and dirt. Still, he had never seen such a beauty.

His hard scowl softened somewhat. "I guess I deserved that. We are even now. Bout one is over. But, my little flower, don't try me again. I'm used to having my women around to share my bed and cook my food, but never to interfere in my life."

"Interfere in *your* life? What of *mine?*" she shrieked. "First you shoot me, then you kidnap me, then you strike me! And now you accuse me of interfering in your life! What utter audacity!"

Azim could see that she had a point there, but, damn, didn't she know that he was trying to help her? Rebecca couldn't possibly think he meant her harm.

"When do you propose to have me cook your meals?" she continued her tirade. "Surely a dead woman cannot prepare food! And about sharing your . . . your . . ." Her voice trailed off as, red-faced, she proudly strode off to tend her mare.

Azim watched her gather her dignity and show her back to him. He thought he should go to her but dismissed the idea. Rebecca needed time to think, then she would realize he meant her no harm. And about the bed, well, he would retain his English chivalry—at least he would try.

The day wore on in almost total silence. Once Rebecca had to find some privacy and she hoped that he would allow her to spend a moment to herself. Azim never doubted her need for a minute, but he could not resist the urge to see her blush.

"Ah, little blossom, do you think that I should allow you to be alone?" he teased. "I think not! Perhaps you will try to escape me again. No, I think I shall accompany you." He was laughing now, watching her increasing discomfort, and Rebecca knew he was teasing her.

She pinkened, snapping, "You have no decency! You're a barbarian, a wild animal. A . . . A . . ."

"Go find your privacy, and for God's sake, cease your everlasting temper!"

Rebecca found her way back to the horses, and ignoring his amused stare, she determined not to talk to him again that day.

Afternoon was rapidly giving way to evening. She hoped that they would stop soon for the night. She was starving, thirsty, and totally exhausted. She found herself gazing at him from time to time. He was incredibly handsome sitting astride his black Arab stallion—proud English-bearing cloaked by the dress of his adopted countrymen. She stared at his long sinewy thighs, made strong by the years of hard riding. Vaguely she wondered if he would kill her tonight. Why hadn't he already done so? Suddenly it occurred to her. He was taking her back to his village. Her friends in Kabul had warned her of the fate she could meet on the trail. He must have some primitive ceremony to perform on her, and the villagers would join in. Yes! That was why he had saved her life! Saved her for a fate worse than death! Envisioning rape, terror threatening to drive her frantic, she was forced to reality by his voice.

"We'll camp here for the night. If you will dismount and see to your horse, I'll begin teaching you how to survive this harsh climate."

Rebecca wondered why he should bother to teach her survival when she had already guessed his plans for her. She dismounted and sullenly went about feeding Alia. She watched him, warily, as he tended his huge ebony stallion and likened his thick dark hair to the rich hue of Khaled's own shining mane. How alike man and beast were, as they stood together, powerful muscles working in the late afternoon heat. Sweat trickled down Azim's neck, dark rings of perspiration showed under his arms and soaked his opened shirt. Rebecca, also feeling the intense warmth, took off her dirty blue jacket. She tried to slip her sore arm out of the white sleeve of her lawn blouse. Azim noticed her futile efforts and approached her.

"Here, before you open your wound again, let me have a look."

"Thank you, but I can manage," she faltered, trying to ignore his hard stare. Her fingers, shaking slightly, undid the tiny buttons and she slipped her arm out of the sleeve. With her free hand she discreetly covered her half-bared breasts.

A sly grin on his lips, he brushed her hands aside. "You can't possibly see the wound yourself. Now hold still and let me apply some salve to it. Know one thing, little flower, if I wanted to harm you in any way, you could hardly protect yourself against me." He smiled widely at her alarm, knowing that she realized exactly what *harm* he referred to. Rebecca's blush was deep, extending all the way to her swelling breasts. His eyes traveled lower still, to her nipples pushing hard against her light chemise. Azim felt a tightening in his groin. *Gods above! I can't even be near her without growing hard. She has bewitched me!*

The bandaging done, Azim was certain that by morning her arm would be all but healed, although somewhat stiff. He felt a certain regret that he would no longer be able to gaze upon her nearly naked flesh. Dismissing the notion, he went about the chore of showing Rebecca how to build a fire.

After a tasteless meal that she had choked down to stave off her hunger, Rebecca stood and stretched her graceful, but sore, limbs. Having slept only a short while on horseback the previous night, she fleetingly wondered what the sleeping arrangements would be. But she was too tired to really care.

Finding a not too uncomfortable spot on the hard ground, she lay down for just a moment and fell fast asleep. Her last thoughts were not of Azim, who sat brooding quietly by the burning embers, but were of her friends. Perhaps their bodies were already covered

with hungry insects. She slept restlessly, unable, even
in repose, to keep the ugly scene from her mind.

Azim sat for a long time, gazing at the dancing lights
of the stars. He watched Rebecca toss and turn,
wanting to take her in his arms and comfort her. Azim
was, after all, Alex Drayton, he mused. Did he really
court visions of her naked body writhing beneath him?
Would Alex Drayton picture her begging him for
fulfillment? He cleared his mind of the image and went
to toss a blanket over her sleeping form. He swore
under his breath. "Damn, if only I hadn't been fool
enough to seek her out at the ball—kiss her—she would
never have recognized me."

The next day was one of the hottest Rebecca had
ever experienced. It was mid-June and they had
descended to the immense open plain of the northern
steppes. Sun was scorching her bare head and shoulders, sweat drenched her heavy riding skirt, which she
had slit up the front to ride astride more easily.
Rebecca had shed her jacket earlier in the day. She
longed to undo her soaked blouse but thought better of
the idea. Azim seemed not to mind the heat. He just
kept leading them further into the opened landscape.
Once, they came to an oasis-like spring. Trees grew
nearby and Azim allowed her to rest shortly in the cool
shaded area.

Late in the stifling afternoon, about the time that
Rebecca longed to stop, Alia picked up a small,
irritating pebble in her hoof. Azim stopped and
checked the filly's gait. He removed the stone, but
knowing the importance of a horse in this barren land
he decided to give the animals a night's break. Rebecca
was grateful for the respite, although she said nothing
to Azim.

Camp was quickly set up and Azim took a few
moments to rest his sun-reddened eyes. Rebecca sat
staring at his long form, relaxing in the still afternoon
heat. He was covered with grime from the hard days on

the road. Still, he looked unbelievably attractive, his features softened in rest. A dark wave of hair fell over his brow and he lifted his eyes to catch her looking at him with a pensive female gaze.

Azim rose languidly, stretching his long arms in a relaxed gesture. "I'm going to bathe some of this grit off. There is a deep pool beyond these rocks. Would you care to join me?" She shot him a mortified glance. "No? Well then, I trust you have learned the folly of trying to escape me. Listen, Rebecca, you would not survive a day out there alone, so don't try anything stupid."

With that he casually strolled away, leaving her alone, and very filthy. Rebecca was aching to follow him and cleanse her tired body in the cool waters. She thought that it would be best to wait until he was asleep that night. Then she could sneak through the rocks and spend as much time as she wanted lazing in the pool. The image of delightfully chilly water surrounding her scorched flesh was almost unbearable but she knew that she would wait.

Thinking back later, Rebecca knew that it was her sharp tongue that had begun the argument. Azim had returned from his bath and looked so clean and refreshed that she spat jealously, "I hope you are comfortable now, sir! Here I sit, alone, hot, and tired and you selfishly go off for a swim!"

Azim's face looked menacing. The muscles in his cheeks tightened. He came swiftly up to her, his wet shirt clinging to his broad chest, his voice dry. "By God, woman! Did I not offer to let you bathe? What a little harridan you have become! If it's a swim you want, then you will have it . . ." He snatched her up into his strong arms and easily began to wind his way through the boulders to the edge of the dark pool. Rebecca could feel the sinews of his arms tense. When she saw his face was dark and raging, she began fighting him in earnest, trying to twist out of his arms. When she had begun her tirade, she had not imagined that he would attempt to drown her! For there was no doubt in her mind that he was going to heave her directly into the still waters.

Azim almost hesitated, knowing that her temper had soared due to the heat. He couldn't really blame her for that, but still she did need a lesson and he saw no harm in giving her a soaking. Swinging her light frame easily, Azim tossed her struggling body high in the air, far from the rocks at the water's edge. She shrieked as she felt herself flung from his strong arms and dumped unceremoniously into the coolness. The water was not deep and she righted herself with as much dignity as was possible under the circumstances. What a sight she made standing there, hands on hips, hair dripping wet, blushing furiously.

Rebecca saw no hope in the situation. There was only one route open to her. Wisely she decided that her revenge would have to wait.

Almost too sweetly, she cooed, "As long as I'm soaked, I may as well bathe. I can hardly complete the task with you glaring at me! Would you mind leaving me in private to finish what you started?"

If Rebecca thought to mollify Azim with her sweet tone, she was wrong. He had begun to feel a little ashamed of his action, until she had risen from the water. Her voice bypassed his ears, for all he could see was her frame outlined by her clinging clothing, every tender curve alluringly visible to his eyes. He felt himself stiffen involuntarily, taken over by a desire as old as time, a primitive urge that must find relief in the body of a woman. Moments before he had been Alex Drayton, gentleman; now the years of moral refinement peeled away and he was driven only by his desire for this beautiful virgin standing vulnerably before him.

Decency leaving him altogether, Azim slowly stepped into the pool. Rebecca's face showed terror, for she could not help but read the naked lust written plainly on his features. His eyes were narrowed, his nostrils flared like a wild beast. He whispered hoarsely

through his teeth, "Take your clothes off!" When she
awkwardly began to back away, hampered by her
heavy wet skirt, he commanded again, "Take them
off!"

Fear gripping her, she stammered, "Azim! No!
Listen to me! I . . . I have not been with a man
before . . . You cannot do this to me . . . Please . . ."
Her voice trailed off as she knew words would be of no
use. Still, Azim came relentlessly toward her. He was a
stalking cat bent on devouring his prey.

Rebecca suddenly began to shed her years of proper
upbringing. Centuries of respectability fell away like
autumn leaves. She stood before him, her fear as
intense as his own desire. She was fighting for her virgin
pride, like so many women before her, and she knew
the animal instinct of self-preservation.

Azim's hand shot out and stopped her retreat. His
other hand took hold of her blouse, ripping it down the
front. Rebecca scratched frantically at his dark face,
managing to draw blood on his cheek, but in doing so
she forgot to defend herself against his hands tearing at
her clothing.

"Nooo . . . Stop! You can't take me this way! If you
touch me, I'll kill you!"

He whispered through whetted lips. "Who are you
saving it for? St. Claire? Or has he already had a taste
of your flesh?" Azim tore her chemise and skirt in one
swift hard motion. His lips parted. He stood back and
surveyed the results. Holding her still, gray eyes raking
her body, he saw her breasts rising and falling, boldly
tipped, pink peaks glaring back at him. Her breasts
were creamy and glistening with a sheen of water. If
Azim could have stopped himself before, he had gone
much too far now.

Pulling her toward him, Azim found her quivering
lips. He kissed her with a passion meeting the intensity
of the flaming sun overhead. Rebecca's head reeled,
her mouth was burning, not at all like she had felt with
William, but with a new and frightening sensation. Her

terror was ebbing, and a new emotion, as yet unnamed, was taking its place. Involuntarily, her mouth opened to meet his thrusting tongue, her arms reaching up to encircle his neck. Azim roughly pulled his head away and looked into her searching eyes. She feels it too! he thought. Never have I wanted a woman like this!

Azim quickly shed his breeches and shirt. The water was waist high, hiding his manhood from her gaze. She braced herself for his next attack. He bent his head and nibbled her neck with his teeth. He took her into his arms again and his dark head traveled down to her breasts. His tongue scorched her sensitive flesh, leaving Rebecca nearly swooning.

Long afternoon shadows set the surrounding rocks in relief. Rebecca opened her eyes and tried to think of William, her father, anything to take her mind off this animal who was carrying her to the bank of the pool, lips still leaving a trail of fire on her breasts. Her body burned with an unknown desire but her mind told her to fight for her honor. She was on the brink of a maelstrom, the bottom deep and terrifying.

Azim tenderly laid her cool slippery body down onto the warm earth. He stood over her, eyes narrowed, and drank in her beauty. Rebecca came to her senses; blushing profusely, she covered her body with her hands.

"I made a grave mistake, Azim. It won't happen again. Please allow me to retrieve my clothing. You cannot have what is mine only to give."

"Too late! You're a treasure I shall have for myself. No man will ever possess you as I now shall—"

Rebecca cut his words off as she rolled to the side and almost succeeded in eluding him. Before she could scratch or kick at him, he had pinned her down to the ground. He held her arms tightly over her head while his free hand stroked her bosom. Slowly, but deliberately, his knee parted her thighs. She struggled uselessly against him, but her movements only served to arouse him further. He lifted himself, positioning his body above hers. Rebecca could then see, with real fear, the imposing size of his manhood.

"Oh, my God! No!" Vainly she crept backward in the dirt.

Her pleas were futile. Azim's passion had risen beyond all control. "Come now, my beauty, stop twisting." His free hand held her hips still and he patiently found her tiny entrance. Pausing above her, Azim knew she would continue to fight him so he decided to take her quickly. Rebecca could feel his hardness enter her slightly. His gray eyes held her dark frantic ones. Time hung suspended over the two naked figures. They were, at the moment, the only man and woman on the earth. Rebecca's writhing had ceased as she gazed into his eyes. The primeval desire to know this man almost overcame her again, but her common sense told her to fight him.

"I belong to no man. I beg you to stop!" Rebecca again turned this way and that, but he was already inside her, his member at the tip of her womanhood. Rebecca's movements, although she could not realize it, drove him to a frenzy of sexual desire.

He groaned and whispered soft words into her ear. Suddenly she felt a sharp, stinging pain and then her insides were filled with him. Azim did not move himself for a few moments. Rebecca let herself sob aloud, as she felt a sticky wetness flow over her thighs.

"The pain is over, love. Let me take you now to the heights of pleasure."

"I'll never forgive you for this! You have shamed me . . . You have ruined me . . ." Rebecca wept uncontrollably. Azim could not hold back his movements another minute. He tried to contain himself for her sake, but realizing that she would not enjoy the encounter, he decided to relieve himself as quickly as possible.

He moved himself inside her but it brought little pleasure to Rebecca. She lay like a porcelain doll underneath his sweating body. His perspiration mingled with her tears, tasting salty in her mouth. Her face felt hot. When would it end? Suddenly his frame stiffened and he moaned words in Pashto, spilling his seed deep within her.

As quickly as he could, he rolled off her and stood naked in the fading light. He looked back at Rebecca, whose voluptuous body shook and trembled from the rape. His eyes roamed over the scene. Streaks of blood were visible on her thighs, and Azim knew a sadness that he attributed to the aftermath of love-making. He dove into the cool spring and lazed in the refreshing waters.

Rebecca knew that what was lost could not be replaced. She wept for all the ravished women before her, but mostly she cried for herself. Her tears finally spent, she turned to look at Azim, unashamedly dressing himself on the bank. Rebecca rose, hurting, held her head high and stepped into the water. Her stomach ached, not so much from the pain, but from a feeling that she could not, or would not, acknowledge. Rebecca washed herself thoroughly, taking care to keep her eyes from his.

Watching her scrub away the fresh blood of her maidenhood, Azim slowly returned to reality. He did not regret taking her, but rape? That was a new experience for him. But he would be damned if he would apologize to her! If only she could have enjoyed it! God knows, he had. If she hadn't been such a little bitch! Was he actually starting to feel regret? Would Alex Drayton have raped Rebecca? What the devil was the matter with him anyway?

Rebecca noticed a sharp movement out of the corner of her eye, startling her. Azim jumped quickly from his position on the ground and, abruptly, smashed a clenched fist into a rock. Blood spurted from the bruised knuckles, but he did not even acknowledge it as he turned again and strode back to camp, a dark, brooding scowl on his face, crimson drops falling from his hand.

Rebecca could not fathom what went on in the depths of his mind. She found the rags that minutes before had covered her and tried to restore some semblance of order to her torn blouse and skirt.

When she made her way back to join him she was determined to keep silent. Perhaps she should have flung herself into the pool and tried to drown herself. On the other hand, Rebecca did not feel suicidal. After all, not all women made it to the altar before they bedded a man. Was rape really a fate worse than death? Maybe it was, but then again, maybe she was different from most women. At any rate, she squared her shoulders and purposefully strode into the campsite.

Azim was crouched over the fire absentmindedly stirring the embers with a twig. He felt Rebecca's presence. Nevertheless, he chose to avert his stare into the burning logs. Azim was feeling a faint tremor of guilt which was shaking his hard facade and leaving him with a sick irritation in the pit of his stomach. He reflected back on his many years on the steppes. His love for the people and the harsh life were a passion with which no cold English bitch was going to interfere! Any other Afghan, in his present position, would take the woman again right now and leave her weeping in the dust. His last thought, before returning to the current situation, was that a warring tribesman such as himself would cut her throat after he finished with her body so that she would not live to bear more sons for the enemy.

The remaining hours of the evening were spent in total silence. Both Rebecca and Azim were lost in their unending trains of thought. They went through the motions of eating and resting, but their minds reeled with private doubts and a growing hatred for one another.

By daybreak, neither one really rested, they set out toward Azim's village. The small settlement was locat ed in the broad expanses of the northern Afghanistan plains. Rebecca did not know how near they were to her former destination, Mazar-i-Sharif. Azim had not decided what to do with her. Although he had toyed with the idea of ridding himself of the girl, his early upbringing in London would not allow him to do so. *Azim* would have tumbled her again and again, as his desire for her naked body underneath his own had not faded, but *Alex* would have no part of that contemptible behavior.

Rebecca desperately hoped that he would answer some of her questions, but she was damned if she would open her mouth to him. The only conversation between them was stilted, uncomfortable. "We'll camp here. See to the mounts. Cook this slowly. Relieve yourself over there by those rocks," etc. etc.

After an eternity of silence between them, Azim spoke brusquely. "Tomorrow we'll arrive in my village. You are to act subservient to me and to keep your bold eyes away from the men. I'm greatly respected by my comrades and I'll not have you shame me in my home!"

Her pent up angers and fears found a release at last. "Shame you! Don't make me laugh! I don't give a damn what they think! Azim, you can just go . . . to . . . go to everlasting hell!"

Furiously rising to her bait, he answered her, a snarl on his lips. "So now you have learned to swear! How ladylike! Take care, little hellion, or I'll put you in a veil and send you to the women's quarters! We'll see how you'll like that!"

Azim laughed loudly at her reaction, for Rebecca had none too gently nudged Alia and bolted off ahead of him. They did not speak two words that day, nor did he talk to her when, the next afternoon, they rode into his village. Rebecca was deep in apathy as the natives eyed her suspiciously. She pictured her father's reaction on learning of her abduction. She wondered if William would still want her in her used condition.

The veiled women of the village gathered around her, jealously surveying the captured ferangi beauty. The men shot her lusty glances. Azim noticed their reactions immediately, but Rebecca was still lost in contemplation—she was still in Kabul. It was centuries ago.

CHAPTER 13

William waited several days following Rebecca's departure before he tackled the job of seeing Lawrence Merideth. He wanted to assure himself that everything would go well in this all-important interview, as he knew Rebecca would not marry without her father's blessing. He never stopped to consider whether he loved her or not since that emotion was a foreign one to him. He desired her luscious charms, certainly, but above all, he wanted control of her inheritance and the fateful jeweled box waiting for her in the bank vault in London.

He sent a note to Lawrence requesting that he be allowed to call at eight o'clock on Tuesday evening to discuss a matter of great importance to them both. He carefully abstained from even a touch of brandy, arrived at the Merideths' and was ushered into the sitting room.

"Good evening, William," said Lawrence, rising to greet him.

"And a good evening to you, Mr. Merideth. How do you fare without the company of your beautiful daughter?"

"A bit lonesome, I must admit. Even in this short time I have grown used to having her here. And Nur Mustafa has gone back to making his wretched mutton stews again!" replied Lawrence with a wry smile.

"She will return in a few short weeks, bursting with

stories of adventure, and you will be thankful to remember the peace and quiet here now," laughed William. Then, becoming more serious, he broached the subject he had wanted to discuss initially. "It is about your daughter that I wish to speak, sir. I'm sure you are aware of my deep feelings for her. I would hope to venture that she has warm feelings for me, also. She asked me to speak to you while she was gone and said she would give me an answer when she returned, depending, of course, on what you decide."

Lawrence Merideth frowned. He had been afraid of some such confrontation when he got William's note requesting a meeting. He put his fingertips together and stared at them for a few minutes before he answered.

"Mr. St. Claire, it is my definite opinion that my daughter is too young to marry at this time. It may be that I am selfish in not wanting to lose her so soon after finding her again. That may be . . . There is also the fact that your work keeps you in one of the most dangerous spots in the world and I really would never forgive myself if anything happened to her because of that."

William felt a sinking sensation. "But, Mr. Merideth, she loves it here. More than I do myself, I fear. Certainly, I don't plan on remaining here forever. I have only begun my career," he protested.

"Nevertheless, William, I cannot and will not give her my permission to marry for awhile yet. I'm afraid that will have to be the end of the matter."

The younger man turned white. If Lawrence could have sensed what was whirling around in William's brain he would have drawn back in horror; a maelstrom of seething emotions like one of the snake pits of legend, a twisting, writhing mass of deadly serpents raising their poisonous heads to the outside world.

William controlled himself with great difficulty. He managed to rise, mumble some vaguely polite words and take his leave. He let his feet carry him wherever they would. As he walked slowly around the British compound his head sunk on his chest, his hands clasped behind his back, thinking deeply of his plight.

If only Lawrence had not taken this unreasonable dislike to him! He knew he could persuade her to marry him without her father's influence against him. How could he change the man's opinion of him? Perhaps, cause her to be put in some false danger of his own devising, then rescue her from it? Seduce her and get her with child? She was a passionate woman under the demure pose, he was sure. It might not be too difficult. But, no, there was no assurance in that plan. Sometimes it took years for women to conceive! What would absolutely assure him of her hand in marriage?

A small thought crept into his head like the tiny but deadly viper slipping among the writhing bodies of the larger serpents. What was needed was the removal of Lawrence Merideth, the permanent and irrevocable removal of the one individual standing between him and his most cherished, nay, most necessary, goal. The only irreversible method of ridding the world of a person was by somehow causing their demise. An accident! In this godforsaken and war-torn land, accidents were commonplace. Small skirmishes, robbers, bandits of all types, disease, bad food were all possible here.

William continued walking, his brain proceeding in its tortured logic. A fully detailed scheme rose unbidden to his mind. It seemed to him that all he had learned and felt in his life was leading him inexorably toward the culmination of his plan.

The next day, William knew, Lawrence Merideth was to attend a meeting with the Afghan Emir at his palace to discuss trade policy. Lawrence would be returning alone, near dusk, to the British compound. There was a small cluster of ruined huts at one point along the road where an assassin could conveniently hide until the victim passed by. There was, however, no one who William could trust as an assassin, nor had he the money to pay such a person. He would have to do this particular task himself. His decision reached, William felt a load lift from his shoulders for the first time in months. He smiled in the darkness, a surprisingly boyish grin, and set off purposefully for the bazaar. He needed one small item . . .

At six o'clock the following evening, Lawrence Merideth was riding toward home, exhausted by a long tense session with the Emir and his translator, but pleased, nevertheless, with the results: a signed manuscript in his saddlebag promising to grant the British certain trading rights in Afghanistan and promising *not* to give these same rights to the Russians. A tired glow of success filled Lawrence, and he reflected upon the future of his country's relations with this turbulent land.

Passing a familiar group of mud huts, his thoughts turned to Rebecca, wondering where she was. She should be nearly at her destination by now if all had gone as planned. With Thomas Mansfield in control he felt quite satisfied that his daughter was well cared for.

Lawrence felt his horse shy. Out of the corner of his eye he glimpsed a dark figure leap at him. He was conscious of a sharp, excrutiating pain explode in his back. Then, surprised, he felt himself helplessly falling . . . falling . . . All went dark.

William stood over the body, his chest heaving with effort and excitement. His sallow cheeks were splotched with red and his eyes gleamed like an animal's. He realized with faint surprise that there was a hardening in his groin. A pent-up breath escaped his lips in a rush.

He knelt and checked for a heartbeat. None. There was a red stain spreading on the back of Lawrence Merideth's coat. The knife handle stood up like a sinister decoration in the expanse of light cloth.

Looking carefully around him to see if anyone had witnessed the murder, William took Lawrence's purse from his pocket, shuddering as he touched the dead man. He wanted the assault to appear to be a simple robbery. He quickly walked back to where he had left his horse hidden behind a mud wall, mounted, and rode in a large circle to return to the compound from a different direction.

His initial burst of excitement had faded and he felt as though he were shrinking in size. He had felt himself larger than life, invincible, until now. The reaction to his deed began to set in. By the time he saw the walls of the British compound his face was pale and slippery with sweat. His hands shook with a dreadful fear.

At least I will have Rebecca, he thought. No one can stop me anymore. He tried to concentrate on her gleaming white body, losing himself in her creamy flesh, burying his face in her golden hair and between her breasts. The image of the knife handle standing up like a phallus in the dead man's back suddenly came to mind and dashed away his dream.

CHAPTER 14

The sunrise was particularly radiant this early summer morning at the end of June. Rebecca watched the warm rays filter through the window, casting just enough light for her to see Azim's sleeping body. When at rest he seemed peaceful, but she had learned to fear his waking hours. His personality could change on a moment's notice: one minute, dark and sinister; the next, wild and carefree.

She silently said a prayer as she slipped quietly from her separate bed. Recently, Rebecca had found herself asking for God's help in returning safely to civilization. Even though days had passed since they had arrived at his village, Azim would not answer her questions concerning her future. At least he had not touched her since that evening by the pool's edge. For that one small favor she was immensely grateful.

In a few moments, she knew, an elderly veiled woman would appear at the door. She would silently go about preparing Azim's food and tend to whatever chores there were to be done. Azim had so far seemed content to let Rebecca stay in bed late in the mornings, sometimes crying, sometimes staring bleakly at the ceiling.

This morning Rebecca had decided to come out of her lethargic state and had risen before Azim. Besides, she thought, that old hag shuffling about makes me nervous. I'll just go walking this morning. Then at least I won't have her strange eyes following me! Clothing herself in native attire, Rebecca had quietly sneaked away and was enjoying the fresh, cool morning air.

Her flowing robelike dress was belted at her narrow waist by a sash. Its color was a soft shade of tan. The morning breeze caught the skirt and swirled it up around her thighs. Azim would be furious if he could have seen the display of ankle and calf, but she was content this morning and did not want to spoil the mood by thinking of what he might say.

For days she had pensively followed Azim around the village, wishing that he had allowed her to stay in his house. The women would have nothing to do with her as Rebecca refused to wear a veil, but she did not really care what *they* thought. The men, on the other hand, leered at her. Azim seemed to enjoy the embarrassed way that Rebecca dropped her velvet eyes when the looks got too rude.

She saw their great respect for the brave young chapandaz, Azim. He held the position of horse trainer, a much skilled and envied job, in addition to being one of the best buzkashi players. Even the children gathered around him and he chuckled easily with them in his adopted Pashto language.

Rebecca arrived at the stables. She thrilled to see Alia standing there groomed and apparently well-fed. Mares of many colors stood nursing their young foals. Great stallions kicked up dirt in the early light and nipped at one another. She was reminded of her grandfather's estate, although it was a contrast being green and lush in the English tradition.

She spent a short time with Alia, then roamed without direction toward a grassy knoll nearby. A flower caught her eye—one lone yellow flower in the expanse of grasses, but such a delicate blossom to be here among the coarser growth—a flower of the steppe. I must ask Azim what sort this is, she thought, her hand reaching out to pick it. No! She snatched her fingers back. It is too beautiful to be plucked, it will only droop and fade. Better to let it grow and seed itself again.

The fat-tailed sheep grazed lazily in the high grass,

and she noticed a shepherd boy silently keeping his vigil. Suddenly, two huge beasts bounded at her in long leaps, growling viciously. Even the hackles on their backs sprouted fury. She stopped, terrified, thinking them demons. Their heads were large and strong but had no ears! A piercing whistle split the air causing the beasts to stop instantly and meekly trot back to their master. Rebecca relaxed, almost smiling. They were only dogs, their ears cropped to give the wolves no hold should a fight ensue over the protection of the flocks.

She approached the boy then, avoiding the dogs, and smiled into his young face. He was delighted that the ferangi woman should pay him any attention at all. They sat down together and easily enjoyed the companionship of one another. He wondered why such a beautiful lady should seek out his company, but he was too wrapped up in her smiles to think long on the enigma. He was not frightened of her, just fascinated by her pale hair and skin.

The sun cast its long sleek shadows on the great expanse of the plains as both Rebecca and the lad sat pensively, savoring this splendid morning. She did not hear Azim come up silently behind them.

"So here you are! I thought you had slipped away in the night, but I see otherwise," he noted sarcastically.

"I decided to rise early today, and the steppe looked so tempting." Hoping to pacify him, she added, "Then I saw this boy, and he looked so lonely, as I am. After all, Azim, no one in the village, except Mahmud, pays me any attention."

Azim realized that she had indeed been excluded from the life here. Perhaps Rebecca would stop sulking and moping about if he included her in his daily life.

He spoke to her pleasantly then. "Today you can accompany me when I work with the horses. The men will not like it, but if you do not intrude, they will soon come to accept you."

Rebecca wondered when he had taken the time to worry about her. There was perhaps a lot about this man she had not taken into account.

"Tonight you will share the food around the fires. But remember, my treasure, do not leave my side. The men would like nothing better than to take advantage of an unveiled woman—a ferangi."

Was he really warning her? Did Azim seek to protect her? Rebecca began to wonder if he really meant her harm, or was he only going to hold her captive, then ransom her?

They left the knoll, Rebecca throwing the shepherd boy a winning smile. Vaguely, Azim wondered if she would ever flash him such a charming glance.

An easy truce developed between them that day. She was once again caught up in the excitement of this strange land. She felt more at peace with herself than she had thought possible. Several times during the chores she began to do, Rebecca stopped and wondered why she was in such high spirits. After all, it was only days ago that she had thought happiness would never again be hers. She refused to feel guilty lest the sensation spoil her mood.

Azim was pleased with the new attitude she had taken. When she was smiling, he had never seen a more radiant sight. He longed to roll with her, laughing, in the high meadows. Dismissing the notion, he went about finishing the day's business.

Azim was one of the most respected trainers in the village. His knowledge of medical aids far surpassed that of Mahmud, as Azim knew more about tending wounds and illnesses. The balms that he carried in his leather pouch were no mystery to him, but what sane man would give his secrets away? He had found a cure for wounds quite by accident.

Years before, Azim had received a long gash on his arm. While playing the game of buzkashi he had torn his arm on a branch. He had always noted the quieting effect a certain weed had on the nerves of the sheep and horses, so, playing a hunch, he had applied the noxious weed to his cut. The results were remarkable; his arm had all but healed within a day. After that, Azim began applying the salve to the animals with much the same results. The villagers were astounded by his powers. Even Mahmud smiled proudly on him, never asking what his powers really were.

Azim related this tale to Rebecca while they were rubbing the same balm into a nip on one of the stallions. She was enchanted by the story and cheerfully giggled at the simplicity of his cures. Azim delighted in telling her the truth of his powers, for in England they had been applying medicines made of herbs for many years! She could see Alex's personality emerging as he laughed easily with her. They might have been in a drawing room somewhere.

Azim had, for the first time, a vague impression of what his mother and father must have enjoyed together. The sensation was pleasant, but somehow, it was also alien. He repressed the growing impulse to look back on painful memories and went on cheerfully bantering with Rebecca. Azim did not wish to lose the joy of the moments they now shared.

As Azim cared for the animals, Rebecca could not help but notice one of the younger stallions who shuffled and snorted in a corner, as if challenging Azim to touch him. The young stallion was mostly white with dark muzzle, dark flashing eyes, wildly flaring nostrils. He was magnificent, Rebecca thought. Then an idea came to her and her lips curved impishly into a smile.

"Azim, why do you not ride that one? He looks as if he needs some exercise." She pointed toward the white stallion.

"That one? He is only just broken and I've never ridden him. He looks a handful, doesn't he?" He cocked his head and looked quizzically at her. "What have you in mind, Rebecca? Would you like me to break my neck?"

"Why, are you afraid of him?"

Azim saw the spark in her eye and knew that he must meet her challenge.

He grabbed a bridle and walked toward the horse, speaking soothingly to him. The stallion's ears perked and his long tail swished madly as Azim softly approached. Watching the horse stiffen in anticipation, Rebecca almost wished she had not dared him to mount the half-tamed beast. But still, she had little doubt that Azim could handle him, and she loved to see a fine horse in action.

Some of the men gathered around to watch the spectacle, for the steed promised to be a good match for Azim. The villagers needed little excuse to drop their chores and view a more interesting scene.

Then they began wagering on the outcome of the ride. The bet seemed to be for how many seconds Azim could remain seated on the angry horse's back. Mahmud was trying to explain to Rebecca, mostly in gestures, what kind of bets were being placed.

"That man," Mahmud pointed, "bets a chicken that Azim stays on two minutes."

"Is that all?" asked Rebecca, surprised.

"Oh, this very, what you say, wild horse," explained Mahmud.

The excited babble of voices surrounded her, and for the first time, she wished that she could understand them. More and more people descended upon the area, bringing coins, dragging unwilling goats or sheep to wager on the outcome of Azim's ride.

"Is nearly even," said Mahmud, "those who think he make it and those who say he fall."

"Mahmud," said Rebecca suddenly, "I bet this necklace that the horse unseats him quickly!" And she unclasped a silver chain from around her neck and held it out.

"Ah, little lady, you, too, like to play with us! Yes! I bet spring lamb Azim stay on!"

"It's a wager!" said Rebecca, smiling at the fierce Turkoman. They clasped hands on it. The contest began.

Azim stilled the nervous animal and leaped on his arched back. The horse reared before Azim had even seated himself firmly. The crowds cheered furiously as Azim's strong hands and legs fought for control. Round they went, circling the walled enclosure over and over again. Rebecca grew frightened when the stallion suddenly stopped dead in his tracks, quickly surveyed the height of the walls, then headed straight for them. Azim had not anticipated this move. Few horses had ever tried the seven foot structure. He knew that it meant a swift death for the steed if he tried to jump with a man on his back, and the horse's mouth was too untrained as yet to stop him from attempting the barrier. Azim instantly flung himself from the horse, giving the terrified animal a chance to clear the barrier. The sleek white stallion leaped high into the air and luckily did manage to avert impending disaster, his hooves barely scraping the wall.

The crowd cheered for a long time, as everyone present realized the forbearance shown by Azim. The contest meant little compared to the worth of such a grand horse. Azim was the hero of the day. A feast was set for the fires that night with the wagered livestock generously donated to the cause. Azim was satisfied that he had managed to save the stallion, and he proudly strode up to Rebecca and Mahmud.

"What a devil that white beauty is, eh, Mahmud? I have seldom seen such courage in a horse! Tomorrow we shall begin to train him for the games. Do you agree?"

Mahmud nodded affirmatively. "I think your Khaled may have to work very hard now, is that not so?" Azim agreed, replying in Pashto and translating the exchange for Rebecca.

She asked Azim to relay a reminder to Mahmud with a twinkle in her dark eyes. "Please tell Mahmud that I would also like to donate my lamb to the feast tonight."

With a raised eyebrow, he barked, "What lamb?"

"Why, the one I just won from Mahmud, of course!" She was laughing, tears of mirth streaming down her pink cheeks. Mahmud, understanding the gist of her glee also joined in the merriment.

"I don't need to ask who *you* wagered on, Rebecca." Azim, thoroughly enjoying her success, knew that

Mahmud had, of course, bet on him. Azim was beginning, more and more, to enjoy Rebecca's lively wit. She was a challenge for him and he needed the mental stimulation. The English women he had known in Kabul wanted only one thing—a wealthy husband to assure their social standing. On the other hand, the hard life of the veiled village women had left most of them without humor and old beyond their years. Rebecca was like a first ray of sunshine following a dark sleepless night. Azim was dimly conscious that his life was coming to a turning point, but he shrugged off the idea.

Rebecca was combing out her long hair after washing it in preparation for the festivities. The shadows in the room were deepening and she rose to light a lamp. As twilight descended on the village she felt a dark curtain drape her bright mood. Azim had gone to fetch the lamb and help slaughter the animals for the feast. She tried to shake the brooding feeling that was threatening to spoil her evening. She told herself that as long as she was being held here, what possible harm could it be to relax and make the most of the experience? She pictured Azim's tall suntanned body, his hard muscles, and flat stomach. When his face was in repose or when he was performing a well-liked job, he was incredibly handsome, even the scar on his face seemed to add to his charm. She could also picture him in a rage, face a stone mask, scar white against a stern facade, handsomeness giving way to coldness and severity.

Rebecca dismissed the picture from her mind. At least at the moment he was soft and gentle, sharing a portion of his life with her. She began to form an idea in her mind, the notion growing on her like a vine, writhing, alive. If she could charm him enough, perhaps he could be persuaded to return her to her friends. Yes—that was it! How stupid she had been! Why any schoolchild knew the lesson—you always caught more flies with honey! Her mood was lightened instantly, impending success lending a sparkle to her eye. The plan was perfect. Rebecca only saw one dark side to the brilliant idea. What if Azim was no longer interested in her? After all, he had used her once and then he had stood his distance. Was it possible that having tasted her charms he had tired of the game? Now she hoped not. Tonight was the perfect time to try her plan on Azim.

As she was formulating her plot, Azim was knee-deep in the messy preparations of slaughtering the animals. He hurried through the ugly job and went straight to the *hammam* to wash, for he was anxious to return to the hut and watch Rebecca perform her nightly toilette. Although he had refrained from touching her, it was not because he did not desire her any longer—quite the contrary. He was afraid of wanting to depend on her solely for his male needs. Before Rebecca, he had been able to bed a different woman every time he needed relief, but since that night at the ball she had been the only image in his mind when he lay alone at night. At first he had fought the vision, but then he had allowed himself to fantasize about a make-believe encounter between them. When he had seen her luminous brown eyes gazing fearfully up at him during the ambush, he had known that he was going to kidnap her. If only he hadn't had that damned English notion of honor tugging at his conscience he would have used her enough by now to have tired of her!

The atmosphere around the fires that night was light and carefree. Food and drink were plentiful and the sound of cheerful laughter rang clearly throughout the village. The people of the north were a hearty lot who loved a good wager and told stories with an equal fervor. They would not be called wealthy by any standards, but they did have a rich and full love of life. Rebecca was caught up in the gaiety. Mahmud had even dragged her to her feet and insisted that she learn a native dance. Rebecca was enchanted by the strange music, her feet and body moving deliciously to the rhythm.

When she was finally breathless from the dancing, Mahmud sat down with her near the fire. He motioned for Azim to come close and spoke to him in Pashto at length.

"Mahmud wishes for you to understand our way of life. He wants to relate the story of buzkashi so that you will know what we live for here in the steppes. He has asked me to translate."

The villagers began to gather around Mahmud. He was a famed storyteller, and they were confident that he would not disappoint them.

Mahmud settled himself comfortably, closed his eyes, and began.

"Picture an endless plain, so huge that only the sky forms the boundaries. Picture this plain covered with sweet grass, grass as far as the eye can see, waving, stirring gently in the wind that comes from the huge land to the north. The land has a life of its own. This is the steppe. Nowhere here will you find the terrible walls of rock, the deep canyons, the sheer drops. No, here is only the fertile openness of the mother of us all, nurturing us in her wide bosom, nurturing us all, men and beasts alike." He paused to let Azim catch up. The listeners were spellbound although they had heard the story many times before.

"Picture the northern horizon of the steppe fill with men and horses, wagons behind them carrying their women and children, their yurts and their goats. This was the army of the mighty Genghis Khan, conqueror of half the world and of our own land. His soldiers lived, died, ate, made love. Their small shaggy ponies were tough—strong and bighearted enough to conquer the world with their riders. When the men had finished their killing and raping, their bloody war against the whole of Asia, they looked around for something more. They devised a game with which to amuse themselves, to play in their new life of peace, of too much leisure. The game was as dangerous as battle; their fierce instincts would be sated by it. Their horses were also part of the game. The game of buzkashi."

The listeners' voices repeated the name softly to themselves, savoring it, tasting it, as if it were a new word. They breathed the word lovingly. Their eyes glistened in the firelight with unshed tears. Rebecca felt herself carried on the wave of his narrative also. She was drained when his voice finally stopped.

She turned to Azim as he finished translating for her. "What a wonderful story. I do understand why you can stay here, Azim. It is a life that comes out of the past unsullied, with no pretense to it."

Mahmud could see that she had been affected by the story. He was proud. Perhaps his friend, Azim, and the ferangi woman would find a measure of peace. He would have been disappointed if he had known what Azim was thinking at that moment.

Azim's eyes could not tear themselves from his captive. Every movement she made was achingly, unbearably sensuous in his hot eyes. His body felt a great need for hers. Cold-bloodedly, he decided to lower her natural defenses with alcohol, being certain that Rebecca also wanted him. Azim was suffering from the age-old pride of the male race. He knew that Rebecca had not enjoyed his love-making, and he was determined to bring her body to the same heights of desire that he had felt. Tonight he would make her want him with a passion equaling his own.

Rebecca finally disentangled herself from an overactive dance partner and sat down again with Azim. One of the village girls who was serving slices of mutton was throwing Rebecca vicious glances over her veil. Rebecca had grown used to their ugly stares, but this young woman was insolent.

Curiously, she inquired, "Azim? See that young girl over there serving the meat?" His eyes followed the direction of her hand. "She seems to hate me. I mean,

she looks at me in a fearfully ugly manner. Is she . . .
was she . . . something special to you?"

His gaze dropped to her full pouting lips. He replied
too casually, "You're asking me if I slept with Diyeh?
Yes, and others as well. I'm no saint."

"Oh, I see. I suppose they think that we are, well,
you know what I mean."

"Yes, little blossom, I know what you mean." His
eyes crinkled in amusement and he had a humorous
grin on his handsome face. Rebecca wished she had
never mentioned the jealous hussy.

Azim saw the awkwardness of the conversation and
decided to change the subject. He thought that now
might be the time to offer her something stronger than
tea. He poured her a hearty shot of the brew and
offered her a cup.

"Try some of our native drink. I think you will find it
mellow and to your liking." He put the earthen mug to
her lips and helped her to take a first taste. Rebecca felt
the fluid burn all the way to her stomach, but the
sensation was not unpleasant and she began to slowly
sip some more.

Azim soon began to wonder if his idea might be
going amiss, for she was enjoying the new feeling
brought on by the strong liquor and he feared that she
was overindulging. He did not want to have her pass
out on him! He reached over and gently took the mug
from her hand.

Rebecca looked at him in surprise. "What are you
doing? I was enjoying the drink and I feel like finishing
it!"

"You've had enough. That light-headed feeling you
have now will turn into a vicious headache in the
morning. Come, let us go. It's late and I have work to
do early tomorrow." He helped her to her feet. She
protested weakly. The stars were the only source of
light to guide them to his hut. Rebecca felt delicious all
over. Azim had his arm around her waist and was trying
to keep her from stumbling. He also was sensing the

effect of the brew. He longed to touch her soft whiteness, but he would wait, as he was determined to take his time with her tonight and let his own needs come second.

Once inside he lit the lamps deciding against a fire. There would be no need for extra warmth tonight. He would see to that.

Rebecca stretched lazily, exposing her soft curves to Azim's hungry eyes. Previously, Azim had always allowed her a moment of privacy so that she could change into her shift, which a serving woman had silently handed her one evening. Rebecca noticed that he was reluctant to leave and sobered instantly.

Azim saw her body stiffen. Fearing her mounting tension, he crossed the room hastily. "You're a little unsteady. Here, let me help you." Rebecca's head was fuzzy from the alcohol she had consumed, her feelings confused. She stood still and allowed him to have his way. Her body was rigid as he lifted her dress over her head, but she kept remembering her intentions to "catch flies with honey." She did not want to make him angry, for she intended to ask him to let her go. In fact, she had taken the drink hoping to stiffen her resolve enough to broach the subject this evening. She tried to relax but could still feel a hot surge rise to her cheeks.

She smiled shyly when Azim's eyes traveled to her breasts. She looked for her nightgown, as the scanty chemise she was wearing did little to cover her. Soon she began to search frantically. It seemed to have disappeared.

"Is this what you're looking for?" he asked, holding the gown out toward her.

Rebecca saw a dangerous look on his face. He was incredibly masculine as he stood there beckoning to her. She suddenly realized that if she dared to approach him, he would have his way with her. Dear Lord, she thought, he has mistaken my affability for more than I would offer! I cannot go through with this!

He spoke, his voice strangely hoarse. "Rebecca, you

have nothing to fear. Stop fighting me . . . I'll teach you what it means to be a real woman."

His meaning escaped her, but his husky tone inflamed her imagination. God, he is handsome, thought Rebecca. It must be the drink. I cannot, no, I shall not let him take me again! But her unspoken words were not convincing.

"Relax," he continued slowly, but deliberately. "Let me show you Rebecca. Your body was formed to make a man burn. If you would only give in—just once—I'd show you what a woman needs."

Her answer was simple, the meaning of her words not even striking her until the statement was out. "I don't want that, Azim. I want to go home." There, she had named the price. She was bartering her body for freedom. But would this one act be so sinful if it brought her safely home? After all, he had already had his way with her.

Rebecca's body was cold and trembling but her mind was made up. "Azim, I shall sleep with you, here, tonight. But you must promise to return me tomorrow to the Mansfields. In turn, I shall give myself freely and without a battle . . . And I promise you that no one shall ever know your identity. You can trust me."

Though the thought of her selling herself was distasteful, he had to weigh the alternative to her deal. He could have her with a bitter struggle but then she would hate him again, and soon he would have to return her anyway, or he could strike the deal with her and take her as many times as he wanted, pleasurably.

A contemptuous smile curled his lip. "So you would sell your soul to the devil of lust? The bargain is struck, then. You are mine to do with as I please until the sun rises."

He was treating her like a whore! But what did she really care now? She could close her mind to the act and she would survive it—she had before. Slowly, Rebecca took her chemise off. She spoke not a word, but flushed hotly from head to toe. God, how she wished she could prevent herself from doing that all the time!

Azim whetted his lips at the sight of her standing naked in the lamplight before him. She was a rose bud ready to open, her skin glistening in the flickering shadows of the room. Her eyes were fearful but challenging. She held her head high and met his gaze. His eyes roamed over her body freely and deliberately stopped at her breasts. The swelling mounds rose and fell heavily, the pink enticing tips beckoning him. Azim went to her.

At first he did not touch her with his hands, but stood slightly apart from her and bent his head to caress her nipples with his lips. The effect was completely unexpected by her. The pink tips rose involuntarily to meet his tongue. She was suddenly aware that she longed to have him touch her with his strong hands, but still he kept a tantalizing distance. His tongue began to travel down to her belly, sending shock waves of pleasure upward making her head reel.

"Your body was made for love," Azim murmured, voice low. "Tonight you will learn what it really means to be a woman."

She reached down to his head shakily and put her fingertips in his thick dark hair. Slowly, she began to move her fingers through the deep brown waves, then lower still, to touch the cords of his neck. While caressing him, she was unconsciously moving his head to pleasurable spots on her belly and breasts. Azim was aware of her growing desire and took his time with his kisses. Finally, when Rebecca was visibly trembling, he raised himself back to his full height and swept her into his powerful arms. He was still dressed and she felt slightly ashamed to realize that she ached to feel his skin next to her own. Did a whore think this way? she dared to wonder.

Her thoughts were dashed away when his lips took hers. Her belly gave a quiver that sent waves shooting through her. His lips took hers more deeply still, and then roamed to kiss her nose, ears, eyes. He gently placed her on his bed and quickly undressed. Azim's magnificent body was tanned deeply. He stood before her, erect, tense, surveying his prey.

"Do you want me, Rebecca? Say the words, little flower! Tell me what you feel."

She moaned. "I feel strange all over . . . I'm frightened, but I want *something*. I don't know how to tell you."

"Just say you want me. Just say it."

"I want . . . I want . . . you." Was that her voice? Was she really playing the harlot for him? Surely it was only the drink. Rebecca Merideth would not behave so abominably.

Azim crouched over her lithely, a cat ready to strike. Rebecca was trembling with anticipation and fear, but she could not prevent herself from letting him have his way.

Azim entered her slowly, taking his time when she moaned from the small pain of entry. He poised his body over hers and held himself above her, arms straight and muscular, hands next to her shoulders. He looked into her eyes, whispering slow tender words of love. He saw in her eyes the blossoming of a girl into a woman. He saw a promise of growth from bud to full bloom, a woman's total glory in fulfillment.

She felt a throbbing inside herself unlike any she had ever known before and a desire to have the ache eased. She started to move, her back arching slightly, her hands finding his buttocks and moved him deep inside her. Deeper and deeper he drove, following her rhythm. She was mindless now, and only sought to satisfy her overpowering sensations. Slowly, then more rapidly, she felt the burning urgency spread to the core of her very being. A small explosion, then another larger one, a spiraling whirlwind, raised her to dizzying heights. Her whole body stiffened and arched and held itself suspended in time. A great void was filled and she came spinning back to earth. Azim quickly followed suit and Rebecca clasped him tightly to her, unmoving now. They lay entwined and fell serenely into a blissful sleep. The stars moved serenely above, and soon faint streaks of light would usher in a new day.

As dawn stole silently through his window, Azim propped himself up on his elbow and studied Rebecca's face. She was more beautiful to him than ever. His fingers lightly traced the fading scar on her upper arm. She had become a fulfilled woman last night, and in spite of her bargain, he could never think of her as a whore. Who knew better than he that she had been virginal before he had deflowered her? The knowledge brought a swelling pride to his chest. He sighed and let the true happiness of the moment envelope him. Rebecca stirred slightly but slept peacefully on.

Azim was certain that her bargain would be meaningless to her now that she had discovered his love. Perhaps he would tell her that he loved her and she could join him in his life here. They might even marry. The notion no longer frightened him; he almost felt a certain comfort in it. He looked at her long golden hair, spread like soft English wheat on a blanket of earth. Her dark lashes fluttered. She awakened to find Azim looking tenderly into her eyes.

Rebecca was instantly reminded of their love-making of the night before. She reddened at his gaze, but remembered how easily he had agreed to return her this very day. Her body was totally satisfied and she felt no shame for the deed. Looking into his gray eyes, she felt a deep attachment for the comely man. Perhaps he would even settle down and they might see one another in Kabul. She dared to think that he might even marry her. After all, he was of the highest birth. And, her father would be delighted with a man who shared both the love of Afghanistan and his daughter.

Brushing a stray lock of his hair from his forehead, she said, "Azim, shall I pack my clothes. Will we be leaving soon?"

His face darkened. "I naturally assumed . . . that

you would not want to leave . . . Quite so soon, that is." Then the full truth dawned on him. "I see . . . You really did sell your treacherous body, didn't you, love?" He continued, a contemptuous curl on his lips, "And I was stupid enough to think that little bargain was a cover-up for your high English morality!" he ended with a sneer.

Eyes brimming with tears, she cried, "I just thought that after last night . . . Well, I mean . . . I thought that you cared a little . . . *I* did, you know."

"Oh, you mean to say that you allowed yourself to feel?" he mocked her in a hard voice. "Come now, Rebecca, a good whore would never let that happen. Don't worry, bitch, the deal was well-struck! In fact I've grown tired of your pretense. I'm not done with you. The night is not yet over!"

His face was a hard mask, his muscles tensed—he hated her. Rebecca was frightened to death by his sudden turnabout. What made him so cruel to her? Did he imagine that she would continue to sleep with him and live in his village? Surely he could see the impossibility of *that*. The man was an arrogant fool. He could kill her on the spot, but she would be damned if she was going to give in to him again! Not without a fight!

She swung her long legs over the side of the bed, and, tossing her hair back, she hissed at him. "Go to the devil, Azim. It's dawn and I've done my part."

He gave her an icy look. "Get back in the bed! If you don't, I'll thrash you here and now!" With that he grabbed her arm and pulled her to him. Rebecca panicked and clawed at his face. Without warning he soundly slapped her. Then he was bruising her shoulders and arms with his strong hands. She started to cry uncontrollably. He pushed her onto her back and roughly, brutally entered her. She gasped with pain, her body twisting frantically.

Azim hoped her agony was great. Still, he thrust deeper into her body, until Rebecca was sure she would faint. He was visibly enjoying her agony and was determined to continue. She had severely cut him with her callous words when he had thought to keep her with him. The little tart had truly sold her body, not for desire of him, but for freedom from his caresses. Azim's male pride would not endure such an affront; he rammed into her body.

He grunted, "Why aren't you wrapping your legs around me, sweetheart? Play the slut you really are." With that he began a more rhythmic movement and held himself in check. There was no doubt in his mind that the sobbing bitch would begin to respond. He would have the last laugh yet.

Azim's lips found her neck and his teeth nibbled at the spots he had memorized only last night. His mouth moved lower still and found her heaving bosom. The nipples responded instantly, rising to meet his tongue.

"No . . . Please don't shame me this way." She had felt her own response. Against her will, her control was slipping.

Suddenly he pulled away from her. He pushed her knees up and held her flailing arms. He crouched down between her thighs and began to caress her parted flesh with his mouth. Rebecca was mortified, her resolve crumbled, her shame complete. Her body traitorously continued to respond. She felt shock after shock of burning delight, culminating in one long flow of ecstasy, leaving her shivering all over and crying his name aloud.

Unfulfilled, Azim stood up and leaned over her. Rebecca tried to cover her body with her hands. He swept them away.

Tossing his head back, he laughed at her although the tone was not humorous. "You see, slut? You even respond to *this!* Look at yourself lying there. You're a spent whore and don't try to deny it." He snarled, "Now get dressed before you make me sick, and pack your belongings." He ripped off a small portion of her petticoat. "Write a few words on this. I'll have Mah-

mud deliver it to your friends so that they won't worry
about your safety any longer. I'll return in an hour and
you will be with your precious friends as soon as I can
possibly get you there. Remember this well, Rebecca,
if you breathe a word to anyone about my identity, I'll
find your slim neck and cut your throat." He left her
then, weeping, humiliated. At that moment, she knew
true hate for him. She also knew lust.

CHAPTER 15

William St. Claire considered himself very fortunate, indeed, to have been able to join an East India Company caravan traveling to Mazar-i-Sharif. Otherwise, he would have had to wait until Rebecca returned to Kabul, or travel alone, which was unthinkable in this hostile land. It had been so easy to feign astonishment, shock, grief as David Mountstuart told him the next morning of the foul murder of Lawrence Merideth.

"It was another case of these damnable natives robbing a lone man. His purse was found to be missing and the knife was of local workmanship. So, there is no doubt about that. I only wonder why they did not take his horse, too."

"Perhaps they were afraid someone would recognize the animal later," suggested William quickly, sorry that he had not thought to take the beast and sell it to some horse trader.

"Yes, of course, I'm sure that was it," said Mountstuart. "These Afghans are becoming more subtle in their evil ways lately. We have very little hope of finding the culprits. We're so helpless in these matters!" He paused. "However will I break the news to Rebecca?"

"I would be willing to take that painful matter out of your hands, sir," suggested William, inspired. "You must have suspected that Miss Merideth and I had an understanding, so I do think it is my duty to tell her. The dear child will be devastated. And poor Mr.

Merideth was always so worried about *her* safety! If only he had cared more for his own!"

The journey to the North had been exceedingly difficult, William thought. He wondered how Rebecca had withstood it and how she was feeling *now* about this inhospitable place. He had spent the night, uncomfortably, in the East India Company's temporary camp, not wanting to arrive at the Mansfields' hot, dusty, and bad-tempered. He was aware that the grief-stricken girl would have no one to turn to but him, and he wanted to be thoroughly prepared to take advantage of the situation.

He rode through the bare and ugly little town as he had been directed, and arrived at a pleasant, rambling house, surrounded by the ubiquitous mud wall. Someone had planted a rosebush by the front gate, but it was drooping in the heat. A neat young servant opened the door at his knock and showed him to the cool patio behind the house where Catherine and Thomas were breakfasting.

He walked toward them with a smile on his face about to utter a greeting, but the words were frozen on his lips by the sudden shocked whiteness on both faces.

"Dear God!" exclaimed Catherine, "It's Mr. St. Claire!" And she buried her face in her hands.

"Please excuse me, Mrs. Mansfield," said William quickly. "Perhaps I've come at a bad time . . . I'll return later . . . I've just arrived from Kabul and must see Miss Merideth about something . . ." His words fell on ominous silence. "Is there . . . is there something wrong?"

"I'm terribly sorry, Mr. St. Claire," answered Thomas Mansfield finally. "Excuse me for not rising to greet you, but I've had the damnable misfortune to have received a ball through my leg."

"Dreadful," put in William. "I hope it's not serious. How did it happen?"

"Sit down, St. Claire," Thomas said with a long sigh. "I'll tell you exactly what occurred."

When he had finished telling of the attack on their

camp and of the abduction of Rebecca, William's face was white and strained. This time, he had no need to feign surprise and horror because he felt shocked to his core, sick with frustration and thwarted hopes.

"And do you lead me to understand," asked William at last, "that Rebecca disappeared that night and no one has seen or heard from her since? Have you done nothing to find her?" His tone began to rise in panic.

"Yes, of course, Mr. St. Claire," replied Catherine tearfully. "We have done everything we can, everything! We have been hoping, praying, something would turn up . . ." She put her face in her hands again and wept. Thomas tenderly patted her head and murmured something.

Addressing William he said, "Calm yourself, Mr. St. Claire. We have every spare soldier in the garrison out right now searching for her, and asking in villages. I've even sent messages to the other towns along our route to watch for her and to listen for news of her fate. We've done everything we can, everything humanly possible. I'm only sorry I cannot go myself, but this leg has been giving me a devil of a time. Why, we were lucky to have escaped the ambush at all. I don't like to think what poor Catherine went through, getting back here with Meera, a handful of the men, and me delirious with fever." He paused, his face thoughtful. "We have not given up hope, St. Claire. She may be unharmed, she may be held for ransom somewhere— that we will hear soon—or she may be on her way here. You must, like ourselves, hope for the best."

William wondered what the "best" could be at this point. It seemed that his plans were spoiled again. Damn that girl! She laid waste to each of his schemes as though on purpose! Well, there was no reason to keep his news any longer. The Mansfields were sure to hear sooner or later.

"I actually came here for a very sad reason," confessed William. "I was sent by the governor to tell Miss Merideth of her father's . . . death."

"Oh, no!" broke in Catherine, raising her tear-stained face from her hands. "That can't be true! That would be too cruel!"

"I'm afraid it is true," William went on. "He was found one morning with a . . . foully murdered . . . his money gone. It was a terrible shock to everyone . . . but, now, this news . . . I don't know what to do. Can I be of any help in the search?"

"No, Mr. St. Claire. I'm afraid you don't know the area well enough to be of much assistance. But you must stay for awhile; you need a rest after your trip. What a terrible affair this has turned into. If I had not offered to take Rebecca with us, none of this would have happened." Mansfield's voice was painfully full of self-accusations.

"You must not blame yourself . . . too much, Col. Mansfield. Afghanistan seems to hold danger for all of us. What a fearful place!"

William could think of nothing else to do but to remain in Mazar-i-Sharif until they had word, one way or another, of Rebecca's fate. He arranged for one of the Mansfields' servants to pick up his bag at the East India Company camp. Then he stayed in his room all day, hiding from the fiery sun. Evening brought some respite, but William was restless and ill-at-ease. Was there no way out of his dilemma? He drifted off to sleep that night with visions of Rebecca, captive in a dirty village, dragged by the hair through the dirt, lying dead at the bottom of a ravine, set upon by wolves, or men, all chances of recouping his mother's box dashed.

Meera tossed and turned, dozing fitfully in her small room off the kitchen of the Mansfields' house. She had not slept well since the attack and was barely able to do any work, breaking into tears at the slightest provocation. She felt personally responsible for her Missy Sahib's predicament and was sure she could have persuaded her mistress not to go on the ill-fated journey. If only she had tried harder to dissuade her!

The other servants, all men, had grown tired of her everlasting tears and sad brown eyes, and had left her alone. They preferred a more substantially built woman than Meera anyway, even though they had given her some admiring glances and some even more flirtatious pats and pinches before growing weary of her weeping.

She woke once more in the dark room and lay there, praying with fervor to a myriad of Hindu gods and goddesses to keep her mistress from harm. When a tear slipped from under an eyelid her hand rose to brush it away and froze in midair. She heard a sound at the shutters which covered her window, and a black shadow blotted out the little bit of moonlight that had filtered through the slats. It must be the fearful Kali coming in the night to take her away and punish her evilness! Her breath came fast and the blood drained from her head. She could not move an inch. It was as though her limbs were made of stone. It is the hand of the deity, she thought, freezing me as the cobra stills his unfortunate victim before pouncing!

The shutters opened slowly. An ominous shadow crept silently over the window sill. It moved on cat feet to her bed, reaching out a hand, covering her mouth. The other lit a candle by her bedside.

In the flickering light Meera could see a pair of black eyes under bushy brows, a large black mustache. This was no god, but a very dangerous looking man! However, the rough hand over her mouth was gentle and the man surprisingly did nothing more than to stand there gazing at her for a moment. Finally, he made a motion for her to be quiet. He whispered, "Missy Sahib—Rebecca," while taking his hand from her mouth.

Meera instantly sat up, forgetting her half-dressed condition, forgetting even her veil in the explosion of joy his words had evoked.

"Missy Sahib all right?" she asked frantically. "Where is Missy Sahib? Tell me quickly!"

"No English. No talk English," said the strange

apparition. From inside his long coat he took a soiled and faded piece of cloth and offered it to her. In the faint light of the candle, Meera could see nothing remarkable about the piece of material until she recognized a scrap of lace on one corner. Surely this was a portion of Rebecca's petticoat! She gazed up at the fierce-looking man with a question in her eyes. He carefully unfolded a corner revealing words written in charcoal on the cloth. Meera immediately began to study the words, which were difficult to decipher, being smudged and dirty.

It definitely was from Rebecca. She could not explain much in this note but she was alive and well and would be arriving at the Mansfields' in a few days. It went on to say that the bearer of the letter was Mahmud, a friend, and that he was to be well-treated, but not made known to Catherine and Thomas.

"Missy Sahib?" asked Meera, holding up the piece of cloth. "Missy Sahib good?"

"Yes, Missy Sahib good," replied Mahmud with a wide smile to show that Rebecca was indeed unharmed.

Meera's eyes widened in discovery. "You," she pointed, "you man go bang! Bang!" and she made a motion as if shooting a gun.

Mahmud hung his head in embarrassment. He knew that she was referring to the ambush on Mansfields' camp that night.

"Yes," he whispered, "Me go bang, bang! But no bang . . ." He made a motion of breasts and hips and long hair.

"Ah, you not be shooting ladies!" Meera said with pursed lips. "I am seeing now Sahib Mahmud!" She took his arm and led him through her door to the kitchen, empty now that the servants were all asleep. She motioned for him to sit at the table. She would return.

As she hurried back to her room, Mahmud followed her with his eyes, noticing the small waist and rounded hips of the slight girl. Meera returned in a moment with her sari wound around her body and her veil properly in place. He could only see her large brown eyes fringed with thick black lashes. At least they no longer held the paralyzing terror he had first seen in them.

"Meera fixing you *chai* and *nan*." She made eating motions. "Go back to Missy Sahib. Say, Meera happy!"

Somehow Mahmud understood what she meant even though he did not understand the words, and he liked the sound of her lilting voice as she chattered away while bringing him tea and flat bread with slices of cold mutton.

Mahmud ate in silence but with many appreciative glances at Meera. She, in turn, noticing his attention, began to feel very self-conscious, a blush rising hotly under her veil.

He finished, thanked her politely in Pashto and left, quickly melting into the inky night. Meera could hardly believe he had been there at all. Only a scrap of cloth and the dirty dishes on the table remained as proof of his visit. As she began to clear the table it occurred to her that maybe Mahmud *was* a god, appearing in human form to bring her the news of her mistress's safety.

The Mansfields had barely seated themselves on the patio where they habitually had their breakfast served when Meera appeared, waving a piece of cloth in excitement.

"Sahib Mansfield," she cried happily, "My Missy Sahib is well. She is coming to us in a few days! I am feeling so happy now."

Catherine and Thomas looked at the scrap Meera held. They deciphered the writing, finally glancing up at each other in surprise.

"Who is this Mahmud, Meera?" Thomas asked her. "How did you get this message?"

"Letter coming in night by Sahib Mahmud. He friend of Missy. Very nice man. Letter says be treating him well, so I do what letter is saying. This all right, Sahib Mansfield?"

"Yes, Meera, of course, but it certainly is a mystery. Where is she and how did she send a letter with this man, Mahmud? I suppose we'll just have to wait and ask her. I do hope this is not a hoax of some sort."

"What do you think is a hoax of some sort?" William St. Claire's voice reached across the patio.

"See for yourself, St. Claire," answered Thomas, handing him the note.

William read it carefully, then sat down quickly in a chair, rereading the words again and again to make sure of their meaning. He looked up with a frown of concentration furrowing his brow.

"I can hardly believe it is true. Are you sure this is from your mistress, Meera?"

"Oh yes, Sahib William, this is coming from Missy's petticoat for sure."

"I pray to the dear Lord that this is true and that Rebecca is well as she says," said William. "I suppose we can do nothing but wait patiently."

"Amen to that, St. Claire," said Thomas Mansfield fervently.

Two days later, one of the Mansfields' servants ran into the dining room where they were having lunch with William and announced excitedly that a ferangi lady had been seen riding alone through the town on a dapple-gray horse. The Mansfields and William immediately hurried to the gate to see if it was Rebecca. There was nothing but a deserted street. Then a gust of hot dry wind swirled a cloud of dust around the angle of a high wall. A dim figure emerged from within the billows, catching the morning sun on her bright hair. They hardly knew the girl—her blue riding habit was so torn and filthy as to be unrecognizable, her hair tangled and riotous around her pale face. When she finally looked up to see them standing there, she stopped her horse and sat looking at them wildly and fearfully.

William was the first to recover. He held out his arms and spoke her name softly, hoping that she would turn to him in her trouble.

Rebecca slid off Alia's back, almost falling to the ground, tottered toward William and flung her arms around him, crying hysterically as he held her to his chest, stroking her hair, assuring her that she was safe.

Azim had followed Rebecca from a secure distance to make certain that she reached her friends safely. It was a great relief, he told himself, to be rid of her at last. He had no time or inclination for a woman, especially one as contrary as this!

Watching from a discreet distance, he was surprised at the hot anger that flashed through him when he saw Rebecca clasped tightly in St. Claire's arms. His brows drew together, a muscle in his jaw jumped as he reined Khaled around roughly and set out, retracing his path to the village.

CHAPTER 16

"William, oh Lord . . . It's just that I haven't seen a familiar face in so long!" Rebecca finally had enough control of herself to push William gently away and attempt to smooth her hair and skirt.

"Catherine, Thomas," she said turning to the Mansfields. "I had no idea whether you were alive or dead! I'm so thankful to find you here. It's been awful . . . I can't begin to tell you how glad I am to be back!" Her words tumbled out feverishly while she continued to arrange her tattered clothes.

"Rebecca, Rebecca, thank God you are safe!" Thomas soothed her, putting a paternal arm around her shoulders. "You look marvelous considering what you must have been through. We were so relieved when we got your note. You'll never know how frantic we have been. I assure you, Rebecca, that I accept all blame. No thanks to me that you are safe and well, now . . . but, I think—"

"Missy Sahib! Missy Sahib!" a familiar voice cried joyously. "You are coming back to Meera at last!" Meera was sobbing with joy. After awhile she took control of the situation and said in a broken voice, "Goodness sakes, you are needing bath and new dress!" Her faithful servant could not wait another minute but wanted to hustle her inside instantly.

Catherine embraced her friend warmly. "Meera is right. What Rebecca needs is a good soak, a long rest, and a hot supper. We will talk later when she feels more like herself."

Rebecca thankfully followed Meera to her room. She could not imagine how she would answer all the questions that they were bound to ask. At the moment, she was too exhausted and drained of emotion to even come up with evasive answers, and to tell them the truth was unthinkable!

Once in her room, she allowed herself to be handled like a child—undressed, seated in a large tub of blissfully hot water, and scrubbed all over until her flesh was tingling, while Meera chattered constantly and shook her head over the state of Rebecca's clothes. Eventually, Meera wrapped her into a large soft towel, combed the snarls out of her wet hair, and rubbed her body with a sweet-scented oil, leaving her relaxed and drowsy. She was helped to the large inviting bed, covered with a soft bolster, and quietly left alone to rest.

Rebecca snuggled down deeper into the soft bed and endeavored to let her mind go blank. She wanted only to forget the past weeks and start a fresh new life, from this moment on, but her mind refused to forget the incredible events that she had been part of; the awakening of her body to a woman's excitement, the intense but conflicting emotions she had felt, even the mere fact of her survival was enough to keep her mind occupied with thought.

The image of a darkly tanned face, sardonic smile curling the wide sensual mouth, rose unbidden to her mind. She gave a sigh of exasperation and buried herself even deeper into the bed. In spite of her attempts to sleep, vivid scenes kept drifting through her head, especially the haunting picture of her last moments with Azim.

They had finally reached the outskirts of Mazar-i-Sharif, a most unprepossessing place it seemed to her. He had stopped their horses under one of the rare trees a short distance from a chaikana.

"Follow the main street until it veers to the right. You'll see a house with a rosebush by its gate," he began matter-of-factly. "The Mansfields' residence is easy to find." He paused and looked at her for a long moment. His eyes feasted on her features. He felt the chill of desolation descend upon him, catching him unaware. Rebecca saw a faint, undefinable smile on his sculpted lips.

"I almost wish the circumstances could have been different . . . Another time, another place . . . Perhaps . . ." He paused again. "Take care of yourself, my passion-flower." And with this enigmatic statement he had turned abruptly and left her. She watched his muscular form receding until he rounded a corner. She felt, strangely, a sudden sense of loss, an unexplainable ache in the pit of her stomach . . .

Meera's soft knock on the door woke Rebecca several hours later. She was surprised to realize that she had actually slept. Soon she was dressed in one of her own summer frocks that had been packed in her trunk so many long weeks before. She felt rested, clean, and almost carefree for the first time since leaving her father in Kabul. She would begin a brand new existence from this point on and try to forget the painful episodes of her past.

The Mansfields and William had been waiting for Rebecca to appear with a certain amount of nervousness. The three of them had decided not to break the news of Lawrence's death to her until they had finished their evening meal.

Finally she appeared, looking youthful and refreshed in her white dress and golden curls. All three knew that the meal ahead would be exceedingly difficult to endure. Catherine suddenly had to attend to duties in the kitchen, William averted his eyes and took a long swallow of brandy, and Thomas found he could not think of a single thing to say.

Rebecca wondered why her friends did not appear to be glad to see her. The atmosphere was awkward and strained. It abruptly occurred to her that they were embarrassed for her. They must have suspected or even heard stories of her capture and subsequent treatment. It was no wonder that Catherine had disappeared so quickly into the kitchen!

Thomas saw Rebecca's happy smile fade as she hesitated in the doorway and a wave of pity for her washed over him. "Come in, my dear, we were just waiting for Catherine to announce dinner. Are you feeling better after your nap?"

"Yes, Col. Mansfield, I am . . . But, still, it feels so strange to once again be with civilized people and clean clothes and polite words . . . You have no idea—" She broke off suddenly, afraid to continue. She might inadvertantly give Azim away—best not speak about it at all.

"Of course, Rebecca, we understand. There is no need to talk about your terrible experience if you prefer not to. There is no point in bringing it all back to mind. It is best to forget such things sometimes," he said kindly.

"Thank you so much. I hope to forget and start anew. I should consider myself fortunate, I suppose, for being returned at all. At least I didn't turn up in one of those slave markets I've heard so much about!" She attempted to laugh, but the sound emerged more like a hiccup.

Fortunately, Catherine returned from the kitchen just then to announce dinner, and the four sat down at the pleasantly arranged table. They were ill-at-ease; conversation was both difficult and forced. Catherine could not help but stare at Rebecca with such pity in her eyes that Rebecca thought she would scream. The two men attempted desultory conversation, but found it difficult to finish a subject once started, or to include the unfortunate girl in the conversation. Their minds kept reverting to the sad news they must impart to her after dinner.

Rebecca could see that they were extremely uncomfortable. What did they expect her to do, she thought, weep and wail and tear out her hair? She had more dignity than *that,* she hoped! After all, the whole awful mess had not been in any way her fault. She had only been an innocent pawn in a dangerous game, and now they silently implied that it was her failing in some roundabout way. How unfair! Nevertheless, she thought, I shall keep my pride and face the world squarely. I shall show them that no one can make me bow my head!

Rebecca raised her eyes from her plate and said brightly, "Has anyone sent word to my father that I am safe? Does he even know what happened? Oh dear, I expect he's been terribly worried about me."

The sudden silence that descended was palpable, having a cold and sinister form of its own. Thomas and William shot quick glances at each other over Catherine's bowed head.

Rebecca's face went white. How could she face her father after what had happened? The awful truth of her predicament hit her like a blow. She felt weak and sick to her stomach.

The meal continued interminably. Catherine talked little and ate less. Rebecca played with her food and could swallow nothing. At one point, William's fork accidently touched his crystal wine glass. The sharp ring falling on utter quiet pierced Rebecca's ear like a knife thrust. She thought she would faint.

Finally, William glanced at Thomas meaningfully. Thomas nodded.

"Rebecca," said William, "it seems that none of us has an appetite. Will you come out to the patio with me? I have something to discuss with you." He rose and helped her with the chair. Holding her elbow, he led her to the garden. The darkness was comforting and she was thankful to him for rescuing her from a difficult situation. Together they seated themselves on a bench near the terrace while William held one of her hands. He was quiet for awhile.

"What did you want to say, William?"

"My dear girl . . . I'm so sorry to have to be the one to tell you . . . We thought we should wait till now, you understand . . . Give you a chance to recover a bit, you know . . ." By God, this was even more difficult than he had thought it would be! "Rebecca, your father met with an accident a few weeks ago—"

"Father! An accident! What are you trying to tell me? What is it?" Her voice was frightened, demanding.

"Rebecca, your father . . . I'm afraid . . . died." There, it was out. It sounded so flat, so impersonal. "He was . . . ah . . . slain . . . by an unknown assailant, a robber. I'm so dreadfully sorry. You know I'd do anything in the world for you. I hate to be the bearer of bad tidings . . ." His voice trailed off. Outwardly, she appeared to have no reaction whatever. She sat still and white in the darkness. The shadows lent to her face a gaunt and sorrowful cast. William pressed her cold icy hand which he still held. "Rebecca? Are you quite all right? Can I get you something?" Why didn't she cry or scream? Anything was better than this uncanny silence.

"Rebecca!" He shook her shoulder lightly.

She turned, startled, and looked through him. Her eyes suddenly filled with tears. They spilled over onto her cheeks, making glistening pathways where the light caught them. She stood up and cried, "Father," weakly, then crumpled and slid down onto the ground in a deep faint.

Rebecca came slowly out of her world of blackness and silence. It was painful to ascend from the safety of unconsciousness, but a force stronger than herself drew her toward the light. She heard voices; Catherine's, William's, Meera's, praying in Hindi. As the voices became clearer, she suddenly remembered why she had wished to remain unknowing. Her father was dead. It was a realization holding such anguish for Rebecca that her mind fled from the concept. She was alone in the world—her grandfather dead and now her father, too. Who could she turn to? Who would care for her? Where should she go? There was not even anyone left in England.

She reluctantly opened her eyes to see Catherine hovering over her and Meera wiping her forehead with a cool damp cloth.

"Oh, thank goodness!" said Catherine with obvious relief. "She's come around at last! Rebecca, how are you? We were so worried . . . Poor William felt it was all his fault . . . Oh, dear, I am rattling on—"

"It's all right, Catherine. I shall be fine in a moment. It was just such a shock. My poor father . . ." Her eyes filled with tears again. "You must tell me exactly what happened. After all, I should know."

"Later, dearest," broke in William. "Right now you should rest and try to recover from this tragic news. You frightened us terribly, Rebecca, and I want you to take care of yourself. You must not worry about a thing. I will see to everything that needs be done. You are to stay here and recover."

"I will do precisely as I wish!" snapped Rebecca, feeling smothered by William's condescending manner. "Oh, very well, William, I suppose you are right. I would like some quiet for awhile—everything seems so confusing . . . I must think of what to do . . ." She seemed on the verge of tears again and raised trembling hands to her forehead.

"Please, at least tell me about his funeral—where he was buried."

"He was interred with all due ceremony in the British cemetery about three weeks ago, and even became the hero of the day. He had just succeeded in getting the Emir to sign an important trade agreement and the paper was found in his saddlebag. He was thanked officially by Governor Mountstuart. It is terribly unfortunate that he was not alive to hear it. The entire British community was at the service. You know he was a well-loved man. I miss him myself, even knowing him such a short time." William lost himself in his own fabrications.

"Thank you for telling me, William. I shall be quite well now, really . . . I think I'd like to sleep." Her eyes were dark pools in her white face.

William felt his heart contract with pity for her. He had momentarily forgotten that he was the cause of her grief. He was very pleased with the way she had turned to him for comfort and assurance. He would soon have her in the palm of his hand.

"You must try to rest, Rebecca," said Catherine. "Meera will be in the next room if you have need of anything. Gentlemen, let us go now. She needs her sleep."

Rebecca was grateful to be alone. She drifted into restless slumber, dreaming of her father whirling through the sky pursued by a tall dark figure on a black stallion, while she ran, trying desperately to reach them both as her feet grew heavier and slower, finally losing them both in the darkness.

CHAPTER 17

Rebecca had become completely listless by the time William delivered her to the front door of her father's house in Kabul in mid-July. She had made the trip back in a state of detachment, going through the motions of eating, riding, even conversing with William and Meera. Later she recollected the journey as being a blur washed over with misery and loneliness. The Mansfields had wanted her to stay with them, but she felt an urge to return to her father's home and face her existence there. She had no thought as to what the future would hold nor any special wish to return to England for the time being.

Meera had tried futilely to cajole Rebecca into eating more, but her appetite had disappeared. Her face and figure became more angular and there were dark circles under her eyes. Rather than diminish her beauty, her suffering caused her to emanate a more mature and unearthly grace. Her large dark-fringed eyes became pools of fascination to all who looked into their depths.

William had been very kind and attentive to Rebecca since they had left Mazar-i-Sharif and she was grateful to him, but could find nothing in her heart to offer him. She was empty and dead inside. Vague stirrings sometimes nudged her consciousness, telling her this was better than to feel the full extent of her wretchedness.

Rebecca tried to re-establish her normal life in the

capital, but her days seemed endless and useless. Since she was in mourning for her father, she could not attend social affairs, although she did see a great deal of William. The English ladies were kind and visited her often at first, but found her singularly cold and uncommunicative, so that she soon found herself in solitude much of the time. Meera tried to cheer Rebecca in every way that her happy nature could devise, but Rebecca was merely polite in spite of the well-meant efforts.

Meera noticed that Rebecca had been sleeping erratically and was barely touching her breakfasts. She lay abed half the morning and only began to move around the house after lunch. Often, her evenings were claimed by William.

St. Claire found himself unable to take his eyes off Rebecca these days. He felt that her air of slight dissipation was extraordinarily attractive. Although she was pale and thinner than ever, her breasts were still large and voluptuous. She seemed docile, fond of his company and dependent on him to a great extent. He felt that he had accomplished his goal—Rebecca was pliant and weak, ready to accept any proposal he might make to her. He decided that he had given her enough time. He would ask for her promise of marriage at their very next meeting.

One warm July afternoon, Rebecca was in the dining room, arranging the table very carefully. It gave her something to do and occupied her mind for a time. William liked a nicely set table; he had mentioned it casually on several occasions when he had taken meals with her. She found herself, of late, thinking more and more often of what William liked, or what William disliked—always trying to repay his kindness.

She had just returned from the kitchen and another hour-long argument with Nur Mustafa. The man was really incurably stubborn and probably should be dismissed. He still refused to cook anything edible unless she stood over him all the while. And lately,

Rebecca's stomach did not take kindly to his greasy pilaus. Yet, she looked forward in a way to her daily contests with Nur Mustafa. They were the high point of her day and took her mind off her grief.

She had just convinced the cook to roast a chicken and some potatoes instead of his perpetual rice because she knew William found it more palatable. She put a finishing touch on her flower arrangement and stood back to admire her handiwork, head cocked to one side. It would do.

Rebecca slowly went upstairs to change her dress for William. Surveying her closet full of black, she sighed. No more bright summer cottons this year, she thought, and her eyes filled with tears at the memory of her father. Angrily, she wiped the drops away. She cried much too easily these days.

Putting on one of her new black gowns, Rebecca surveyed herself in the mirror. The unrelieved black made her look tall and thin and accentuated the pale luminosity of her skin and the gold highlights in her hair.

She heard a male voice downstairs, which she knew to be William's, talking to Meera. She stopped brushing her hair for a moment and stared, unfocusing, into the mirror. It was strange how Meera had taken a dislike to William. She did not say very much, but Rebecca could tell that Meera had no great liking or respect for him. Oh well, she thought, Meera does not have to sit across the table from him and make polite conversation, *I* do! She looked forward to William's visits. Lately, they were her only link with the outside world. He brought tidbits from the governor's mansion: who had recently come from England; who had had a baby; how negotiations were going with the Emir; where a new skirmish had taken place with the Afghan rebels.

Rebecca finished brushing her hair and gathered it together at the nape of her neck in a black snood. She looked very respectable and almost severe, a far cry from the exuberant young girl who had first come into this house, seeking adventure in an exotic land.

She descended the stairs to find William seated comfortably in her father's favorite red leather chair with a snifter of her father's brandy. He had made himself quite at home in the familiar surroundings, as was his wont lately. He rose with a smile of pleasure, took both of her hands in his and kissed her gently on one cheek.

"You look beautiful tonight, my dear, but you are still a little wan. You really should try to get out more, ride Alia perhaps, or walk in the public gardens. Meera will accompany you."

"I suppose you are right, William," she sighed, "but I have no heart for it yet. Perhaps in a few weeks."

"You really must, Rebecca. We cannot have you pining away. You have to keep your strength up, especially in this dreadful climate."

"Yes, William." It was easier to agree than to argue these days, she thought. "Shall we go into dinner? Nur Mustafa has outdone himself tonight, or at least I hope he has." She said, smiling.

They ate leisurely, William praising the various dishes and wines and relating the newest gossip from the diplomatic circle. Rebecca did not say much, but listened, and surprisingly felt quite hungry this evening. She ate with pleasure and drank several glasses of wine which William made certain to keep full. She felt sleepy and relaxed after the meal despite the fact that her stays pressed uncomfortably into her tender skin.

Rising, William suggested they go out into the garden, as it was cooler now that darkness had fallen. He poured himself another brandy before they strolled out to sit under the one tree the garden offered.

Rebecca leaned back in the chair, her eyes closed, the warm evening air caressing her. She could hear, faintly, the *muezzins* of the city calling the faithful to their evening prayers. It was, oddly enough, a comforting sound.

"Rebecca, I have something to ask you," began William. "You must know that I have loved you ever since we first met and, of course, I have wanted you for my wife. I know you are still in mourning, but given the circumstances—a young girl alone in a strange country—I think we should marry very soon. Indeed, I think we shall. You cannot stay here unprotected much longer."

She was silent, staring straight ahead. Finally, she said, "William, I know you are right, but I am still too full of grief to be a wife to anyone. I have known you loved me . . ." She looked down at her hands. "I am not certain I can return a full measure of love. I feel so very empty inside."

"I understand, my dear. You are sad—a natural reaction. But I will help you to get over your sorrow. I want to put the laughter back in your eyes and the bloom in your cheeks. You are too young to go on like this. Time will dull your sense of loss, and then you shall have me to love and cherish you. You will learn to love me in the same way."

"Do you really think so, William? I would hate to burden you with the sad person I have become."

"Rebecca, my dear child, you would never be a burden to me. You are my true love, my one and only cherished darling."

She looked up at William. His eyes were on her, warm and adoring. He would make a good husband, she thought. He would be kind and considerate, charming and thoughtful. They could return to England and have a full social life. He would fit into society anywhere. She was going to inherit enough money to keep them both comfortably, as she knew his family had lost its fortune. Why should she continue on, alone and terrified of the future, when all she had to do was say, "yes," and her future and place in society would be assured. She was even beginning to detest this country with a fervor to equal his own. Why struggle on by herself when she would be cared for, pampered,

relieved of all her worries? And to forget that rogue
. . . How simple it would be to marry.

William watched her, in an agony of suspense. Had
he asked too soon? What thoughts were going through
that proud and exquisite head of hers? He could hardly
believe his ears when he heard her voice, soft and
trembling.

"Yes, William, I shall marry you."

The wedding had been set for the end of July.
Rebecca was busy with preparations for it was to take
place in her father's house. It would be very small and
quiet, as she had no heart for a large festive affair. In a
way, she was content to have made her decision. All
her insecurities and fears were put to rest. William
would see to her future.

Only one thing marred her contentment during the
wedding preparations. Her health did not seem to be
returning to normal. She was often tired; her stomach
was queasy and bilious in the morning. Indeed, lately,
she had even been sick in the chamber pot several
times. Yet, by afternoon, she was so hungry that she
could hardly wait for tea. It must be a reaction from all
the terrible events that have happened here, she
thought, and tried to dismiss it from her mind.

Meera, however, could not help but notice Rebecca's
symptoms. She was also aware that the periodic
evidence of a female nature had not occurred last
month. Of course, it could be attributed to her grief
and shock, but Meera had a much better idea of what
had happened to her Missy. She would have to ask her
if it were true. It could not be hidden from Meera any
longer.

The next morning, Rebecca awakened to her usual
morning nausea. She lay in bed for awhile and tried to
will away the feeling in her stomach. She got up, put on
her robe and sat in front of her vanity mirror. Her
reflection was quite green. Meera's gentle knock came
at the door and Rebecca bid her to come in.

"Missy Sahib, look what I am bringing you this fine morning!" said Meera, carrying in a tray of steaming food. "I have been yelling at that lowly jackal of a cook to be making kidneys for my mistress! I know English are loving kidneys for breakfast!"

The sight of the innards was enough to send Rebecca dashing for the chamber pot again, as her heaving stomach could stand no more. Meera put down the tray with a tinkle of china and ran to her. When Rebecca was through, she sat down in a chair, pale and spent.

Meera thought the time had come to broach the subject of her mistress's illness. "Missy Sahib, are you wanting to tell Meera why you are being so sick lately?"

"Oh, I don't know, Meera," answered Rebecca, annoyed. "I suppose it's the excitement and the dreadful things that have happened. Why do you ask? It's not important. It will go away. I've always been healthy." She had not yet caught the meaning of Meera's words.

"Missy Sahib, perhaps this sickness is being more important than you are thinking," said Meera, growing very solemn. "Is it being . . . uh . . . possible . . . that Missy is having baby?" And she patted her own flat stomach.

"A baby!" burst out Rebecca. "Oh, no! Oh, dear God, it surely isn't a baby! You don't think—" She suddenly sat up straight, thinking deeply, with a frown creasing her brow. Then she fell back into her chair with a gasp. She looked up at Meera, tears welling in her eyes.

"Whatever shall I tell William? What can I do? Oh, this is so unfair!" And she began to sob hysterically on Meera's shoulder.

"Now, now, Missy. Having baby wonderful thing! Mother should be happy."

"Happy!" shrieked Rebecca pulling away. "How can I be *happy*?"

"You are being sure this not Sahib William's baby?"

"Of course not!" snapped Rebecca, "I wouldn't

. . . didn't . . . let him touch me! And don't ask me whose it is, because I won't tell you, ever! It wasn't my fault . . . I was forced . . . I couldn't stop him. Oh, Meera, what am I to do? I can't marry William. I can't marry anybody! I'll be disgraced, and the child will be a . . . a . . . a bastard!"

"Can you be telling father of baby to be marrying you?" asked Meera.

"*Him!*" spat Rebecca. "I wouldn't marry him if he were the last man on earth! After what he did to me?" Visions of him, standing over her, spitting vileness rose to mind. "He will never find out about the child, never!"

"You will have to be talking to Sahib William, Missy. Maybe he is being nice man and marrying you anyway."

"You're right, Meera. I shall have to tell him, but I certainly can't expect him to marry me. Oh, poor William . . . Meera, get me my writing paper. I shall write him immediately and invite him for lunch today . . . What can I say to him?" she wailed.

William knocked at Rebecca's door promptly at one. He wondered what was so important that she had to tell him immediately. She opened the door herself and stood looking at him. William could see she had been crying; her eyes were red-rimmed and swollen. She had a delicate lace handkerchief in her hand that she kept nervously twisting. William felt a sudden foreboding. What had happened now? By God, were his plans to be ruined again?

"Rebecca, what is the matter? I can see something has upset you." He took her arm and lead her into the sitting room.

"William," she faltered, "I must tell you something . . . It is difficult to say this . . ." She gave a sob and wiped her eyes with her handkerchief.

William went to the sideboard and poured himself a

brandy. It certainly looked as if he would need it. "What is it, my dear? You know you can tell me anything."

Rebecca took a deep breath and looked straight at him. "I am with child." Her eyes searched his face, looking for shock, hate or, even worse, disgust.

William felt the blood leave his head. He could think of nothing at all to say. He took a deep swallow of his brandy. Feverish thoughts rushed through his mind. Sudden white-hot anger flared in his breast—for her, who had deceived him, and for the man, whoever he was, who had tasted her white body before he himself could. But to give her up would deny him his long sought goal. He *must* have her regardless of her condition. But, by God, he would make the bitch pay!

Her eyes were still on his face, silently imploring him to say something, anything.

"I must admit, this is quite a shock to me . . . I had thought . . . ," he attempted.

"You thought I was untouched!" She spat bitterly. "Is that what you were going to say? I *was,* I swear it, until I was kidnapped by that . . . that . . . savage and . . . raped . . ." Uncontrollably she burst into tears again.

William forced himself to bend over her, raise her tearstained face with his hand and kiss her on the forehead.

"My dear child, do not distress yourself so. As I said, this is a shock to me, as I'm sure it is to you." He gave a short laugh. "But I asked you to be mine and I still want you. Never mind this new . . . uh . . . development . . . We will marry, and I will raise the child as my own. No one will be the wiser." He suppressed the growing urge to strike her, to lash out at someone. "After your child is born, Rebecca, we shall return to England where I can be certain of your safety . . . Come, now," he reached toward her, "all will be well."

"You can't mean that, William," cried Rebecca through her tears. "You couldn't want me after what has happened!"

"Yes, I still want you, no matter what has happened. After all, it wasn't your fault . . . you . . . an innocent young girl . . ." A scene of Rebecca, white legs wound around a man's torso, moaning with pleasure, leaped into his mind. He clenched his jaw. Damn the cheating wench!

"The wedding will take place as planned. This will be our little secret. Never fear, I will love and cherish you as my own."

"Do you really mean it? Do you still want to marry me?" she asked, her large eyes begging him, her lashes glistening with tears.

"Yes, Rebecca," he said impatiently. "Now I must return to the governor. Take care of yourself, my child, you have a new reason to watch your health now." He forced a smile, kissed her cheek, and left her sitting there, still twisting her handkerchief.

Outside the door, he let out a long breath, whistling through his teeth. He laughed a short harsh bark. He had held in check his own passion for her all these months, trying to win her trust, only to have some other man take her virginity by force! The joke was on him, perhaps, but he would see to it that she paid. Yes, he would unquestionably have his pleasures, too!

CHAPTER 18

The morning of Rebecca's wedding had at last arrived, the summer day already stifling, even for Kabul. Rebecca was glad that Polly and her few friends had helped to arrange the affair, but she wondered idly if she would feel some measure of happiness as the day wore on. The wedding was set for five in the afternoon, with a light supper planned for afterward. Rebecca was not even certain how many people would be present; few had been invited under the circumstances of her mourning.

William had been an absolute dear for the past week. His attitude about her pregnancy was still a mystery to her. She was, to be certain, exceedingly grateful for his love. If only she could return some small measure of it! This morning, of all days, she knew that she could not sit in bed and muse. In any case, Meera would not allow her to do so. Already she was fussing about the room trying to take Rebecca's mind off of her sorrows.

Meera smiled and indicated the pastel blue dress that hung in readiness. "Missy, you must be getting ready for great day. Up now! Must not be sad or baby will be coming out with sorry faces on!" Meera had not meant to say anything about the baby; the words were forever slipping out unbidden. It was just that she was certain that Rebecca would love the child dearly when it came. Having lost her father, Rebecca would need the tiny infant to comfort her. Meera was forever optimistic, forever cheerful.

Rebecca finally stretched her arms and slipped out of the soft bed. "Do you think that I shall be comfortable in father's rooms? I don't know . . . Meera, will you put as many of my things as possible there. I don't think I can stand many more changes in my life."

"Missy will be thinking she is in own rooms!" Meera immediately began to gather up Rebecca's odds and ends and scurried out to place them in Lawrence's old room.

Rebecca donned her black day dress and hoped that William would not want to lunch with her today. She did not feel up to receiving company this morning, needing to gather her strength for the wedding that evening. She mechanically went about her toilette, then descended the steps to the entrance hall where she found William already waiting.

Rebecca frowned. "I did not realize that you were here. Why, it's bad luck for us to see one another today!" She felt the beginnings of a throbbing headache.

"Dearest Rebecca, I only wanted to make sure you are feeling well for the occasion. I think that we shall retire early this evening. The guests will understand the strain you have been under." He continued, a too wide smile on his lips, "At any rate, I've brought my belongings and had hoped to place them upstairs."

Rebecca groaned inwardly. "Of course, William, I was simply not thinking. Feel free to have one of my . . . our servants carry them for you." Rebecca realized that her conversation was stilted, but she could not feign interest.

William bowed with a flourish and went about firmly planting himself in her home. He was so near to victory that he could taste the sweet nectar that soon would be his. Shortly, he could quit Mountstuart and head home to England where the jeweled box awaited him. He could then destroy the certificate proclaiming him to be half-caste, and he would also reap the benefits of Rebecca's abundant fortune.

Just the thought of her yielding body beneath his own brought a cruel twist to his mouth. The fact that she was soiled goods only made him desire her more, for he had been recently practicing his skills on the local bazaar harlots and found that his expertise was increasing. He could now cause his victims a great deal of discomfort while enjoying the acts immensely himself. But whenever William was with his women, he could envision only Rebecca's face. Perhaps he could make her bend to his whims, too.

Rebecca did not choose white for her wedding dress. This decision was not made solely because she was in mourning, but partly because of the shame she had felt that early dawn in the northern village; the experience still fresh in her mind. She knew the joys of womanhood now. She also knew the degrading things a man's body could do to her. No, she would not wear white today.

Her gown was simple, a skirt of soft silken folds and a close fitting bodice with a modest neckline. The long-sleeved dress was comfortable to wear on this hot summer evening, the front trimmed delicately with off-white Venetian lace. Rebecca had brought the gown from England and it would serve her well tonight. Her hair was piled in a chignon style, loosely pinned to the neck. The veil was a simple embroidered *Schiffli*, the same lace as her dress. She looked lovely, but ghostly and Meera had to apply a rouge to her cheeks.

The guests had arrived and William waited impatiently for her to appear at the top of the stairs. David Mountstuart was to give the bride away while his wife, Eleanor, anticipated shedding tears of happiness when the ceremony was completed. Polly Swanson had returned to the drawing room after having helped Rebecca with her wedding finery. She was concerned over the girl's pale features, but discreetly said nothing.

When William and Rebecca finally stood before the army chaplain, she felt empty and faintly annoyed at all the fuss. What did they want her to do, blush like a virgin, look knowingly and lovingly into William's eyes? She felt none of these emotions. She would not pretend to. Let them think what they would!

The chaplain droned on. "And do you, Rebecca, take William St. Claire to be your . . ."

Rebecca mustered the strength to reply, "I do." The deed was done. Her fate was sealed forever—bonded to this stranger who stood proudly next to her. Rebecca realized that she really knew little of St. Claire. He had befriended her on board ship, even declared his love and ambition to make her his. But what did she really know of his family and background? Rebecca knew that Lawrence Merideth had disliked the man intensely. However, she saw him as a kind protector who was always available in her hour of need. He would make a fine husband, not exciting, but she had had enough adventures to last her a lifetime. William would also help to raise her child, saving them both embarrassment and ostracism.

Bringing her thoughts back to the wedding, she heard William speak. "Rebecca, won't you kiss me now?" He lifted her veil and gave her a rather wet kiss on her cool lips. Voices of their friends drifted to her ears and she turned from William's caress. She allowed the men to embrace her with hopes for a prosperous future, the ladies to wish her well with tear-streaked faces. Outwardly, Rebecca smiled.

Supper went well, considering the poor cooking of Nur Mustafa. Meera and Rebecca had insisted that he allow them to select the menu. Nur Mustafa was not happy about the interference, but because the mistress was to be wed, he bowed and let the stupid ferangi females have their way. Meera had watched over the preparations and was scurrying around the kitchen busily when she saw a figure standing in the door leading to the back entrance. She looked closer. By the sacred waters of the Ganges, it was Mahmud!

She was shocked into total silence. Her feet felt as if they were made of rock and would not move toward him, even when he beckoned her. So far, Nur Mustafa had not noticed Mahmud's presence. Meera recovered herself and quietly slipped outside and away from the house. Her heart pounded frantically in her chest and she prayed that Missy Sahib would not notice her disappearance.

She spoke first, trying to convey her feelings in a few common words and gestures. "You have come seeing Meera. Meera very happy."

Mahmud smiled broadly. "Happy see Meera. Azim want know Rebecca fine?"

Meera's face blanched underneath her veil, Azim! She began to put two and two together. The kidnapping was done by the same man who had caused her Missy to become so angered that she had heaved a hair brush at her the day after the ball. It was that romantic Englishman-turned-tribesman who had stolen her mistress! No wonder Missy was so heartbroken lately. So he was the father of her child! She now knew that Mahmud was a friend of Azim. Meera was stunned by her discovery. She seriously doubted if Azim knew he was to be a father.

Meera suddenly became distraught, remembering that her mistress had just been married. Her kind, romantic heart went out to the lovers who were forever separated by a legal ceremony. She began to weep. Mahmud did not know how to comfort this pretty creature.

"Meera no cry . . . Mahmud help." He brought her tiny body into his protective embrace and let her sob.

She finally managed, "Missy marry William today." She indicated a ring around the marriage finger. Mahmud understood immediately and he shuddered to think of Azim's reaction to this news.

"Azim, he not happy Rebecca go. He not talking, he not liking . . . ," said Mahmud referring to the symbolic action of Meera's hands.

The pair clung to one another until the Indian girl broke away and tried to go into the house. Mahmud stopped her and begged. "Meera see Mahmud. Mahmud coming dark time."

Not knowing why, she braved, "Yes, Meera be waiting." All he really understood was the "yes," but that was enough for the moment. Mahmud disappeared around the corner, wondering if he should tell Azim. He thought not.

Meera stole back into the kitchen to find Nur Mustafa mumbling angrily at her disappearance; he shot her a murderous glance. She was terribly upset, not knowing whether to tell her Missy of the visit or not. She had no doubt that her mistress was in love with Azim, but she also realized that Rebecca was not aware of the emotion. Meera knew that for many people, love was closely related to hate, so close, in fact, that the two were often interchangeable.

Rebecca was going through the motions of entertaining her guests. As the hour grew late, Rebecca was growing fearful and anxious to have the wedding night behind her. She had wondered about William's reaction to her soiled condition, but he had vaguely mentioned it some days before the wedding, saying softly, "I love only you, dear, have no fear of my reaction on our wedding night, as I think only of your happiness." These words now brought reassurance to Rebecca as she and William escorted their guests to the door and thanked them for attending the ceremony.

Meera, standing behind her, wanted to tell Rebecca about Mahmud's visit. "Missy, Meera bringing you chocolate to bed tonight? Missy not eating dinner and need food."

"Meera, William and I shall retire tonight without your assistance. Now go to bed, and thank you for all your help." She dismissed Meera and began to ascend the stairs.

William discreetly remained in the drawing room. He badly needed a drink to celebrate, for this was the moment he had awaited so many months, and he was determined to savor the victory. He drank a touch more than he had planned to and was unsteady by the time he entered their suite. Rebecca noticed his stupor, but said nothing as his gaze fell to her soft breasts, creamy and silken in the glow of the lamp as she sat at her dressing table. Her nightgown was of the palest shade of yellow with an open bodice and flowing sleeves, the sheer material leaving little to the imagination. William felt himself stiffen at the sight of the exquisite display and quickly went into the adjoining room to change into his burgundy robe. When he emerged, his dark eyes were glazed with emotion. Rebecca began to dread the encounter, but she tried, nevertheless, to calm her nerves and went about combing out her long golden curls.

William slipped up behind her and caught her stare in the mirror. She could see open lust in his slightly protruding eyes. She spoke politely, "William, I think perhaps you have had too much liquor. Would you care to retire tonight? We shall both feel better in the morning." Rebecca knew that her ploy had failed, for William had boldly reached over her shoulders and was kneading her bosom. She stiffened and drew away instinctively.

Who the devil did she think to fool? He would have no part of her cat-and-mouse game. Certainly she was not going to play the sainted virgin with him!

"Come now," he slurred. "You must not pretend to be the shy one, Rebecca. We both know better." He spun her around, grabbed at her gown, catching the neckline and tearing the front to her waist. It fell to the floor in a heap. Rebecca was shocked, seeing a new side of his nature for the first time. What had she married—an animal? She realized that she had almost spoken aloud, but at the moment she was too horrified to care.

William was not so drunk that her expression escaped him. It angered him and he went on fondling her breasts roughly. She slapped his hand, furious. She would not submit to rape again, especially by her own husband!

He lifted her struggling body, carried her unceremoniously to the bed and deposited her there.

"Shut your mouth. You seem to forget that I am now your husband, Mrs. St. Claire, and I'll have my rights or by God you shall suffer! Shall I tell all Kabul how you were pregnant already when I first took you to bed?"

Tears of hysteria rolled down her cheeks. She had married a monster, far more unfeeling than the last man who had touched her! Horrified, Rebecca watched him disrobe. Then he was on her, his manhood pressing into her cringing flesh. She twisted frantically from him so that he struck her, leaving an ugly red welt on her tender hip. William then rolled her back over and spread her thighs with his knees.

"Hold still, trollop! I shall have you."

William hit her in the face then, drawing blood from her bottom lip. Rebecca prayed aloud, but she did ease her squirming and let him have his way. If he beat her further the baby would surely come to harm. All she could do now was to endure his drunken love-making and pray that he would remain sober in the future.

William was elated when Rebecca finally ceased her struggles. He entered her, causing some little pain and began his irregular pounding into her flesh. Rebecca felt sickened and fought back her tears. He disgusted her so completely that she suddenly knew that her body would respond to Azim's caresses, but never to her own husband's. At last he moaned loudly, bit into her nipple and quickly withdrew his deflated member.

Sleep did not come to Rebecca that night. Nor did she rest on subsequent nights, for William was always waiting for her. He was almost kind when the sun shone, but at night he would force her to succumb to his whims. The days drifted by, unending. Polly Swanson even commented on her haggard appearance. Meera was distraught, and finally conveyed her concern to Mahmud on one of his nightly visits. She did not mention the pregnancy for her devotion to Missy was total, but her concern for Rebecca's happiness was primary.

Azim awoke one morning, a couple of weeks into August, to find Mahmud gone, his blanket still folded. They had made camp outside the city, for Mahmud disliked the hustle and turmoil within the limits of Kabul. Where the devil is he now? thought Azim. He's been slipping away at night and has a sly grin on his face in the morning. In fact, we should have purchased the arms already and been long gone from here. Mahmud was purposely delaying the departure. Azim would confront him when he returned this time.

The weeks had passed by slowly since he had returned Rebecca to Mazar-i- Sharif. Azim had been unable to shake his brooding and Mahmud finally suggested that they travel again to Kabul, purchase arms and supplies for the winter, then return home late in September. Mahmud thought that the journey would occupy Azim's mind, taking it off Rebecca. Azim had not mentioned her to Mahmud, but all the signs were present. He had gone about his daily chores with less and less enthusiasm, had begun to snap at everyone, and lived a celibate life in the village. It was then that Mahmud announced his own desire to travel to Kabul before the possibility of early autumn snows.

Azim was attending to the grooming of their mounts when Mahmud marched decisively into camp. His face was a mask, and Azim took notice of his comrade's unusual manner.

Azim began in Pashto, "Your bedding was unused last night. Have you perhaps found a lovely woman to warm your bones?"

Mahmud dreaded this moment, but he felt words were necessary. "I have much to tell you, old friend. Please let me speak without interruption. Last week I went to find Meera, she is the Indian lady who attends Rebecca, the one I told you about when I delivered the message to Mazar-i-Sharif. I found that they had returned, unharmed, to Kabul."

Azim did interrupt, a dark scowl covering his true emotions. "Mahmud, I have no interest in whom you see. That is your business. If you want to stay here, do so, but I am returning to the village as soon as I can."

Mahmud spoke harshly to his younger friend. "You will hear me out! Let me tell you, Azim, for your own sake. Do not try my patience, but face my words like a man, not as a boy who will not listen to logic." Having won his point, he continued. "Rebecca has married a man named St. Claire whom Meera tells me treats his new wife cruelly. Meera tells me also that her mistress is almost out of her mind with sorrow. She does not talk to anyone and has bruises on her arms and back."

Azim was visibly shocked. His tanned face turned white and his features twisted. He told himself that he didn't give a damn if she had married Allah, himself, but the thought of a man abusing her was unbearable to him.

"Meera told me that Rebecca's father was stabbed to death here in Kabul when she was with us at the village. Since the father's death, Rebecca has been a stranger and this William has taken advantage of her grief. What are we to do? I will not stand by and let this man hurt the girl even if you will! Meera has asked me to help. They have no one here in Kabul to turn to."

Azim, thinking he saw a plot, sneered, "Come now, Mahmud. Do you expect me to believe that Rebecca was forced into a marriage, then beaten, and stood back letting it all happen? No, even in her grief, Rebecca is a strong woman, and she would undoubtedly seek the help of Governor Mountstuart."

Mahmud went on, correcting Azim. "No, my friend. I also thought that. This St. Claire fellow, he has threatened to expose Rebecca's condition when he married her." He left then to give Azim time to gather his wits.

Azim sat alone for a long time. He had seldom known such misery; his heart ached from the pain Mahmud's words had brought him. No one knew better than he that Rebecca's pride would never allow her to breathe a word of her shame to Mountstuart. Clearly and truthfully, he let himself see the justice of her actions. First he had kidnapped her, raped her, and ultimately made Rebecca bargain her body for the freedom that was rightfully hers. He let himself see the degrading position he had placed her in when he last took her body.

Azim almost felt relief when he realized that most of her actions were caused by his own arrogance. He must go to the governor, as Alex Drayton, and find out how much truth there was in Meera's words. But Rebecca was married! What possible right did he have to again interfere in her life? Hadn't he only moments ago, reprimanded himself for doing that exact thing? Azim was torn between his two worlds. One side of his alter ego said, "If there is truth in Mahmud's words, kill this William and have her for yourself." His other side told him, "Hold back, see Mountstuart, don't interfere where you may not be wanted."

Mahmud interrupted his anxious thoughts. "I see Meera again tonight. I'll find out much about this William."

The two men went on with the day's business, but Azim was seething inwardly and had decided to see Mountstuart himself. He knew he could say little or Rebecca's reputation would suffer, so he planned to talk with the governor about his brother's activities in England. It would do no harm to confront Mountstuart on a more civilized level. Most of the day Azim spent picturing Rebecca responding to her husband's embraces. The thoughts threatened to drive him insane: He tried to dash away the notions and went to the governor's mansion. He dressed for the role in newly purchased English attire of the latest fashion. It had been nearly fifteen years since he had worn his countrymen's clothing: The feeling was both assuring and threatening to him.

He was ushered into Mountstuart's office by an open-mouthed servant, one who had never before seen him in anything but native attire. Azim took the governor's outstretched hand and shook it warmly, for he genuinely liked the man.

"David, how are you?"

"Alex, my boy, what brings you to Kabul—a bit late in the season for you, isn't it?"

"Yes, I've been escorting some rather valuable . . . ah . . . mares to the market," he lied expertly. "Any news from my brother?"

"No, not this time—those blasted ships take so long. But, Alex, I'm glad you've stopped by. You may well be able to give me some advice."

"Advice?" laughed Alex. "And what sort of advice might I give *you?* Isn't it your role to give *me* advice?"

"Yes, usually," said Mountstuart wryly, "but this time it is about the tribes. The foreign secretary in London wants a report on the natives—whether they will accept our rule without too much bloodshed, or whether we require more troops here. That sort of thing. I thought you could tell me the feeling in the villages."

Alex's brows drew together. "I can only say the same thing I've known all along—I mean no offence to you, sir, but there are many shortsighted cronies in the colonial service—leave the tribes alone. Do not try to rule the steppes, for they will defeat you in the end and you'll have nothing but loss of life to show for it."

"Hmm, I feared you would say something of that sort, Alex. You know, tension has been building up lately. Another caravan was ambushed back in June and the guns they carried were stolen." Mountstuart stopped abruptly, eying the younger man speculatively, tapping his fingers on the desk top. "By the way . . . you wouldn't happen to know anything about that?"

Alex looked him straight in the eye and growled, "No, of course not."

"No, you wouldn't," said Mountstuart shrewdly.

Alex noticed William St. Claire enter Mountstuart's office, leave a stack of papers on his desk and start to leave.

"So, mother England is worried about us," said Alex. "Good. It's what we hoped for. And what is going on at home these days? The usual scandal and corruption in the hallowed Houses?" Alex looked around: St. Claire was ostensibly tidying a stack of books in the corner of the office. "Would you mind leaving us, sir? The governor and I have private matters to discuss," he said to William, who hastily withdrew.

"David, I wanted to ask you something, actually. About Lawrence Merideth's death. Can you tell me how he died?" He added hastily, "I am only interested because he was a fair man, one of the few who treated the natives with respect."

"Yes, he was a well-loved chap. Tragic, tragic the way he died. And his daughter had just arrived from England after years of separation . . . Well, his body was discovered by some ruins—knifed in the back, horse still there, money stolen. Obviously, it was a robber, and no signs of struggle, so it must have come as a surprise to the ill-fated man. But, you know we'll never find the guilty party, for these natives are closemouthed and would never give away one of their own."

"How strange," mused Alex aloud. "Unusual, I mean, for one man to be attacked like that, and a European, especially one as well known and liked as Merideth. I may ask around. Perhaps I'll come up with some answers . . . And how, how is the daughter taking it?"

"As well as can be expected, as the old saying goes. Poor child . . . the fire's gone out of her. She was a saucy lass when she arrived—as you well know, having vied for her attentions at my ball—but now she's pale and gloomy. Eleanor worries dreadfully over her for the girl sees no one but St. Claire and he seems reticent to speak of her welfare. It seems a pity, Alex. Why, we don't even see her riding out on that pretty mare anymore."

"Yes," Alex replied tightly. "It is a pity . . . Tell me, what is this St. Claire fellow like? I mean, is he an all right chap?"

"I would say so. He is quite competent here at the office. But between you and me, he's a bit of a bore. I would have thought the girl would wed someone more exciting. And another thing about him, he seems to loathe the natives; never refers to them any way but 'dirty wogs'. Such a beautiful girl . . . find it difficult to understand her choice."

"Yes, I suppose so. But then, I hardly know her."

"Just so, Alex. Well, she's out of your game now, isn't she?"

"She certainly is that, David," said Alex dryly.

Meera was helping Rebecca to arrange her hair for

the evening meal. She feared that bringing up any upsetting subject might do Rebecca mental harm, but some things were best brought out in the open.

"I must be making confession to Missy Sahib. Meera has been seeing a man. I am behaving like lady, though." She waited for her mistress's initial reaction.

"That's fine, Meera. But I hope you do not find yourself in love with someone who could not provide for you." She continued, a growing fear that Meera might leave her, "If you wish to marry, please, have him work here. I'll pay him well."

Meera saw Rebecca's worried look, "No, Missy, I am not leaving you for any man! But this man you are knowing. He is Mahmud."

"Mahmud! But I don't understand . . ." Rebecca was visibly excited, but she whitened as the memories flooded back. Was Azim in Kabul? Had Meera seen him?

Meera knew the thoughts that plagued Rebecca, so she hurried on, "Azim is in Kabul, too. Meera is only seeing Mahmud, though. Meera has been liking him since he is bringing news that Missy Sahib alive and well."

"Does Azim know of my marriage? Oh, Meera, I don't know why I care what he thinks! I hate him for the shame he has brought me. This marriage of mine is all *his* fault. But he would blame me, and call me unspeakable names. No, I don't care what he thinks! I despise the man!" She ended her tirade with a burst of tears.

Meera decided to let it go for the present. Rebecca at any rate, would not listen to her point of view.

That night at dinner, William was pleased with himself. He had had a good day at the governor's offices, and was hoping to receive news of a replacement to a position in England. As always, William was anxious to return. He related his good news to Rebecca who sat pensively wondering how he could be so sinister at times, so like a loving husband at others. She absentmindedly rubbed the latest bruise on her arm. William had given her that one several nights ago when she had once again refused his attentions. He could be almost tender with her when he had abstained from drink, but when he took to his bottle, his mood turned, leaving him vicious and cruel.

William brought her back to the present. "Imagine who dared to visit the governor today?"

Rebecca was bored by the game. "I don't have the slightest idea."

"Why, that same upstart who caused you to faint sometime back. Remember?"

Rebecca remembered all too well and blanched at the thought. So Azim was at the governor's today. She must not show too much interest lest William suspect something. She remembered Azim's words to her: "Find your slim neck . . . cut your throat."

"I know you remember him, dear, in fact he always dresses in native attire. Well, today he was wearing the latest fashion of Europe. Can you imagine it? Think of the gossip he must cause his brother, Lord Blackstone, to endure! I overheard their conversation today, at least until this Alex fellow asked me to leave! Imagine the audacity of the chap! Anyway, he was concerned about the political news in England. Do you suppose he plans to return there?"

"I really have little interest in the maneuverings of the man. After all," she lied coolly, "I have only seen him once."

Dinner that night continued on in the usual fashion. The conversation was restrained and as soon as she possibly could, Rebecca retired to the questionable haven of her room. William would spend the evening hours, as usual, drinking alone in the drawing room. His normal habit was to come to Rebecca in a state of intoxication and force her to accept him in low debasing ways. After he was finished with her, he would fall into a deep and dreamless slumber, while she lay awake dreading the next encounter. He had used her body in every way possible, or so she thought.

That night, Rebecca slept soundly for several hours. She awakened once and found herself alone in the bed. Rebecca was grateful for the respite. She cared nothing for William's whereabouts and fell back to sleep.

Early rays of light crept silently through the windows when William finally stumbled up to bed after having passed out in the study some hours before. Rebecca felt the bed dip heavily. William rolled over on top of her. Unfortunately for Rebecca, she was sleeping on her stomach then. He grunted something unintelligible and began to fondle her backside. She would not tolerate that! She struggled to free herself.

William moaned in her ear, "Ah, my beauty, your charms have captivated me. I have been concerned over the health of your infant and have decided to show you a new way that a man may pleasure his wife at such times."

God! What had he planned for her this time? Rebecca twisted and turned but could not budge his large bulk from her back. William pressed Rebecca's head into the pillows, nearly suffocating her. He held her hands tightly over her head. With his free hand he reached beneath her and pulled Rebecca's belly up toward him and tried to enter her from behind.

She screamed, but her voice was muffled by the pillow. The pain was excruciating, and would not cease no matter what little care he took in entering her. William pushed and shoved at her, whispering the foul words of his pleasure in her ear. He actually thought Rebecca was enjoying it! Why hadn't he thought of it before?

Finally, William shuddered and pulled away. He rolled over and fell asleep, where her sobs barely reached his consciousness.

Rebecca rose stiffly from the bed, trying desperately to regain a measure of her dignity. When her weeping would not cease, she went to her old room and lay on her bed, shaking uncontrollably. Hours later when Meera found her, she still lay there semiconscious.

Meera's heart skipped a beat when she saw her mistress lying on the bed, bloodstained gown, half-opened eyes. Rebecca had a vacant stare about her that frightened Meera.

"Missy Sahib, please wake up! Is it the baby coming?"

"Oh, it's you, Meera," murmured Rebecca. "I couldn't sleep and came in here to see if my old room . . ." Her voice trailed off and she collapsed into Meera's outstretched arms. Rebecca sobbed and sobbed, all the while telling Meera of the disgusting acts William had made her do. She let her hysteria pour out, both in tears and in words.

Meera noticed the waves of crying begin to ebb. "Meera first met Missy when Missy was very happy lady. Now Missy is crying all the time and is not being the same person. You must please stop the weeping and be a strong lady again. That William, he is weak man. Missy can be making him do anything she wants." She went on, daringly, for she could see that Rebecca needed her help. "Please sit up now, and Missy Sahib be starting to grow strong again. Meera help. Together we will be thinking of ways to stay away from nasty man."

Rebecca almost laughed at Meera's simplicity, but the truth of her words was undeniable. Why hadn't she seen it before! She was the strong one! She had even saved his life once on the Khyber Pass. It wasn't William who had tamed her and broken her spirit, it was Azim! He had unwittingly broken her one early dawn, not by his actions, which proved her to be human, but by his false and cutting words. She had been allowing William to vilify her body because Azim had called her a whore. Well, she was no whore, and she would not be treated like one!

Rebecca banged the bedroom door open, startling William into a sitting position. He snapped, "Rebecca, haven't I told you never to awaken me!"

Rebecca boldly answered him. "You forget this is my house, too. If I wish to enter our chambers I shall do so. You thought to intimidate me, for God knows what reasons, but I shall no longer allow you to do so."

William stretched and opened his eyes. "My dear, I never meant to intimidate you. Of course these are your chambers too. I think you should try to revive your spirits. As of late you have been terribly listless."

Rebecca braved further, "Also William, I know that you now control my estates. Under the law, I naturally have little to say. But if you continue to abuse my body, I promise you that I shall disappear into the streets! I would prefer a penniless death to anymore of your . . ."

William saw that she was angry. He really did find the old Rebecca more to his liking and he did not want her to escape him, not just yet. He calmly replied, "Why don't you go visiting today? Take Meera with you. In fact, dear, I'm planning a small trip north in a couple of weeks. You will accompany me."

"Wouldn't you rather travel alone? I might be a hindrance. Don't you think I best remain here?"

"I absolutely forbid it. You will stay by my side at all times."

Rebecca was not sure she wanted to travel, but the prospect of making a journey by caravan was certainly a way to get out of the house and start to live again.

"Of course, if you want me along, I have little to say. I'll begin preparations." She paused, then continued with her original purpose. "About your nightly attentions, William, I'm quite serious. I'll leave you if you touch me drunkenly again." She hoped that he believed her, for Rebecca saw little joy in the idea of wandering the streets alone, without funds, but she had decided to bluff in the hope that he might cease his drinking and treat her fairly.

Suraj Mal had been trading in arms and slaves for as long as anyone could remember, his carpet shop in the Kabul bazaar lending him a perfect cover for his illicit business. His close-set eyes bored into Mahmud's. Mahmud had never trusted the fat bandit who smelled like rancid mutton grease. He saw the man's filthy white turban and the gaping holes in his over-large mouth. The trader revolted Mahmud, but Azim paid little attention to the man's appearance. They needed him. He provided them with many guns and ammunition, and in return he was well-paid. Azim pointed all these facts out to Mahmud, but Mahmud would never trust the man.

This hot summer day in August was to be the final contact with Suraj Mal. The sweat-drenched merchant was pleased with the deal and would deliver the arms within a week to a prearranged destination. The tall Englishman could not know it, but Suraj Mal had devised a plan to betray him. Suraj had difficulty finding guns to sell lately and planned to have no further dealings with Azim. What a perfect time to ambush him and to re-sell the arms to another buyer who was patiently waiting with a fat purse!

Suraj Mal chuckled at his cleverness. He spoke to Azim, emitting a foul odor from his mouth as he did so. "Ah, my friend, the goods are on their way. I'll have them in your hands soon, but I must insist that you pay me half the price in advance. My suppliers have grown greedy, you understand?"

Mahmud spoke first. "You fat greedy swine! You shall be paid upon—"

"Come now, Mahmud." Azim broke in. "Suraj Mal would never cheat us! He has been our close friend for years. Besides, he would not like his chubby little

throat slit." He turned to Suraj Mal, "Would you, good
friend?"

Suraj Mal narrowed his small beady eyes. "Cheat
you! By Allah! Why should I wish to steal from my
friends who pay me so well?" But he had, indeed,
planned that exact thing. Now to persuade them to
travel in the Englishman's caravan. This would not be
so simple.

He began, matter-of-factly, "You must take special
care this trip. I hear that the soldiers are checking many
travelers for arms. If only there were a troop caravan
leaving Kabul soon, but alas, there are none." He
drooled offhandedly, "Only a governor's small emis-
sary, one going as far as Khulm."

Azim thought he detected a note of urgency in Suraj
Mal's voice, but perhaps he only imagined it. After all,
the man had not yet cheated them. He may only have
been concerned that if the arms were detected, his
name would most assuredly be linked to the illicit
weapons.

Suraj Mal went on. "Check carefully, my friends.
Find a good cover, for I would not wish to lose my best
customers, no?"

"This government caravan, how many men? When
does it leave?" Mahmud suspiciously inquired.

Suraj Mal was still setting his trap. "Two weeks time
it will leave. I hear through my ears at the governor's
mansion that one William St. Claire will deliver
dispatches to Khulm. It is a very small group this time, I
think."

Azim's mind whirled, his white teeth clenched under
taut skin, his scar a thin white line. St. Claire! Would
Rebecca accompany him? If Suraj Mal was planning a
trap, then so be it! There was little reason to believe he
would do so, but precautions could be taken.

Closely covering his emotions, Azim replied, "We'll
see, friend. For now, just meet your end of the
bargain." He handed the obese little man a small purse
and rose to leave the bazaar compounds. Mahmud

followed closely behind, a worried look on his face. He feared that Azim would jump at the chance to be near the St. Claires. Mahmud smelled danger.

Rebecca felt the perspiration trickle down between her breasts; the bazaar was oppressive today. Her black high-necked dress threatened to choke her. She was determined to make a success of her shopping excursion in spite of the heat. Her face was visibly whitening, the dark circles under her eyes deepening. Meera feared her mistress would faint and begged her to return home. Rebecca would not hear of it, and continued her shopping spree.

She was examining a piece of delicate lace when the spell overcame her. The fine white lace slipped through her fingers. The bazaar roof was spinning; Rebecca sank to her knees on the hard floor. She did not pass out, but her perception was hazy and she felt terribly nauseous. Voices faded in and out and someone was insisting that she lie down.

Azim and Mahmud had just left the carpet shop when Mahmud heard Meera's frantic cries. He rushed through the door to find Meera sobbing helplessly over her Missy's crumbled form. Azim was close on his heels thinking that his comrade was assisting a woman in trouble.

Then he recognized Rebecca and crossed the distance separating them in one easy stride. He dropped to his knees and pressed her shaking body to his own strong form. Sweeping her into his arms, he hurriedly carried Rebecca outside into the fresh air. In the light, he saw her weakened condition. She had become thinner and her delicate skin was pale and wan, with signs of many sleepless nights. By God! He would murder that bastard, St. Claire! What had the man done to her?

Rebecca began to come around a little and she

nestled into the strong arms that held her. Her head tilted back and she saw a blurred vision of a tall handsome Englishman. He looked vaguely familiar. She shook her head and forced his features to come into focus. Gray eyes met hers and the realization of his identity flooded her ashen face.

Rebecca mustered what little strength she could. "Put me down . . . I'm fine . . . Don't touch me, I can't bear anymore!"

Azim, seeing her panic, tried to steady Rebecca as he set her on her feet. She was so weakened that he dared not upset her further. Had his mind not already been made up to join the small caravan heading north, nothing would have stopped him.

Rebecca was trying desperately to stand on her own. The proximity of his hard muscular body only brought back agonizing memories and left her even more dizzy than before. What was the attraction he held for her? Was she bewitched?

She whispered weakly, "Stay away from me. Let me be . . . I despise you!"

But her faltering words did not convince Azim. He let her stand alone and surveyed her unsteady figure. He spoke to her with great tenderness. "You'll be all right now, Rebecca. Is there anything I can do? Would you like me to talk to your . . . husband?"

The words fell on her like sharp chips of ice. She steeled herself. "You shall not speak to William! I'm quite capable of living my life without your interference. Excuse me. Meera, come." Her voice was barely audible. She had turned to leave before Azim could read the truth in her eyes. Rebecca's tears, however, had not escaped his notice. Azim's heart skipped a beat at the brave front she presented.

Rebecca and Meera returned home and, exhausted, she retired to her room. Later at dinner, William again announced his intentions for her to join the travelers going north.

Rebecca sullenly replied, "I've reconsidered, William. It would not be healthful for me to travel so far in my condition. I should remain here."

Coldly, William turned to her and in clipped tones said, "That, my dear, is entirely your problem. It might even be better for all concerned if something . . . uh . . . accidental happened to your baby . . ."

Rebecca drew back in horror.

"Don't worry, my dear, I'm sure you will survive this trip. But, most assuredly, you *will* accompany me!"

CHAPTER 19

It was much cooler this trip as August slipped into September and autumn came early to the mountains. At the top of the Shibar Pass they had seen trees that were already turning color and once Rebecca had seen a small pocket of snow in a shady spot, left over from an earlier snowstorm. In the mornings, their breath froze in the cold air and the horses were frisky and hard to saddle.

Meera suffered from the cold, not having been away from the sultry climate of India for long, but Rebecca thought the weather delightful—a reminder of home in the fall, fox hunts and weekends at country estates. She was feeling energetic. The exercise seemed to improve her health and the morning sickness had disappeared. She had fresh color in her cheeks and the beauty of pregnancy's first bloom. Rebecca would have enjoyed this excursion greatly except for the discovery she had made on the first day out from Kabul.

Of all the incredible coincidences, she thought. Azim was traveling with the caravan! She had been mounted on Alia, riding behind William, when they met several Afghans on horses, leading their camels. It was common for travelers heading in the same direction to proceed together for reasons of safety, so Rebecca had paid little attention to the men, taking them for ordinary merchants, or perhaps servants taking goods to their masters. They stayed at the rear of the caravan and she did not see their faces at first.

When the party stopped for a short rest, Rebecca tied Alia to a bush and picked up her left forefoot to check it for stones as Alia seemed to have been favoring it slightly. Approaching with its ungainly sideling gait, a stray camel startled the horse. The gray filly tried to shy, jerking her head up and throwing Rebecca off balance. With a smothered oath, Rebecca landed on her rear, her riding skirt flying up over her thighs.

"I am awfully sorry, Mrs. St. Claire," insolently drawled a well-known voice.

Rebecca looked up, taken aback, and encountered a pair of familiar gray eyes, crinkled with laughter.

"I had no intention of letting my camel frighten your animal, I assure you, but these cantankerous creatures will wander about. Please let me help you up. You look rather undignified sitting there with your mouth open." He gently helped Rebecca to her feet, his face showing no emotion, although a smile was threatening to break through his serious expression.

Rebecca could hardly stand, the surprise of seeing him there paralyzed her for a moment. She looked so pale and frightened that Azim feared she would faint again.

"Are you all right, Rebecca?" He asked, concern breaking through his coolness.

She had recovered her poise sufficiently enough to answer him. "Yes, I am fine." Then, "What are you doing here? Must you plague me forever? Why can't you leave me in peace!"

"Ah, Mrs. St. Claire, so many questions! I cannot answer them all at once, but suffice to say I am a lowly camel driver returning to my village with supplies for the winter." He smiled irritatingly at her. Then went on, "Excuse me, Mrs. St. Claire, but I must get back to my camel, and no doubt your *husband* is looking for you."

She could not mistake the deliberate emphasis on the word "husband." She prayed that he knew only of her marriage and not of her pregnancy and that he would leave her alone. She blanched as she thought of the consequences if William found out that Azim had been her abductor and the first man to possess her body. If William did not kill her, then Azim surely would, thinking she had betrayed his identity. Above all, she must give William no hint that she knew Azim as any other than a mere acquaintance. She must remain calm and stay away from him as much as was possible in the confines of their camp at night. She prayed that it would be easier during the day.

She led Alia back to William's side and tried desperately to see who the other men with Azim were. One she was sure was Mahmud, especially when she caught sight of his jug-headed roan, Ghazal. She hoped fervently that neither Azim nor Mahmud would pay her any attention, or even glance in her direction.

The days passed slowly for Rebecca who was tense and terrified. William noticed her nervousness and attributed it to fear of a miscarriage. He baited her about it, telling her that the baby would be better off not being born, or contrarily, that the little "thing" would probably be too stubborn to abort. She bore this silently so as not to antagonize William further.

Meera had also recognized the men, and was as nervous as her mistress about the situation. She tried to ignore Mahmud for her Missy's sake, but his broad smile followed her everywhere.

Although they shared a tent at night, William generally left her alone. One night, nonetheless, he had become slightly intoxicated and took Rebecca's arm firmly to lead her from the fire. She went with him in an agony of nervousness, sensing Azim's eyes boring into her back as she was led toward the tent.

Azim was seething and his gray eyes were dark and menacing. Mahmud feared that he would follow the couple to the tent, but Azim only stood tense and brooding. By God, he would murder that bastard St. Claire if he dared harm Rebecca! Azim felt that something must happen to bring a confrontation between them soon.

Long before the sun had erased the pink streaks of dawn from the sky, the caravan was inching its way over the pass. Plumes of frozen breath from man and animal alike hung briefly in the thin air, dissipated, then formed whitely again. As they began their lung-relieving descent, they passed the spot where Rebecca had been abducted by Azim. She gave a shudder, remembering the terrible events that had taken place there, but the rocks remained silent this time and the caravan passed on to stop for the night much further down the trail.

They stopped earlier than usual to appease their hunger, ravenous in the cool air. They were in the habit of sitting around the fire before retiring, William usually drinking brandy from his own personal supply, while the others talked. Mahmud normally kept to himself, but Azim often joined in the conversations. William feared pushing the fierce man too far although he had been treating him in a condescending manner. Azim tried to ignore this to keep the peace. He had difficulty keeping a rein on his temper and often stalked, smoldering from the fire. Rebecca cringed inwardly when she saw the proud Azim accepting veiled insults unflinchingly. Only his flinty eyes proved how hard this forebearance was for him.

It was barely dusk when they began to gather at the fire. William was searching for his second bottle of brandy while Meera was washing some things out in the stream. Rebecca was resting by the campfire when she saw Azim approaching her. She immediately rose to leave, but he reached for her arm and held her: Just as he was about to speak shots rang out in the clear mountain air.

A bullet whistled by, not a yard from Rebecca, ricocheting off a rock behind her with a whine. She stood motionless, stunned. Azim swore under his breath viciously, furious that he was so far from his rifle, still sheathed in his saddle. He shouted back at Rebecca to take cover while he ran, dodging bullets, to get his weapon. He momentarily wondered how Mahmud was faring in this crossfire, but he had not much time to think of anything while trying to reach his horse.

Rebecca heard Azim's shout as if from a great distance, but was still unable to move. She stood paralyzed in horror as bullets flew around her. A vaguely familiar man next to her, reaching for his gun, was suddenly hit in his throat. He made a hideous gurgling sound and toppled over backward, his gushing blood spraying Rebecca's skirt. She remained frozen, the back of her hand pressed against her mouth, her eyes unable to move from the gaping black hole in the man's neck. She was not conscious of the two men stealing up behind from the trees until one of them had covered her mouth with his dirty hand and pinned her arms to her sides. She tried to scream but it was cut off. Frantically she kicked backward at the man, but he laughed shortly and dragged her off toward his horse.

Azim had just reached Khaled when he heard her strangled cry. He spun around in time to see her being drawn back into the trees. Without a moment's hesitation, he flung himself on Khaled and galloped after Rebecca's abductor. A white-hot rage had swept his body when he saw her in danger, all else deserting his mind.

The two men had wasted no time in putting distance between themselves and the camp, pleased with their lovely hostage. They knew that Suraj Mal would pay well for her, or her family would ransom her back. Either way, their greed would be satisfied.

Rebecca was half-stunned, held tightly in front of the hired mercenary. She had fleeting, terrified thoughts. What would William do? Would he attempt to get her back? The moments in the camp had passed in stop-motion, each picture etched clearly in her mind: the bullet hole in the man's throat, the puffs of smoke from rifles, the plunging horses, and scattering men. What had happened to Azim, to William, to Meera? She shuddered in helpless terror. Where were they taking her?

Her abductors were following a seldomly used path, obvious to only someone familiar with it. It led ever deeper into the mountains, winding around rocks, clumps of trees, crossing streams and gravel slides. It seemed as if they had been traveling for hours and the western sky was turning dark. Rebecca was so exhausted that she dozed off several times due to the lulling motion of the horses' slow gate. She awakened periodically to find that her nightmare was a reality, and the two men were carrying her on and on into the wilderness.

Finally, they stopped their lathered horses and set about making a fire, assured that they were safe from pursuit. The flames lit up a partially ruined mud hut and an enclosure for the animals. It was cold by now and Rebecca was grateful for both the blanket they threw her and the cup of tea that they brewed over the fire. They gave her a piece of flat bread and motioned that she was to sleep in the hut while they kept watch outside.

How long would it be until one of them tired of the vigil and came to her in the darkness? She shuddered at the thought. Before retiring, Rebecca put her fears aside for the moment and realized that she needed some privacy to meet a call of nature. Embarrassed, she asked the men with gestures if she could go out of sight for a minute. They laughed rudely and told her to go, unconcerned about her escaping into the black mountains surrounding them. On her way back to the hut, she thought she heard a movement in the bushes and hurried toward the fire, envisioning bears, wolves or other wild beasts. She entered the musty one-room hut, wrapped herself in a rough blanket and tried to sleep. Rebecca could hear the men conversing in Pashto around the fire as she drifted off.

She was awakened a few minutes later by the sound of a shot echoing off the canyon walls. Terrified, her heart thudding uncontrollably, she lay unmoving, afraid to look outside. She heard cries of fear from her jailors, a scuffle, another shot, a grunt of pain and a terrible gurgling scream, cut off suddenly. Then there was the sound of a horse breaking through the underbrush. Still, she cowered in the hut, afraid to let her presence be known. There was complete silence for a moment. Then slow irregular footsteps approached the door. She closed her eyes unable to face another horror this night.

Unbelievably, she heard a voice call softly, "Rebecca! Rebecca! Are you there?"

She did not trust her ears. Was it . . . could it possibly be *him?*

Again she heard the voice, just outside the door.

"Rebecca, it's me . . . Azim . . . Are you in there?"

It was him! Relief, a flash of an unnamed emotion poured through her. She pushed back the blanket finally to rise and answer him.

Her voice came out weakly, she could hardly recognize it. "Azim, I'm here . . . I'm all right . . . Oh, thank God, you've come." Tears began to run down her flushed cheeks as she ran to the opening.

He stood outside the door, silhouetted by the firelight. He was in a strange position, she thought, leaning against the wall of the house, his head bowed, one hand on the wall, supporting himself. He looked up as she emerged from the dark opening, a crooked smile twisting his lips.

She stopped short, looking at him. Something was wrong. She saw a body on the ground, the firelight reflecting off the knife handle in its throat. Azim followed her eyes then gave a harsh laugh at her shocked stare.

"He would have done the same to me, Rebecca, and you, too, if he had been paid enough. Don't waste your tears on him. I just wish I'd gotten the other one too, but he got away." He shifted his weight and a low groan escaped his lips.

"What is it, Azim? Oh, dear God, you've been hurt . . . Let me see!" She tried to find where he was wounded.

"It's nothing, my little flower. I've had worse injuries playing buzkashi . . . I'll recover."

Her practical nature asserted itself. "You will come over to the fire and let me look at it . . . Right now!"

"I expect you're right . . . but you will have to help me, I'm afraid. If the truth be known, I'm not sure if I can make it or not." A wry smile pulled at his lips.

She let him lean on her shoulders as they made their way the few yards to the fire. He winced at each step and leaned heavily on her. Rebecca thought she would collapse under his weight, but was able to help him to sit down close to the heat. It was obvious he was in great pain, although he remained silent.

"You'll have to get the knife to cut . . . the seam of my pants." He gestured toward the corpse.

She blanched. "I can't do it . . . It's too horrible! I couldn't—"

"I'm afraid you'll have to, my sweet. It's the only knife I have." His gray eyes looked into hers; his forehead was beaded with sweat.

She saw the pain he was in and knew that she must do it. Steeling herself, she strode quickly to the body and grasped the handle. It took all of her strength to free the blade as if the body wished to keep it in an unearthly grasp. She was panting and shaking by the time she succeeded.

When Rebecca returned to the fire, Azim was lying back, his head leaning on a log, eyes closed, his wounded leg stretched out in the patterned light. She tore a piece off of her petticoat and wiped the deadly instrument clean, then carefully cut the seam of his trousers up to his thigh. Pushing the fabric aside, she saw a wound in the muscle, the edges angry-looking and purple. She gasped in shock.

"I'll have to clean it," she said looking at him from

her kneeling position. He merely nodded, not opening his eyes.

She tore the rest of her petticoat into strips, and wet one from the stream nearby. Gently, she began to remove the caked blood from around the bullet hole. His body jerked involuntarily once when she pressed too hard.

"I'm sorry . . . Am I hurting you awfully?" She stopped, afraid to touch him again.

"No, go on." His voice was a whisper. "Someone has to do it, and I certainly can't."

She continued her task until the area was as clean as she could make it, then wrapped strips of material around his muscular thigh. Finished, she sat back on her heels and looked at his face. His eyes were closed so that she could study it at her leisure. He was breathing shallowly, a sheen of perspiration on his forehead. His curving black brows were drawn together in a frown, but his mouth looked boyish and unprotected in the firelight. *This* was the man who had stolen her, ravished and humiliated her—the father of her child!

He opened his eyes after a time, surprised to find her staring at him with a quizzical expression on her face.

"Rebecca, come here," he said. She rose, then kneeled by his side, still watching him carefully. He put his hand up to touch her disheveled hair, then gently traced the tear-paths on her cheeks with his strong fingers. His eyes held hers for a long moment, then he merely said, "Thank you."

Rebecca reached up with her hand to touch his, and she felt his fingers close over her own and press them. She knew a warmth, a softening and opening of her heart that she had not felt since she last saw her father.

"Azim . . . Azim . . . will you be all right now?" she asked imploringly.

"That depends . . . The bullet is still in there . . . If it doesn't get infected and I can reach Mahmud or someone to get it out . . . yes. If not, well, maybe," he answered grimly. Then seeing her lips tremble and her eyes brim with tears, he said quickly, "You're not to worry, Rebecca. I told you I've suffered worse wounds than this in the games." He smiled at her. "Now, my charming little beauty, help me inside. We can't do anything until morning anyway. We both need some sleep, I'll warrant."

He pushed himself up and leaned heavily on her while he limped to the hut. Once inside, he lowered himself to the ground stretching his bandaged leg out with a groan that he tried to muffle. She put her blanket over him and went back outside to get the other one left by the man who had escaped. Wrapping herself in it, she lay there, tense and very aware of his breathing so near to her.

His voice came softly through the darkness. "Rebecca, come closer . . . Damn it, Rebecca! Please." It was obviously hard for him to beg.

"What is it? Do you need anything?" she asked, moving closer.

"Come here, love. Don't be afraid, for God's sake. I'm in no condition to do anything to you now!"

He reached out and felt her arm, then pulled her to him. Unresisting, she brushed her mouth with his. Suddenly she realized that his lips were cold, his body shivering underneath the blanket. She lifted the cover and crawled under it next to him. She pressed her body to his, trying to warm him and stop his shuddering. Eventually they both fell asleep, pressed closely together, sweet breath mingling with sweet breath.

The sun finally woke Rebecca. She felt refreshed and happy until she remembered the events of the day before. It all came back in a rush and she turned with a gasp to find Azim still asleep, but breathing irregularly. She shook his shoulder to wake him, feeling the heat of his body through his shirt. He half-opened his eyes; they were unfocused and bleary.

"Rebecca? . . . You still here?"

"Yes, Azim, how do you feel?"

"Leg hurts like the devil." He licked his dry lips. "

feel hot, burning . . . Must be a fever . . ." His voice broke off, frightening her in its weakness.

She turned back the blanket, removed the strips of cloth and looked at his leg only to discover the wound was swollen and ugly. Red streaks radiated out from the hole.

She said nothing, but felt her stomach rise toward her throat. Even with no experience, she could see that the wound was dangerously inflamed.

He broke in on her thoughts. "It's infected, isn't it? I thought so . . . There's only one way, one thing to be done . . . Rebecca. You'll have to get the bullet out, then cauterize the area."

"I can't . . . I've never done anything like that . . . I'd hurt you," she wailed. Then, gaining a measure of control, she looked at his face again. "I have to do it?" she asked weakly.

He looked at her, holding her eyes with his. "Yes, you must do it. There is no one else."

He explained what she had to do. "There's a flask of liquor in my saddlebag, get it and bring my medicine pouch, too. Boil some water and put the knife in the fire. That's my girl, you'll do fine."

Rebecca knew that he was trying to be reassuring, but the thought that his life depended on her made her hands fumble and her face become ashen. Rebecca got his flask and left him drinking it in long gulps while she built up the fire. She put on a kettle, brought by her captors, to boil and stuck the blade into the glowing embers.

When she reentered the hut, he tensed visibly. "Go ahead . . . Do it now!" He closed his eyes and tried to make himself relax. Rebecca looked at him for a long moment, then turned to the wound. She was afraid to dig with the knife, so she had decided, instead, to probe with her fingers. Taking a deep breath, she poured the alcohol over her hands, then stuck her fingers into the unsightly wound. She could feel him flinch.

Rebecca almost stopped her probing but she managed to push deeper still and finally felt a hard object. That was it! She grasped the bullet as tightly as she could and pulled. Don't lose it, she prayed. Please, let it come out. Her fingers held on and she freed it; a black irregularly shaped ball. She sighed with relief, but remembered the rest of his directions. She went to the fire, grasped the knife handle and jerked it from the flames. The blade shone red-hot. Trying not to dwell on what must be done, she walked quickly into the hut and drew the hot blade across his wound. It sizzled and the smell of burning flesh rose to gag her. His body stiffened, and mercifully, went limp.

It was over. She put some of his herb salve on the wound, bound up his leg again in clean strips and sat by his side most of the day, wiping his forehead with cool wet cloths. She got up only to eat a piece of bread, see to Khaled, and relieve herself.

Azim was burning with fever and delirium. He mumbled continuously but she could understand little, for it was often in Pashto. But once she could understand his words clearly.

"Father . . . I'll take you home. But why is there so much blood . . .?" Rebecca sat perfectly still while he continued. "I can't bury you, I'm sorry—ground is so hard . . . the rocks . . . the rocks . . . Father. I'm sorry . . ." What did he mean? What terrible event was he reliving in his ravings?

Several times he called her own name. Once she heard him say, "St. Claire, I'll kill you," and he struggled to rise, opening his wound again and making it bleed. She tried to lie across his body to keep him still, and only succeeded then because he was so weak.

Eventually, Rebecca slept, huddled in the corner of the hut. She awoke in the dark, stiff and shivering with cold. She crawled under the blanket with him and realized with great relief that he was no longer burning with fever, but was resting peacefully. She fell asleep again, deeply and dreamlessly, until morning.

Rebecca woke in the cold gray dawn and noticed with satisfaction that he still slept calmly, his face relaxed and young-looking, his skin cool to the touch. She busied herself, building up the fire and brewing tea, searching his saddlebags and even the dead man's bags for food. She found some hard goat cheese, bread, and more tea.

She washed at the stream, tried to comb her hair with her fingers and straighten her riding habit, which was showing signs of wear. She felt amazingly well, especially now that she thought Azim would recover. She sensed, in a way, that she had evened the score between them. He had rescued her from the two men, but she had saved his life, too. Maybe he would feel some respect for her now.

Returning to the fire, she poured cups of tea into the rough mugs the men had carried, laced them liberally with their precious sugar, and carried them inside. She saw that Azim was awake, drawn, but clear-eyed in the dim light.

"So you didn't leave after all," he muttered. "I thought that you had decided to return to St. Claire."

Ignoring his mention of her husband, she replied, "*You* may leave helpless people alone, but *I* do not!" She snapped, "It's only fair that I take care of you since it was my fault you got into this fix in the first place!"

"I apologize, my fiery little lady. I misjudged you. Now come here so that I may properly thank you." He smiled wickedly.

"Oh! You're impossible! Besides, you must have something to eat, to strengthen you. Here, I've brought you some tea." Her face was flushed to a degree that only he could make her do.

"My, what domestic talents you have, my sweet. I would never have guessed." Giving ground, he took the drink and gulped it down quickly, then ate some of the bread and cheese.

Rebecca helped him out into the warm sun and sat

with him while he rested, the effort of moving having exhausted him. She was sorely tempted to tell Azim about the baby, but thought better of it. He was still too weak to bother with such news.

He sat in the sunlight and dozed most of the day, regaining strength, while Rebecca busied herself cutting grass to feed Khaled and the dead man's horse. She also performed the difficult but necessary task of burying the corpse, as he had begun to attract more than his share of flies.

Rebecca was beginning to have a sense of pride in her accomplishments. For the first time, she felt in control of the situation, and it was a good feeling. She scarcely gave a thought to William, even feeling guilty once or twice that she cared so little about his fate. But she was worried about Meera. What had happened to her? As for what the future would hold, she refused to even think about it.

Rebecca was pleasantly tired by dusk, when she noticed massive blue-black clouds building up over the mountain peaks, and lightning flashing in the distance.

Azim noticed her glances at the threatening sky. "It will rain soon. We can hope that the roof doesn't leak tonight. These storms are violent sometimes in the mountains."

"Will the horses be all right?" she asked, worried.

"Yes, our horses are accustomed to this weather. They turn their tails to the wind and wait the storm out."

They retired to the shelter, Rebecca helping him again: This time he leaned on her much less and was stronger than before. They rolled up in their blanket and fell asleep like children.

In the early morning hours, the storm broke in its full fury. The wind lashed at the ruined hut, rain slashed in the windows, thunder reverberated along the mountain valley. They both awoke simultaneously, with a particularly loud peal of thunder. Rebecca started in fear at the sound, dreaming of gun shots.

Azim reached over to touch her face, reassuringly. "It's nothing, Rebecca—only thunder, come here."

She moved without thinking into the comfort of his strong arms. His mouth came down over hers—tender, searching. She sighed, accepting his kiss as a long-awaited reward.

Rebecca felt lost in the grip of a fierce emotion, stronger than herself. She returned his caresses, felt every inch of his body with trembling fingers; tasted his mouth with hers. An ache grew in her core, spreading until it was unbearable.

When he entered her, she gave a soft cry of relief, wanting him with her whole being. They rode together on the crest of a wave of sensation, rising and falling in rhythm, abandoning themselves to passion.

They slept again, the rain beating on the roof, and awoke, clasped in each other's arms. The storm had spent itself; the sun was shining once more through the clouds.

Azim smiled at her, no bitterness, no pride between them, only happiness and peace at this moment. Time stood still, holding them together in a world of their own making.

Rebecca thought again of telling him about the baby, but the moment passed, and she hated to spoil the magic of their special world. She snuggled happily up to him, forgetting all but the realization that she was wantonly, deliciously, incredibly in love. Nothing else mattered.

"Rebecca, my passionate little blossom," he laughed. "I cannot keep this up without sustenance. Is there any food left?"

"How can I get you breakfast when I have nothing on?" she teased.

"Put on my shirt, and hurry! Or I shall expire from weakness!"

She did as he said, feeling ridiculous in the long sleeves and tails falling to her knees. The fire was out, but she found some bread and cheese that was relatively dry. They ate in the musty little hut, tasting nothing of what they swallowed. She traced the muscles on his chest with her fingers, felt his beard-stubbled face.

They spent the day exploring each others bodies, reaching heights of pleasure neither had dreamed of before until they were left spent and trembling to sleep and begin their odyssey of love again.

Rebecca was happier than she had ever been before, and refused to consider what the future held for her. Azim had begun to laugh and joke with her. He was relaxed and had forgotten his bitterness and hate. He had asked her once what she felt for her husband, but she turned suddenly serious and refused to discuss it.

Once again she almost told him about their child, but was afraid to destroy the mood. It could wait. She was sure she would find the right moment to tell him.

The next few days passed blissfully, the lovers discovering the depth of their passion for each other. Azim was able to hobble around and set some simple traps in which he caught a rabbit. He cleaned and gutted it and cooked a stew. Rebecca thought that she had never tasted anything so delicious. The outside world had no reality for them, they dwelled in a closed universe of their own devising. They loved unashamedly under the sun.

One morning at dawn, Rebecca awoke entwined in her lover's arms. She quietly rose and went out to build up the fire, hoping to surprise him with a fresh cup of tea. She walked to the stream, a smile on her lips, and knelt down to splash the cool mountain waters on her face. Before she knew what had happened, a rough hand covered her mouth from behind and she felt a blow to her head. Everything went black.

CHAPTER 20

The only communication between Rebecca and her captor had been the single name, Bukhara, that ancient and notorious city that still dealt in human flesh. Rebecca would never forget those terrifying days on the road to that city. Even the small children of Kabul had heard of the slave markets there. The town sat to the north across the Russian border near the Oxus river. As far as the Emir of Bukhara was concerned, anything that brought profits to his province was good for him, too. Lawlessness ruled in the area and as Rebecca approached her destiny there, she wished that she had the nerve to take her own life.

Her captor, thank God, had not lain a finger on her. Rebecca was surprised at the careful way in which he handled her. They had been several weeks on the road and she was hot, tired, and bedraggled. Her hair was snarled and hung to her waist, so when they passed a fellow traveler on the road, her abductor would pull the veil of the native garb he had provided back into place. He wanted no one to recognize her, however, she prayed that someone, anyone, would notice that she was different from other local women.

Long after dusk one night, her captor finally pulled the horses to the edge of the road. She had named him Mastiff, for the lack of any other name to call him; and because of his curiously cropped ears, she was reminded of the huge sheep dogs of the steppe. There was a stream nearby and she longed to cool her hot body in the tempting water. Yet, she feared that Mastiff might attack her, and tried to think of a way she could lose him if only for a few minutes.

Mastiff surprised her by indicating the water. His huge stature no longer intimidated her, for someone must have instructed him to deliver her unharmed, or perhaps he was the type who preferred only men. Rebecca knew that her white burnoose, once wet, would provide him a tempting view of her figure, but at this point she cared little.

As nearly as she could guess, Rebecca was now three months along in her pregnancy. Other than her swelling breasts and her slightly rounded belly, she was certain that no one would notice her condition. She had told herself to think only of survival and not the days to come in Bukhara. With that thought in mind, she went to the stream and began to wash the filth and grime off her body. The job proved difficult for she had remained dressed as Mastiff was still on the bank watching her.

He was large and muscular in form, middle-aged and with a face not unpleasant to look on, except for the odd ears. His many missing teeth presented a contrast to his respectable appearance, which was ordinary enough so that any onlooker might take them for husband and wife traveling together.

Rebecca finally emerged from the water, somewhat cleaner, much more refreshed. Her skin had at last lost its white pallor when her morning sickness had ceased and she looked vibrantly alive again.

The evening meal was large and nutritious. In fact, she thought, most of her meals were surprisingly so. Rebecca had the distinct feeling that someone wanted her in good health and untouched when they reached Bukhara. Could it be an enemy of her father's, or perhaps William's? Was it someone who wished her healthy for the slave market? The very thought made her shudder.

Rebecca had no way of knowing if Azim had

followed her. For all Azim knew, she had run away from him. Her mind reeled at the thoughts he must have had when she had failed to return that morning. She did her best to keep her nerves calm by remaining optimistic. Vaguely, she wondered what she and Azim would be doing now if this had not happened. As they had been blissfully happy when she was abducted, could he really think she had run away? Did he have the strength to follow her? Her mind was tortured.

A week ago, Rebecca had tried to leave a sign on the road. She had planned to drop a piece of torn chemise and hoped that the finder would recognize it as being European. If word of her abduction was out, then perhaps . . . Of course she knew how impossible her plan had been, for Mastiff had caught her movement in his eye and snatched the material up off the ground before a lone, wandering wayfarer could notice it. He chastised Rebecca in words that she could only guess at. Since that attempt, she realized that her efforts were futile for Mastiff was a highly experienced jailor and saw through every ploy she attempted to devise.

They had traveled further and further into the majestic Hindu Kush. The air, for a while, had been cooler and she was becoming stronger by the day. She had only one regret. She should have told Azim about the baby, but they had been on the fine edge of a discovery and she had not wanted to spoil it by announcing her pregnancy to him. Oh! Why hadn't she told him!

After the meal, Mastiff indicated that she should rest, so Rebecca went to her blanket and tried to sleep. Tomorrow, she surmised, they should be near Bukhara, for the strange land had flattened out and the people on the road were a different lot from those who traveled the Afghanistan caravan routes.

She slept restlessly that night; visions of cool grassy English meadows filled her dreams. She was naked in the high lush grass. A tall faceless man dressed like an Afghan, strode leisurely up to her, then bent down and

kissed her. She woke up with a start for she had not
wanted to finish the dream. She did not want to know if
his caresses would have aroused her.

The next afternoon, they reached Bukhara. Rebecca
had hoped to stay on the trail a bit longer but as the
familiar mud huts of an Asian city began to crop up, she
knew that her fate would soon be sealed. They passed
unnoticed through the outskirts of the city.

Arriving in front of a large house, Mastiff unceremoniously lifted her down from her mount and ushered
her inside, leaving Rebecca alone while he went to tend
the horses. She quickly appraised her surroundings and
wanted to run, when she saw that she was not alone.
An unveiled servant woman, not unattractive, appeared and led her out into an open courtyard. The
serving girl sidled over to a grotesquely fat figure who
turned to pinch the girl's wiggling backside. The young
girl giggled and left them, disappearing again into the
house. When he finally turned to face Rebecca, she was
revolted by his ugliness.

The fat little man was of middle age, and wore filthy
clothes and a dirty once-white turban. Even the turned-
up toes of his slippers were black with grime. He smiled
at her and drooled from a nearly toothless mouth.
Rebecca thought that she had seen him somewhere
before, but where?

He finally spoke to her in passable English. "My
name is Suraj Mal. I am your master now."

She had been expecting something like this, but to
hear the words spoken aloud left her cringing with fear.

"I demand that you release me immediately!" She
would not beg him and squared her shoulders. "There
has been a terrible mistake here, I assure you. I am
Rebecca St. Claire and—"

"No mistake has been made, little beauty!" Suraj
Mal sat perfectly still with his small round eyes never
leaving hers, his fingers clenched whitely together
cracking his knuckles.

She ignored his lewd gaze. "I will have an explanation!"

Suraj Mal could hardly contain himself and chortled with glee while he bragged. "But of course you will have a full account! My own cleverness will not go without proper acknowledgment." He reached over and grabbed her arm, pinching her tender thigh with his other hand. She let out her breath in a gasp.

"I have had to pay my man dearly to fetch you here, but you will return my investment a thousand-fold, my beauty. You have caused Suraj much trouble and anger! When that stupid man of mine returned to Kabul, wounded, dripping blood all over my priceless carpets, and then told me of his failure to keep you . . . Well! Suraj was quite furious."

Rebecca struggled to free herself from his grasp. "I don't know what you mean!"

"Of course not. Women are only useful for affairs of the heart. My ingeniousness has escaped you, I fear," he continued his bragging, "for it was I who planned the attack on Azim. You understand now? Even a lowly water boy knows the value of a white woman . . . But alas . . . my men were overcome by that clever Azim! You see why I sent my most trusted assistant to retrieve you? And now that I have you my purse will bulge anew!"

She was beginning to realize that her predicament was no accident but a well-planned scheme.

Her nerves were ragged. "But my husband and the governor will find me. I know they will!"

Suraj Mal laughed, his breath choking her. "No . . . No, you must not think me so stupid. Already my man is returning to Kabul to spread word that you were taken away by Azim. Tell me, who will be the viser?"

She knew that he was right, Meera would even think her with Azim. The situation was hopeless.

He grew bored with his explanation. Releasing her

hand he said, "And now, my little fair one, we must make you presentable. I have arranged a small sale for you to enjoy and you must look your best! Off to rest now, you must be exhausted!"

His laughter rang in her ears. He meant to sell her, and to even make her presentable! Where had she heard that voice before?

Rebecca was ushered off and found herself in a dimly lit room on the eastern wing of his house. Once inside, two old crones stripped her of her filthy clothes and deposited her into a shallow tub. The bathing was humiliating to say the least. And to make matters worse, one of the hags had noticed her condition and the two were giggling between themselves. Oh Lord, thought Rebecca, if they notice, I must have grown in these last weeks. What would become of her and the baby?

After the bath, they dressed her in an obscene pink gown, her every curve enhanced by the sheer material of which there was little. Her swollen bosom could be clearly seen in the light and the neckline was low on one side with material draped over the other shoulder. She was sickened by her reflection in the mirror. She looked like a whore! Even her glowing hair was allowed to flow freely about her shoulders. She wondered when the sale would be and if she could bribe her buyer to return her for twice the money he paid. Her mind was in turmoil. She prayed for her unborn child.

On the morning of Rebecca's abduction, Azim had been anxiously awaiting her return. There were so many things that he had left unspoken and he was beginning to feel that perhaps he could confide both his doubts and his joys to her. But then she had not come back.

Azim had arisen and limped to the middle of the clearing. She was nowhere in sight. His fears increased by the second, for he saw unshod hoof prints in the sand by the stream and whoever had made them had tried to cover the marks up. Azim knew that a lesser horseman than himself would not have detected the signs. Rebecca had definitely been taken away. But, by whom?

His mind was still foggy from the fever but for her sake he shook the haziness from his brain and started to think. He knew that her kidnapper must have planned the deed well; He also knew that the man was headed north, for in his haste he had overturned a stone on the path, leaving the earth underneath a different color. Azim was certain that he would find evidence of another horse tethered nearby. The man must have been strong or he would have seen signs of a struggle, a broken twig, something, two sets of footprints neatly covered up. No, her kidnapper had been strong enough to subdue her cries and, while holding her, he had done a passable job of covering his tracks.

Azim searched his memory. He personally knew of a few men who could carry the plot through. These men would had to have known of her approximate whereabouts and they must have had a week to plan the deed. The flash of truth came to Azim. That was it! Only the ambushers could have known where she was. And the man he had wounded did get away!

But who was behind the ambush? Azim remembered that at the time of the attack on the caravan, he had seen a familiar looking man with close-cropped ears. Cropped, undoubtedly by a master who feared the man had heard too much, but still valued his services. Azim had seen those telltale ears before. It was years ago, yes, at the bazaar. No, specifically at the shop of Suraj Mal. God! That was it. Who else could have planned the ambush so cleverly. Hadn't Mahmud warned him?

Azim was nearly drained from the emotions that whirled through him. He prayed that his logic would be correct, for Rebecca's life depended on his clarity. Again and again he came to the same conclusions. Suraj Mal had obviously masterminded the whole affair.

Only one question remained unclear in his mind: Where would Suraj have taken her? To Kabul? Or perhaps to his well-known quarters in Bukhara? Azim decided that if he were in that man's place he would definitely take her to the slave market and fatten his purse. Having made his decision, Azim painfully pulled himself onto Khaled's back and started to head north. Suddenly he stopped his horse, realizing that he had no money and one did not travel to a slave market without funds! First he must return to Kabul, secure money, then ride to Bukhara and hope that he would be in time to save her. His trusted Khaled could easily make the long journey but Azim prayed that he, himself, would also have the strength.

Azim rode directly to the governor's mansion when he finally reached Kabul, and within an hour had signed a promissory note and was headed back out of the city before nightfall. He had neglected to ask Mountstuart to inform St. Claire of his own intentions to rescue Rebecca. Let the governor worry about her husband. He would be damned if he was going to take the time to bother with that bastard, St. Claire!

Azim made excellent time on Khaled; the steed was strong and could endure the long trek better than most horses. He was mainly concerned about his own stamina. The journey thus far had been bearable, but what if his leg gave out? Azim decided that he would face that, when, and if it happened.

Once he had made it past the point of the ambush, Azim took the time to question some of the caravan leaders and travelers. He had spoken to numerous people and was beginning to give up hope that one of them had noticed her when he met a young wanderer. The youth had indeed seen a strange woman and large man with cropped ears some days back. It seemed that the burly Afghan had been chastising his wife for carelessly dropping some object and the traveler had only taken notice when he glimpsed a stray lock o golden hair escaping from under her veil. Azim gave the boy a few coins and in return the lad, a musician, offered a poetic tune. Good manners insisted that Azim listen to the boy's sad song, but he was soon on his way again, assured that he was on the right track. He prayed that Rebecca's abductor would not touch her, but dismissed the tormenting thought as anger would surely lead to mistakes.

It was early one cool morning—the sun would not illuminate the eastern sky for hours—as Azim was crossing the Oxus river, close to Bukhara, that a pair of robbers waylaid him.

He had been half-expecting an attack, for the reputation of this borderland was known far and wide. His decision to go on in these pre-dawn hours was made with the knowledge that he would be in danger. Azim readied his pistol and took one of the bandits down before the man ever knew what was happening. The other was not frightened off and jerked Azim down from Khaled's back, jarring his wounded leg. They rolled by the water's edge for some minutes, but Azim's determination and superior strength finally won out. He held the husky man's face totally submerged in the river. For a split second, he thought to show mercy to the bandit, but knowing that the man would most assuredly kill and rob again, he held the struggling body under the rapid current until all life flowed out of him. Azim breathlessly dragged the corpse onto the bank and left him for the wolves. No one in this land would take much notice of the dead man's body for it was a cruel and heartless territory. He felt very much a part of it.

Rebecca tried to fortify her mind against the degrading and terrifing experience she was about to undergo. Earlier that morning she had been taken to the bazaar area of Bukhara where she had been thrown in with men, women and children of all ages, colors and shapes. She likened the bazaar to a huge jar of assorted confections, with a variety of human beings instead of sweets. Even the hungry leers of the onlookers reminded her of eager shoppers in a marketplace. The majority of humans to be sold that day were passive enough, but Rebecca was in the minority; she screamed, tried to kick and bite her jailors.

Suraj Mal had at last arrived for the event with prospective buyers to view the merchandise. She was taken out of her cell to afford the men a better view. She still wore the pink gown—one bared shoulder, little fabric. The bright color enhanced her own rosy complexion, her hair, golden shining ringlets hanging to her sashed waist, her eyes widened in the terror of her predicament.

Mercifully, the prospective buyers were not allowed to sample the soft flesh that tempted their greedy hands. Suraj Mal would stand for no tampering. He did, however, bare one of her breasts for their lascivious stares. Rebecca was mortified, tears of humiliation slipping down her blushing cheeks. She would have suffered even further had she known that Azim stood in the crowd, hurriedly disguised as a merchant, trying to look on passively with the others. He would have to wait for the appropriate moment, but his face was grave and his jaw clenched with suppressed fury at the outrage.

Rebecca was unable to focus her wet eyes on anyone. She hung her head shamefully and stared vacantly at the cold stones beneath her feet. Was no one to save her? Her mind reeled as the market slaves ushered her into the auction-block area. She was to be sold next. Her hour of greatest abasement had come.

The auctioneer began his normal harangue. "Next, my friends, Allah has brought us a rare white gem. She is more lovely than the goddesses of ancient Greece . . . she has the grace of . . ."

Rebecca did not hear his words. The slaves had lifted

her onto the narrow platform, a single dark-skinned slave holding her arms behind her. The bidding began. She did not know, nor did she care about the high figures being placed upon her. She did, however, hear gasps of delight from Suraj Mal, but she still had her head hung low unable to face her degradation.

As if the horror of her present predicament were not enough, Suraj Mal indicated to the auctioneer to reveal her breasts and torso while he licked his puffy lips and nodded his head. The auctioneer reached over to her gown and tore the flimsy material down to her hips, exposing her luscious bosom and belly to all who hungrily watched.

A sudden hush had fallen over the crowd, then slowly the bidding had commenced again. Many of the men had dropped out when the sums being bid went too high; only two remained vying against one another for the prize. Rebecca thought the bidding would never end. Her whole body ached in anguish, her pink nipples stood erect, defying the crowd.

A deep commanding voice came to her ears. "For this flower, I shall pay . . ." The voice could belong to none other! It was Azim! He was here! She regained a small measure of composure. It would not do to show anyone how rapidly her heart beat.

The auctioneer was well-pleased with the enormous amount bid on her, but he saw an opportunity to drive the price higher still. The man had one more device in mind. He coaxed loudly. "Come, come friends. Can our eyes not see? This rare jewel comes with a bonus! Look at those swollen breasts. Friends, you will receive two slaves for the price of one!" He poked a finger into her rounded belly. "Is there a better buy for your money? She is worth a fortune in gold."

Azim was stunned. By God! How could he have been so deceived by the bitch! The cheating whore had been pregnant with St. Claire's brat all the while she had given her body so freely to him. He ached inside with a new agony. He was brought back to the stifling hot room. He must make his move now, but she would pay dearly for the ruse.

If Azim had been horrified, Rebecca was doubly so. She had never meant for him to learn about the baby in this dreadful fashion. To have him hear it from this monstrous figure was more than she could stand.

She felt the roof spin, her feet were lead and she could not focus her eyes . . . She fell into the black slave's arms in a dead faint.

When she opened her eyes again her hands went instinctively to cover her nakedness, but she was already clothed. Gentle, but firm hands were helping her to sit up on a rough bed. Where was she? She looked up into hard gray eyes and a handsome tanned face. Unaccountably, there was an expression of hate emanating from it. At first she was overjoyed with relief, but searching his icy gaze she grew fearful. What was wrong with him and why was he purposely trying to scare her?

Rudely brushing aside her arms, he stood erect above her. "We have little time to depart this place, my dear. I suggest that you come around from your latest fainting spell and make haste." He was gathering a few possessions and stuffing them into a leather sack. She was totally confused by his sudden personality change. Had he thought she was selling herself? Impossible! She stood and went toward the door. He threw her a frigid glance. Was he lost to her again?

Eyes brimming with unshed tears, she whispered, "I'm ready Azim. I wish I could change my . . . my dress. I feel . . . so naked."

He interrupted her harshly. "You seem to be at your best when naked, my dear. Now keep quiet while I think!"

That night, when the half-moon had dipped below the horizon, they left Bukhara; Azim on Khaled and Rebecca on a small chestnut he had purchased. They were across the Oxus before midnight. Azim had not spoken once to her since their encounter in his room. She could no longer bear the silence that hung between them like a heavy cloud.

Quietly, she implored. "Azim, why are we stealing away in the middle of the night? And what in heaven's name has come over you! What have *I* done?"

He did not speak at first but eyed her warily for a few minutes. Finally he answered her in cold detachment. "Did you think Suraj Mal would allow me to live? No, sweet, he knows that if he does not kill me then I shall find his fat throat and slit it!" Azim turned to face her, his expression unreadable. "It's best that we leave here as fast as possible. I'll soon have my day to stay and fight. I can wait."

"I know that man from somewhere—"

"Of course, we first met in his carpet shop. Don't tell me you've forgotten so soon?"

The scene came vividly back to mind. So that was where she had first seen Suraj Mal!

"Now I understand everything . . . except why you hate me so. If it's the baby, well, I can explain." She waited for his reaction. She was both tense and exhausted.

Azim studied her face, could she be that naive? Did she expect him to take another man's brat? Aloud, he measured his words carefully. "Rebecca, when I saw you standing there in the marketplace . . . I was out of my mind with shame for letting you be so abused." He turned his head, hiding his eyes from her bewildered stare. "But when the auctioneer made your . . . condition clear for even *me* to see . . . Rebecca, I may be stupid for not realizing you were pregnant, but I am not without pride! Do you care so little for yourself, and for St. Claire that you will allow me to use your body? Is a moment of pleasure all you seek? What of the child?"

Some minutes later, Rebecca was able to sort out his stinging words. She was slow to realize the impact of his statement. Azim thought the baby was William's! He thought her so deceitful that she would use him to pleasure her body with no concern for the infant! How could he think her so cold, so harsh.

Before the words were even formed in her mind, she had decided to damage his pride too; he had insulted her grievously. "Why Azim, I never thought you would stoop to care about the health of an unborn child. Besides, I don't want the baby! Even William had hoped I would miscarry on the road to Khulm, so why shouldn't I? . . . You know Azim I despise you, I always have!" She could go no further as she was sobbing uncontrollably and speech failed her.

Azim had guessed as much. What a heartless little bitch she was. She had only used him to try and abort the baby! And he had, for some moments in the hut, actually thought he loved her! What a fool she had made of him. Azim was already formulating ways to retaliate, but then he remembered the infant. He would not share in their scheme to destroy the child. Let William have her back.

Aloud he said coolly, "In two weeks time you'll be back in Kabul. Your loving husband deserves you, Rebecca. You're nothing more than a wanton bitch!"

She had gone beyond crying, her head bowed. She had endured so much for a gently-bred young woman. The limit had been reached. Blanking out all thought, all emotion, she let the void fill her, traveling through a wilderness of despair.

After several days on the road to Kabul, Azim was feeling a little gentler toward Rebecca. Having brooded for hours over her harsh retort he began to think perhaps she had intended to hurt and shock him with her biting tongue. Well, at any rate, she had achieved her goal. He wished he could recall what he had said to her, but what did it matter at this point? They had been completely silent for days. The rift had widened and neither regretted it.

At supper that night they had camped near a small

village. Azim was growing tired of looking at her in her scanty attire, in fact he was once again observing her enchantingly rounded figure, her golden hair flowing unbound down her back. He began to think that he would go insane if he had to stare at her another minute; her full breasts showed through her gown so deliciously . . .

His voice, breaking the quiet, was harsh, abrupt. "I'm going into the village for awhile. I'm sick to death of watching you! And even sicker of having to avoid all travelers on the road due to your half-naked state! Keep out of sight and I'll return shortly." With that, he leaped on Khaled's back and disappeared into the darkness.

Rebecca was certain that he was going to abandon her. Well let him! He could go to the devil for all she cared! That crude Afghan! She'd been a fool to trust him. If ever he did return she would be long gone, and she never needed him in the first place. Kabul was only a week or so away, she could make it. He was sick of watching her, was he? Well, that was easily cured!

She mounted her chestnut, longing to ride Alia again, and headed in the opposite direction from the village. She had only gone several hundred yards when a couple of very young men accosted her. They appeared to be sheepherders and drunk in the bargain. The boys were delighted with their find. So pleased were they, that one of them roughly dragged her from her horse. They had no idea what to do with her next, but she was a vision out of the heavens and they would not release her.

Rebecca was terrified. If only she had a decent dress to wear this would never have happened. The lads were hurting her and she feared for the infant, but she would not cease her struggling. When it finally dawned on the boys to tumble her, they hurriedly tore her gown off and one of them pounced on top of her.

She clawed and dug at him. Her feet caught the other lad in the britches and set him off groaning, but her strength was fading and she couldn't hold them at bay for much longer.

She moaned and pleaded. "Please . . . No . . . You'll harm my baby! Oh God, no." But they did not understand her words. "My baby . . . Help me, Azim!" By this time her pleas were a scream in the night.

As he had promised, Azim had returned shortly after her departure. He had no difficulty tracing her path. He was furious at her stupidity to take off unescorted. When he got his hands on her, he'd—

Her cries echoed from over the rocks, "You'll harm my baby . . ." and again before he tugged the scared boy from off her naked body, "My baby . . . Help me, Azim!"

He saw the drunken state of the shepherds and let them go on their way with nothing more than a few stern words and sharp cuffs to frighten them. Then he turned to Rebecca who was crouched against a boulder. She was shivering, her eyes welled with tears, and she rolled her head from side to side like a mad woman. Azim was worried that she had lost her sanity.

"Rebecca . . . Rebecca, listen to me." he soothed. "The baby is fine. I'm not going to let anyone hurt you, not now, not ever. Please listen to me. I've been a pigheaded fool."

He gently shook her, hoping his words would get through. How could he believe that she would hurt the baby? She had sought to protect it desperately just now. What an idiot he had been! She had not used him at all, at least not for the reasons he had thought.

Again he tried to break her spell. "Look, little flower, I've brought you some proper clothes." He gently took her stiff body into his arms, rocking her softly while slipping her arms into a white shift. "I only went to the village to find you a dress. A local woman was kind enough to sell me one of hers, see?" He slid Rebecca over his shoulder while he pulled the garment down over her naked thighs, then brought her back into the cradle of his arms. "Rebecca, we're going back to camp. You can sleep all you like once we get there. I won't leave you again."

Although she was aware of his words, she couldn't really understand why Azim was being so kind to her. If only she could speak, but she was afraid to come out of her protective shell. There had been so much pain these last few months. If only she could sleep, forever. The thought alone was enough to make her slip into a semiconscious state so she did not realize that Azim had carried her to their camp, nor did she stir when he took her in his arms and lay next to her.

Azim finally drifted off into a restless slumber himself. Later, he awoke thinking of all the events that had thrown them together these past few months. He tried to realistically see her point of view. Each time they had met he had protected himself from her natural charm by offering a cold front, but more often then not, the facade had melted away and turned into a desire for her. Did he fear the beautiful creature who lay beside him? Did he fear losing his way of life to a more gentle English one? His mind refused to answer. Perhaps there was no solution.

Tiny, sharp rays of light, tugged at Rebecca's eyes. Gentle hands stroked at her womanly form. She fought the instinct to sleep on endlessly. Her dark lashes stirred and she opened her eyes. Little of the previous night came back to her. When she became frightened, Azim murmured words of assurance. She did not have the fortitude to fight him, or hate him. She clasped his body tightly to her own while he kissed her eyes, her throat—he whispered words of love, desire, and need of her. Rebecca answered with her body. With the silent response of desperation she clung to his maleness. There was security in his arms, and oblivion.

Her voice, when it came, was barely audible. "Take me to our special place . . . I must live again. My baby must survive."

Azim slipped her shift off, taking great care not to break the spell. She was right. She must survive. He took his time with her, slowly, gently bringing her to a response. His lips seared her skin where they touched. Though his passion demanded urgent release, he stopped himself at her entrance, remembering the last time he had taken her that way. Instead, he sought her breasts. Her nipples readily replied to his tongue, her back arched, she wanted him.

Azim entered her slowly, with great care. He would not harm the infant. He moved inside her, rhythmically, tenderly. He felt the stirrings of life both from Rebecca and from the baby and was moved beyond desire. Never had he wanted and adored a woman this way. He had taken his time with her and she was having wave after wave of ecstasy, culminating in one long ebb of bliss. Azim reached his peak instantly upon feeling her final response.

They lay together, unspeaking, for a long time. The yellow autumn sun bathed them in gold. She was the first one to speak. "Azim, I don't know what you must think of me . . . Perhaps you were right about my wanton ways. I can only thank you for bringing me back to life again. I'll be fine now, but still," she paused, "I feel that I'm on the edge of an abyss, and I can't stand much more."

"I won't touch you again." he replied softly. "I do understand, Rebecca. Soon you'll be home. Meera should be there. I saw the governor briefly in Kabul and he assured me that William and Meera made it safely back home. I'm sure Mountstuart told them of your capture and of my intent to free you." He was quick to see her alarm. "It's all right, we won't tell them about the stay in the mud hut, or the slave market either."

Azim was so careful with her that she began to cry. He let her, no, wanted her to sob, for he knew that she was seeking release. They could travel tomorrow, for the present she needed to rest from the emotional exhaustion. He looked at her swelling stomach, her fully rounded breasts, deeply longing for the impossible. It was with great difficulty that he forced back his own sense of loss for what could never be.

Rebecca was withdrawn for the remainder of the journey, her breakdown behind her. He had been treating her with extreme care. She felt like a frail china doll for he was always at hand to assist her. His manner was brotherly, but his eyes betrayed him. She was certain that Azim wanted her, desired her as much as she did him. Why couldn't he say the words? She would tell him of her love and the baby, she would follow him to the ends of the earth. The situation was impossible, for they would be in Kabul in a short while and Azim would return to the northern steppes. She was married, her husband controlling her estate; no good could come from her confession. He would only turn hard and accusingly toward her.

One late afternoon, only several miles from Kabul, they stopped at a chaikana, one of the many rest stops along the caravan routes which served both tea and food. They sat outside in the brisk autumn air and sipped their tea. Rebecca could not believe that they would be ending their journey so soon. She held onto the moment, indeed, she clung to the time they would be together before riding into Kabul. Azim spent the hour sitting with his back propped up against a rock, his knees hugged by his arms. Rebecca thought that he had never looked so handsome, so relaxed, in the atmosphere of the caravan trail. He talked at length about the various travelers, the myriad of people who used the ancient routes.

Rebecca smiled at him, her eyes catching the golden afternoon light. "My father loved the caravan life, too. He spent hour upon hour telling me about the land and people. It's pleasant to hear stories again, for William doesn't—"

She cut the words off and sipped at her tea instead. Why spoil the magic of their moments discussing how much William loathed the land!

Azim studied her face, the delicate way her neck

arched up into her chin. She was exquisite, serene now in her enjoyment of his tales. "Rebecca, I never told you how deeply sorry I was to hear of the tragic loss of your father. He was an intelligent man and I admired and respected him greatly. Lawrence was one of the few men who appreciated the proud life of the Afghans. He even went so far as to encourage their struggles against the British. Yes, I know you must feel a dreadful loss—"

Rebecca flew to her feet. How dare he speak so admirably about her father, when he wouldn't even show her one ounce of respect! Why if her father were alive he would thrash Azim for his treatment of her! How easily he could smugly sit there and talk about Lawrence, without one kind word for her feelings or her respect for the people. She turned her back on him in a temper and strode away.

Azim was dumbfounded by her reaction. He shrugged his broad shoulders and returned the tea mugs to the chaikana. Who the devil could understand a woman anyway?

The next day, entering the British compound, Rebecca slowed her horse and turned to Azim. "I apologize for my rude behavior yesterday at the chaikana. It was uncalled for." However, she offered no explanation for her actions.

Azim studied her one more time before coming up her drive. He smiled at her show of pride, the fact that she would not bother to explain herself.

"Apology accepted, little flower. But now let me think of how best to approach St. Claire. Do me one small favor, and let me do all the talking." He thought of William and let the long unspoken question form into words. "Rebecca, tell me truthfully, does St. Claire beat you?"

"Not that way! I mean . . . not with a whip or anything. It's just that he drinks a little sometimes and comes to me at night—" She broke off, seeing an unreadable mask cover his face. Why had he asked her if he was only going to brood over her answer?

She took her eyes from his grave expression to see Meera running from the house with opened arms, nearly dragging Rebecca from her horse. William emerged also, but his features did not reveal pleasure. His face was wooden with an artificial smile.

CHAPTER 21

Cold, unreadable eyes, outstretched hand, Azim dismounted and approached him. "St. Claire, we have never been properly introduced, my name is . . . Alex Drayton. If you care to be civilized about this, I suggest that we—"

William drew back in surprise, then smoothed a displaced strand of hair with nervous fingers.

"I think, sir," he said coldly, "that I can take care of my wife from now on. Thank you for delivering her home safely. Now, I'm sure if there was any financial responsibility you had to bear, I can take care of it—"

Azim shouldered past William escorting Rebecca into the house.

Her gaze flew to Azim's face in horror as they entered the sitting room. What on earth would he tell William? But no, he had promised to handle the explanation, and she was not to be afraid.

He was turning to face William, saying between clenched teeth, "St. Claire, you are amazingly fortunate to have your wife back at *all*. It does not seem to me that you have been very successful in taking care of her. I hope you manage to do better in the future." His tone was scathing.

Rebecca feared that they would come to blows. "Azim . . . Mr. Drayton, please!"

William's heated words interrupted her, "Now, see here, Drayton! I'll not have you speak to me like that! I was almost killed in that attack, I'll have you know!

What could I do in this uncivilized country to find her? I refuse to take any blame! And now, perhaps you will leave us . . . My wife can tell me anything I wish to know about this . . . adventure . . .," he threw a sidelong glance of disgust at her.

"Rebecca . . . Mrs. St. Claire does not owe *you* any explanation. She was captured and held for ransom by some very greedy men. It was pure luck that I happened to find out where they took her."

"I'm sure she can tell me herself!" William glared at her.

Rebecca sat huddled in a chair, wondering whether to interrupt the two angry men. She was tired and shaken and badly wanted to escape, but was afraid to leave them together in the same room. She prayed Azim would not try William's patience too far, or she and the rest of the household would suffer for it.

Azim glanced at her and saw her fear and misery. He felt a wave of pity for her, but hardened his heart. After all, she was home, reunited with her husband, the father of her child. This was the life she had chosen for herself.

"I doubt if Mrs. St. Claire is enjoying this scene, sir. I think we should spare her any further distress. If you will forgive my abrupt departure, I shall leave you both to your joyful reunion." Turning to her, he said in an icy tone, "I hope your health remains good, Mrs. St. Claire."

He spun on his heel and disappeared through the doorway. Rebecca gave a sigh, made up equally of relief and regret. Now she had to deal with William.

He was eying her with fury. "How *could* you bring that dirty native into my house? As if you haven't caused me enough trouble, you have to disappear, *again,* and be returned by *him*! It embarrassed me greatly, Rebecca, and I don't take kindly to that!" He stalked up and down the room, his sallow face growing purple with rage. "You've upset my plans for the last time, my dear, from now on you will be a model wife, quiet and demure! You will stay at home and you will never see that filthy turn-coat again!" He stopped, a vicious smile lit up his face. "Is he your latest lover, Rebecca? What vile things have you let him do to you? You're a slut at heart, aren't you?"

She had sat with bowed head during his tirade, but his last accusation was to much to stand. She summoned whatever dignity was left to her and looked up at him.

Her brown eyes flashed. "If you ever touch me again, William, I promise that you will pay!" Her words were quiet, icy. "I shall remain here for the sake of the baby and for appearances and I shall be a dutiful wife to you in all respects. But if you ever dare to lay a finger on my person, you will find yourself quite alone." Her eyes did not flinch, and was gratified to note a shadow of doubt flicker in his face.

"Don't you threaten me, Rebecca!" He blustered. 'I'm your husband!"

"I am not threatening you. I am offering you a compromise that will work for both of us, a bargain, if you will . . . And now, I really am exhausted. I want to see Meera, have a bath and a good night's sleep. Will that inconvenience you terribly?"

He muttered sullenly, "No, go ahead, have your bath."

She knew she had won her first battle. She kept her head high and her back straight as she left the room and climbed the stairs. She went directly to her old room and collapsed on the bed, sobbing at last, her emotions taking over.

Meera flew into the room like a whirlwind a minute later, threw herself on her knees in front of Rebecca and hugged her, crying, "Missy Sahib, Missy, you are back. I am being so worried! . . . Oh, Missy . . . is baby being fine?"

"Yes, Meera, the baby is fine, and I am well, too. My body is, at any rate . . . I am so glad to see you. What happened when we were attacked? It was so horrible. It seems like years ago!"

"Oh, Missy, guns terrible! Noise everywhere, but Mahmud was saving me. He was throwing me behind tree and shooting back at bad mans! Oh, Mahmud very brave man! He was bringing Sahib William and me back to Kabul. Oh Missy! Sahib William being so mad! All the way he swearing and cursing. I was being afraid gods come down and punish him soon."

Rebecca could picture William furious at her disappearance, being guided back to Kabul by the silent Mahmud. Although it certainly seemed that Mahmud had impressed Meera, if not William. What was going on here? Was Meera truly serious about Mahmud?

"Meera, have you been seeing Mahmud all this time?" she asked suspiciously.

Meera's eyes were fixed on the floor, but Rebecca could see the dark flush spread up to her forehead.

"Yes, Missy. I am liking Mahmud so much. Very hard talking to him but I am learning some words of Pashto and he is speaking English words. Are you not being angry at Meera?"

"No, Meera," laughed Rebecca through her tears, "I think Mahmud is a very nice man, too."

"I am being glad, Missy." Meera looked up, dark eyes shining. "Mahmud is asking me respectfully to be his wife, but only if Missy says this is being all right."

"Oh, Meera! That is wonderful! But whatever will I do without you?" She thought of the lonely months ahead of her, married to William, without even Meera for companionship. Her heart gave a throb.

"Don't be worrying, Missy," Meera hastened to explain. "Mahmud is promising to live in Kabul all winter so I can be staying with my lady while she is having baby. I am not leaving you, Missy"

"Thank God, Meera! I couldn't face William all winter without you!"

Meera said nothing but went about preparing a bath for Rebecca, and laying out a fresh nightgown. She felt very sad for her mistress and had often talked to Mahmud about her. Yet, she had never voiced her suspicion as to whom the father of Rebecca's baby was. If Rebecca wanted Azim to know, she would tell him, or perhaps she had told him and he didn't care. Oh, her poor mistress!

Rebecca went to bed that night, her body clean and refreshed. She had almost forgotten what a soft bed and clean sheets felt like. But even though her body was comfortable, her mind was bludgeoned by misery. She had been abandoned by the man she loved. Yes, she had to admit even to herself that she loved him.

But worse, he thought her a deceitful lewd female who had lain with him while carrying another man's child! How unfairly he judged her! If only he had listened when she had tried to explain. If only she had been able to overcome her pride and confess the truth to him. But really, what difference would it have made? She was married to another man for better or for worse and she would have to face her years of marriage with whatever courage she could summon. She drifted off to sleep, wishing she were back in the uncomplicated universe of a half-ruined mud hut somewhere in the Hindu Kush.

At breakfast the next morning, William was withdrawn and cold. He ignored her with studied rudeness and departed for the governor's mansion. She filled her day with resting and reading from the small collection of books her father had brought with him from England. That day she immersed herself in a copy of Dickens' *Oliver Twist,* one of her father's favorites.

William returned late and began drinking brandy immediately. By the time supper was served he was glassy-eyed. Rebecca had noticed that liquor always had the effect on him of making him surly and oversensitive. His state of inebriation disgusted Rebecca, but she decided to say nothing. He would only react badly to anything she might venture.

William finished eating and pushed away his barely-touched plate. He leaned his elbows on the table and stared malevolently at her while she tried to choke down her meal. His glare made her nervous; she fumbled and couldn't swallow. Finally she gave up and put her fork down.

"What's the matter, dear, lost your appetite? From the pounds you've put on, it doesn't look like you've lost it!" He laughed loudly at his witticism.

Rebecca blushed profusely, aware of her growing belly. She wanted to hide. She must be an affront to William every time he looked at her, and he would never let her forget it.

"Excuse me, I'm very tired. I think I'll go to my room."

"Go on! What do I care? You're not much good anymore anyway. The whores in the bazaar are better than you are!" he shouted, slurring his words.

After she left, he sat at the table continuing downing brandy until he fell asleep in the chair with his head on the linen tablecloth.

Her days soon took on a sameness that was only bearable to Rebecca because William was home very seldom. He worked all day, came home late, and began drinking immediately. His face was beginning to look puffy and unhealthy, criss-crossed by a network of broken capillaries. When fortified by alcohol he insulted her, even in front of the servants and tradesmen. Only Meera's presence made him hold his tongue.

William devised a new torture, asking Rebecca over and over again what had happened when she had been abducted. She refused to answer, but her silence only had the effect of infuriating him more. He berated her, offering his own version of what had transpired during her capture. It was always of degrading and repulsive acts of licentiousness which he described in full detail to her. Rebecca listened as long as she could stand it, then fled from the room, her hands over her ears.

William took to leaving the house at night with increasing frequency to consort with the bazaar prostitutes. He was very obvious about it, not trying to hide from the neighbors when he returned in the morning. Rebecca was past caring what William did, so long as she was left in peace. She attempted to arrange her days so as to come in contact with him as little as possible.

Rebecca's body rounded gradually and her health remained good. She often walked out to the stables to bring Alia a lump of sugar. The filly was restless and fat having had no exercise in weeks. She wished she could leap on the horse's back and gallop toward the mountains, light and free as the air, to another time, another existence. The bright cool air of autumn on the high plateau was invigorating, but she felt trapped in her own small world, closed in by convention, by her gender, by hate and disappointment. Her large eyes often turned of their own accord toward the Hindu Kush. The peaks were beginning to whiten as they collected their winter mantle. Each day now they shrugged their mighty shoulders to accept a heavier burden of snow. She thought of the hasty grave of the dead man she had buried near the ruined hut and pictured it covered with snow, the cold bones frozen into the iron-hard earth. The flowers would all be dead.

Rebecca had put her emotions into a locked vault. She tried to keep her mind occupied with household activities and plans for the baby. She had begun to sew tiny garments for the child. Meera helped her with this activity, being an expert with the needle.

The women chatted gaily over their sewing while William was absent. Mahmud and Meera's approaching wedding was her favorite subject.

The ceremony would be in a week. Mahmud had insisted that it follow the Turkoman tradition of the northern steppes. There had been some argument about this, as Meera was Hindu and Mahmud Moslem, but she had given in to his desires as Afghanistan was to be her adopted country from now on, and she wanted to accept their customs with her usual good grace. She was very excited about her impending marriage, and

Rebecca envied Meera her happy future. Hers still stretched unendingly, bleakly into the future.

As Meera's wedding day approached, preparations continued feverishly, for the wedding party would arrive at the St. Claire's residence in the morning to partake of a meal before "spiriting" the bride away to her new husband's home. Nur Mustafa, at last, was in his element. He made it very clear that he would stand for no ferangi women in his kitchen while he prepared the refreshments. For this feast, only his own artistry was needed! He scurried around his kitchen all day, muttering and cursing in Pashto and Persian, lifting lids of steaming stews, adding seasonings to his rice.

Meera was preparing her own wedding garments. She was to wear a crown-like hat covered with trailing scarves of bright colors and a circlet of heavy silver ornaments and bells. She would be hidden under this regalia while she traveled by camel from her present home to her new life.

William finally noticed the preparations one day and asked about them. When Rebecca explained to him what would take place, he became furious.

"Do you mean to say that you are going to allow a troop of heathenish lice-ridden natives in my home?" he yelled, his face contorted in rage.

Rebecca drew a deep breath and tried to control herself. He had been drinking again and would turn vicious if she angered him in any way.

"William, please. Meera has no family to give her away and she will lose face if there is no home to offer hospitality to the wedding guests when they come to fetch her. It is very important to her . . . I implore you, William."

He gave in with bad grace being a little afraid to push Rebecca too far, knowing how close she was to Meera.

"Well, at least I'll be at my office and won't have to see the filthy peasants." he retorted.

Rebecca said nothing but was very glad that Meera was away on an errand at the time.

The next morning, William went through the household accounts and spotted a large withdrawal. He had an idea what it might be and strode purposefully to Rebecca's room to confront her. He threw open the door without knocking. She was half-dressed, her robe hanging open over a revealing petticoat. She looked up, startled by the intrusion, and gasped. He was quite sober, for it was morning, but his bloodshot eyes were devouring her ripening figure and loose golden curls.

She pulled her robe around her tightly and braced herself for an unpleasant encounter.

"And what, may I ask, is this withdrawal for one hundred pounds?" He was eying her accusingly, thrusting the account book out in front of him like a dagger.

"That is for Meera's dowry. She needed linens and household items to start a new home, as all women do, William." She answered him coolly enough, refusing to give ground, but her heart beat fast with trepidation.

"I thought it might be something like that! It is out of the question! I am not her father and I shall not allow you to spend a shilling on her! Why, she's only a servant!"

"William, Meera is my friend. She deserves a dowry whether she is a servant or a great lady. If you will not provide money for her dowry, then I shall just have to sell some of my jewelry at the bazaar. Just think what people would say of you then! William St. Claire is so close with money, his wife has to barter her jewelry! And may I remind you, William, the money you refer to is really mine, left to me by my father and grandfather. You might be a little less niggardly with it!"

"You wouldn't dare sell your jewelry!" he hissed.

"I would do it in a minute for Meera. Don't doubt my word!"

He looked at her for a moment, fury etched on his every feature. She was afraid he would strike her, but she stood tall and refused to waver in front of him.

He turned suddenly and stalked out of her room, slamming the door so hard that a vase of flowers fell off of her table with a crash. She sank down onto her bed, trembling with reaction. She wondered how long this could go on.

The morning of Meera's wedding dawned clear but with a hint of frost in the air. The trees were covered with leaves in jeweled tones, smoke drifted up in lingering trails to lie on the clear autumn sky and the far-off cry of the muezzins could be heard. Luckily, it had not rained lately, so the streets were dry, not the morass of mud they usually were in the fall.

Meera was so excited that her trembling fingers could not fasten the complicated wedding garments and she humbly asked Rebecca to help. She chattered incessantly the whole time, sometimes in Hindi, sometimes in English, sometimes in Pashto, practicing the phrases she would have to repeat during the wedding ceremony. Her lighthearted mood was infectious.

"Missy, will Meera be liking wedding night? I am being so afraid, not knowing what men and ladies doing together."

"Meera," said Rebecca blushing, "I'm sure you will be delighted with your wedding night. Mahmud will know exactly what to do."

"Missy, will Meera be getting baby like you? What fun, having babies together!"

"Oh, Meera, stop asking questions and let me fix this veil. It doesn't seem to fall correctly. There!"

Meera was ready at last, her happiness hidden by her veil and headdress. She had become a mysterious figure, the archetypal woman of Asia, voluminous and rich fabrics concealing the woman awaiting fulfillment.

The camel caravan was led by Mahmud's second cousin, Holkar, as the eldest family member present. Rebecca and Meera could hear the tinkling of the silver bells that decorated the festive harnesses of the camels as they approached. Rebecca could see nothing of Meera's face behind the veil, but she could feel Meera's hand squeeze her own and hold it tightly.

Some members of the procession were on horses,

others on camels, but all were laughing and joking, teasing the gruff Mahmud until he grinned with embarrassment. Azim was in the crowd, also, but preferred to stay out of sight at Rebecca's house.

They fought a mock skirmish at the door of the house, the ceremonial "abduction" of the bride. Rebecca watched with fascination, not wanting to miss a thing, as she could not join in the festivities at the bridegroom's house because of her pregnancy. She wondered if Azim were there, and surreptitiously searched the crowd for his tall figure, but could not find it.

The wedding party then partook of the feast that Nur Mustafa had created, all except for Meera, who could not eat until her veil was removed later that night.

Afterward, Holkar led a camel up to the door. It was bedecked with finery and provided a wooden platform to hold the bride. Then he helped Meera to climb onto the platform. The women of Holkar's family who had come along wished Meera prosperity and happiness as she was led away, and the men prayed to Allah to bless the marriage. Meera and the merry cavalcade, bells tinkling, voices babbling, disappeared down the street toward the groom's home where the marriage ceremony would take place. Rebecca watched them go, her heart laden with both a great happiness and a great sadness. She felt that a part of her life was gone forever.

At the house that Mahmud had provided for his new wife, the party had another meal: endless varieties of pilau, lamb, sour milk cheese, and fruit. After dinner, Mahmud approached his bride with a *mullah*,, a Moslem religious man, and two witnesses, one of whom was Azim. They all retired into another room as the ceremony was brief and private.

The short questions asked and answered, the mullah blessed and congratulated the newly married couple and they were left alone for the night.

Azim left the room with the mullah after the short

ceremony. He joined the festivities, but was noticeably restrained in his behavior. He wanted to leave shortly, his present depression contrasting sharply with the merriment of the wedding party, but knew it would be an affront to Mahmud's family. He wanted his friend's wedding to be perfect in all respects. A night to be remembered fondly for a lifetime.

CHAPTER 22

It had been difficult for Azim to watch the loving glances that Mahmud bestowed upon the nuptial-veiled figure that was Meera in her wedding finery. Mahmud's decision to marry had weighed heavily on Azim, for he knew he would miss the man's comradeship in the long winter months ahead. But even more than that, the happiness, the hope etched in Mahmud's face made it achingly clear to him just what he could never have. He tried to tell himself that it didn't matter, but the burden of realization remained. His only chance for love was lost in another man's arms.

Even as he took part in the festivities, his thoughts were tugged back to the ugly scene of the previous night. Vengeance and hate were strong emotions, Azim had learned, often leading a man into dark alleys, only to come face to face with himself in the end. He had lived the days since his return to Kabul with little else on his mind but revenge, and now he found that the wedding was marred for him by the memory of his own bloody deed.

After Azim had left Rebecca in the uncertain care of her husband, he had rested only briefly at Mahmud's house. His days and nights were filled with possible plots against Suraj Mal. Azim had put the fat mendacious man from his mind when they left Bukhara. Then, his only concern had been for Rebecca's welfare, but now he let the hate wash over him like a surging tide. The desire to carry out the vendetta flooded over him, drowning out all other emotions.

The plot was basically simple. His only problem had been to get Suraj Mal alone, away from his band of cutthroats. Azim knew that would involve a third party, a man trusted by Suraj, but one that could be manipulated.

Several days had passed before Azim thought of the perfect conspirator. He had gone to Governor Mountstuart to thank him for his assistance and discretion while Azim was obtaining the funds to save Rebecca. There hadn't been enough time to explain, and Mountstuart had openly and freely helped Azim sign a note that the bank had not questioned.

Azim had been in the process of thanking the governor, when a young corporal entered Mountstuart's office with some papers to be signed. Azim sat back in a comfortable leather chair observing the scene. Suraj Mal's words came swiftly back to him, "I have my ears in the governor's mansion!" The problem was nearly solved! If only the identity of the traitor could be secured, he could force the man to betray Suraj Mal. The man would surely want to save his own neck!

Leaving the mansion, Azim delayed for a moment to question the doorman. As casually as possible, he inquired, "Who here is closest to the governor?"

The discreet doorman, not wanting to tell tales, at first refused to talk about Mountstuart's private affairs, which forced Azim into telling a blatant lie—the governor, himself, had personally asked Azim to review his nearest confidents. "You understand the problem, it's to be done discreetly. I'll count on your ability to keep a secret."

With a sense of pride and duty, the loyal man replied in a low voice. "But of course. You need only have given your credentials. The men closest to the governor are, Corporal McBain, his Secretary William St. Claire and possibly one or two others."

Azim thanked the man, bid him keep his mouth

closed and left the mansion. He spent the next few days checking out the information. He quickly dismissed St. Claire and turned his attention to McBain. Spying was not to Azim's liking, but he would wait the soldier out and hope he had properly judged the situation. The waiting was rewarded on the third day, for Corporal McBain, out of uniform, strode silently through the night to the bazaar area. Azim was awaiting him when the man emerged from Suraj Mal's quarters.

Urging McBain into a dark alley, knife pricking in his ribs, Azim hushed him. "If you value your worthless life, you'll keep silent."

McBain nodded his head.

Azim released the hold on the man's mouth and continued, "Your game is over, McBain. So far, only *I* have guessed your connection with Suraj Mal. You can keep things that way or you can have your traitorous neck stretched! Which is it to be?"

"How can I trust you? What do you want of me?"

The trap well-laid, Azim answered in a slow, steady voice. "Set that pig, Suraj Mal, up for me. We'll decide on a plausible story for him, one that will overly tempt his greed. I need only a few minutes alone with him and I'll even give him a fair chance to save himself, for I'm no murderer. Once the man has met his fate you can return to your job. No one will be the wiser. You have my word. Besides, you have no choice."

There was truth in the hard stranger's words, so McBain readily agreed to assist. He would miss the flow of cash, but the dangers to himself had become a strain, and frankly, McBain would be more than glad to be rid of Suraj Mal. Steven McBain had told Azim as much, and Azim had every reason to believe him. The conspirators agreed on a time and place to meet the following evening, McBain promising to have a scheme prepared. They had parted warily . . .

Azim had forgotten the wedding. "What makes you brood so, my good friend?" Mahmud was concerned that Azim did not approve of the marriage.

"It's unimportant," Azim smiled at his host. "I was only thinking about the past. And, where is Meera? In my native land, the friend of the groom is allowed a kiss! Bring her to me, so that I may claim her lips!" Azim chuckled merrily at Mahmud's reaction.

"Meera would never kiss you! Have you lost your senses?" Mahmud did not know if he were serious or not until Azim's rumbling laughter told him that his young English friend was truly jesting. Mahmud relaxed and grinned.

He felt a deep love for his friend. If only the man could be as happy as he was at this minute. But to bring up the subject of Rebecca would only cause much pain. Mahmud kept his silence and joined the other guests.

Absentmindedly picking up a slice of roast lamb, Azim thought back to the events leading up to his encounter with Suraj Mal. McBain had proven himself to be a man of his word. When they met again, McBain had formulated a sound method to get Suraj Mal alone in an abandoned hut outside the city. His plan involved a story of gold and silver being transported by caravan to the governor's mansion. A greedy camel driver wanted to make a profit on this trip, but did not want to steal the gold himself. He wished only to allow the robbers to have their way, and then they could split the stolen goods. The fabricated camel driver was old, and fearful that his identity would be revealed. Above all, he sought to protect his reputation and would meet only with Suraj Mal, and alone.

Azim thought the story was reasonable enough for Suraj to lick his fat lips and think only of a tidy sum to line his purse. Azim and McBain worked out the minor details of the plot, then parted company. McBain trusted the tall Englishman and thought that Azim must hate Suraj Mal very much indeed to go to so much trouble.

The meeting between the camel driver and Suraj Mal was planned for the following evening. Azim dressed for the part, and counted on the corporal to keep his end of the bargain. Azim had gone so far as to tell McBain that if anything went wrong on his part, a letter would be delivered to Mountstuart the very next day. McBain did not believe Azim, but who really knew?

The last glimmering rays of light illuminated the walls of the crumbling mud hut. Azim was unrecognizable; he wore the garb of his fictitious camel driver, stooped, and let one arm hang loosely. His appearance was aged by ten years. He had gone so far as to procure a camel and tethered the smelly beast nearby. The sun remained longer than Azim had counted on, but darkness was beginning to blanket the eastern sky.

He let out a sigh of relief when he saw Suraj Mal approaching the hut astride a horse. If Suraj were not alone, Azim would face that detail when, and if, it arose. He had prepared for the encounter as best he could.

Azim's nerves were wound tight, his muscles tensed, his lithe body ready for the clash. He could already taste the sweet flavor of victory. Suddenly Azim was a primitive beast, stalking his prey, savoring the moments before success. A small doubt flickered through his mind; it sprouted, seed-like, and grew strong. Azim recalled his mother's gentle readings of the Bible. But why now?

Her soft voice spanned the years and reached his consciousness—but he did not want to listen. "Vengeance is mine, sayeth the Lord!"

Azim fought the eerie impression, shaking her warning off. He honed his nerves as if they were blades. A devil possessed his body. Nothing would stop him.

Suraj Mal steadied himself on the mount when he saw the camel driver. His wide, hairy nostrils flared slightly. Had he smelled a deception? No, he doubted it. Many people sought Suraj out to further their own desires; this was no different. His close-set eyes scoured the area for a possible trap, but could perceive none. If this old man had laid a trap, then Suraj had a weapon on his person. One shot would bring his men who waited impatiently nearby. Suraj dismounted some yards away, studying the stranger.

"Inside . . . someone may see us . . . I have my reputation, you know!" the camel driver croaked in Pashto.

Suraj Mal felt for his concealed gun. It was in place. Cautiously he entered the hut.

Azim had his strong arm around the obese man's neck, choking off his air before Suraj could react.

His voice was dry, emotionless. "Suraj Mal, stealer of women, traitor to men, you have neatly fallen into my trap. I knew only a greedy pig such as you would respond so readily."

With that he tightened his forearm, causing the man's small eyes to pop like tiny black beads. He could feel Suraj Mal's drool on his own arm. The bulbous man sickened him. He would be done with him.

"I should cut your thick neck this minute," Azim jeered, "but that would be too easy. Instead, I give you the chance to kill me!" He raked Suraj Mal's nerves with his low laugh.

When Azim's grip loosened, the merchant fell back against the wall with a heavy thud. His hands went to his throat and rubbed the white layers of fat. He waited for Azim to make a move. Azim leered at him, waiting for the man to reach for a concealed weapon, for he knew that the insidious coward would have certainly come prepared.

Suraj Mal slowly lowered his hands to his sides. He hoped to deceive Azim with his words, all the while reaching for his pistol. "Come now, Azim. Perhaps we can make an arrangement. I would hate to have you spring on me without first explaining my motives in the case of the lovely Rebecca!" Suraj had hoped to set his opponent off guard with the mention of the girl. Noticing that Azim had narrowed his eyes, he continued to taunt. "She has an exquisite body, yes? Her breasts like ripe fruits in my hands . . ." He reached for his pistol when Azim's mouth tightened menacingly.

However, Azim was not fooled by the ploy. His foot and leg shot upward, catching Suraj Mal's hand and cracking the bones. The pistol dropped to the floor.

Suraj was in great pain, and prayed that Allah would deliver him, and clutching his hand, continued, "I even extracted her full response when I spread her soft thighs and entered—" Azim had him around the throat with one hand and bloodied his lip with the other. Suraj Mal slid to the floor, groping for the pistol, but Azim continued to wrestle with him on the stone.

Finally Azim untangled himself and stood over Suraj. He knew that the pistol was within the man's grasp, yet waited. Suraj grabbed for the gun just as Azim's high-heeled boot ground his hand into the unyielding floor. The sound of crushed bones could be heard in the still night.

Suraj moaned. "Why not just kill me now? You are enjoying this, aren't you?"

Azim reached down, slowly, to his leather boot, and pulled out a curved knife. Crouching down to the man's shrinking form, Azim spat directly in his face.

In Pashto, he said, "You're quite correct, fat little man, I am prolonging your agony. Let no man make a fool of me, for he shall know of my wrath!"

With his left hand, Azim shoved Suraj Mal's head into the ruined wall. With his right hand, he calmly, expertly, slit Suraj Mal's throat. Azim let his hands soak in the blood of his enemy. Quickly, he put aside the notion to cut the man's heart out and present it to Rebecca. He knew that the violent act would pleasure himself; he doubted that Rebecca would be pleased with the barbarous gift.

Meera approached Azim with a frown on her veiled features. He was so white that Meera feared he was suffering from his wound. "Sahib Azim, you must be resting leg or you being sick again. Mahmud not liking Azim to be passing out at wedding!"

Azim was unquestionably pale. Not from his injury,

but from the memory of his recent murderous act. Only last night, he had gone to a stream and washed Suraj Mal's blood from his hands. He vaguely wondered if the cool waters would ever wash away the memory of the brutality to which he had succumbed.

"I'm sorry, Meera. I fear I have put a wet blanket on your good mood. My leg is fine, and I won't ask where you found out about it in the first place. I was only thinking of the coming snows and of the long journey home."

He had almost said, *back alone,* but he knew that Mahmud had enough difficulty justifying his decision to remain in Kabul for the winter. Suddenly, Azim longed to wipe the filth of the city from his feet and return to the steppes where a man could think clearly in the beauty and solitude of the land.

"Azim, Missy St. Claire is being sad lady. Will you be seeing Missy before going to village?"

Azim had asked himself that same question a hundred times, but not a week ago he had sworn to stay out of her life. There were a few questions he would like her to answer. Only Rebecca could give him the peace of mind that he sought. Suraj Mal's insinuation that Rebecca had slept with him rankled his composure.

He confided in the newly-wed girl, "Yes, Meera. I think I shall see your mistress again."

Azim drank himself into a stupor that night. Before he staggered to his bed, he wondered what powers Rebecca possessed that caused her men to resort to drink.

CHAPTER 23

Azim had several loose ends to tie up before he began the trek back through the pass. The trees in Kabul had long since shed their leaves, leaving the ground blanketed with color. The earth smelled fresh and alive to him, even as the rotting foliage imbedded itself in the mud. Contrarily, he felt a rebirth of his spirit. Autumn held a note of sadness, but the soon-to-fall snows would usher in a new spring, a new life for all nature, a new beginning for Azim.

On one such crisp morning, he walked to the Mountstuart's in order to say his farewells before the onslaught of winter, which would prevent his return. He ambled slowly to the mansion, taking in the brisk air, shuffling his boots through the crackling leaves. The sun was high and bright, shining golden on the bared branches. The weight of the love he had just recognized lay heavy on his shoulders. Yet, he also felt a fresh horizon opening to him. He would seek out Rebecca this very day, for the last time, and then he could renew his chosen life in the northern steppes.

The doorman ushered Azim into the governor's drawing room. Before he turned to leave, he gave Azim a knowing smile. If the poor man had only known to what use his information had been put, Azim was certain he would have been mortified.

Some minutes later Mountstuart came rather hurriedly into the room.

"Oh, Alex! I'm happy you stopped by. We really did not know where to reach you, but at any rate, I have a letter here from your brother, Lord Blackstone." He handed over the weighty packet and excused himself to afford Azim some moments alone to enjoy the letter.

Azim seated himself comfortably on a sofa, and started to read the message that had been written six months ago.

London, May, 1882

My Dear Brother,

I should hope that this dispatch will reach you before winter, but with the piracy on the high seas these days, it may take years! My lovely wife, Carla, is expecting our fourth child in a matter of hours. Haven't I always written to you on these occasions? It helps me to pass these difficult times.

I am hoping for a daughter, the three boys remind me too much of yourself. Pardon my impertinence, but they are really quite wild! Robert forever talks of his "romantic" Uncle Alex; the boy would fly to you immediately, but I try to discourage his notions. Alex and John are well, but they are forever in their tutor's hair.

The estates are more profitable than ever this season. When you return, you will be a very wealthy man in your own right. Oh, have no fear, I pay a handsome fee to your namesake, Alex. He does little, but I thought you would want to contribute some monies to his schooling.

The doctor has just informed me that Carla has hours to go yet.

Azim chuckled silently to himself. He read on and on. His brother, Stuart, was a kind and considerate man, never a vile word for anyone. He was, however, devious in his methods to convince Alex to return to England. Always the newsy letters, pretending that Alex had left England only yesterday, never the mention of the gossip that must, most assuredly, have reached his ears, never a word about their lost parents.

Azim's eyes dropped to an interesting note in the lengthy letter:

> By the way, do you remember our friend, George Merideth? I'm sad to tell you that he passed away rather suddenly a few months back. The man was grandfather to a lovely girl of about eighteen or nineteen. At any rate, she went to Kabul, of all places, to join her father. Perhaps you know the chap, Lawrence Merideth? Some high position with the East India Company, I believe. We shall all mourn the loss of his father, George.

Azim reread the paragraph, knitting his brows together in concern. No wonder she had been so distraught! First losing her grandfather, then, almost immediately, her father. Odd coincidence. Would she always be shrouded in grief? He hoped not.

The letter ended, as usual, with the birth of the baby. Azim laughed to hear that he was once again an uncle, the gods having smiled favorably on Stuart and Carla—the baby girl was named Charlotte. Alex felt a pang of pride in his nephews and now his niece. Azim shuddered inwardly at the awesome responsibility.

Once he had related the news and gossip to Mountstuart, who always took an interest, he bade good-bye for the season, and left to see Rebecca. Prior to departing, however, he had purposely asked the doorman if Mr. St. Claire was at work today. He was.

Azim walked rather than rode the distance to the St. Claire's, needing the time to formulate the words he knew he must say. He told himself that for Rebecca's sake, and her unborn child, he would stay away from her. He silently prayed that he would have the courage to see his words through. Azim looked up into the sun, crinkling his gray eyes and speaking silent words of Pashto. In the Turkoman tradition, he gathered strength from the sustaining earth, the damp and fertile soil beneath his feet. Let him have the courage to face her and bid her a last farewell. The brilliant blue sky shone in his eyes, turning their color to light blue, reflecting the boldness and depth of the heavens. He felt ready to face her now and headed purposefully into her drive.

Since Rebecca's return, William had been consistently cruel toward her. She could stand his biting words and accusations, as long as he left her alone physically, but there were moments when she was ready to blurt out the truth about her kidnapping, simply for the pleasure of seeing his expression. William had nearly convinced her that she was heartless and conniving, caring little for anyone other than herself. She wondered if she were as selfish as William made her out to be. Perhaps he was right.

What were his stinging words one day? "You are cold, Rebecca. Like all beautiful women, you think only of your beauty. You use a man to flaunt your greed for recognition." She had become upset, but William made her hear him out. "Why do you think I drink so? You drive a man to it, Rebecca!" He had looked scornfully at her over the rim of his glass.

She had bolted from the room, crying. "It's not true! I'm not all those things!" William's bitter laugh had followed Rebecca to her room. She sobbed for a long time, his accusations having cut deeply, especially as she could see the ruins of her life spread out in front of her. William, on the other hand, was delighted to have found another weapon to use against her. The next few days, he had spent rubbing the salt into her wounded feelings.

She had gone over his words a thousand times in her mind. She couldn't possibly be as heartless or as vain as he said. But still, she remembered the many parties in London where she had certainly flirted outrageously with all the single men, knowing that they found her irresistible! She had even gone so far as to bat her eyelashes at them, trying to extract promises of undying love under the sharp eyes of her chaperon. Her girlfriends had giggled for days with her over the incidents. Even Azim had told her of her beauty. She had thrilled to hear his tender words. Did that mean she was insensitive to others?

What of forcing men to drink? Certainly William was driven. In truth, he had first approached her on the ship, intoxicated, declaring his love. Was that her fault? Both her grandfather and her father had enjoyed an occasional brandy. Was it a sickness she brought to men who were saddled with her?

She had let her imagination run rampant, sitting for days, unable to stem the flow of thoughts. Meera had asked her several times to open up her heart, but she knew that Meera was too busy with her own wedding preparations, and too happy to be burdened with Rebecca's latest problems.

When Azim turned the corner and strode toward her home Rebecca was sitting in front of her mirror. She had been unable to pin her hair up properly this morning, being all thumbs and lacking the assistance of Meera who was still away. Rebecca smiled on at the thought of the innocent's first encounter with a man. But the smile quickly changed to a frown at the thought of her own initial experience—wet, naked in the fading sun, ravished. She tried in vain to pin up her stray locks, but they only fell softly back to her shoulders. The effect was wanton; partially arranged, half-flowing curls with a will of their own. How did Meera manage?

Rebecca's dark eyes stared brightly, too brightly back at her from the mirror. Her cheeks were rosy this morning, the color enhanced by the deep shade of her crimson velvet dress. It had a high neck with long fitted sleeves, trimmed in beige lace, and the skirt had been altered to accommodate her swelling stomach. There was also a sash of the same soft velvet tied below her full bosom. Her hands were white and slightly swollen this morning, her wedding ring weighing heavily on her finger.

A sudden, far-off rumble of thunder brought her to her feet in a startled reaction. From the window she could see huge black clouds descending from the snowcapped peaks. The sun was still shining brightly on Kabul, but rain was imminent. In October, the city could be cloaked in sunlight one minute, then masked with cold rain and sleet the next.

She saw him then, coming up the drive. He was so handsome, so lithe, with his long sure strides. He was dressed like a European, so unlike the clothes that he had worn in the Bazaar that fatal day. The rays of autumn sun gilded his dark hair, and she recalled a time when she had likened his hair to the glossy mane of Khaled. His dark suit and waistcoat fit him perfectly. She could picture Alex Drayton entering a drawing room anywhere in London. He would certainly turn the ladies' heads. Rebecca had never known a man so vital, so attractive, in spite of the things he had done to her.

Snapping back to reality, she wondered anxiously why he had come. Her heart was pounding so that her full breasts threatened to break the seams of her gown. Thank god William was not here. Where were the servants? Then she realized that they disliked William anyway, and would say nothing of the unexpected visit. A slow, reverberating clap of thunder made Rebecca's heart jump as she made her way quickly down the stairs.

I must compose myself, Rebecca thought, as she threw open the front door. Why is he here? Her face showed her pleasure even as she tried to fight the emotion. She hadn't felt so alive in weeks.

Azim was slightly taken aback when the door opened unexpectedly. He had just been about to tap the brass knocker. He smiled warmly into her brown eyes.

Lord, but she was a treasure, her honey-colored hair cascading to her shoulders, her breasts large and rising with breathlessness.

"Rebecca? Aren't you going to ask me in?" he asked, clearing his throat.

She blushed. "I probably shouldn't. Azim . . . I suppose, for just a few minutes." Her voice had faltered. What in heaven's name had come over her? Did merely seeing him make her lose all reason?

Pushing the question out of her mind, she led him into the sitting room. He relaxed easily into William's favorite red leather chair, facing the fireplace. She seated herself on a small couch opposite him, the deep ruby in the Afghan rug picking up the color of her velvet dress. Azim took in every detail. She was growing more lovely with each day of her pregnancy. If only the child . . . but he dismissed the idea.

Awkwardly, Rebecca broke the silence. "I wish you wouldn't look at me that way. It . . . well, it's not at all fair . . ." Her voice was broken, her nerves raw.

Azim chuckled at her discomposure. "What way is that, Rebecca?" He teased her. But he knew that this meeting was not going as planned. His nerves did not feel as steady as his voice. How easily he had learned to conceal his emotions, he thought.

She stood and went to the window, her hands fumbling with her sash. She hesitated then went on. "Azim, you should not have come. If William were to find out, he would . . . be v⌄ry angry with me," she finished uneasily.

She turned and saw an ugly frown on his face. "If that bastard touches you, I'll murder him! Do you doubt me?"

"Not for a moment. It's just that you were the first to—" She could not finish, her words cut off by a burst of thunder.

Azim waited for the deafening noise to cease. He measured his words carefully. "That is why I came today. I wanted to see if he had believed my stilted version of the truth, or if he was harming you in any way. Rebecca, you don't have to put up with—Never mind. Just set my mind at rest. Are you all right?"

"I am quite well. He really doesn't harm me bodily. It's simply that he always says cruel things. Cruel, yes, but some of what he says is true. It just hurts to see yourself through someone else's eyes."

Rebecca studied a drop of rain spattering on the window. The sparkling drop blew diagonally across the glass, leaving a little of itself behind. Rebecca likened the weakening drop to her own life; she had already left a portion of herself behind. Death had claimed a small share, Azim had claimed his portion also. How much was left to her? She had almost been whispering aloud. Azim could not hear her musings, but he felt saddened for the lovely young woman who had been a part of his life. That was over now. In a few moments he would have to strengthen himself to make the break. His whole being felt empty, a void, unfulfilled.

Azim wondered what that bastard was saying to make her doubt herself. "What lies is he filling your head with?" His voice cut into her thoughts, low, menacing.

Rebecca finally answered him. "William says that I am shallow. Too beautiful to care for anyone but myself. He says that I drive him to drink and that I do things to anger him. I suppose he's right, Azim. Maybe I am unfeeling . . ." Tears of frustration spilled over her eyelashes. She hadn't meant to tell him that, but the words were out and rung true in the silence that hung between them. She shook involuntarily. Sleet was pounding against the glass. She was miserably chilled.

Azim stood, seeing her shiver in the damp air. He went to the fireplace and began absentmindedly to build a flame from the dying embers. From his stooped position, he motioned for Rebecca to sit down near the fire.

Then he laughed, a forced sound. "I suppose you believed him, didn't you? Rebecca, you are naive, maybe a little gullible, but you are not cold! Trust me, sweet, you are far from cold! Fiery, alive, and giving, yes, but never shallow!"

"But William said . . . and in a way he's right. I know that I'm pretty." She blushed at the immodesty of her statement.

Azim loved to watch her become rattled when she spoke too bluntly. "You are pretty, my blossom, very very pretty. Don't let William plant a seed of doubt in your mind. He's only using subtle forms of torture to bend you to do his will. Perhaps I have no right to say this, but from what I can gather, William is a weak small man." There, it was said. A plain statement of jealousy. To what had he lowered himself? Yet, he could not stand by and see her spirit broken by that coward.

The fire was raging now, throwing off a splendid warmth. Azim still crouched on his haunches poking the blazing logs. Rebecca looked at him, genuinely seeing the man. Yes, he was outrageously handsome, his strong profile glowing in the firelight, but he could also be tender, caring. Her head spun from his words. Was he jealous of William? Or was he simply comparing his own strength to William's weakness? Rebecca knew her hopeless love for this strange man and wept inside, torn by her deep feelings. Her fingers nervously twisted her wedding band. She wanted desperately to tell him that the baby was his. Her lips even parted, forming the words. He turned his muscular frame and stared at her. She looked into gray eyes and knew she could not tell him; he was a fool not to have known in the first place. Another woman might secure a man by getting herself with child, but what would happen when he realized that he didn't love her, and only took her with him because of the baby? No, she would never tell him. If he truly cared for her, he would have known that she would not come willingly to his bed carrying another man's child. Damn him anyway! Why couldn't she stop her heart from pounding?

Azim rose from his cramped position and casually

rested an elbow on the mantle. He saw her hands resting on her belly and thought that he could see the baby move when her fingers jumped slightly. Rebecca seemed very swollen for such a short pregnancy. She would undoubtedly bear her husband a strong male child. If only he had chosen a civilized existence, but life had shown him that his fate was with his adopted people. God, how he ached right now. He turned from her agonized gaze to pick up the brass-handled poker, shoving it into the flames.

Turning back to face her, he seated himself on the edge of the leather chair. He reached out one strong hand and took Rebecca's own trembling one. A current of feeling flowed between them. They clung to the emotion, their eyes telling the truth that their voices could not.

Azim's eyes never left hers, and when he spoke his voice was ragged. "Rebecca, I came to say good-bye. I leave this afternoon for my village. The winter snows will keep me from interfering again in your life." He pulled a gold ring from his finger and handed it to her. She took the ring and turned it, sudden tears filling her eyes, blotting out the details. It was a man's ring, bearing a family seal.

Azim continued, his bronzed hands clutching her white one, crushing her fingers against the ring. "If you ever need me, my flower, send the ring. Mahmud will bring it. Promise you'll summon me?"

Rebecca could hardly speak she was so choked with emotion. "I promise." She had to ask, "What if I'm in England? William wants to leave as soon as the baby can travel."

"I'd circle the earth ten times if you needed me. Never forget that, Rebecca." Azim released her hand and stood to lean against the mantle, gazing deep within the flickering lights.

Did he love her? Why couldn't he speak the words? But Rebecca knew that he would never utter what she longed to hear. It was useless.

Azim turned and looked at her as she sat gazing past him into the dancing flames. The storm was brutally beating down on the house, the wind whistling around the corners, and howling through the bare branches of the trees.

He spoke quietly. "Before I leave, you should know that you no longer need to fear our mutual friend, Suraj Mal. Before he expired—" Rebecca gasped in surprise. He went on, "No, I won't tell you the details. I'm not proud of the act. Let us just say that he made some insinuations about you. I'm afraid that I allowed him to anger me." Azim's face became like a hard stone mask.

Rebecca wondered what bloody deed he had committed. She knew and feared this dark mood of his. She almost pitied Suraj Mal, that obscene replica of a human being.

"What insinuations?" Her back stiffened. "Are you going to ask me if Suraj Mal bedded me?"

"I didn't really believe him, but still . . ."

He was actually asking her if she let Suraj Mal use her! What a joke. How like Azim to think the worst of her! Rebecca threw her head back, laughing wickedly in his shocked face.

She was half-hysterical. "But of course *you* would want to know! I let him have his every way with me. I enjoyed it! He was a great lover . . . He brought me to heights of pleasure . . ." Rebecca had crumbled under the violence of her own speech. She pulled her shaking knees up under her, hung her head, and wept again.

Azim was at her side in one long stride. He kneeled and forced her to look at him. Rebecca struggled against his hands.

He was ashamed. "God, I'm so sorry. I should have known that you would never let that pig touch you. It was just that he made me so damned mad—he sealed his own death warrant. Can you understand how I felt when he described your body? Forgive me, dearest." He was pleading and she felt him take her face between his palms and kiss her tears away. Would they ever be able to get along without the contest of passion between them?

The kiss of tenderness slowly became a kiss of desire. Azim's mouth covered hers, his tongue opened her lips and took her. Rebecca's lips involuntarily responded to his while her arms found his back and caressed him. He lifted her into his arms and carried her to the leather chair where she seemed to melt into his lap. They clung to each other as he murmured words of love in her ear. Her spine tingled as his head bent and kissed her breasts.

"I still want you, damn it—"

Rebecca found his mouth, hushing his thoughts. She could feel him hard and moving underneath her thighs. She was so hungry for him.

Azim's fingers found the tiny pearl buttons at her throat. One by one he undid the objects, kissing her naked flesh beneath. Her fully rounded breasts sprang, barely contained, above her chemise. He eased the thin material down underneath her bust, his lips taking one nipple while his hand stroked the other breast. Rebecca was confused by her own response and pressed his head to her satiny skin, arching her neck backward and moaning. Inside, the logs crackled madly, while outside, thunder roared and howling winds swept wet leaves against the windowpane.

Gradually, Rebecca became conscious again of the comfortable dimly lit room, warm and secure against the storm. She gently lifted his face with her hands, causing their eyes to meet for an unending moment. The fire had burned low and they knew that they must face parting. He slowly began to re-button each tiny pearl, hiding her soft flesh inevitably from his gaze, then straightened his own attire. Neither spoke.

Rebecca silently walked him to the door, firmly clasping the signet ring in her hand. Azim's face was a blank, tiny white lines surrounding his mouth. He stopped to study her. Silence hung in the air; the storm had lulled. Sheets of cold autumn rain still poured across the ground, turning the hard earth into mud.

Finally Azim gathered the courage to speak. "I'll leave you now. I meant what I said—I shall not interfere in your life again. I wish you a safe confinement. Good-bye, Rebecca."

She watched his tall form push through the waves of rain—dead leaves clinging to her skirt and feet getting soaked. The bare trees bowed their heads to the fury of the gale. Later she could not recall whether or not she had said good-bye also. She only remembered clinging to the door, bitter cold drops of rain pounding on her face.

CHAPTER 24

It was cold and clear on the steppes, the ground frozen hard, the tufts of grass white with hoar frost. There was to be a game of buzkashi tomorrow. The Turkomen never played in the hot summer months, but only in the fall and winter, until the snows were too deep. Azim was giving Khaled a final rub-down, a measure of grain and his six daily eggs for strength. He loved the silky feel of horseflesh beneath his strong hands and the pungent odor of horse dung, sweat and urine in the stable. It was a familiar aroma, reassuring and relaxing to him because it was a basic part of nature.

He missed the company of Mahmud in the next stall, doing the same for Ghazal, laughing and joking about how he would beat Azim in the game. Yet, he felt the lack of more than the male companionship of Mahmud. He found himself missing the society of Englishmen, even those in Kabul. His thoughts often focused on Stuart and the family. How did his new niece fare? Was his namesake Alex similar to him as a boy? It reassured him somehow that there was an Alex Drayton in England—an alter ego of sorts.

Images of Rebecca, standing in the doorway of her house, buffeted by the autumn rain came to him at odd moments: when he woke, in the bathhouse, or riding Khaled over the frozen steppe. There had been something strange about their last meeting. He had the nagging feeling that she had left something unsaid, something she wished him to know. How ridiculous he was, mooning over a married woman like a love-sick boy! But somehow, his life in the village did not have the same pure flavor it had always had before. It did not leave him satisfied.

Azim gave a short laugh out loud. Khaled looked around at him curiously.

"Don't worry, my *kara Khan*, my black king, I'm only thinking of how long it's been since I had a woman. A willing wench in bed will cure all my ills!"

He stroked Khaled's glossy jet-colored neck. "Just like you, my beauty, I too grow restless in the winter. But I don't have to wait for the mares to come into season! There are *some* advantages to being a man!" He laughed again, a bitter note creeping in, mocking his observation.

Azim continued talking aloud to the great stallion, whose ears flickered alertly at every word as if he were indeed listening to his master's conversation.

"I would like to relax this afternoon in the hammam but it happens to be Tuesday, the women's day at the bathhouse. Damn! I am bored unto death!"

He stroked his newly-grown beard, an idea coming to him. He would make a visit to the barber, hear the latest gossip from under a hot, steaming towel, and have his new beard trimmed.

"A perfect thought!" He left Khaled, giving the horse a slap on the flank. Khaled swished his tail, irritated.

Azim set out across the village to the barber's shop which was actually a room in the man's house. The village was quiet under the clear skies, the air dry and crackling with energy. Smoke lazed upwards from the chimneys; women were cooking over their fireplaces and some homes had a *bukhari* going. These primitive stoves burned wood for heat, but wood was expensive here on the open plains and few people could afford to keep them going all the time.

Azim passed the home of Diyeh. She was no doubt busy in the women's quarters of her father's house. He could remember her slanted ebony eyes watching him ever since she was a child. She was a child no longer, however. He had noticed how she had grown up this last year and had taken advantage of her natural urges once or twice. Diyeh was ready for a man of her own, but so far none of the young men in the village had pleased her, or they had not had enough money for the bride-price. She was doomed to spend several more years weaving rugs with her mother and sisters. Azim was very much aware that she preferred him to those who asked for her hand.

He remembered also how Diyeh had glared at Rebecca when she was in the village the previous summer. He also recalled the question Rebecca had put to him about his relationship with the young girl, and his answer. Why had he been so cruel? He could have lied, or softened his brutal words somehow. No wonder Rebecca had always been so ready to think the worst of him. He had been harsh with her, had insulted and hurt her. What a fool he was! He had virtually thrown her into St. Claire's arms.

Azim shook his head in annoyance. There was no use in endlessly hashing over the past. He needed a new interest, why not take up with Diyeh again? He recalled her youthful inexperience, her passion, more attractive in a way because of her naïveté.

Arriving at the barber's, Azim had to stoop because of his height to enter the sweltering and odorous room. The bukhari was going full blast, and the customers' bodies gave off a strong smell from their sheepskin coats. The barber's small son was running back and forth, bringing hot towels for the customers.

Azim waited his turn, hearing several interesting tidbits of news from the men gathered in the stuffy little room.

Buri's favorite mare was near to foaling—much too early—and would probably die in the harsh winter.

"Feed her *raki* in her grain!" shouted another man. "The alcohol slows their birth-urge."

Rahim's oldest wife had just been delivered of another fine baby boy. His circumcision ceremony was to be next week.

Yalavich needed a new chapan. His lowly wife could not sew properly. Where could he have one made cheaply?

Azim traded news, gave encouragement or advice where needed. The men liked and trusted him, both for his prowess at buzkashi and his fairness with them. It cheered him up to be surrounded by this friendly group of men that he had known for fifteen years.

A vision of the gently-bred Englishmen at his father's club leaped into his mind. He had been there once with his father when just a boy, and had been terribly impressed by the frock-coated, bewhiskered men, dignified and silent in the gloomy hall. His two existences separated in his mind, merged, then separated once more, tearing his being into fragments which would not be reconciled. He left the barber's room before his turn came, unable to bear the stifling atmosphere any longer. The men looked questionably at his departing figure.

The next day dawned cold and cloudy; a few snowflakes, delicate and lonely, drifted out of an overcast sky. Fortunately, the afternoon brought a break in the clouds, perfect buzkashi weather. The men and horses were nervous, breath pluming white in the cold air. Single words, too loud, emerged from the group.

The animals stamped, snorted, flicked their tails— they also knew what was coming. Azim, among the veterans, the *chapandaz,* of the game wore his honorary fur-trimmed hat. The mullah blessed the men and horses. The players mounted and approached the halal the circle of justice.

At the signal, each man began his personal battle each horse his own form of combat. Azim stood aside waiting for someone to break free. His beard hid the grim smile on his lips, then, finding an opening, he entered the melee, fighting, shouting oaths, bent on maiming and destroying. The crowd heaved and flowed, a gigantic beast with a hundred arms and two hundred legs, each bent on destruction. The goat's carcass was torn and bloody already; it passed from man to man, over a horse's neck, under a belly, torn apart in the fury of the game. A new carcass had to be provided and the game continued for hours, on into the gray evening.

Khaled was becoming impatient to enter the fray; Azim had been holding him back for awhile to save his strength for a final attack. The goat had passed around one pole, and was held by an expert chapandaz under his thigh while he raced for the second pole. Careening around it, his horse straightened out for the dash to the halal. He had not reckoned on Khaled, nostrils flaring, hooves pounding, approaching him from the right. The outstretched necks of the two horses raced side by side as Azim, whip in his teeth, leaned to his left, keeping his balance only with his left foot in the stirrup, and snatched the goat away. He galloped easily to the halal and threw the goat into the circle, then stopped his lathered mount, raising his arms in victory. The crowd roared its approval, never having seen him play with such skill and ferocity.

Azim was able to find forgetfulness only in the life-death situation of the games; it wiped out his conscience, his upbringing, his divided self, and provided him with an interlude of peace.

He went back to the village with the rest of the chapandaz, and handed Khaled to a groom. The women awaited them there, for they were never allowed to view a game even though their eyes habitually followed the chapandaz with yearning.

Diyeh was there, also, welcoming the men with a cup of the local brew, but with eyes only for Azim. He looked tall and majestic to her, even with a torn sleeve, muddy boots and a darkening bruise on one cheek. He was the hero of the day and she was aglow with worship of him.

Azim took the cup from her with a swift smile, downed it and turned to see her tilted black eyes devouring him with adoration above her veil. No one was watching him, so he spoke to her quietly, lest her father see and punish her for being unchaste.

"Little jewel," he said softly, "meet me tonight in the empty stable when the midnight hour arrives. I will await you with a very great desire. Do not fail me."

She lowered her lashes demurely and answered him breathlessly. "I should not, Azim, oh great chapandez, for my father would beat me if he knew . . . But for you I would brave anything." She moved off, her narrow hips swaying enticingly beneath her robe, to pour cups for the rest of the tired players.

Azim was waiting in the empty stable as the moon rose, throwing a square of white light through the window to rest on the strawcovered floor where he had spread a blanket. He saw a slim shadow flit across the courtyard and slip through the door. Diyeh flew into his arms, unveiled, her lips cold from the night air. She was breathing hard from emotion and from her hasty trip across the village.

He held her at arm's length after their first embrace, looking keenly at her perfect features and light brown skin, lit by the moonlight. She was beautiful in an Oriental way, slightly slanting eyes and high cheek bones betraying a Mongolian ancestry. Her hair was straight and black and heavy.

He could not help but compare her body to cream skin, golden curls and voluptuous curves. He put this train of thought out of his mind with a frown.

"What is it, Azim? Do I not please you?" Her voice was anxious.

"Diyeh, you please me. Oh yes, little jewel, you please me very much." He pulled her close and kissed her hungrily, willing himself to bury all thought, all logic, in sensation.

They sank to the floor, embracing. He pulled off her sash and undid her robe; she wore nothing underneath. Her narrow hips and small breasts felt strange to him, but her beauty excited him afresh. He traced the line of her hip, making her moan with pleasure, then gently moved his hand nearer to her dark triangle. She bit his ear lobe, whispering Pashto endearments. Her hands traveled over his body under his chapan, touching him like molten butterflies on his muscular belly, slim hips. He quickly shed his clothes, ready, and plunged into her, wanting only the annihilation of awareness.

Winter in Kabul was a dreary time. Often, the frigid wind howled across the plains, whipping the snow into a fury of tiny white projectiles. The peaks of the Hindu Kush were visible on clear days, brilliant white and shining in the pale sunlight. Rebecca shivered as she looked at them from her window; no human being could survive in those mountains in the winter.

Her thoughts took wing, flying over the frozen barrier to a village in the north. What was Azim doing? Had he forgotten her? Somehow, she felt that his thoughts reached across the great mountains to caress her being with longing. Her hand rested on her swollen abdomen, feeling the quick jump of her baby, their baby, flesh of her flesh and yet blood of his blood. The poor child would be born into a household of hate and tension. She wondered whether William would take his evil nature out on the defenseless infant. With a sigh, she realized that he most probably would. A rush of emotion passed over her, a love so strong and fiercely protective that she was surprised at herself.

William had become increasingly inhuman. He was drinking heavily, frustrated in his efforts to get back to England, but no one could travel until spring. He took all of his failures out on Rebecca, never striking her, but coming close on numerous occasions. She was not even sure why he held back any longer, but she stayed out of his way as much as possible.

Meera was a great help to her during this time. She lived at her home with Mahmud, but came every morning to be with her mistress, knowing how Rebecca depended on her. She was unfailing in her cheerfulness and devotion to her Missy, providing a bright focus in those dreary months.

The winter days were short and bitter cold. Rebecca went out occasionally for a walk in the bleak, snow-covered garden. She was tired lately, her body having grown awkward and heavy. Often, she would sit in her room, reading one of her father's volumes. Just as frequently, she would find the book resting in her lap, her eyes staring out the window toward the Hindu Kush, an enigmatic smile curving her lips.

Day followed day, each alike in the monotony and tedium of waiting for her child. When the baby was born, she felt sure she would be able to leave Kabul, return to England and create a separate life for herself and her infant. She would simply have to convince William that it was the best solution for them. She felt that she could no longer live with his abusive nature. It was becoming more and more difficult to put up with his moods, his accusations, his humiliation of her. Thank God he never approached her room at night; he was usually too drunk, or visiting one of his whores. She wondered what would happen once the baby was born, but pushed the thought from her mind.

She had no one to talk to but Meera, whom she confided in to ease her own loneliness. Meera was worried about her Missy. She could see that William was becoming more unbalanced every day. He could easily turn violent. She shuddered to think of the consequences, quite aware that William kept a loaded pistol in his dresser drawer. One of the servants had whispered that piece of information to her.

One morning at breakfast William seemed to be in a better than usual mood. He had teased Meera, asking her if she were pregnant yet. Meera blushed and quickly excused herself to the kitchen.

He turned to Rebecca, surprising her. "Rebecca, you are looking well this morning."

"Thank you." She looked up warily.

"Don't look at me like that, my dear. I'm not an ogre! I meant to compliment you."

"Yes, William." It was easier to agree than argue with him.

"I know you don't get out much, my dear, but how would you like to have the Mountstuarts, and perhaps the Swansons, for a small, private Christmas dinner?"

Her wan face brightened perceptibly. "Oh, William, do you mean it? I would so love to have some people here and a little Christmas spirit. I'll invite them immediately! And Nur Mustafa can cook something decent for once!"

"Of course, Rebecca, go on with the plans. It will be a pleasant evening and I will have a surprise for you."

She wondered at her husband's pleasantness, perhaps he was changing for the better. Fervently, she hoped so.

"How wonderful, William, especially since it will probably be the last time I can see anyone before the baby . . . comes." Perhaps she shouldn't have mentioned it, but William did not seem to be disturbed.

He went on, almost gaily. "Have you heard the latest bit of insanity in this foul place? It appears that a pack of wolves is prowling the city at night. They have been forced out of the mountains by the snow, you know. Two nights ago, they tore apart and devoured some old man who was out alone. Can you believe the monstrosity of it all? Oh well, it was only an old Afghan, luckily no one of importance."

Rebecca gasped in horror, feeling the blood leave her face. Wolves in Kabul! My God, what would happen next in this godforsaken place?

William laughed in her face, and left for work, throwing one last remark over his shoulder, almost as an afterthought. "Wouldn't you be a tasty morsel for the wolves, all that flesh . . ."

Rebecca refused to let William dampen her spirits. She planned carefully for the dinner party, locating and paying dearly for a goose for the main course, and decorating the house with greenery. It began to remind her of her grandfather and Faroaks, his lovely estate, during the holidays. She went about the house happily discussing menus and wines and decorations with Meera.

Outside the snow drifts rose higher still and the small English community felt isolated from the world. Christmas went unnoticed in Afghanistan, as the people were Moslems, so the servants looked upon these preparations as somewhat odd, considering the time of year.

Rebecca decided to make a warm dressing gown for William, a kind of peace offering, or perhaps to thank him for the party. She sent for some black and gold patterned silk from the bazaar and lined it with soft wool. It wasn't too difficult to work on it while William was at work; she decided it would be a surprise.

The day of the dinner party dawned gray and ominous. It was Christmas Eve, and Rebecca had all in readiness for the party. She had overseen Nur Mustafa while he stuffed the goose and put it in the oven, not trusting him to do it properly.

She was a trifle worried as it began to snow heavily, but she knew that the Mountstuarts and Swansons lived only a short distance away and was sure they would arrive safely.

The table was laid, sparkling with china and crystal, reflecting the flames from the fireplace. The hand-woven carpets glowed deeply in jeweled tones of garnet, violet, and crimson.

Rebecca was in her room dressing. Meera had promised to stay the night, especially in view of the inclement weather, to help her mistress. She was putting Rebecca's hair up, leaving a cascade of gleaming curls down her back. Rebecca wore a gown of deep gold satin, showing off her alabaster skin, and matching perfectly the gold of her hair. The neckline of the dress plunged to her swelling bosom and the elbow-length sleeves were trimmed in yards of black lace. The full skirt covered the bulge of her stomach, lending a graceful aspect to her figure.

She was quite nervous and excited, hoping that all would go well tonight. She had wrapped William's dressing gown and planned to present it to him tonight, as he had mentioned that he had a surprise for her. She heard the door open and William stamping the snow off his feet in the hall. She prayed that he would not start drinking yet.

Actually, the evening went quite well. William acted the part of the fond husband, even complimenting Rebecca in front of their guests. The goose was done perfectly, the ambiance warm and pleasant, the wines mellow. William indulged liberally in the after-dinner brandy, Rebecca eying him furtively from time to time, trying to determine if he were getting tipsy, but he seemed to be in perfect control, acting the charming host and loving husband. He had a faint smile on his lips all evening and was caught once or twice staring vacantly ahead, turned inward to his own thoughts.

After dinner, the guests sat in front of the fire, relaxing in the warmth of the leaping flames.

"What a terrible storm! Why, I so believe it's the worst I've seen here," said Eleanor Mountstuart.

"Yes, dear, I think you're right," remarked her husband. "I shudder to think that this storm will make the wolves even more daring."

"What a delightful idea of yours," said Polly Swanson, "having this dinner, and you in a family way, too. I'll bet your husband is pleased to be having a child so soon," she continued, patting Rebecca's hand fondly.

Rebecca could not say a word, terrified of what William's reaction might be. She lowered her head and looked at her hands in an agony of tension. Polly mistook it for natural reticence.

William broke in quickly and smoothly. "Yes, Mrs. Swanson, we will both be very proud and happy parents, won't we, dearest?"

"Yes, William," was her muffled reply.

The conversation continued casually, topics of local interest being discussed, or the future of the British empire and the little lady who ruled it, Queen Victoria. Rebecca was very quiet.

Presently William stood up and held his glass high. "Let us drink a toast to a Happy Christmas! Cheers!" He downed his drink in one gulp, then turned to the ladies, excusing himself. "I must fetch Rebecca's yuletide present. I think it is quite an unusual gift and I wanted you to share it with us."

"Oh, William, you must wait! I have a surprise for you, too, and I want you to open it first," said Rebecca, embarrassed by his apparent thoughtfulness. She climbed the stairs to her room and returned to the guests with the gaily wrapped package.

William opened it and gave a great show of praising the dressing gown, even trying it on over his coat for the guests to admire.

"Why, he looks just like an Indian prince!" cried the irrepressible Polly Swanson. William's head turned sharply, his eyes boring into Polly's face. His sallow skin showed a dark flush. There was an uncomfortable silence for a minute, then William recovered himself and spoke lightly, putting everyone at ease again.

"Rebecca, you must open your gift now. I can hardly wait to see your reaction." He handed her a medium-sized flat package, wrapped in gold paper.

She tore off the paper then opened the top of the box. Inside lay a gorgeously illuminated ancient Persian manuscript, all vibrant colors, swirling Arabic writing and delicately etched designs—a gift fit for a queen! Rebecca drew her breath in amazement. William must have searched for months to find such an exquisite piece of workmanship, and it must have cost a fortune! Their guests were exclaiming over the beauty of the book and asking William where he had found it. William smiled to himself and politely refused to answer them. All he would say was that he had his own sources.

"Look inside the book, my dear," he finally said to his wife. "I think you will appreciate the special quality of the pictures."

Rebecca opened the book, delighted to have such a lovely gift. Her eyes fixed themselves on a page and she stopped smiling. She turned to another page and remained unsmiling, ashen. Her eyes found William's across the room; he was grinning triumphantly. She felt a chill run up the back of her spine.

The book was a clearly detailed treatise on the varying sexual positions that men and women could indulge in for their mutual pleasures. Rebecca could feel a hot flush cover to her cheeks and tears start to her eyes. William had merely been playing with her and had neatly ensnared her in his trap, to torment and humiliate her further.

She could not stand to be in the room another moment. She looked around frantically. The Swansons and Mountstuarts were watching her expectantly, waiting to be shown the contents of the book and William was still smiling at her. Rebecca stood up, the book falling to the floor with a thud in the silence and fled from the suddenly shocked expressions.

"Oh, dear," said Polly. "I hope she's not going to be ill . . . the baby . . . Whatever happened?"

"Hush, Polly," her husband whispered.

"Please, Mrs. Swanson, don't be upset," broke in William. "It's only her condition. These spells occur often. Just a little rest is all that's needed, I assure you." He had picked up the book and replaced it carefully in its box.

"I do hope you're right, Mr. St. Claire," continued Polly. "Shouldn't she have someone with her?"

"Hush, Polly," repeated her husband.

"Her maidservant will take care of all her needs,"

said William firmly, and then, turning to the others. "Another brandy, gentlemen? Perhaps a sherry for you, Mrs. Mounstuart?"

The guests, slightly uncomfortable with this strange behavior, excused themselves rather quickly and braved the storm to travel the short distances to their homes.

William was exceedingly pleased with himself. He felt content for the first time in months. He poured himself another brandy and reclined in his favorite chair, his feet stretched toward the fire. He enjoyed the feelings of triumph and power that rose in him when he recalled the stricken look on Rebecca's face.

All of his problems were laid at her feet: her damned grandfather buying the jeweled box, her father rejecting him as a husband, even her pregnancy, which rankled more than he cared to admit. She was the bane of his existence, the focus of his frustration.

William supposed that she was crying in her room; she was occupied that way often enough. He pictured her tearful face, her tumbled hair, her white bosom heaving in the golden gown. He felt desire stir his loins and cursed under his breath. She still had the power to arouse him, haunt him, even in her bloated condition! Perhaps she deserved a visit from him. He had been too kind to her until now, respecting her wishes. A husband had rights to his wife's body—no one could deny him that.

The thought of her pregnancy only stirred his imagination. He had never bedded a woman so far along before. It might prove interesting. It might even rid him of the illegitimate brat she carried, although he doubted *that*!

Another brandy gave him the needed courage to climb the stairs to her room. He knew that Meera and the servants were asleep in the other wing—unable to hear anything from their quarters. He tried the latch on Rebecca's door. Good, it was open. So she had not taken the precaution of locking her door yet. She trusted him that far.

The room was dark. He stood still a moment to accustom his eyes to the blackness. Soon he could see her body on the bed, even make out the pale oval of her face in the darkness. She slept.

He stole closer and watched her in repose. Her chest rose and fell regularly and curls lay in confusion about her face, which still bore the marks of her tears.

William saw his hand, of its own accord, disembodied, move to touch her breast. Rebecca's eyes flew open, widened in fear. Automatically she drew back into her quilt as if for protection.

"I *will* have you tonight," said William quietly. "You will be an interesting experience for me, my dear."

"No!" Her eyes were huge, terrified, like a doe trapped by the dogs. "You promised . . . the baby . . . don't touch me!"

"Frankly, wife of mine, I don't care what happens to the baby, or to you, for that matter. Tonight, you will satisfy me as *I* wish, love."

Rebecca could see that he was completely beyond reason. It would be useless to argue with him, beg or even fight back. He was far past thinking of her in any way but that of a female body with which to satisfy himself. Rebecca felt a chill steal over her at the realization. She was powerless to stop him, even though her body could not help but shrink at his touch. And this was her husband!

William sat on the edge of the bed and drew the coverlet back slowly, savoring the sight of her trembling body. He undressed her, then stroked her smooth skin with his small fingers, down her arm, trailing across her swollen belly, down the inside of her thigh. Rebecca lay still, paralyzed with horror, her eyes shut tight. He kneaded her distended, blue-veined breasts, then bent his head to sip at her nipples until they rose like flower buds. Still she did not move, but shudders swept her body and tears squeezed out from under her eyelids.

William undressed and slipped into bed, his manhood erect and quivering. He was panting rapidly and his breath smelled of brandy. He mounted her, driving into her harder and harder. His weight pressed the mound of her child up into her lungs, and she thought she would suffocate before he finished and rolled off her.

A moment later she heard him say, "That was lovely, dearest wife, but only the beginning. Let us see what else you know how to do!"

The night was endless. He forced her to depths of degradation she had not known existed. Her mind fled her body, leaving it behind to perform the vile acts that he desired of her. She was never to remember that night clearly; it became a blur of his hot flesh and whispered orders.

He left her sometime during the early morning hours. She had no recollection of his departure.

When Meera knocked and entered Rebecca's room in the morning, having carefully rehearsed herself to greet her mistress with "Happy Christmas," she found a dry-eyed, vacantly staring ghost of the woman she knew. Rebecca would not answer any of her worried questions, but requested hot water for a bath and scrubbed herself viciously for an hour, then retired to her bed for the rest of the day.

CHAPTER 25

Spring in the Afghanistan mountains could be either violent or mellow. The magnificent Hindu Kush could gnash her teeth and spew forth a steady flow of brutal spring snows, or she could gracefully bow her head in rest, letting the warm yellow sun melt her white cloak, sending rivulets of water down her slopes to feed the vast valleys and streams below. Her massive drifts of white, an open book written on the snows by a myriad of tiny paws, revealed an ageless story in hieroglyphic paths. At lower altitudes, patches of brown frozen earth dotted the hillsides facing south. Occasionally an early bud showed itself through the snow; it was doubly precious in the cold air.

Azim studied the pink-tinted clouds that formed that morning over the craggy ridges above. The storms had lessened in early March, but he feared that the clear conditions would not hold. This would be the most difficult day of his journey. He must make it over Shibar Pass before sunset. However, Khaled could not be rushed over the heights. The horse became too winded in the thin air, so he would have to take great care and rest his mount often.

He purposefully set off from his camp that cold spring dawn, bracing himself against the frosty morning air. Khaled was full of energy and stepped briskly along the rocky path, shying at imaginary shadows.

By the time the sun stood overhead they were

halfway up the steep slopes and the clear sky was growing dark and threatening. Great clouds laden with heavy spring snows had begun to gather overhead, hanging oppressively on the high peaks. By mid-afternoon Azim and Khaled were nearing the summit of the pass amidst a raging blizzard, flurries of blinding snow and wind making visibility nearly non-existent. Azim had dismounted several times to walk Khaled even though he feared that they would not make the lower slopes on the other side by nightfall. But he shook the notion and continued forcing his horse upward through the driving sheets of snow.

Icicles had formed on his mustache and beard; Khaled's mane was thick with frozen snow. He had thought once to stop and build a shelter from the fury. The drifting snow would afford a protection against the winds, but he knew that his trusted horse would not be able to survive the night.

On and upward they struggled, familiar landmarks long since buried by the ferocious weather. He no longer had any idea how near they were to the top, but the terrain seemed to be leveling out. Time passed, unending in the violence of the storm. Held in the grip of white vertigo, he realized that Khaled's labored breathing had eased—they must be descending.

The sky darkened further; he did not know whether it had blackened due to nightfall or if the storm had grown worse. Still they went on . . . moving a few pitiful feet a minute. He knew that he was nearing his limit to endure. His body sagged in the saddle, clinging there by sheer will power. The cold beckoned him into its blessed embrace. What utter release it would be to succumb to the chill, to let its icy fingers surround him, to sleep.

Azim spoke aloud to Khaled, to the snowflakes that piled high in his lap, trying desperately to stay awake. He felt his mind slipping; sleep threatened to overcome him. The long glacial arms of winter called to him, enticing. His lids became heavy . . . oblivion claimed him. Everlasting blackness held peace and security.

Much later, when bleak rays of light pricked his eyelids, Azim mumbled to them, "Go away . . . Leave me to my rest." A faint, barely perceptible warmth touched his brow. He sat up with a start. Merciful Allah, he had allowed himself to pass out! The first rule of the mountains—so easily broken! He tried to stand, but his legs would not move. His feet were frozen, numb. It was only when he saw Khaled standing near-by with the snow-crusted saddle still on his back that he realized he must have fallen while asleep. Khaled raised his perfectly formed head and gave a snort.

Sun peeked out of the clouds, indicating that the storm was over. How long had he lain unconscious? A minute, an hour? He would never know. But he did know how few had ever awoken from the embrace of frozen death. Visions of a power greater than the storm flooded his perception, an inner peace filling him. He was, for the moment, at one with the raging elements that had nearly taken his life. With a new awe for the omnipresent forces that had spared him, Azim found the courage to stand on his frozen feet. He remounted Khaled and began down the snow-drifted trail.

The late afternoon sun melted the frost from his beard. His mind began to function rationally again and he surveyed the landscape. Yes, over there, that was a well-known peak. Somehow they had made the worst of the descent and would reach the safety of the valley before dark.

Like the handful of survivors before him, Azim had stared into the black face of death and emerged into the sunshine of the living. The experience would never leave him, for he had been spared and left to live out his life, to fulfill a scheme . . .

Azim rode into Kabul the next day, not the same man who had begun his journey, forever changed, forever a part of the mighty Hindu Kush. He felt reverence for these grand mountains of legend. The snow-capped peaks had spared him and had commanded him to take his place in the world.

He rounded a corner in a narrow street and saw Mahmud's home where Ghazal was tethered in front. Azim smiled to himself. It would be good to embrace his old comrade once again.

Mahmud recognized Khaled first—the bedraggled figure on his back unfamiliar for an instant. The man had not only grown a beard, but looked so feeble that Mahmud stood motionless, taken aback. Azim nearly collapsed into his arms from exhaustion. His friend's face was a welcome blur through his clouded gaze.

In a matter of moments, Mahmud had half-carried him inside and wrapped him in warm blankets. He gently stripped off Azim's wet boots and eased the frigid feet into a copper bucket and slowly poured warm water over them. Azim almost passed out from the excruciating agony.

Mahmud's worried expression finally turned to one of joy. "The pain is good, my friend, for you will keep your feet attached to your body." Azim winced at the waves of unbearable pain. Mahmud went on, "The blood is in your toes, yes? In a few minutes you will be fine. Your feet already shed the cold skin, see?" He lifted a foot from the bucket.

Azim replied, gritting his teeth, "Yes, I suppose I am very lucky but, God, it hurts! I had forgotten about the frostbite. I suspect when they froze I no longer realized the danger."

Mahmud looked down into Azim's gray eyes and new-bearded face. The man was somehow different; older perhaps? No, Mahmud thought, not older. But an inner strength radiated from the man, a knowledge gained through suffering.

Mahmud looked on him proudly. "Azim, let me warm you with some drink and food. I will join you and listen to the story of your winter. I have missed you and my village these months. This city is a fetid place! I shall take my wife back home soon."

Azim did not want to dwell on the past, lonely season. He did, however, convey the dissatisfaction and boredom of his winter. Mahmud listened quietly, only interrupting to ask about an old friend, or how the buzkashi games had come out. Still Mahmud had the feeling that Azim was holding back something. He did not want to pry, but curiosity bested him.

"You have not told me all that has happened since we last saw each other. I would not ask, but somehow you are not the same man that left Kabul in the fall."

Azim gazed through Mahmud; his voice was low and searching when he finally spoke. "Yesterday, I suffered a kind of rebirth in the cold snows of the pass. I cannot put it into words just yet, but I was given a second chance. My life was returned to me by the mountains. I can only say that you are correct. I am no longer the same—a new side of me was revealed by the Hindu Kush. The man who descended this side is changed . . ."

Mahmud finished for him. "I would say that the man, Azim, came out of the mountains with wisdom. Is this not so?"

Alex looked long and hard at his comrade. "Yes, my friend, I haven't faced the truth before, but I hope I have gained a small measure of knowledge now. My misbegotten dreams died in the storm. God, I feel so strange."

Exhaustion took over; his head sagged down onto the soft pillows. His eyes closed and he slept until the next morning.

Mahmud mourned the loss of his young comrade; he celebrated the birth of the man, Alex, who had been hiding from his true identity for so many long years.

Long after the sun had touched Kabul with its early light, Alex rolled over and stretched his arms. He sat up abruptly, the aroma of freshly baked bread assailing his nostrils, making him realize how famished and

refreshed he was. Alex had not had a full night's rest
for over a week. The few cat-naps he had allowed
himself had not been enough—it felt good to be rested
again.

He watched Mahmud tend the meal. "Ah, Mahmud!
I see that Meera has taught you the fine art of cooking!
Do you also do the laundry?" Alex was chuckling aloud
at his friend's confusion.

"If you had risen earlier, you would have seen Meera
prepare our food," retorted Mahmud, insulted. "She
has gone to the St. Claire's house as the birth is
imminent. She told me to tell you how happy she is that
you have returned. Meera says we would be very
displeased if you do not stay with us." Mahmud smiled
proudly at his offer of hospitality. Alex could not refuse
him.

He swung his legs over the side of the bed and stood,
slightly wavering, on his sore feet. His expression had
sobered. "Ah, yes, the baby . . ." He shook off the
ache. "Of course I shall stay with you, old friend! We
have much to catch up on!"

They ate a hearty meal and talked at length about the
winter months. Mahmud was annoyed at Alex for
having braved the pass before April or May, but Alex
convinced him that he had been much too restless to
remain in the village. After unpacking his few European clothes from the leather saddle bags, Alex washed
and changed his attire. He felt certain that Mahmud
would comprehend his feelings of contentment now
that he had discovered his new identity.

He explained himself quietly but with a firm sense of
purpose. "I've come to an awareness about my own
actions for the past fifteen years. Mahmud, you must
see that fighting the British with guns and swords has
only temporarily set them at bay."

Mahmud knew, even before Alex spoke, that the
young Englishman was going to return to his former
way of life. He nodded wisely.

Alex continued, "I'm planning to write my brother a

letter this very day. He should be able to secure a position for me with the foreign minister. Mahmud, I feel I must begin to fight for your, *our,* country in a new fashion. I despise politics but, on the other hand, this is the only way to assure that our people here will have a fair chance to survive the English threat unchanged." Alex hoped that his best friend would see the truth of these words.

Mahmud not only agreed, but was pleased that his friend had seemingly risen above his painful confusion of the past months. He conveyed his delight to him and they planned for the future. Alex assured him that he would return to Afghanistan soon and that they would ride again, rejoicing together in the sun of their beloved steppes.

As Khaled was in need of a rest, Alex decided to walk to the governor's. He knew that David Mount-stuart would be thrilled to hear that he was intending to return to England.

The sky was crystal clear that day and there was a hint of warm spring wind from the north. Alex had never felt more at peace with the world. He walked with a perceptible limp to the mansion. As he was passing the garden, a dark cloud descended upon his light mood. Nearly a year ago he had met a bewitching young beauty here and he had been overbearing and rude, trying to bend her will to his own. Then he had abused her, not just once, but many times. Alex realized at that moment he could have had Rebecca for the taking. If only he could turn the clock back, how differently he would behave. Oh, maybe he still would have taken her virginity, but he would have married her, over her protests perhaps, and the child that she would bear St. Claire would have been given life by his own seed. The girl had been given little choice but to succumb to St. Claire. What an utter fool he had been!

As he entered the mansion, Alex tried to put aside all thoughts of the past. He could not change the facts as they now stood. His new wisdom forbade him to feel guilt for the deeds of his past. He vaguely thought of going to Rebecca and declaring his love, but what possible good could it do her now? Would she find solace in his words? Did she even care?

Dismissing the idea, for he had promised to stay away from her, he reached out his hand and warmly greeted David Mountstuart. Mountstuart was baffled by Alex's sudden appearance so early this spring.

"Alex, what has brought you to Kabul before the summer? I'm delighted to see you, of course, my boy. I almost didn't recognize you. The beard is new, I trust?"

"Yes, it is. I've undergone some changes . . . Actually, I've come to draft a dispatch to my brother and shortly thereafter I hope to return to England."

"But, my boy, that's grand news indeed! I shan't ask why the sudden turn-about, let us just say that my best wishes go with you even though Eleanor and I will miss you. Here, come into my office and write your letter." He showed Alex into his comfortable library and left the man to compose his draft.

Alex began his letter in a gentle way, not wanting to shock Stuart too suddenly. The words began flowing easily and he conveyed his overwhelming desire to meet his nephews and niece. He did, however, explain that although he would return to Afghanistan periodically, his life would now be centered in England. Alex hinted at his wish to join in an active political venture to squelch the British oppression in his adopted land. He knew that Stuart Drayton would fully agree and assist him in any way possible.

Having finished his draft, Alex thanked the governor and left the letter to be sent in the first dispatch to leave Kabul. The Khyber Pass would soon be open to caravan travel and Alex planned to leave in time to catch a ship to England before the monsoon season.

During the next few days, Alex and Mahmud spent much time together. He planned to leave Khaled in the trusted care of Mahmud when he was in England. Meera was in and out of the house, as nervous as a cat for her mistress. Alex tried not to listen to her chatter about the St. Claires for his heart always gave a jump at the mention of Rebecca as he knew that it always would.

One day, while listening to Meera babble on, he caught mention of a sinister scheme that William had perpetrated on the unsuspecting Rebecca. Meera was chattering while preparing supper.

"Oh, so many times Meera be thinking her Missy losing baby. Why, after your Christmas, Missy sick for weeks. I am not liking that Sahib William for shaming my Missy before her guests."

"What did the Sahib William do this time?" Alex could not help himself from interrupting. His eyes were menacing.

Meera looked hesitantly at Mahmud, who would offer no way out of the situation, so she related to Alex the details of Rebecca's Christmas party and the incident of her vile present.

Alex's features blackened with fury. That dirty bastard St. Claire! He should ride over there immediately and drag the man through the streets of Kabul! Alex said as much aloud and Meera grew afraid of the consequences to her mistress.

"No, Sahib Azim!" she pleaded. "Sahib William will be killing Missy! He is not even caring about baby! He will be drinking too much and slaying us all! I am begging you not to be interfering!" Meera sobbed at her stupidity in speaking too freely.

Alex knew that unless he killed St. Claire, the filthy coward would certainly vent his wrath on Rebecca. Besides, he had promised to stay out of her life. If Rebecca needed him she could always send the ring. Alex shrugged off the thoughts and forced a smile.

"Don't worry, Meera. I was only thinking aloud what I should like to do. I shall not cause your mistress any undo troubles."

For the remainder of the week, Meera, who was seldom at home now, kept silent on the subject of the

St. Claires. She greatly feared that Alex would carry through his threats. In a way, she secretly desired to see him do precisely that, humiliate Sahib William before all of Kabul.

If Meera had been pestering Alex and Mahmud with her prattle, she had also been torturing Rebecca with comments about Alex.

Upon Alex's unexpected return to Kabul, Meera had blurted out to Rebecca, "Missy, I am bringing good news today. Sahib Azim has come to Mahmud's! Mahmud is being very happy."

Rebecca's heart leaped involuntarily. Then she swept Meera's hands away from her hair. "I don't want to hear that man's name mentioned in this house, Meera. Do you lack any sense at all?" In truth, she wanted desperately to ask if he was well, if he ever mentioned her . . . Instead, she hardened her heart.

But Meera was not to be stopped so easily. "Sahib Azim is going back to England. He is looking very handsome Englishman now. He had wondrous experience in mountains, Mahmud was telling Meera that he is being very different. He is having beard now."

Rebecca cut her words off sharply. "Meera! I just told you not to mention him again! You must listen to me!" Softening her voice she continued, "I don't mean to scold you but my . . . my acquaintance with Azim . . . Alex Drayton was over a long time ago. I have the baby coming and the infant's future is my primary concern. Understand that if William finds out that you have Alex staying with you, well, I don't know how he will react. Enough said, now let's finish my hair." She could not stop her imagination as easily—his face swam in front of her eyes, so familiar in a way, yet as far removed from her life as if an ocean separated them. Well, he would have to remain there, she thought bitterly. There is no place in my life for him.

On the sixth day after Alex's return to the city, the first dispatch bags arrived from Bombay, stuffed with official and personal letters. The news of the arrival of long-awaited correspondence circulated rapidly around the British compound, although there was so much mail that it took several days to sort the mess out.

Alex and Mahmud were in the bazaar area one afternoon when Steven McBain approached them. McBain had been sent by Mountstuart to fetch Alex, but was not happy to encounter him again, having tried to put the Suraj Mal incident out of his mind.

McBain excused himself and directed his words to Alex. "Sir. Nice to see you again. I saw you come out of this shop and would not have intruded except that Governor Mountstuart has been looking for you. Something about a letter, I believe."

Alex saw the corporal's discomfort, so he simply thanked him and assured him that he would go to the mansion that very afternoon. The cool encounter totally by-passed Mahmud, who knew nothing of the plot against Suraj Mal save that Alex had revenged himself on the fat little man.

Some hours later while sitting at the governor's mansion, Alex's world was once again shattered. Reflecting on the occasion, he would remember only a hideous black rage overcoming him, a fury so strong that all other emotions had been washed completely away. He had never before, or since, that fateful afternoon known such a hate and loathing for another human being.

The letter from Stuart Drayton had begun simply enough. Carla was once again expecting a child . . . when would Alex cease his wanderings and come home . . . the political gossip in the House of Lords was . . . etc.

Turning to the third page of the long epistle, Alex noticed a newspaper clipping attached.

Recently uncovered facts concerning last year's death of one esteemed George Merideth have come to light. The police have traced the elusive William St. Claire to the remote and exotic city of

Kabul, Afghanistan. The gentleman in question is being sought in connection with the sudden death of Merideth. Although the police had been previously unable to contact St. Claire, the matter was not pressing until yesterday when a strange fact was uncovered. It would seem that St. Claire had sought information from the auctioneer at his father's estate sale. The auctioneer came forward to tell the police that he himself had given the name of George Merideth to St. Claire. The man told the police also that St. Claire was visibly shaken and seemed unduly upset at the time. It has already been established that one William St. Claire had been at Faroaks estate the very day of Merideth's peculiar and fatal attack of apoplexy. We must congratulate the police for their fine powers of deduction, for most assuredly, St. Claire has been involved in a sinister plot. This paper will follow the investigation with keen interest.

It only took Alex an instant to realize what the article implied. Not only had St. Claire been involved in George Merideth's death, but he had followed Rebecca to Kabul for God knows what motive, and then suddenly her own father was murdered mysteriously! *Who* then ends up with the entire estate of the family? Why none other than St. Claire himself! My God, thought Alex, Rebecca has been alone with the bastard for months!

Alex did not remember leaving the mansion, nor did he recall Mountstuart chasing briefly after him. His last memory of the incident had been watching the clipping float slowly, feather-like, to the blue carpet.

CHAPTER 26

Alex became cognizant of his surroundings only when he stood before the entrance of Rebecca's house. He looked up, shocked that he was standing there. He paused barely long enough to knock, then impatiently burst through the door. One of the servants was hurrying toward the commotion but stopped in surprise as he saw a tall, bearded man stalk into the hall, his mouth grim and his dark brows drawn together in fury.

"Where is Mrs. St. Claire?" Alex demanded of the boy in Pashto.

"The mistress is upstairs in her room," answered the frightened servant hesitantly.

"I will see her immediately, if you please."

"I don't think that she can see anyone right now, effendi. She is resting in her—"

His words were cut short by a muffled shout from upstairs, then a woman's voice pleading, crying, the words indistinct. The male voice continued, harsh, as if he were cursing.

Alex stiffened, then, shaking with suppressed wrath, he turned on the boy, his voice intense.

"Is that your mistress?"

"Yes, effendi." The youth quaked.

"Is her husband up there with her?"

"Yes, effendi." He spoke barely above a whisper.

His next words were stopped by a shrill scream, cut off sharply by the unmistakable sound of a blow. Alex

297

wasted no more time; his towering rage carried him up the stairs in long strides. Which room was she in? Instantly his question was answered when he heard a sob and the man's voice, cruel and low, demanding.

Alex threw his full weight against the door, splintering the hard wood with the strength of his anger. He burst into the room, taking in the situation in a split second. St. Claire's horrified glance was turned toward Alex; he was holding Rebecca's arm tightly, twisting it over her head. He was poised to strike her again. She cowered, half falling onto the bed, her distended stomach making her awkward, unwieldy, her features drawn with terror.

"Drayton! What the devil . . . !" William's face was tinged purple with fury. He still wrenched Rebecca's arm, hurting her.

"St. Claire," hissed Alex, every ounce of the revulsion he felt contained in his words. "Let her go, you filthy coward." His tone was quiet, deadly.

"Get out of here, you bloody native! This is *my* wife!"

"Let her go! . . . Now, St. Claire. Never lay a finger on her again or I shall break your vile neck!" The words were so low that William had to strain to hear them, but the meaning was unmistakable.

"How dare you charge into my house, into my *room*—threaten me! Why I'll have the soldiers hang you from the highest tree in this hell-hole!" William had worked his way slowly to his bureau, dragging Rebecca with him. He opened the top drawer and quickly snatched up the loaded pistol he kept there, aiming it point blank at Alex.

"*Now,* why don't you try to break my neck, Drayton? Come on, you fool, protect your whore. She's not much good to me anyway," he taunted suddenly shoving Rebecca sharply into a corner, where she crumbled into a heap, gasping with pain.

Alex was aware of only a fine red mist transforming his perception; his heart almost burst within him shooting flames of white-hot fury through his body. He flung himself at William with a cry of bestial rage on his lips, knocking the gun from William's hand to the floor. William made a dive for the pistol, landing on top of it, trying desperately to turn it toward his assailant. Alex threw himself on William; they struggled, panting with exertion, as they fought for the gun.

Rebecca was frozen in the corner. Searing pain twisted in her belly and she felt a hot gush of liquid soak her skirt. She watched the fight in horror, trying to comprehend why Azim was there at all. She was stunned and confused by his sudden appearance, even embarrassed that he should see how her husband treated her. Still, she could not take her eyes off of the weapon. It seemed huge and black, wickedly, cunningly made to kill and maim. She realized with a part of her mind that her labor had started, but could only watch, unmoving, as the two men clashed on the floor, clutching at the gun.

Her body jumped involuntarily from the sudden sharp report of the weapon. Both figures remained still on the floor for an endless moment while she held her breath as another birth pain mounted.

Interminably, she waited for one of the men to rise. When he finally stood, her shrieking nerves gave way and she began to sob hysterically.

"Rebecca, my God," whispered Alex in a tortured voice, "I . . . I've killed him, the father of your child . . ."

Rebecca did not answer him immediately; her head was bowed, her breath came in gasps as her contraction came to its peak, then slackened. She looked up at Alex, her eyes full of tears, the words welling to her lips before she could think.

"Alex . . . Oh Lord, Alex . . . it's yours . . . The baby is *yours!*"

She could hear his suddenly indrawn breath. His eyes were fixed on her, disbelief, wonderment, finally realization playing across his features.

"Dear God, Rebecca . . . I had no idea . . . What an utter fool I've been . . . My love, can you ever forgive me?" He approached her, his arms out to gather her up from where she still crouched.

"Rebecca, can you stand? Let me help you up, my angel, we'll go away together . . . Rebecca?"

"It's my pains. They've started! Please . . . call Meera . . . She'll know what to do."

Alex helped her to the bed, her body heavy, ripe with child—his child. He felt a burst of tenderness for her pride, her strength, her dignity, then a gnawing fear. What if something should happen during the birth? He steadied his voice.

"Rebecca, I'll be back in a moment, I'll fetch Meera. Will you be all right?"

"Yes, of course," she said, smiling faintly, then turning inward again, breathing heavily, she left him, another pain taking her.

He rushed out of the door, stopped short, then dashed back into the room to drag out William's body and put it in the other chamber for the time being— death had no place in a room soon to see the beginning of a new life. Rebecca averted her face, concentrating only on the birth-pang.

Racing down the stairs, he found Meera in the kitchen, cowering in a corner, crying. Nur Mustafa was at his stove, wide-eyed with fear, trying to ignore the strange events taking place in this ferangi house.

"Meera! Rebecca has begun her labor. You must go to her!"

She looked up at him, terrified, her large eyes red and swollen from her tears.

"Meera, little one, for the love of God, get yourself together and go to your mistress. She needs you!" He shook her, finally seeing comprehension dawn on her face.

"What is happening, Azim? What is this shot I am hearing? Is Missy being all right?"

"Yes, Meera," he said more gently, "your Missy is fine . . . but her baby is coming! What shall we do?" He told himself that he must keep control for Rebecca's sake.

Meera thought he was quite pale under his tan. Did he know yet? "Yes, yes . . . I am going. Nur Mustafa, you crawling worm, heat some water! Get some clean cloths. Hurry!" Meera was very calm now. She knew exactly what to do, having assisted at many births in her home village.

Over her shoulder, as she bustled around, she asked, "Where is Sahib William? Is he knowing?"

"Never mind St. Claire at the moment, just go to Rebecca!" He was almost shouting.

Meera realized that he was very worried about Rebecca *and* the baby?

"Azim," she said softly, "many ladies having babies every day. That is why we are being so many Indians! Having baby easy thing to do. Ladies made for that."

She gathered her clean cloths and water and went up to Rebecca. Alex followed her closely, visibly nervous. They found Rebecca resting easily; she smiled at them. Meera helped her into a clean nightgown, discarding her wet skirt. She noticed a blood spot on the carpet, but kept her own counsel. They would explain about the stain when they were ready, and besides, Sahib William deserved the fate she suspected he may have met. She made Rebecca as comfortable as possible, then left the room for a few minutes on some pretext, to allow them a moment of privacy. She was sure that they must have important things to say to each other.

As the door closed quietly behind her, Rebecca said, breathlessly, "Azim . . . !"

He broke in softly. "It's Alex now."

"Alex . . . How . . . Why are you here? Now, of all times. I don't—"

"Hush, my love," he interrupted soothingly. "I left

the village early this year, and almost finished myself in the process. Now I know why I was brought here. The fates have finally treated us kindly."

Rebecca breathed a great and satisfied sigh. "Thank God you know. . . . I tried to tell you before, so many times. I thought you despised me, didn't want the baby . . . I thought—" Her words were stopped by another contraction.

Alex sat by her side and held her hand. He knew that he would never let her go again, as long as he was alive to protect and cherish her.

She began again as soon as she could, still breathing hard. "William . . . he . . . he . . . abused me. Made me do disgusting things . . . " Her voice trailed off. "I grew to hate him long ago. I . . . I'm glad he's dead . . . There, I've said it! He tortured me, humiliated me . . . " Her head rolled back and forth on the pillows, tangling her damp curls.

Alex soothed her, stroking her hair, murmuring assurances. "You never need to fear him again, my blossom. I'm here to take care of you . . . and our child." His brows drew together as he thought of the newspaper clipping his brother had unwittingly sent him. He would not tell her about that yet. She had something more important to think of at present. In any case, William could no longer harm her or the babe.

Her hand gripped his fiercely as another pain took her; her knuckles turned white. Alex began to feel apprehensive. Where was Meera? What if something happened while she was out of the room? He could not let anything happen to Rebecca. He had just found her again after treating her so cruelly, throwing her into St. Claire's arms, leaving her alone with him—a depraved monster, murderer, God knew what else. Alex realized that he was grasping her hand much too tightly.

She was looking at him in a strange way, and had murmured his name several times. "Alex, are you glad about the baby? I mean . . . you don't have to . . ."

He looked at her, tenderly, lovingly, the way she had wished he would look at her so many times before when he had been bitter and hateful instead. He covered her small white hand with his strong ones.

"Rebecca, I've never said these words to a woman, but I say it to you. I love you, my flower. And I will love the child we have created between us, never fear."

Her face, etched from painful effort, lit up with a brilliant smile. "Alex, you have made me so happy . . . I think I've loved you since the first moment I saw you. Remember, in the garden in Bombay?"

"Yes, love, I remember."

The door opened and Meera entered, her attempt to cover her frown pathetic. "I am sending servant-boy for the English doctor, but not being sure he will be here in time. Never be minding, we are good doctor, aren't we, Azim?" She smiled at Rebecca to give her confidence.

The labor continued for several hours, growing in intensity, Meera and Alex never leaving Rebecca's side. In between contractions, her face, despite its pallor, was peaceful and glowing with an inner joy. Not a sound escaped her lips. The job of bringing this baby into the world was difficult, but worth every moment of the intense strain.

Near dusk, her body covered with a sheen of sweat, she began to bear down strongly. The birth was imminent. Meera fretted that the doctor had not arrived but was secretly glad as she wanted to be the one to help her Missy.

When the baby finally entered the world night had almost fallen; the sun had set gloriously in the west, a few lingering rays still gilding the peaks of the Hindu Kush and stretching across the plain to Kabul.

Rebecca lay spent, her long travail over. Meera held the tiny slippery body in her hands. Alex stepped up to her in one long stride, taking the baby gently from her and slapping the tiny form on its backside. Instantly, the infant began to cry. It was a loud and lusty bawl, fitting for the son of a chapandaz, thought Alex with great pride.

While he stood in the center of the room holding his naked child in his arms, a lone ray of the setting sun pierced the window, lighting up the tableau with an unearthly glow.

EPILOGUE

Easter came early the spring of 1884. It dawned cool and gray, faint rays of light breaking through the heavy clouds. Rebecca drew aside the heavy bedroom drapes and yawned into the bleak morning. She turned and let the curtain cloak her in semi-darkness again. Alex's eyes followed her movements, a tender curve on his lips.

When he spoke, his voice was husky from having just awakened. "Little flower, do you think that perhaps we can take a year or so off from your pregnancies?" He swung his legs over the side of their bed and continued to tease. "I vow that I have rarely seen you without a full belly! In fact, I cannot recall what your hips and breasts looked—"

Rebecca had tossed a satin pillow in his face, commencing their morning play. She jested easily with him. "And I suppose I got myself in this condition all by myself!" She turned sideways affording Alex a view of her rounded shape. She wore a blue silk night dress which did nothing to hide her figure. Her full breasts were revealed clearly through the filmy material.

Alex coughed and averted his interested stare. "I'm going to the nursery to see little Lawrence. At least *he* takes my mind off of my . . . uh . . . urges." Alex put on his handsome maroon dressing robe and started to leave.

"Oh, Alex, is that all you ever think of?" Rebecca

laughed. "Besides, we must hurry this morning, for I'm sure that Stuart and Carla will be here before noon. Oh, why can't the sun shine today?" She sighed, then brightened. "I'm *so* glad the Foreign Minister gave you a few days off. We shall have to make the most of them."

Rebecca began to bustle around the lovely old house, preparing for the family gathering. She did not really have time to open her mail today, but she noticed a letter from Catherine Mansfield in Afghanistan on the silver tray holding her correspondence and could not resist opening it. A smile lit her face as she scanned the contents rapidly. The Mansfields were coming home to England in a few months time! Oh, she would be so glad to see Catherine again, with none of the sadness that had been present in their last meeting. Well, she would simply have to be satisfied with this news and finish the rest of the letter tomorrow, she thought, swirling around to check the library for dust.

By the time that Alex's brother arrived, shortly after noon, the sky had cleared and the day was perfect. Rebecca was delighted and ordered the servants to set the Easter table out on the stone veranda. Her grandfather had been an avid outdoorsman and naturalist; his gardens and elaborate terraces were the pride of Faroaks Manor.

Alex was relieved when his family's carriage arrived because Rebecca finally had to cease her busy preparations and join the festivities. The proud mothers exclaimed over the growth of each other's children in the few months since Alex and Rebecca's return to England. They had only had time to visit each other once as Rebecca was unable to travel with her second baby due in a few weeks time.

Young Alex, who was fourteen now, tagged along after his uncle, begging for tales of the exotic steppes. Rebecca was charmed by her husband's family and the older children loved her easy manner.

That evening during the Easter meal, the Drayton'

youngest daughter, Charlotte, was crawling under the dining table. Lawrence George Drayton, only a year old, but very like his father, Alex, caught and pulled a lock of her hair. Charlotte, who was a full year older than her cousin, screamed so loudly that the entire family ducked their heads under the linen cloth to scold the children. Alex looked lovingly at his son who would not release the girl's long hair. The child was obviously the apple of his father's eye. He had dark hair and gray eyes, nearly the color of his father's. Rebecca grew tired of the commotion and summoned the nanny to tend the small children while they finished their meal. Alex, however, would have none of it and suggested that he withdraw from the feast, taking the small tots to his library.

With one under each arm he dropped his gaze to Rebecca. "The children only require a small amount of attention before bed," he fabricated. "I'll simply entertain them for a moment and be back to the table shortly."

Rebecca laughed at his attempt to further spoil the little imps, but she secretly loved him dearly for the open affection he showed his family.

The two toddlers soon made a shambles out of the tidy library. Alex built a blazing fire to keep them comfortable and sat back in his leather chair.

The day's journey to Faroaks and the excitement of the Easter meal had taken its toll on little Charlotte. She crawled up into her Uncle Alex's lap and fell into a deep sleep. He relaxed deeper into the chair and watched Lawrence tear the room to pieces.

The boy eventually found a single trinket to amuse himself with, and as any toddler will do, plumped himself down on his backside to play with the toy.

Alex would have retrieved little Lawrence's plaything but he feared that any movement would awaken Charlotte, so he let his son go on banging and examining the small jeweled box.

Rebecca will have my neck if she finds him toying

with her treasure, he thought. Hadn't she told him that her grandfather had purchased the Indian relic for her a few days before his death? Alex was about to chance disturbing Charlotte's rest when he noticed two folded pieces of paper fall out of the box and float to the floor. The baby was delighted with his find and his little fingers turned the documents over and over.

The door to the library opened and Rebecca stood in the portal ready to scold Alex for allowing the tot to run amuck. The normally immaculate library was totally disarranged, and to make matters worse, the baby was playing with her priceless jeweled box! How could Alex let these children take such advantage of him?

"Rebecca, love, before you begin your lecture, please bring me those papers in our son's hand. They fell from your box and I couldn't rescue them." He indicated his confined position with the little girl.

Rebecca contained her annoyance for a moment, having never seen the documents before. Where had they come from?

She stooped over the baby and firmly loosened his grip. Little Lawrence let out a piercing shriek but was soon distracted with another toy that his father handed him. Rebecca read the papers, a frown on her face. She read them over again to make sure of the contents. This was not possible! But the papers were official—one, a marriage certificate announcing that Philip St. Claire, Englishman, had married an Indian lady of the Brahman caste named Lakshmi in the year 1850. The other document was even more stunning—the birth certificate of a male child named William born in 1851 to Lakshmi and Philip St. Claire. Race: mixed.

Rebecca looked up at Alex, who was watching her horrified expression with puzzlement. She sank to her knees before him, her dark eyes glistened with tears. She was trying to calm herself enough to explain, the papers dangling from her nerveless fingers.

"Oh, Alex, this is the reason William . . . This i

why he married me . . . murdered them. Why he hated me so . . . I never knew . . . he must have been so bitter. Look!"

She handed the papers to Alex. He scanned them, then eased Charlotte into a curled up position in the large chair and drew Rebecca to her feet.

He held her for a long time. They clung to each other, silently reviewing to themselves St. Claire's treachery. They knew at last why the malevolent man had been compelled to murder both her grandfather and father. The mystery of William's compulsive pursual of Rebecca had always bothered Alex, but now he understood everything. William had been trying to gain control of the destructive knowledge contained in the box.

"Oh, Alex, I feel, at last, that I can put the past in its place now that I understand William's demented behavior . . . I always wondered what he wanted of me," Rebecca said tearfully.

"Think of the dreadful events that brought us together," she continued. "It's a terrible thought, but if William hadn't come to see grandfather—well, I never would have been in Kabul and . . ."

Alex stroked her golden hair and soothed her with his words. "Sometimes the beauty in our lives must be born of great pain and sorrow . . . We have so much now. We shall return to the steppes someday, the dark clouds lifted."

Rebecca looked up into his beloved face and tenderly placed her small fingers in his strong ones. "Yes, we have each other, a lifetime. . . ."

ENJOY ALL OF THESE TITLES
FROM PARADISE PRESS

LOVE'S FRANTIC FLIGHT by Joan Joseph. She escaped to a new world in search of the man she loved.

A DREAM OF FIRE by Drusilla Campbell. Her beauty warmed Scotland's green hills—and a warrior's fierce heart!

NOW IS THE HOUR by Joan Joseph. In New Zealand she found wild beauty, savage splendor, and her heart's hidden desire.

THIS RAGING FLOWER by Lynn Erickson. She was an exotic English blossom in a land barren of all but the wildest passions, the boldest men.

CONQUER THE MEMORIES by Janet Joyce. 1847: The Mexican-American War. A spirited English noblewoman braved the perils of battle and her own unbridled passions.

RED ROSES FOREVER by Amanda Jean Jarrett. 1875 - On the night of the first Kentucky Derby a fiery southern beauty encounters romance and intrigue— and a lover with a startling secret.

OUTRAGEOUS DESIRE by Carla A. Neggers. Summer: 1874 - The rich and powerful of Saratoga Springs held little allure for this beautiful reformer. Then, who was this charming, handsome stranger who came to town with his outrageous behavior?

ENJOY ALL OF THESE TITLES FROM PARADISE PRESS

ISLAND OF PROMISE by Madeleine Carr. 1779: Georgia in turmoil. A beautiful Savannah heiress—imprisoned in an exotic house of pleasure—was determined to escape and find her island lover.

PASSION'S HEIRS by Elizabeth Bright. In the rugged wilderness of the new West, she was caught in a whirlwind of danger and passion by a masked strange she met at a costume ball.

THE PASSION AND THE FURY by Amanda Jean Jarrett. 1872 - On a vast plantation in South Carolina a spirited Southern girl and the suddenly appearing mystery man from the North face a strange and dangerous destiny.

FORTUNE'S TIDE by Gene Lancour. A proud, beautiful woman pays the price of passion over a man with a fearsome secret.

THE SILVER MISTRESS by Chet Cunningham. Silve City, Nevada 1870: A sensuous and resourceful woma fights to save her silver mine.